CHAUCER
DICKINSON
AND THE
TIMBERSCAPE
OF MEMORY

The **HERETICS IN OCCUPIED EDEN** Trilogy:

Book One: **THE FLOATING BOY**
Book Two: **THE STRANGE ANGELS**
Book Three: **THE DANCING CHURCH**

The **HERETICS COMPANION** Works:

Book Four: The Mansion of Our Undressing
Book Five: Chaucer Dickinson and the
                     Timberscape of Memory
Book Six: The Book of Zara (forthcoming)
Book Seven: The Heretics Appendix (forthcoming)

CHAUCER DICKINSON
AND THE
TIMBERSCAPE OF MEMORY

HERETICS IN OCCUPIED EDEN
BOOK FIVE

KENNETH ALAN MOE

STRANGE ANGEL PRESS
Phoenix, Arizona
strangeangelpress.com

Copyright © 2015
Kenneth Alan Moe

Cover, interior design and cover photos by Ethan Moe
Cover photos were taken in the Superstition Mountains, Arizona
Jackrabbit photo taken by Matt Lavin

Printed in the United States of America
First Printing

ISBN: 978-0692328712

For Radec, Nyrb, Yeroc, and Neelloc

Wouldest thou see a truth within a fable...
Then read my fancies.
John Bunyan

Magical Arizona with its rose-amethyst mountains
...the mountains in a fairy book.
George William Russell

What does it matter where my body happens to
be? My mind goes on working all the same.
Lewis Carroll

LEGEND

GYMNARYKUM

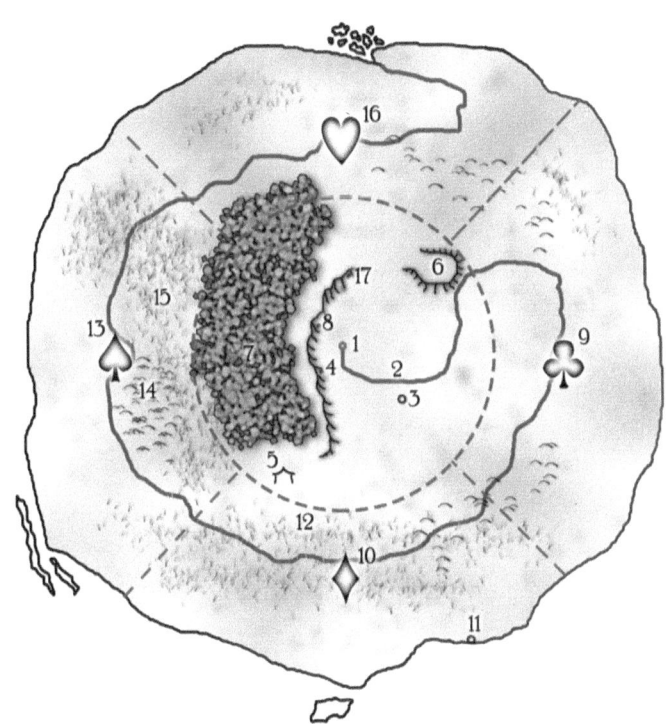

The Universal Sea

CONTENTS

CHAPTER 1:
BOXING DAY

How News must feel when traveling
If News have any Heart
Alighting at the Dwelling
'Twill enter like a Dart!
Emily Dickinson

"**Boxing** Day feels like it should be the first day of the year," Chaucer Dickinson said to her husband, Ving Valborg. Her vividly blue eyes flashed determination as she pulled her long red hair into a ponytail and expertly wrapped it in a band. Thus girded, Chaucer began gathering into a large plastic trash bag pieces of torn wrapping paper, ribbons, garment boxes, and other residue of the previous day's celebration. "The day after Christmas is a time to begin letting go the disappointments of the old year and clear out the excesses of the holiday season and start anew. Yesterday we gave each other wonderful presents, but in other ways, 1983 has felt so…unsettled."

"Well," Ving said, "since you brought it up -starting over that is- I have something to say." He bowed his head in a confessional posture. "I've been wanting to say this for a while now, but it seemed wrong to do it before Christmas." Unconsciously, he ran his right hand lightly over his head to reassure himself that his blond hair remained neatly in place. "Shortly before we were married, I…told you about my bisexuality."

1

"I remember that moment with crystal clarity," Chaucer said, as a stoic and glum expression descended upon her face. She had indeed brought up the subject, very much desiring to clear the air and now determined to withstand the pain.

"But it was *you* I wanted, only you. It was you I chose to be with," he whispered. "I so much wanted it to be you."

Chaucer remained silent, mentally noting the conditional nature of wanting it to be her as opposed to *knowing* that she was the one.

"But of course, that's not the whole story," Ving continued. "I need to say a little bit more. I told you the truth, but not the whole truth."

She stared at her husband, dreading and yet welcoming the words she was about to hear.

"I thought I was bi," Ving confessed. "At least I desperately wanted to be, but at a deep level, I knew even then that I'm really not. Not truly so. I am a gay man who has tried faithfully to live a lie and to love you as you deserve to be loved. I do love you in a way. You're the dearest sister a man could have. But when we have sex it almost feels like incest. I'm haunted by a sense of guilt after making love with you. I have failed you, Chaucer. I have cheated on you, and you have every right to hate me."

"I don't hate you, Ving," Chaucer said calmly. "But your dishonesty hurts so much it tortures my heart."

"You've known all along, haven't you?" he asked.

"Yes, I suppose so," she said. "I guessed when you told me you were bisexual, but I wanted so much to be married that I buried the thought. I wanted a man like you who was straight. I decided I could settle for bisexual. That was *my* lie. The marriage began with each one of us withholding what we knew." Chaucer paused before asking a frightening question. "Is there someone else?"

"There have been some passing flings," he answered, not looking at her. "The thing is, when I said my wedding vows to you, I intended to be faithful. I *wanted* to be faithful. I convinced myself that I *could* have an exclusive relationship with the most wonderful woman I had ever met.

"But as time passed I wanted more, and somehow you and I

became ships passing in the night, never quite connecting. So cheating was easy to rationalize. And now I've met a darling man that I'm totally in love with, and I want to settle down and enjoy domestic bliss with him."

Chaucer managed a rueful chuckle. "Where do we go from here, big brother?"

"I'll move out tonight. Crandall has given me an open invitation to move in with him," Ving said. "I'll be as generous as I can afford with a divorce settlement. I only ask one thing of you."

"Which is?" Chaucer asked with genuine curiosity at what he might want.

"Don't tell my dad I'm gay," he said. "We'll come up with a cover story to explain the split. I'll tell Dad that Crandall and I are roommates sharing an apartment to cut down on expenses. Two ex-husbands with alimony payments and all that. All I'm asking is that you just go along with it."

"That sounds suspiciously like *The Odd Couple*," Chaucer said.

"Dad always liked that show, so he should buy the story," Ving replied. "Although, Crandall and I are both more like Felix, so we wouldn't actually be odd."

"What about your mom?" Chaucer asked.

"Mom knows, or at least she knows that I'm bi. I guess I should say that she knows I've been trying to pass for bi. She never believed that I am truly bisexual, and she almost told you so before the wedding, but I begged her not to."

This last admission cut Chaucer so deep that her stoicism faltered and she winced with physical pain.

Ving dropped to his knees in supplication. "Please, Chaucer, I'm begging you. If dad finds out I'm gay, he'll cut me out of the business, and then I won't be able to afford alimony."

In an instant she knew what the divorce would cost her, and she was willing to pay the price. "I don't want alimony, Ving. I have a good position and am fully able to support myself financially. I will give you this much. I won't go out of my way to disagree with anything you tell your father. But if I ever find out you've cheated on Crandall the way you've cheated on me, I might find it easy to drop by the agency in Phoenix to say hello and let something accidentally slip."

Ving visibly cringed at her words.

"You're really afraid of your father, aren't you, Ving? Physically afraid," she said.

He hung his head, feeling enormous shame. "Yes."

"And it's not really about inheriting the business, is it?" she asked.

"Not about the business," he agreed. "I want him to love me and be proud of me, and that will never happen if he knows I'm gay."

"Yeah," she said with bitterness, "I know all about that story."

Ving moved out that evening, genuinely relieved that she would not ask for alimony but recognizing that she still held considerable power over him.

After his departure, Chaucer took a book to the toilet and experienced somatic relief, ending a week of constipation with a massive bowel movement.

Though now more comfortable physically, Chaucer slept fitfully that night and toward dawn experienced a nightmare in which she fainted in a classroom full of her colleagues and was strapped to a gurney and taken to a hospital emergency room, where she was diagnosed with AIDS. The dream startled her awake and for several hours she paced the apartment trying to forestall panic. Being left for another man was a pain she could deal with. She could get over that. The idea of being infected with a fatal disease was a geometrically higher level of magnitude. Terror and rage competed for dominance within her mind. At noon, she telephoned her gynecologist's office for an appointment, only to hear an officious message that the office was closed for lunch. She slammed the phone down in a fit of frustration. Mid-afternoon she called again and was able to get an appointment for the following Thursday.

CHAPTER 2:
IMAGINARY FRIEND

My whole heart is bent
On helping you, if only you consent,
And if your troubles I cannot amend,
For consolation, please, on me depend.

Geoffrey Chaucer

Chaucer Dickinson was born in Phoenix, Arizona on April 27, 1950, the second child of Banky and Norah Dickinson. According to family lore, the labor went so quickly and the pain of delivery so much less than the excruciating experience the first time Norah had given birth, that she nearly forgot she had a second daughter. With Chaucer safely tucked away in the care of maternity ward nurses, Norah woke from a nap momentarily wondering why she was in the hospital. She later told friends that it felt almost as if she had temporarily left her body for an airy voyage through the corridors of Good Samaritan Hospital during her labor.

Norah and Banky had given their older daughter, born in Phoenix two years earlier, the equally literary name of Marlowe. A son would be born to the Dickinsons two years hence, and he would be named Spenser.

Marlowe and Spenser were golden haired children, while Chaucer, the middle one who had slipped so quietly into their lives, had inherited the red hair of her father's Irish mother. Unfortunately for Chaucer, Norah Jaxon Dickinson disliked her mother-in-law, and by

5

extension the Irish people in general, although she made an exception for Irish writers and playwrights, because these artists, she rationalized, mostly made their marks in England or by elegantly using the English language rather than what she thought of as lowbrow Erse.

Of course she deeply loved her husband, but regrettably, she freely admitted to many people, he had inherited the gift of blarney from his freckle-faced Catholic mother, and this trait was the one thing about Banky that irritated her. Banky's father was a non-practicing Protestant with a judgmental streak and a desire to be deemed sophisticated by social elites.

The strongest bonds holding Norah and Banky together were mutual disgust for organized religion and appreciation for the arts. Flouting common wisdom, they discussed religion on their first date, and Norah was delighted to hear Banky say of the Church, "It's all bullshit." He had no objection to people believing anything they wanted, but he became hostile when they insisted their church owned the exclusive truth about God. He had been raised Catholic but repeatedly argued with the priest in catechism class and spoke disparagingly about church doctrines and traditions. Even so, the philosophical Monsignor had let that behavior slip by.

However, in Mass one Sunday, Banky listened as a priest rushed mumbling through the Latin rite, and the idea came into the boy's head that the priest sounded like an auctioneer. When the cleric raised the chalice, Banky stood, used a missal to rap the back of the pew in front of him, and shouted, "Sold! to the lady in the blue hat."

For that he was excommunicated. His mother was furious with him for weeks, but Banky felt relieved to be out from under what felt like a smothering creedal regime.

Chaucer loved mockingbirds. One lazy afternoon when she was four, she wandered into the living room while her dad was listening to the Les Paul and Mary Ford recording of "Mockin' Bird Hill" and in a burst of whimsy, he scooped Chaucer into his arms and whirled her across the carpet in a theatrical waltz. The back of her head tingled and she laughed with great joy, and for the first time felt truly loved. Sadly, however, this was the last time Banky ever danced with his middle child.

Nevertheless, the notion that mockingbirds congregated on peaceful hills stuck in the girl's mind. "Do mockingbirds live around here?" she asked her mother one Sunday morning in the spring.

"Sure they do," Norah said.

"Where?" Chaucer pressed. "Can I see them?"

Banky had come home in the wee hours from a gig with his dance band and was, as usual, sleeping late. Norah felt restless, wanting to get out of the house and go somewhere -anywhere- and so instead of brushing off her middle daughter, she said, "Encanto Park. I can take you there if you like."

"Yes, please," Chaucer replied eagerly.

Norah gathered up her children, Marlowe, Chaucer, and Spenser, and drove to Encanto Park, where she found a bench overlooking one of the canals spiraling from the main lagoon. From this perch, she pointed out the mockingbirds taking off and landing from tree branches on the other side of the water. "They look a lot like doves, but there's a way to tell them apart. Look for the white stripe on each wing, parallel to its body," Norah explained.

Chaucer, however, was the only one paying attention to the bird-watching lesson. The entire conversation was over the head of Spenser, who kept jumping down from his mother's lap while she repeatedly scooped him up again. Marlowe wanted to ride the train in Kiddieland and ultimately got her wish.

But before that happened, Chaucer managed to ask her question. "Why do they call them *mocking* birds?"

"Well, it's because they imitate the songs of other birds. They mock the sounds that other birds make," Norah explained.

"Why do they do that?" Chaucer continued. "Why don't they just sing their own songs?"

"I don't know," Norah said with a slight tone of irritation. "They say the mockingbird covers up a broken heart by pretending to be some other happy bird, but that's an old wives' tale. It's a fallacy to think that birds know how to pretend to be something they're not. They don't think at all but do everything by instinct."

Chaucer thought the legend was probably true, for she already knew from experience how to hide disappointment and pretend to be happy. It was as instinctual with her as it was with the mockingbirds, she decided.

She got on fine with her siblings, but somehow it seemed that her parents rarely found any time just for her. Thus it was easy for Chaucer to imagine that some birds -beautiful birds with white-striped wings- were also ignored by their parents and only pretended to be happy when they sang. That this outing in the park had been at her instigation was an exception to the usual household dynamics.

Marlowe, a serious-minded and very pretty blonde, had needs that always managed to be high priority. And as Spenser grew older, his status as the only boy generated a disproportionate amount of parental attention. Chaucer tried very hard to please her parents but generally felt benign indifference in response. They were never unkind to her, and the clothing and toys she had were as nice as those bought for her sister and brother. But it felt to Chaucer that their care for her lacked energy and enthusiasm.

So she managed life on her own and turned for nurture and affection to an imaginary friend. The conversations began one night in bed when Chaucer was seven. All day she had been feeling sorry for herself and emotionally abandoned. Deep down she suspected it was her own fault that her parents ignored her. Surely something was wrong with her that no one would tell her about. Though not able to conceptualize her feelings in this particular word model, she did not like being the odd one out in the family constellation.

What if, she thought in the darkness of her room, I could invent a mom or dad to love me? She knew a girl at school who had an imaginary friend with whom she carried on long conversations. How about an imaginary parent?

No sooner had she asked herself this question than a voice entered her mind that only she could hear. The voice came from an adult but sounded strangely like her own child's voice. "I'm not your parent, but I am happy to be your friend," the voice said.

"Are you *my* imaginary friend?" asked Chaucer.

"I am indeed your friend," the voice said. "And I care for you very much. You are a precious child to me. And I can be as real or imaginary as you wish." The being who had initiated this telepathic conversation with Chaucer was at that moment seated in the lotus posture in a shack in the desert west of Phoenix.

"If you're real, can I ever see you?" Chaucer continued.

"For now, I must be real only inside your brain," the voice answered. "Can we still be friends if you don't see me?"

"Oh I want a friend very much," said Chaucer. "What is your name?"

"I have a long and unusual name that you would not be able to pronounce," the voice said.

"Well then, is it OK if I give you a nickname?" she asked.

"That is a splendid idea! What would you like my nickname to be?" asked the voice.

She wrinkled her brow and nose as she tried to think of a name she liked. "Let's see, you are my real imaginary friend. R-I-F. Rif. I could call you Rif."

"That sounds good to me," the voice said.

"But I want you to stay a long time," Chaucer continued. "Real imaginary friend *forever*. R-I-F-F. Riff! If it's alright with you, I'll call you Riff."

"So it shall be," said Riff. "I will happily respond to Riff whenever you have need to call upon me. And now, it is time for you to fall asleep, Chaucer. Before you nod off, though, I want you to know that your parents do love you, but for now they are easily distracted by other demands. In the meantime, when you need a hug, just call me in your mind, and I will cuddle you and hold you in your imagination."

Telepathic exchanges between Chaucer and Riff took place about once a week for several years, each one filled with encouragement and affection for the little girl. Chaucer yearned for this relationship to become real but accepted that it was all within her own head. Although she never mentioned this to Riff, she pictured her mental friend as a giant Teddy bear. Riff was aware of this, although the entity she called Riff looked nothing like a furry toy animal. Rather, Riff appeared vaguely human, with long fine white hair and penetrating turquoise eyes.

The existence of Riff became Chaucer's deepest secret, which she hid even from her siblings.

<><><>

Banky and Norah's wedding took place in a Phoenix orange grove in 1946. A Justice of the Peace officiated, and Norah's best friend Nissa and Nissa's new husband Onan Verrall stood with them as witnesses.

Bancroft Dickinson had been born in Phoenix in 1924 and graduated from Phoenix Union High School in 1942. Immediately, he enlisted in the Army and served in a Special Services unit for entertainment and morale until he was discharged in late 1945.

Thursday mornings were golden for him in grade school, because the teacher would hush the class to tune into the Standard School Broadcast of classical music from the San Francisco Symphony Orchestra. The classical pieces entranced him and made him avid to pursue a career in music. He began writing clever tunes in high school, when he discovered that this talent made him popular. His skill with piano, violin, and drums bordered on virtuosity, and he was a passable singer with a pleasantly raspy voice, all of which accounted for his assignment to the Special Services. While still on active duty, he composed a novelty song that was picked up by a major swing band and became a substantial hit. "The Sally and Rose Comedy Shows" mocked the radio patter of propagandists Axis Sally and Tokyo Rose as essentially funny and sarcastically thanked the enemy broadcasters for their unintentional morale boosting humor.

Between 1945 and the early fifties, Banky penned several more novelty songs that became minor hits. After the war, he established a dance band in Phoenix and performed at resorts, country clubs, and veterans' organization halls all over Arizona. He met Norah Jaxon at a country club gig. She had come to the dance with a club member but left at three in the morning with Banky. From their first meeting, Norah was taken with the idea of being married to a talented musical artist.

Norah, also a native Phoenician, was a year older than Banky but looked younger. She graduated from North High in 1941, along with her closest friend Nissa Vennlig who came from a family of nudists. Norah thought that Nissa's naturism was a splendid lifestyle, but never participated in the practice herself. She imagined that most of the great artists and poets were nudists, thus elevating the lifestyle in her mind. While they were in school together, Nissa had invited Norah to nudist picnics, but since she was a minor, Norah never had the nerve to approach her Christian fundamentalist parents with a permission slip.

During the war, she worked off and on as a clerk and secretary, while in her free time she wrote poetry and fancied herself a bohemian. In the early 1950s, Norah joined the Phoenix Poets Society and contributed readings of her works at the organization's meetings at the library. However, her free-flowing lines and stream-of-consciousness images were not popular with most other members, who preferred classical verse structures. Norah was tolerated by her fellow Phoenix poets but never achieved the inner circle of celebrated local bards.

To demonstrate persistent devotion to her art, Norah regularly sent copies of her poems to magazines such as the *Atlantic Monthly, Harpers*, and the *Saturday Review of Literature*. None was ever published, even in the local *Phoenix Gazette* newspaper. Nevertheless, she maintained a folder full of rejection slips from notable publications, and these documents somehow confirmed in her mind that she was a professional poet. While building her distinctive artistic persona, Norah also, in contradictory fashion, sought rising class respectability. That meant being attended by one's personal physician rather than simply the family doctor. This image of gentility was further burnished by consulting with her own new car salesman, who would bring vehicles to the house for inspection. Dropping the names of these two symbols of professional success, she knew, demonstrated that she and Banky counted in Phoenix society.

Several times in the late forties, Nissa and Onan invited Norah and Banky to go with them to nudist resorts, and the bohemian side of Norah was open to going, but Banky balked, so to the relief of her striving-for-respectability side it never happened.

Her marriage with Banky produced children every other year from 1948 until 1952, after which, with two girls and a boy on her hands, Norah had her tubes tied.

CHAPTER 3:
ANATOMICAL RESPONSES

She did not sing as we did –
It was a different tune –
Herself to her a music
As Bumble bee of June
Emily Dickinson

Citrus groves inside the city limits were becoming scarcer as the 1950s unfolded in Phoenix, but a surprising number of fields of orange, lemon, and grapefruit trees continued to resist the inexorable wave of destruction that was making room for housing developments. The orange grove three blocks from Chaucer's home was her favorite place for make-believe games.

Hidden amid the fragrant trees in the grove, she fashioned an open-air lounge out of produce crates and cardboard boxes. There she carried on extensive conversations with Riff, after which she always felt better about her life.

One day she invited a boy from her third grade class at Osborn Elementary School to play with her in her arboreal parlor. The game they agreed upon was "I'll show you mine if you show me yours." He pulled down his Levis and underwear and she pulled up her skirt and slipped out of her panties.

The boy had not been circumcised. "Hey, what's that thing on your weenie?" she said with avid curiosity. "My little brother's weenie doesn't look like that."

"I'm not Jewish," the boy said.

She had no idea what that had to do with penile differences. Perhaps he was changing the subject. "Neither am I," she said.

After the boy left, she reflected on the strange reality that some boys were born with covered penises and some with uncovered ones.

That day they had not touched one another, but on a subsequent occasion, they did gently rub one another's private parts. The boy giggled from the tingly sensation of Chaucer's hand, but Chaucer cooed when he tickled her.

Early on a Sunday morning, Chaucer slipped out of the house and trotted down to her grove in time to see a coyote emerging from the trees and dart down an alley. Chaucer watched in fascination as the cagey animal pounced on a garbage can to knock it over and then rummaged through the dinner scrapings inside. Coyotes are smart, she thought. They usually find food in the wilds but can find it in the...what? Mentally she paused to come up with an antonym for wilds. They can find food in the tames, she decided.

Enchanted groves, however, are not necessarily eternal, and in 1959, a crew began to remove the trees and prepare the land for new houses. This development upset Chaucer, but she expressed her feelings only to her siblings and not her parents.

"But it's good for the economy," Marlowe explained. "More houses mean more people to buy things to make Phoenix a boom town."

"I don't want it to be a boom town," Chaucer responded. "I want it to be a nice place to live with orange groves that have such a wonderful smell."

"You're just being a dreamer," said Marlowe.

Spenser had no opinion one way or the other.

Soon, however, Chaucer discovered that partially built houses could be nearly as much fun to play in as orange groves. On weekends, when the contractors did not work, Chaucer explored houses that had concrete block walls and two-by-four framing but no interior walls. The rafters, she discovered, were marvelous places to perch and meditate. Thus for a brief interval in the spring and early summer of 1959, Chaucer made use of a series of incomplete houses as safe havens for continued talks with Riff.

While thus occupied on one occasion, the urge to urinate came upon her, but she did not want to climb down and go home to use the bathroom. When this field had been full of orange trees and she had to pee, she found a secluded spot and went. She enjoyed the way it felt to pass water outside in the dirt. Now a wicked idea came to her. She stepped across rafters to the place where the bathroom would be and looked down at the open pipes and holes where the plumbing fixtures would be installed. This is a bathroom, after all, she thought. Quickly she removed her shorts and panties and draped them over a rafter. Then she squatted and allowed a yellow stream to flow, maneuvering her body to aim at the open sewer pipe over which the toilet would soon rest.

Most of the liquid landed in and around the pipe, and she felt pleased and somewhat titillated at her deed. Thereafter, she drank a full glass of water before going out to explore the construction site, so she would have the pleasurable opportunity to aim for the sewer pipe from the rafters above.

When Helene Finn's family moved to Phoenix in 1958, she was assigned to Chaucer's fourth grade class at Osborn School. Chaucer and Helene quickly became best friends, a relationship that would last through high school. Helene was an only child and a bit odd, which is what attracted Chaucer to her.

Helene wore thick glasses, had buckteeth, and usually plaited her fine brown hair in pigtails. Every once in a while, when she was running late or felt like a change of style, she would pull her hair back into a ponytail instead. Her clothes were often mismatched, typically a striped blouse over a checkered skirt. These things were a matter of indifference to Helene, however, because she was very smart and had the highest grade point average in the school. This is what mattered to her.

At the start of summer vacation between fourth and fifth grades, Helene invited Chaucer to spend a Saturday night at her house. They got into their pajamas and stayed up late into the night giggling and telling strange tales from their imaginations and then slept side-by-side in Helene's double bed. In the morning, after a late breakfast in bed served by Helene's doting mother, the girls put on jeans, tee shirts, and sneakers and went out for a walk.

"I really like your mother," said Chaucer as they ambled. "She's so nice, as nice to me as to you. It must be great being an only child and getting all the attention."

"It gets kind of lonely sometimes," said Helene.

Chaucer steered them toward the tract of homes under construction where she liked to play. They climbed in through the window of a house that was fully framed inside with wallboard up in several rooms and part of the attic floor complete.

"I like to hide out in places like this for thinking time and to get away from my parents for a while," Chaucer said.

"Do you ever bring a book and read?" Helene asked.

"Sometimes," said Chaucer. "If I do, I find a place to perch up in the rafters, because there's no comfortable place to sit on a concrete slab. Let's climb up to the attic."

The two-by-four framing for the bathroom was not covered, so they used crosspieces as rungs to get to the plywood floor of the attic, where they sat with their legs dangling over an unfinished portion of ceiling.

"I like these houses, because there are no workers on weekends, so it's completely private," Chaucer said. "I like privacy so I can do whatever I want."

"Has anyone else ever walked in on you?" Helene asked.

"No," said Chaucer. "A gang of boys ride their bikes by sometimes but never stop here. I think they have their own hideout."

"Have you ever taken your clothes off?" Helene continued.

Chaucer was disconcerted by the question, because it reminded her of urinating from the rafters and she had no intention of telling even her best friend about that. But as she considered Helene's words, she recognized that they arose from her reference to doing whatever she wanted in privacy and not to toilet etiquette. "Well, yes, a couple of times."

"Ooh good," said Helene. "Let's take our clothes off."

This they did and lounged nude in the attic talking of daydreams and what they wanted to be when they grew up and enjoying the naughty sensation of doing what they liked in privacy.

"Have you ever seen a boy naked?" Helene asked. "I never have."

"Yes, I have a brother," Chaucer said. "I've seen him naked lots of times. And a boy in third grade showed me his weenie in an orange grove. There are two different kinds of weenies," she continued authoritatively, pleased to be expounding on a subject she knew more about than Helene. "One has skin over the top and the other has kind of a naked bulb at the end."

But Helene was aware of that particular difference. "Oh yes, some boys are circumcised," she told Chaucer. "They have their foreskins removed at the hospital. My mother explained it to me. She thinks I'm old enough to know the facts about sex. It's done, so Mom says, for hygiene reasons. Dirt can get inside the penis cover and they can get infected. Mom says uncircumcised men are also prone to venereal diseases if they have sex with the wrong sort of woman. And Jewish boys are circumcised for religious reasons as well as hygiene, but I don't know what those reasons are."

"Ah, that explains it," said Chaucer, genuinely glad for the information. "Spenser is circumcised even though we're not Jewish."

"Actually, I'm skeptical about circumcision," Helene continued. "Mom is pretty smart about most things, but it doesn't make sense that something that evolved to protect a penis from outside elements would be the cause of disease. And I sure wouldn't want to have part of my body cut off just because I might not have good hygiene habits. I *do* clean myself properly, so it's my decision about my body."

Chaucer looked deeply into Helene's face. "You're really intelligent, you know. I think I'm pretty smart, but you're much more than I am."

Helene sighed deeply. "Thanks, but you have more real life experience. I wish I could actually see a penis sometime. I'm envious that you have."

"How about your dad?" Chaucer suggested.

"Oh no, he's much too shy," Helene replied.

When they grew hungry, they dressed and went back to the Finn house for lunch.

<><><>

The back porch on the Dickinson home had been extended and enclosed to make a music room for Banky's band. Midweek sessions for arranging and rehearsing dance programs were regular events in that household. On summer nights, when school was out, Norah allowed the children to stay up late and sit quietly on a couch on one side of the room and listen to the musicians practice. Chaucer never missed the opportunity, being the only one among them to achieve perfect attendance.

As a result of this experience, Chaucer knew by heart not only a wide array of popular songs from the 1950s, but also standards from the thirties and forties. Adding to her musical education was her faithful watching of *Your Hit Parade* on television the last five years it aired until, unable to reproduce the rock and roll that had come to dominate pop music, it was cancelled by NBC in 1958, picked up by CBS for one more season, and then finally ended in April 1959.

Members of the band were so used to the Dickinson children silently listening from their upholstered perch, that they forgot they were there. As a result, the children often heard scatological language and slang references to drug use, although girl singer Betty Pool nagged at the men to watch their words. Banky was sure that most of the profanity and drug lingo went over their heads. He was not a user, and neither were his musicians, but they all knew plenty of people who were.

Betty had known Banky for a decade and a half. She had been a member of the Four Cuts, a singing quartet made up of people who had been cut from other groups. Together the two men and two women formed what they described as a "stoppable musical force," although they managed twice to crack the Top 100 with Banky Dickinson numbers in the early 1950s. Two of the four, Betty Pool and Benny Quick, now husband and wife, stayed employed as singers with Banky Dickinson's dance band throughout the Eisenhower and Kennedy years and hung on until the whole enterprise fell apart during the Nixon administration.

One night, before Betty and Benny arrived, Banky and his clarinetist, Francisco Xavier, carried on a conversation in Chaucer's presence that later embarrassed Banky when he realized Chaucer had been listening intently. The other musicians had not yet come in, and the two men were shooting the breeze when the talk drifted to World War II, as it inevitably did among men of their age cohort in those years.

"You were damned lucky to get hooked up with that entertainment outfit," said Francisco. "It sure beat the hell out of building airbases on coral atolls."

"Well, you're right, Frank," said Banky. "It was a pretty cushy gig. But it didn't keep me completely out of harm's way. I made it to the South Pacific a couple of times. On one tour, we ended up on a no account island with maybe two palm trees and a huge airstrip. We were doing a show, and two Nip planes buzzed in and dropped a few bombs on the runway and hightailed it before anyone could shoot at them."

"Yeah, but that was pretty tame compared with some of the shit I went through," said Frank.

"Tame? Yeah, alright," Banky replied defensively. "But I got a Purple Heart out of the deal."

"No shit?" responded Frank. "What happened?"

"One of the bombs missed the target and hit behind the makeshift stage they had set up for us," Banky said. "The set was blown apart, and my back and thighs were pierced with wood splinters. It was not life threatening, but it hurt like hell when they yanked them out."

"So you got a Purple Heart! Well, well! You're quite the hero," Frank said. "I never knew."

"I'm surprised you haven't seen it," Banky noted. "I wear a PH pin every damn time we play a VFW or American Legion hall."

"I never looked at it," the other man said. "That little pin in your lapel, that's a miniature Purple Heart?"

"Yeah," Banky answered. "At the time I got it, I didn't think much of it, but now I find it improves the tips and re-bookings. That's why I wear it."

This last remark was what caused him to regret his words spoken in front of his attentive middle child. He knew what he said was cynical and revealed a greedy and manipulative edge to his personality. And he was not nearly that cynical in reality. He simply fell into the flow of words because he did not want to appear overly sentimental or proud in front of a fellow musician. He wanted to be seen as hip.

"What must Chaucer think of me?" he asked himself that night. But after a good night's sleep, he forgot about the incident. If Spenser had heard him say that, he would have taken the boy aside and explained how men sometimes downplay their true feelings and say things they don't really believe. But it was only Chaucer, so he said nothing to her. It was just as well that he let it go, because Chaucer's mind had been exploring images of Pacific islands and dive-bombing planes, and she completely missed the comment about wearing the Purple Heart pin at musical gigs.

Banky preferred performing standards from the thirties and forties, but to keep the customers happy his band had to play current pop music from the fifties. Certain songs he absolutely hated but received so many requests for that his musicians practiced them during rehearsals.

Among his least favorites were "Standing on the Corner," popularized by the Four Lads and "Tonight You Belong to Me," an oldie remade by the pre-adolescent duo Patience and Prudence. Chaucer, on the other hand, thought those songs were pretty good but noticed the grimace on her dad's face when he made the band go through them. He and Chaucer agreed that "Smoke Gets in Your Eyes," a standard given new life by the Platters and an adaptation of a Puccini aria recorded by Della Reese called "Don't You Know" were very good, although Banky thought the Platters' arrangement bordered on being too emotive. The bandleader considered the Harold Rome and Laurent Herpin standard "(All of a Sudden) My Heart Sings" a great piece, but he disliked Paul Anka's youthful cover version, which Chaucer adored.

Chaucer had her own favorites and every once in a while she requested one during rehearsals, thus breaking the condition of silence. Banky pressed his finger to his lips whenever she forgot her place and spoke up, but the band's girl singer, Betty Pool, interceded and suggested Chaucer's choices were worthy of running through. For a time, Chaucer's favorite was Pat Boone's "April Love," but when Johnny Mathis released "The Twelfth of Never," that went to the top of her personal list and stayed there for months.

When she was seven, Chaucer put her dad's wrathful temper to the test by asking if the band ever played novelty numbers. She wanted to hear "The Little Blue Man," a song about a woman who was followed by a blue man no one but she could see. The diminutive creature repeatedly lisped "I wuv you," to her. Chaucer was pleased that there was a song about an invisible presence, because it validated her relationship with the invisible Riff. Unlike the singer, however, Chaucer liked the affection she felt from Riff, while the singer was perturbed by her little blue lover. As she thought about the song, she noted that she did not imagine Riff as a man at all but rather as a creature beyond gender. She had no idea where this concept came from, but she had never conceived of Riff as either male or female.

Even though Banky had written novelty numbers in the forties and early fifties, half a decade later, he drew the line at requests for them, even his own. He wanted his band to have a reputation for playing good, sophisticated songs, which did not include "The Little Blue Man." Chaucer received a barbed rebuke when she asked the band to do it. The following year, he would lose his temper completely and scream at his middle daughter when she asked for "The Chipmunk Song," which made the Chipmunks with David Seville the latest fad. Betty had to intervene again to get him to calm down.

That time, Chaucer slunk out of the rehearsal room and went to bed in tears. Sobbing into her pillow, she decided that she would not stop making requests but would try to ask only for songs she wanted to hear that she knew her dad also liked. "That way, he can't be mad at me," she whispered to herself before falling into a deep sleep.

Except for reading, Chaucer preferred listening to band practice over anything else that happened at home. Both activities made her body purr. Other than *Maverick* on Sunday evenings in the late fifties, she was indifferent to television programs. But she had been caught up in the offbeat bantering of Bret and Bart Maverick, played by James Garner and Jack Kelly respectively. No other Western appealed to her, and she judged *Ozzie and Harriet* stupid, especially the behavior of the boys, David and Ricky. She missed the irony that Ozzie Nelson had been a successful bandleader in the thirties and forties, and Harriet Hilliard had been his girl singer whom he wooed and married.

Discovering the public library at Central and McDowell proved to be beneficial to Chaucer's physical health as well as a feast for her developing mind.

In the spring of 1961, when she was eleven, her sister Marlowe needed to go to the library to get information for a report she was writing for her eighth grade science class and Norah agreed to drive her there on Saturday morning. Chaucer, having gone through all her older sibling's books and who was chronically short of things to read, asked to go along.

Norah took the girls to the main desk and each of them applied for library cards in their own names. After the librarian handed the magic rectangle to Chaucer, the sixth grader set off on her own to explore the stacks.

As she wandered up and down the rows of bookshelves, a sense of awe descended upon her. Room after room of literary treasure beckoned. She could borrow any book she wanted free of charge -a dozen books if she wanted! And quickly she found that a dozen was a conservative estimate. Her emotions overflowed with wondrous gratitude.

Chaucer experienced a physical reaction to being in the presence of so many mysterious, mystical, and transforming words bound up in pages, pages that she in her leisure could explore to her heart's content. Goosebumps covered her skin and her scalp tingled. In response to the feast of volumes set before her to ingest with her eyes and mind, a sense of grateful freedom rushed to her intestines, and she felt a strong urge to empty her bowels.

The first book she read from the pile she brought home that day was a novel based on Harold Gray's comic strip character Little Orphan Annie. *Little Orphan Annie and the Gila Monster Gang* had been published in 1944 in narrative rather than graphic form. Chaucer immediately identified with the redheaded orphan girl, although Chaucer's red hair was fine and straight and not curly like Annie's. Chaucer was not an orphan either, but she thought of herself as least loved in her family. Annie's self-reliance, inquisitiveness, and courage seeped into Chaucer's psyche, leaving a residue of feeling that would become a source of nostalgic reverie for decades to come.

The kenotic intestinal response recurred when she went back to the library two weeks later to return the pile of books she had checked out that first day. She found more books on the second visit and felt the same tingling urge to defecate. In due course, Chaucer learned to rely on the library as a cure for constipation. There was simply no way her body would allow itself to become impacted with fecal matter while sojourning amidst the wordy splendor of the library.

Spending time in the library also stimulated a sense of mystical connection with the universe, and after every visit, her mind became attuned to mental conversations with Riff. Riff seemed to hang around with her, silently, in the library, and then at night in bed, she would talk about books and far away places.

"Oh, Riff, this book I'm reading now is so exciting. It makes me long to live in another time and place," she said. "It's called **Great Expectations** by Charles Dickens, and it's scary, too, and parts of it are sad. But it makes me want to go back to England a hundred years ago and meet Pip and tell him things he needs to know."

"In due time you shall go to England, I am sure," Riff said.

"Do you really think so?" she asked eagerly.

"The eventuality is quite probable," said Riff confidently.

Chaucer had no idea how or when the word *eventuality* had entered her vocabulary, but as it happened, it had been at that moment when Riff put it there. However much Chaucer relied on these talks with Riff, she concurrently felt shame for continuing to carry on with an imaginary friend at the advanced and nearly grown-up age of eleven.

On subsequent trips to the library, she discovered Lewis Carroll's **Alice's Adventures in Wonderland** and **Through the Looking-Glass**, which she inhaled with abandon. Such was her enjoyment of these satirical fantasies that she felt much better about conversing with Riff. After all, she told herself, if Alice can carry on with rabbits, caterpillars, and human playing cards, talking with Riff seems harmless in comparison.

After working her way through the bizarre and violent stories in a compilation of **Grimm's Fairy Tales**, she decided that conversations with Riff were tame, although she was still not ready to tell anyone else about them.

Chaucer wanted to go to the library so often that Norah grew exasperated. "I am not a taxi service," she said curtly.

"Well then, can I go on my bike?" Chaucer asked.

"That's a little far, but if you're careful crossing Osborn and Thomas and stay off Central Avenue, I think you'll be safe enough. You can weave through Palmcroft and cross Central at the light at McDowell."

"Thanks, Mom," Chaucer said. This was a gift of freedom and Chaucer took full advantage of it, filling the basket on her handlebars with loads of books.

Just before the start of seventh grade, in August 1962, Chaucer prodded Marlowe to ask their mother to take her three children to see *The Wonderful World of the Brothers Grimm* at the Kachina Theater in Scottsdale. Chaucer was eager to see the film because she had read a collection of Grimm fairy tales. Marlowe was more interested in the Kachina's wide, curved screen for exhibiting movies made in Cinerama, such as this one, so she agreed to approach their mom. Because it was Marlowe who made the request, Norah agreed. Thus Chaucer became visually absorbed into the lives of these brothers who collected oral fairy tales and wrote them down. This, in turn, awakened a strong desire in her to write her own fantasy stories.

As seventh grade unfolded, Chaucer composed a series of tales about a redheaded girl of twelve who suffered from parental neglect but who escaped into splendid adventures in a place called Always Land, where she discovered that she was a beloved maiden or even a princess. The first story began this way:

Allys had bright and beautiful red hair, but she lived in a dull house in a dull neighborhood. One night when a full moon was shining outside her bedroom window, she climbed up on the sill and thought the moon was so bright and beautiful that she wanted to fly there and see it up close.

Without thinking about it, Allys jumped from the sill and began to fly in the air. She was caught up by a strong wind and carried many miles away. Suddenly the wind stopped and she fell into an eagle's nest at the top of a tall pine tree. Luckily the eagle was not home at the time.

Allys looked down from her perch and saw a strange land below with brightly colored paths and little stone houses with thatched roofs. "Oh, dear. It looks like I will have to climb down and ask for help. I hope nobody minds that I am outside in my pajamas."

When she reached eighth grade, Chaucer reworked some of her stories, making Allys thirteen instead of twelve and changing her hair color to strawberry blonde. That way, she reasoned, she could deny that the stories were about herself. The summer before she started high school, she would change Allys to fourteen and Allys's hair to a more universal brunette. That was a good neutral choice, she thought, because no one in her family had brown or brunette hair.

At the beginning of her final year in elementary school, Chaucer paid little attention to politics -until November 22, 1963. She knew that her parents had voted for John Kennedy in 1960 and had listened to them repeatedly complain at the dinner table about how the **Arizona Republic** had been doing a hatchet job in reporting about the Kennedy administration. But mostly she tuned out such talk.

Knowing how much her mother disliked the Irish, Chaucer thought Norah was a hypocrite for supporting President Kennedy, but the daughter failed to comprehend how many exceptions Norah had made to her anti-Irish bigotry over the years. By now her animus was almost entirely reduced to disparaging her mother-in-law.

However, the president's assassination frightened Chaucer, and from then on she began to listen to her parents' political conversations for words of reassurance that the world would be safe again. It did not feel safe when someone could kill the president and, then someone else could just walk up and kill that person. Where would it end? Ultimately, it was not hopeful words from her parents but their resumption of ordinary life as if nothing had happened that helped Chaucer let go of her fear and overcome the trauma of that violent time.

But on the evening of February 9, 1964, the unspoken cultural alienation that had for several years simmered between Chaucer and her father came into the open. The whole family gathered in front of the television that Sunday to watch the Ed Sullivan Show. The British quartet, the Beatles, performed five songs, and Chaucer was deliriously smitten by their music and their personas.

After the Beatles' first set, Banky said, "That's a flash in the pan if I ever heard one. I dislike rock and roll on principle, but what this shaggy bunch plays is utter rubbish. 'Till There Was You' is a beautiful song. How dare they desecrate it by sandwiching it between two of their juvenile numbers?"

"I think they're great," Chaucer exclaimed.

"Great, my ass," Banky grumbled.

Norah thought the Beatles were charismatic and entertaining but refrained from saying so. Marlowe and Spenser, who enthusiastically agreed with Chaucer, similarly kept their mouths shut.

"Why don't we just turn the TV off now?" said Banky. "We've seen what the noise was all about, and it's just that –noise."

"No," Chaucer replied forcefully. "You always watch Ed Sullivan to the end, even when you complain about the stupid acrobats and hand puppets. You're excused if you want, Dad, but for a change this is something I want to watch."

"Alright," Banky acquiesced. He sat back on the couch and folded his arms across his chest.

However, following the quartet's closing performance of "I Saw Her Standing There" and "I Want to Hold Your Hand," Banky was impatiently irritated. "They'll never last, you mark my words," he prophesied forcefully as he snapped off the television.

The next afternoon, in defiance of her dad's words, Chaucer rode her bike to Bill's Records at Park Central and bought her first but by no means last Beatles records.

CHAPTER 4:

ALLYS IN ALWAYS LAND

There ought to be a book written about me,
that there ought! And when I grow up,
I'll write one.

Lewis Carroll

"The Adventures of Allys in Always Land"
by Chaucer Dickinson

Allys was fourteen years old, and for thirteen of her years, she had been lonely. It wasn't that she had a wicked stepmother or angry stepfather or was given regular beatings or anything like that. Both her mom and dad were her real parents, and they fed her regularly, and most of the time it was food she liked. But except for the food, most of the time they just ignored Allys, leaving her to raise herself.

Allys had bright and beautiful brunette hair and a bright personality, but she lived in a dull house in a dull neighborhood. One night when a full moon was shining outside her bedroom window, she climbed up on the sill and thought that the moon was so bright and beautiful that she wanted to fly there and see it up close.

Without thinking about it, Allys jumped from the sill and began to fly in the air. She was caught up in a strong wind and carried many miles away. Most people would be scared if this happened to them, but not Allys. She spread her arms like an airplane and shouted "whee" as she sailed on the wind. Then suddenly the wind stopped and she tumbled from the sky into an eagle's nest at the top of a tall pine tree. Luckily, the eagle was not home at the time.

Allys looked down from her perch and saw a strange land below with brightly colored streets and little stone houses with yellow thatched roofs. "Oh, dear. It looks like I will have to climb down and ask for help. I hope nobody minds that I am outside in my pajamas," she said.

She tried to be careful as she climbed down the tree, but the pine needles tickled and scratched her bare feet, and this threw her off balance. Soon the back of her pajamas caught on a branch and ripped a hole in the seat, revealing a patch of skin on her fanny. It was only a small patch, but she worried about it anyway. Then on the next step down, she tore her sleeve. Now she was sure that her mom would make her feel guilty for doing this to brand new pajamas. She could almost hear her mother ranting about the high cost of pajamas these days.

When she got to the ground, Allys pulled the twigs from her hair and then looked around and saw that she was in an old-fashioned English village. The full moon lighted the streets, and so she began to explore. For several hours she walked up and down the cobbled streets on aching feet, wondering who lived inside the quaint houses.

As dawn broke, Allys felt hungry and wondered where she could get breakfast. Just then, the door of a house opened and a kind-looking woman stepped out wearing a red flannel nightdress. The woman stooped over to pick up a glass bottle of milk that a deliveryman had left on the porch. Seeing Allys staring at her, the woman said, "Dear me, young lady, what are you doing outside barefoot and in your jammies?"

Allys said, "I see you're in your nightclothes, too."

"Well, as it's before breakfast and I'm only on the porch, it's perfectly appropriate for me to be in my nightgown," she said. "But I don't know you, so you must have come from far away, and since you're not yet dressed, you must not have had your breakfast. Tell me your name and then come inside and I'll fix you a nice meal."

Allys sensed that this woman was kind, and she was not afraid to tell her name. "My name is Allys, and I have traveled through the air from the land of Arizona. I am frightfully hungry, so I will gladly accept your offer of a meal."

As Allys stepped into the cozy warm kitchen, the woman noticed that Allys's pajamas had a tear in the rear. "Dear me, child, how did you rip your jammies?"

"Oh, it was climbing down the pine tree," she answered.

"The one where the eagle lives?" the woman asked.

"Yes, that's the one," said Allys.

"Well, little wonder you didn't rip more than that. After breakfast, I'll mend the rip for you."

"I ripped my sleeve too. See?" Allys said, lifting her arm to show the other tear.

"Oh dear," was all the woman said.

"What is your name?" Allys asked.

"I am Meg," the woman said. "I am a grieving mother, who lost her only daughter to a terrible disease last year."

"I am so sorry," said Allys. "Did she suffer very long?"

"Sadly yes," said Meg. "But she is in pain no longer."

Meg heated up Cream of Wheat, which she sprinkled with cinnamon and brown sugar and set before Allys along with a steaming cup of cocoa.

"My favorites," said Allys. "How did you know?"

"These were my daughter's favorites," said Meg. "You remind me of her, except she had curly locks of golden hair, and you have brunette hair that falls straight to your shoulders. And she had green eyes while yours are blue. And she was a bit chubby while you are slender. But otherwise, you remind me of her. Except for your mouth. Hers was tiny and yours is wide."

At that moment, a man with a walrus moustache dressed in purple polka dot pajamas wandered into the kitchen. "I thought I heard voices," he said. "Aha, someone is here to converse with Meg. Who are you young lady?"

"I am Allys, and I was blown here from another land," she said politely.

"And I am Lute, the man of the house and also mayor of Jix, the capital village of Always Land," he replied genially and offered her his hand.

Allys stood and shook hands with the man.

"Yes, you remind me of my dear departed daughter,"

said Lute. "Except that she was shorter than you and her skin was more pale. You have a nice tan. The land you blew in from must be a sunny clime."

"Oh Lute, they are very much alike," said Meg enthusiastically. "They both love Cream of Wheat and hot cocoa."

When Allys turned to sit down again, Lute noticed the tear in her pajama bottoms and the patch of skin showing through. "Yes, the skin on your rear end is the same shade as the skin on our late daughter's face. You have that in common too."

Allys blushed bright red.

"I'll mend that," said Meg.

"Mend the color of her skin?" asked Lute in astonishment.

"No, silly, the tear in her jammies."

After breakfast, Meg took Allys into her daughter's bedroom to look for a dress that Allys could wear while she mended her pajamas. "Here is one that our dear Alice outgrew, so it might fit you. Try on anything you like, and when you've found something to wear, toss your jammies out to me." Meg left Allys alone in the room.

Allys wondered why neither Meg nor Lute had mentioned that she and their daughter had a name in common and quickly decided that it must be too painful for them to say so. She slipped out of her pajamas and opened the door a crack and pitched them onto the kitchen table. Then she searched through a dresser looking for underwear but didn't find any.

"Ah well," she sighed and picked up the pale blue dress that Meg had suggested. As she held it, a thought came to her that wearing someone else's clothes would feel strange. "But I've worn my sister's hand-me-downs," she said to herself. "But that's more embarrassing than odd. What about wearing the clothes of a complete stranger? By definition, that would be strange. And this is the dress of someone I never met who *died*. That feels creepy."

As she stood there holding the dress up to her chin, the feeling of creepiness faded away, replaced by the idea that kind-hearted Meg wanted her to wear that particular dress.

So, she lifted it over her head and let it fall down her naked body. It was soft cotton and felt good on her skin. A warm and comfortable feeling spread through her body. The fit was pretty good, too, just a little loose, and the hem didn't quite reach her knees, but it would do very nicely for the time she was in Always Land.

"It's not so bad wearing someone else's clothes," she said. "Someone else's clothes could be a good place to hide out for a while."

Allys went back into the kitchen, and Meg told Lute to take Allys on a tour of the house while she fixed the hole in Allys's pajama bottoms and the rip in the sleeve.

Lute led Allys into the living room, which had floor-to-ceiling bookshelves on every wall.

"Oh, I love books," Allys said. "May I look at what you have here?"

"By all means," said Lute. "Feel free to pull out any book that calls to you."

"Books call to me all the time," said Allys. "So many interesting titles."

"In Always Land, books call out in gentle voices," said Lute.

Allys reached for a volume bound in purple cloth and ran a finger down its spine. "I am *The Tale of the Irish Princess*," said the book in a sweet voice. "I am about a princess who was fair to behold who got lost in a dark forest. Please read me!"

"Oh my!" said Allys. "The books really do call to you here."

She put the book back in its place on the shelf and heard it say, "Oh well, maybe next time. I really am a good book."

"I will get back to you," said Allys to the book. "You sound really interesting, but I need to finish my tour of the house first."

Lute then led her to the parlor, where a large record machine played songs. "We have lots of records," Lute said. "So you can request anything you want to hear, and I'm sure we can find it for you. We especially like novelty songs. We just got a new Christmas record by a squeaky-voiced group called The Squirrels. I know you'll like it."

Then Meg came into the room. "Here you are, dear, all mended."

Allys said, "Thank you. I would love to listen to your records and read your books, but I suppose I ought to be going now. They might be missing me at home. I'll change back into these and return your dress."

"Oh no, dear, you can keep the dress," said Meg. "It wouldn't do to go wandering about Jix in jammies in broad daylight. I suppose it would be alright at night. What do you think, Mr. Mayor?"

"Oh yes, jammies at night are fine for going about town. But certainly not in the daytime," he said.

"So, feel free to explore our village. But when you get hungry, you just come right back here and I'll fix you a nice hot meal," Meg said.

"Well, they might have a search party out looking for me by now, so I suppose I should be heading back to my home in Arizona," said Allys. "Do you know how I should go about doing that?"

"Well, if you must, the easiest way would be to persuade the eagle to fly you back," Lute said. "But I have never heard of Arizona. That's a very strange name. You need to ask the eagle if he knows where it is."

"OK, I'd better go do that," said Allys. "Thank you ever so much for your kindness." She went back into the bedroom and changed into her pajamas and pulled the dress on over them. It would make a nice souvenir of this adventure.

As Allys left the house, Meg said, "If you can't find your way back to Arizona, you are welcome to make this your home. I've been praying for a beautiful new daughter, and you fit the bill perfectly."

Both Meg and Lute hugged Allys when she left. When she climbed the pine tree, she found the eagle at home and was not really surprised that the eagle spoke perfect English. But she was surprised that the eagle had never heard of Arizona.

"If you let me ride on your back, I can look for landmarks and show you where it is," said Allys.

"I doubt such a place actually exists," said the eagle. "And anyway, I do not have time in my schedule to search for it. I am, however, free to take you on a tour of a nearby enchanted island where Indians run around in their pajamas in the daytime."

"I didn't know Indians wore pajamas," said Allys. "I always thought they slept naked or in buffalo skins in the winter."

"It is a bad habit they picked up from the English," said the eagle, "although it is still preferable to sleeping in their saris. Of course they would never sleep in buffalo skins, because they worship cattle. That would be a sacrilege."

"Oh, you mean Indians from India," Allys said.

"Where else would they be from?" the eagle said snottily.

"From Arizona and the American West," Allys explained.

"Well, I know everything, and I have never heard of those places, so they must be imaginary."

Allys thought she would not get anywhere by arguing with this eagle but felt secretly smug that she knew some things that the eagle did not. She was also not surprised when she returned to the home of Meg and Lute to find her favorite lunch waiting for her in the kitchen.

The Tale of the Irish Princess was set beside her plate. "We deemed it a probable eventuality that you would like to read while you eat lunch," Meg said.

"I do, I do," said Allys and opened the book as she took a bite of her sandwich.

CHAPTER 5:
KISSING THE BEAST

He dreamed in which he saw a great tusked boar
Supine, asleep beneath the bright sun's heat.
Beside this boar, enfolded in his arms,
Lay bright Criseyde, kissing e'er the beast.
Geoffrey Chaucer

Marlowe was a junior at West High when Chaucer started high school there in 1964. The older Dickinson girl was vice-president of the National Honor Society, a member of Student Council, on the girls varsity tennis team, and very popular with boys, although Norah and Banky had as yet forbidden her to date. They thought Marlowe needed to be protected from the attention of undisciplined young males. Their plan was to allow Marlowe to go to the prom in the spring of her junior year but nothing before then. Once the prom threshold had been reached, they insisted on meeting and approving every boy she went out with, and no one already out of high school was acceptable.

Marlowe took the constraints with outward good humor but was embarrassed by the strictures and yearned to rebel, though she never did.

Chaucer felt invisible amidst a student body of three thousand and took some comfort in this. Though she consistently made the honor roll, she generally sat quietly at her desk, not drawing attention to herself. Helene was in most of Chaucer's classes and quickly became well known for her astute questions and always-correct answers, and Chaucer felt good about that. She and Helene continued as dearest friends in the course of their transition to high school.

One evening while they were studying together at Helene's house, Helene said, "You know the answers as well as I do, Chaucer. Why don't you ever raise your hand in class?"

"I'm not sure," Chaucer replied. "I guess I prefer watching and listening to find out how much other kids know or don't know. Except for you, I figure I'm smarter than anyone else in our class, but I only know that from keeping quiet and paying attention."

"I agree you're that intelligent," said Helene "Actually, I think you're brilliant, but I have a reputation for being a brain and you don't. I think you should try to be more outspoken in class so kids will recognize your intellect."

"Yeah, maybe," Chaucer said. "But part of me wants to fit in, to be liked. You can get away with being a brain and people still like you, but I'd probably come off looking like a know-it-all snob."

"Well, I know what you're really like and think you're great, and I think other people would too, if you only let them see the real Chaucer," Helene said.

Chaucer put down her book and hugged Helene. "Someday, I plan to let the real me out, I promise. But I'm just not ready yet."

Chaucer hovered in the background for two years until the spring of 1966, when Marlowe addressed the commencement ceremony with her valedictorian's speech. At the spring school assembly, the principal had announced that Marlowe had received a full scholarship to Middlebury College in Vermont. All of the faculty were very proud of her, he said.

When Marlowe left for college in the East, Chaucer hoped that now as the de facto oldest child in the house, she would get more attention at home, but this did not happen. Instead, her parents doted even more on the fair-haired Spenser, who began his freshman year at West the same time that a heretofore invisible Chaucer became a junior. Spenser was in the marching band and the all-school orchestra, playing clarinet and saxophone with equal ease. Dinner table talk centered on Spenser's musical activities.

Then things changed for Chaucer. Not at home, but at school. Out from under Marlowe's shadow, she spoke up more in class, became more outgoing, and also paid more attention to makeup and dress styles. This did not feel like an abrupt change to her but more of a natural progression.

Now looking in the mirror more often, she became concerned that her front teeth were a tad crooked, with one tooth slightly overlapping the other. At dinner one night, she raised the subject of orthodontia to straighten this dental defect, but Norah quickly quashed that idea. "It's foolish to spend money to fix something that will fix itself naturally in time."

Apparently, Chaucer's teeth were not a liability, for to her joy, boys suddenly found her irresistible, and popular girls invited her to hang out with their cliques. Members of the band asked Spenser to fix them up with his hot sister.

Helene was pleased that Chaucer was no longer hiding her intellect but dismayed by the change in her best friend's social blossoming. At first feeling abandoned, she soon recognized that she could benefit by proximity to Chaucer's relationship experiences. Thus the friendship continued. Chaucer even managed to help Helene improve her wardrobe and find double date partners for her, though none of these led to Helene acquiring a boyfriend of her own. Helene talked too much about school and the subjects she liked, and even boys who cared nothing for fashion, found her intimidating.

Chaucer decided she liked doing things with groups of people. She found the extraverted lifestyle pleasant and comfortable. With one exception. She made a few study trips to the library with friends and quickly discovered that she much preferred to go to the library by herself. She never felt alone there, however. This was her special paradise where she was surrounded by thousands of intimate friends who happened to exist in pages bound up in covers.

Banky and Norah set no restrictions on dating and no curfew for their middle child. Every weekend, Chaucer found herself escorted by one eager boy or another to movies and Mary Coyle's Ice Cream Parlor, or to the local roller skating rink and Bob's Big Boy. The more enterprising boys discovered that Chaucer would not object to strenuous necking if they could find a secluded place to park. And she was not shy about suggesting a drive up Summit Road in South Mountain Park to Dobbins Lookout to view the lights of the city from on high as prelude to vigorous tactile erotic play.

When her parents seemed indifferent to her coming home at midnight, she pushed that to one a.m. When she found they had gone to sleep at eleven, she stayed out till two or three, if the boy she was with could also get away with it.

On a balmy April night at two in the morning, in the back seat of his Pontiac, Chaucer went all the way with the boy who starred in the school play. This was their first date and her first time. The act was not as painful as she had been told it would be, and she was so steamed up from the foreplay and the risky excitement that she had an orgasm.

The actor asked her out again, and they became a couple on campus for the remainder of the school year and through half the summer, until she became enamored of a boy she met while cruising Central Avenue in Helene's Chrysler Newport. Chaucer promptly dumped the actor.

Helene had suggested they do the Central Avenue circuit, having heard so much about it and wanting to find out for herself what it was like. She also thought that having Chaucer along would aid her in meeting someone, but it was only Chaucer who made a romantic connection. By the start of her senior year, Chaucer was a free agent again and enjoying the attention of a string of boys.

While she was putting things away in her locker one afternoon, a football player sidled up and said, "Hey Saucy Chaucy, how about we take in a movie this Friday and whatever else we feel like doing?"

"What did you call me?" she said.

"Saucy Chaucy," he replied. "I made it up, because I heard you are quite a tasty dish." Seeing the look of displeasure on her face, he quickly added, "Hey, it's a compliment. I didn't mean anything bad by it."

She slammed the locker door shut, replaced the lock, and in a fluid motion slapped the athlete's face. "Take that as a no," she said and walked away. Every student in the hallway stared at the scene.

When he called that evening to apologize, she felt sorry for him and agreed to go out with him that weekend to see *To Sir with Love*.

After the movie she said, "I found the film charming and uplifting." And then to be deliberately provocative she added, "I find Sidney Poitier *very* attractive."

Recognizing her intent to test him about racial attitudes, he replied, "I've played football against teams with a lot of black players. Every one of them are nice guys who deserve respect. And I really like the theme song by Lulu. She's very attractive too."

Having passed her test, after a round of necking, Chaucer rewarded him with hand release. He never asked her out again, which was fine with her.

Reeve Knight, who taught the advanced placement senior English class, was Chaucer's favorite teacher. After the unit on *The Canterbury Tales*, Mr. Knight asked if any students were interested in learning Middle English, and only two responded affirmatively. One was Chaucer and the other a shy boy with pimples. The teacher then formed the *ad hoc* Middle English Club to meet with these two after school in his classroom to study vocabulary and translation methods. Chaucer loved the extra hours spent every Tuesday with the kindly and literate Reeve Knight and became sufficiently infatuated to fantasize about having a relationship with him.

Mr. Knight was always gentlemanly and a bit standoffish in their club meetings, but not in Chaucer's imagination.

Right after Thanksgiving, Chaucer started dating Chuck Wallace, an aesthetically attuned boy who was taking all the art and photography courses his advisor would allow. Chuck could see big things in small details, and Chaucer eagerly engaged him in enchanted conversations about symbolism and artistic expression. Though her affection and admiration for Reeve Knight remained strong, her school-girl crush on him faded as the relationship grew with the more accessible Chuck.

Chuck also proved to be an artist with his hands on Chaucer's body. Most of the boys she dated were not yet skilled at tactile stimulation, generally squeezing, pawing and groping at her breasts and delta. But Chuck was gently deft at unhurriedly exploring the contours of her anatomy, and Chaucer loved his manner.

Over the Christmas break, Chaucer and Chuck took a picnic basket out to a secluded desert area near New River, where they spread a blanket on the sand in a creek bed. The day was sunny but with the temperature in the mid-fifties, a little chilly for thin blooded Phoenicians. Nevertheless, after their meal, they undressed and made love on the blanket. On the drive home, Chuck told Chaucer that he loved her.

She accepted the endearment and said she loved him too, but though she thoroughly enjoyed being with him, she believed they would inevitably go their separate ways after graduation, and she was averse to making any commitments extending beyond high school.

The day before school was to resume, the ***Arizona Republic*** carried a story about a West High teacher who had committed suicide on New Year's Day. Chaucer was stunned to read that it was Reeve Knight. The story did not include a motive for the educator taking his own life.

Her grief heightened when the AP English class was taken over on an interim basis by an eighty year-old retired teacher who made the students memorize patriotic poems and write essays on the responsibilities of free citizens. All of Chaucer's inquiries to various teachers about the reasons for Mr. Knight's death were rebuffed with the comment that he had not left a note.

Emotional pain gnawed at her. She needed an explanation in order to heal. She needed to know that her flirtatious behavior had not contributed to his desperate act. She dreamed about her dead English teacher for weeks, dreams laced with sadness and guilt. Chuck, studies, and school activities eventually pushed this grief into a quiet corner of her mind, but she remained uneasy about the fate of Reeve Knight.

In March, Chuck bought a new single lens reflex camera and burned with eagerness to test it with some truly artistic compositions. Following another enchanted conversation with Chaucer about the erotic interplay of the natural environment and the human body, they returned to their picnic spot late that month, where she posed nude for a series of photographs.

The photos were artfully composed in the hilly desert setting north of Phoenix. Chuck was proud of his skill and pleased with Chaucer's ingenuous beauty as a model. Her pale skin contrasted nicely with the bleached tan of the land and the muted greens of the cactuses, ocotillos, and palo verdes that Chaucer posed amidst. Her posture with her back to a gray boulder blended with the curves and angles of the rock. In one clever shot, she appeared to be holding hands with the arms of a pair of saguaros she stood between.

Gingerly she stepped over to the blanket where her clothes were piled to put on sandals for a hike to another location Chuck wanted to try. As she sat on the blanket, a colorful bird alit on top of one of the saguaros she had been posing with.

"Ooh, what kind of bird is that?" she asked, pointing it out to Chuck.

"I have no idea, but it's pretty, though," he said. "Maybe a cactus wren?"

"No, it's too big for a cactus wren, and they have white eyebrows," she said. "This one has red cheeks and a white breast with black spots all over it. And when it was landing with its wings spread, the underside of its wings are gold. I have to know what species it is."

Chuck raised his camera and took a picture of the bird. Something about Chuck's movement startled the bird and it spread its wings to fly away, and Chuck captured that image as well. "I'll look it up for you when I get this developed."

As they walked toward a palo verde that Chuck thought would make a great backdrop, a pair of jackrabbits bolted from under the tree, and instinctively he raised his camera and clicked.

"Damn! The depth of field was wrong," he said. "It's gonna come out blurry."

"Too bad," Chaucer said. "Maybe they'll come back, or there may be more around here we could flush out."

"What I'd really like is to get you and a jackrabbit in the same frame," he said.

She laughed. "Chaucer Dickinson meets Bugs Bunny."

Chuck looked serious. "No, it's not a cartoon image in my mind. It's two beautiful but elusive creatures together in the natural world."

"That's a touching thought, Chuck," she said and kissed him on the cheek. "How about a picture of you and me together in the same frame? Get your clothes off."

"No, I couldn't," he said.

"Why not? You have a shutter delay don't you? Put your camera on your tripod, set the delay mechanism, and join me in front of the camera. It's very simple."

"Men aren't photogenic," he said.

"Bullshit! The male form is just as naturally beautiful as the female," she replied.

"In principle, I agree with that," he said. "But in reality, I'm shy."

"I've seen you naked, Chuck, and you have a nice body. Time to show it off."

"I…I'm not ready for that yet," he stammered. "I'm no good at posing. I'd look unnatural next to you."

"Men are such prudes!" Chaucer said sarcastically.

"I'm not a prude, just camera shy," he explained.

"That's a statement loaded with irony," Chaucer said. "A photographer afraid of the camera."

"Speaking of irony," Chuck added, desperate to change the subject, "I found out there's a nudist church about a half mile from here."

"What's ironic about that?" Chaucer responded.

"It just seems ironic that religious people would sit in pews naked. It's religious people who are the ***real*** prudes in this world."

"Oh, I don't know," she said. "A nudist church sounds sort of…authentic, like religion was supposed to be in the beginning. I'm intrigued. Let's go over there and check it out."

"They'd probably throw us out," Chuck said.

"We can pretend we're pilgrims looking for the true faith and heard they might be it," Chaucer extemporized. "I'm already naked, so I'd fit right in. Get your duds off and we'll go and see."

"Some other time," said Chuck. "We really need to be heading back home. I'm going to stow my camera gear in the car now." He took a step in that direction and stumbled against a boulder. Seeking to regain his footing, he brushed by a mature teddy bear cholla and let out a scatological scream of pain as its long thorns punctured his right calf.

Chaucer laughed in spite of his injury and quipped, "It looks like a jumping cactus has exacted revenge on the shy photographer who won't get naked."

"That's not revenge, it's sadism," he responded, wincing.

"No matter," said Chaucer. "Come over here and let me take your pants off so I can remove the spines."

Chuck did so, continuing to wince as she unbuttoned his jeans and pulled them down. She then used two flat rocks to capture the nearly invisible cactus needles from his bare leg. First aid mission accomplished, both put their clothing back on and returned to Phoenix, with silence prevailing for most of the trip.

The norm for nude models at the time was posing so that no pubic hair was visible. But Chuck had wanted a more authentic expression of the naked female body, and without hesitation, Chaucer had presented her body fully to the camera. The resulting images were in no way pornographic but stunning as representations of the holiness of the female form.

Chuck developed and printed the shots in his darkroom at home and took the photos of the unidentified bird to the library, where he looked through various avian reference guides until he found that it was a gilded flicker, a woodpecker-like bird found only in Southern Arizona and Northern Mexico.

On a day when no one else was home at her house, Chuck visited Chaucer and showed off a sequence of eight by twelve matte prints of her posing nude, and she asked if she could keep them. Chuck was happy to comply.

"I didn't print all the shots on the rolls I used," he explained. "Some of them didn't turn out good. Wrong exposure or depth of field problems, or just plain bad composition. I might look over the negatives and see if there are good ones I overlooked, but these are the best of the lot."

"Do you have a set of prints for yourself?" Chaucer asked. "For your artist portfolio?"

"Well, yeah," he said. "And I can make more prints for you any time you want them."

Suddenly the idea of nude photos of her circulating around the West High campus entered her brain. And though she had no objection to them being viewed as artistic works, she recognized that this high purpose would be lost on fellow students and any teachers who happened to see them. With trepidation, she asked, "Have you shown these to anybody else?"

"No, would you like me to?" he replied. "These are so good, I'd love to turn them in as a photography class project, but they'd kick me out of school if I did that...and you too."

"But when you get to college? What then?" she asked.

"I suppose I could use them there," he said.

Chaucer was beginning to feel anxious about uncontrolled use of the negatives. Chuck might not be able to resist making extra prints for his friends. "Well, if you already have a set for yourself, after you print any additional ones for your portfolio, why don't you give me the negatives. If you needed them for any reason, I'd lend them to you...for artistic purposes, of course."

Chuck became defensive. "Don't you trust me? The negatives are the product of my artistic work. I need them."

"It's not a matter of trust," she said. "The negatives are also the product of my artistic work as a model. I just think it would be more prudent for me to hold on to them. If you love me, as you have often said you do, I think you should give me the negatives. It would make me very happy."

Chuck assumed a playful demeanor. "Oh yeah, I love you Chaucer. The question is, do you love me?"

"Sure I do," she replied.

"How much?" he said. "Enough to make *me* happy?"

"What would make you happy, Chuck?"

"Love me in a certain way, and I'll give you the negatives."

"It's not love if you have to pay for it," Chaucer said. "But if you give me what I want, I'll feel very motivated to do something to make you happy."

"Well," he said, in a slightly embarrassed way, "we've talked about oral sex, and I...thought it might be time to try it."

Chaucer laughed. "You want a blowjob? I'd have done that anyway.

Sure, Chuck, I think it's a propitious time to explore the world of oral sex. Do you have any interest in going down on me too?"

"You bet!" he said.

She got down on her knees and undid the button on his fly. "Tell you what, Chuck. I'll give you a blowjob right now, and another one at an opportune time of your choosing. And you can choose a time to go down on my bush too."

With more eagerness than skill, she successfully led him to orgasm. Now with her mouth full of semen, she jumped up and ran to the bathroom, where she spat into the sink, gargled with mouthwash, and returned grinning to her bedroom.

As he was preparing to leave, Chuck said, "I almost forgot. That bird was a gilded flicker." He reached into his portfolio and removed another photograph of the bird with wings spread. "It turned out pretty good. This one I can turn in to my photo teacher."

"It's beautiful," Chaucer said. "Can I have a copy too?"

"Of course," he said.

Two days later, he gave her an envelope with all the negatives that contained images of her as well as a picture of the gilded flicker. Though relieved, she nevertheless had an intuitive notion that the photos would show up in some public venue in the future. She had no idea when or where but believed that it would happen. Posing had been fun and adventuresome at the time she did it, but now she wondered if it was a stupid thing to do. Well, nothing to be done now. She shrugged and put the subject out of her mind for the time being.

Back in her bedroom, Chaucer taped the envelope with the negatives to the inside of a King James Version on her bedroom bookshelf, thinking that it was the safest spot in the house because no one in her family would touch a Bible. The only reason she had the book was because a classmate with evangelical intent had given it to her. At the time she felt it was easier to accept the gift and make vague promises to read it than to get into a discussion about her religious objections. After the fact, she thought it was a useful source of literary allusions and so placed it on her bedroom bookshelf.

The photos were considerably larger than the negatives, so she stashed them in the middle of a box of old school papers, souvenir programs, and juvenilia from her elementary school days, placing the gilded flicker on top of the images of her.

Chuck asked for the second act of oral sex on senior ditch day, after they had climbed to the top of Squaw Peak and discovered that for the moment no one else was at the summit. Chaucer accommodated him, fulfilling her part of the bargain. Somehow, throughout the remaining course of their relationship, he never found a suitable opportunity to reciprocate orally with Chaucer.

Back home and in bed one night after making love to Chuck in his car, Chaucer fell into a state of mystical awareness. She was not asleep and yet not fully awake either. As she lay back in pleasant relaxation, she had the sense that she was floating out of her body, hovering above the bed, while at the same time consciously certain that she was not. After all, she could clearly see that her body was sprawled supine in her bed with her eyes open. But how could she observe herself, and more to the point see her face, if she were inside her body? This was a new experience for Chaucer, of a much larger order than her childhood *déjà vu* experiences, but similar to the trance-like states she had often known at the library. Like these earlier mystical states, the feeling of leaving her body did not frighten her.

As she began to reflect self-consciously about what was happening to her, the sense ceased and she knew she was securely back in her body. "Oh, I hope this happens again," she whispered to herself. "It feels wonderful!"

Miles away, Riff smiled.

The carefully planned pregnancy of Donna Cypress, West High drama teacher, did not result in her giving birth the week after the semester ended as expected, but four weeks prematurely. Mother and baby were doing well, but Mrs. Cypress would not be able to return to teach. Thus Rex Fisher was called in as a substitute for the remainder of the school year. Rex was a local nightclub and resort singer and entertainer who had recently been tapped as co-host of a new Arizona Afternoon television program, which would be aired beginning in mid-June.

Chaucer liked him well enough, although she thought he was a tad egotistical. One day he asked Chaucer to remain after class for a quick conference.

"I like the cut of your jib," Rex said to her as she stood across from his desk, "but I noticed you look a little down. Is something wrong? Anything I can help with?"

"Is that why you wanted to talk with me?" she asked, perplexed. "I suppose I look sad because I was just thinking again about Mr. Knight and wondering why he killed himself. It's so frustrating that no one here will say anything about it."

"Oh, I can tell you why, if that will ease your mind," Rex said. "He was being blackmailed by someone who threatened to expose him as a homosexual."

"Oh how awful," Chaucer said.

"Yes, it must be awful to be queer," he said.

"No, I meant how awful being blackmailed," she replied quickly. "Thank you for telling me. It explains a lot. He was my favorite teacher. Is there anything else?"

"Yes, actually," he said. "I'm thinking ahead about my television program and making a mental list of potential guests. Are you eighteen yet?"

"Yes, barely," she said. "What difference does that make?"

"Oh none really. I was just curious," he replied. "What I want to know is if you would be interested in appearing on my show sometime this summer?"

"Why me?" she asked.

"As I said, I like the cut of your jib," he repeated. "I could interview you about what it's like being a student these days, stuff like that."

"Well, I guess it would be fun," she replied. "What do I have to do to prepare?"

"Come over to my house and we can talk about it over a glass of wine," he said. "My wife is out of town, so we can have the place to ourselves."

Now that his intent was clear to her, Chaucer did not know how to respond, so she stammered, "Uh, thank you, but I don't drink."

"Some soda pop, then," he replied.

"I've got too much homework," she said. "And I'm late for my next class. Gotta run."

The previous February, after news of the Tet Offensive in Viet Nam had been repeatedly blared across the land on every national news program, Chaucer discovered the anti-war movement. She had been aware for a long time that many people, especially young men facing the draft, were against the war and some were demonstrating their opposition in protest marches. Now as spring unfolded the subject resonated with her in a more powerful way, and among her peers she became vocal in denouncing the war.

At the school spring assembly, Chaucer was named a National Merit Scholar with acceptances from Prescott College, Anasazi College, and Arizona State University. The principal said she had not yet decided which school to attend. The truth was that she wanted to accept the scholarship and financial aid package of Prescott College, but her parents said they could not afford to have two children in expensive private schools at the same time and insisted that Chaucer go to ASU.

Valedictorian Helene Finn, the principal announced, would be going to the University of California at Berkeley. Chaucer was happy for Helene, but grieved the possibility of never seeing her again, because Helene's parents had decided to move to San Francisco so they could be closer to their daughter, while promising not to intrude on her college experience. They had been childless for so many years that Mr. Finn was old enough to retire when Helene graduated from high school, and there was nothing to hold them in the Valley. Thus there was no reason for Helene to come back during summers.

In May, Chaucer considered attending a protest rally set for Encanto Park, marking what would be her first active engagement in the anti-war movement. The assassination of Dr. Martin Luther King the pervious month had upset her deeply and was pressing her conscience to do something worthwhile. Had not a more directly personal matter been weighing on her mind, she would have gone to the rally.

But her period was late, and she feared she was pregnant.

Ruminating on this situation took up all her emotional energy and sapped her physical stamina. She stayed in her room all Saturday, claiming to be studying for final exams but in fact mentally working out all manner of scenarios about how her life would unfold with an infant to care for.

Chuck picked her up for their usual Saturday night date, and she said she didn't feel like a movie but wanted to have a serious talk. The word serious scared Chuck, because he had been accepted at Occidental College in Los Angeles, and he was planning to break up with Chaucer during the summer so that he could go off to college as a free agent. In his mind, the word serious meant only one thing: a long-term commitment with pledges to be true and wait for one another while they were away at different colleges. He knew he was not suited for such a step. A few months earlier, he would have been eager for a promise to stay together after high school, but his ardor had been waning since then. Oddly, at that moment the thought of pregnancy did not enter his mind.

Chuck drove to Bob's Big Boy at Central and Thomas and parked in the covered area where carhops waited on customers. Other than a halting conversation about what to order, both of them were uncharacteristically quiet.

After their food was brought out, Chaucer munched on an order of fries, not because she was hungry but as a means of stalling. But the fried potatoes tasted funny, making her feel nauseous, and so she stopped eating, looked across at her boyfriend, and spoke softly. "Chuck, I'm late."

"No you're not," he said. "You were ready right on time when I came over."

She grinned ruefully. "No, dummy, my *period* is late. It's always been regular and it has never been late before so I may be pregnant."

Chuck went pale. Suddenly the prospect of breaking up took on a very different significance. "But you're not sure?"

"I have no idea what being pregnant actually feels like," she said calmly, "but I *feel* different from usual. I can't explain exactly how. It's kind of an ethereal feeling. So, my guess is that I am pregnant, but I am not *sure*."

"How late are you?" he asked.

"It should have begun Thursday," she said.

He nodded in acknowledgement of her words but said nothing. His eyes took on a glazed appearance as he processed the information in his mind. Chaucer kept quiet to allow him time to think.

Then Chuck broke the silence with a philosophical sigh, "Well, there goes Occidental. I suppose I could get a job and go to Phoenix College part time."

She kissed his cheek. "Thank you, Chuck. That's all I need to hear for now. I know you don't go to church, but if you're ever tempted to pray, now is the time to pray that I'm only late and nothing more."

"I can do that," he said with the start of a smile. "But you don't go to church either. Have you been praying?"

"You could call it that," she said. "I've been invoking the universal consciousness to bring forth my menses. I think that counts as praying."

"Yeah," he replied, now grinning, "I suppose it's good to cover all the religious bases."

"The only good thing about the timing of all this," she said in an attempt to expand on the lightening mood, "is that graduation is only two weeks away, so I won't show when I walk across the stage to get my diploma."

"Thank God for small favors," he said sarcastically.

"If my period starts, Chuck, you'll be the first to know," Chaucer said.

CHAPTER 6:
THE WIFE OF BATH

And she was fair and very young, ergo
For joy he caught her in his arms, and so
His heart swam in a bath of such dear bliss
That countless times he gave her his sweet kiss.

Geoffrey Chaucer

Chuck had taken her back to the house at ten the previous night, prompting her mother to say, "You're home uncharacteristically early. Did you and Chuck have a fight?"

"Not at all," said Chaucer. She was smiling, which gave credence to her answer. "I just have a ton of last-minute studying to do tomorrow, so I want to get a good night's sleep."

Feeling that her future was in limbo but there was nothing at all she could do about that at the moment, she surrendered to fatigue and slept soundly. The bleeding began Sunday morning.

She telephoned Chuck from home, and not wanting anyone in her family to catch even a hint of a comment about pregnancy, she said, "Hi Chuck. I've been thinking about our talk last night, and although I'm still jealous that you get to go off to Occidental in the fall, I'm genuinely happy for you. It's such a great school. While I'm at ASU this fall, I'll be thinking of you hanging out with all those Hollywood starlets."

Intense study of contraception and safe sex practices began for Chaucer Sunday afternoon, and in a very short span of time, she became an expert on the subject.

49

After school on Monday, Chuck drove Chaucer to Encanto Park so they could walk around and talk.

"I'm touched that you stood by me when I thought I was pregnant," she said.

He looked down at the ground and said, "Yeah, well it would have been cold to do anything else."

"Well, I just want you to know that I'll always remember your gallantry," she said and kissed him gently on the cheek.

"I'm glad you're not pregnant, but the funny thing is," Chuck continued, "when you told me your period had started, I felt a little sad. Like I'd lost something important."

"You like the idea of being a father?" Chaucer asked.

"Maybe," he said. "During the time I thought you were going to have a baby, I felt...virile, knowing for sure that I was capable of fatherhood. Then when I heard you weren't, that confirmation of potency evaporated. That's part of it, but I think it had more to do with art than anything else."

"How so?" she said.

"When I thought about you being pregnant, I thought about the nude photos you posed for and how classy they are, and I got the idea of taking a series of artistic shots of you during the stages of pregnancy. The images would have been profoundly beautiful; I'm sure of it."

Chaucer flushed at the compliment. "Spoken like a born artist. But it's really fortunate that I'm not pregnant, Chuck, because you need to continue your education and learn to become an even better artist. And you couldn't do that while trying to support a family and study on the side."

"Actually, I think I could," he said. "My art would be different as a result, but it would be no less valuable."

"Yes, but I also need to go to college and pursue the literary endeavors that have been calling to me as much as the world of art has been beckoning you."

"Before you told me you might be expecting," Chuck said, "I was thinking about breaking up so we would both be free to date other people while we were away at different colleges. But when faced with the prospect of parenthood, the idea of getting married felt kind of nice. Now I get the sense that you want to do the breaking up."

"It's ironic, isn't it?" she said.

Chuck took the parting with more grace than she had anticipated.

The killing of Bobby Kennedy in June renewed Chaucer's April grief, and her period was late again that month, though she knew for certain that she was not pregnant.

That fall, Chaucer enrolled at ASU, choosing English as her major, and accepting the invitation to participate in the Honors Program. However, the freedom from home life she had anticipated did not fully materialize. As much as Banky and Norah had seemed indifferent to Chaucer's presence in the house during her childhood years, they found a way to keep her there a little longer. They insisted that she live at home and commute to campus in order to save the costs of a dormitory and food plan.

"But I don't have a car," Chaucer said.

"It's all taken care of," Norah explained. "Natalie down the street goes to ASU, and we've worked out a deal with her parents. You can ride with her for ten dollars a week and we'll pay for it. I think that's very generous."

One Saturday morning while Chaucer was studying in her room, Norah entered in search of dirty clothes to fill out a load of white things. Chaucer rummaged through her hamper to extract the requisite items. In the meantime, Norah spied the Kings James Bible on the bookshelf and picked it up.

Chaucer immediately remembered the film negatives taped inside the back cover and tensed up.

"I'm surprised to find this here," Norah said, waving the book back and forth. "Are you going fundamentalist on us?"

"What if I were?" Chaucer responded with a tiny note of defiance in her voice.

"Well...it's your life," Norah said dismissively.

"Actually, I have it for literary purposes. Much of its poetry and stories are literary masterpieces and it is frequently cited in so many other works of literature, that any English major needs a King James Bible for a reference."

"That makes sense," Norah said with a relieved tone in her voice.

"But why should you be upset if I study religious things?" Chaucer said in a provocative manner. "After all, you named me Chaucer, and my namesake wrote extensively about religion and church people."

"Since the church controlled society in those days, there was little else to write about," said Norah with unfeigned sarcasm. "Let the record show, however, that your namesake did not endear himself to church authorities by what he wrote. Take the Wife of Bath, for instance. She was a nonconformist, a strong woman that priests could not abide. I've always thought of her as a very early proponent of women's rights."

Chaucer found herself nodding in agreement with her mother. "Exactly, and her tale is about a knight sent on a mission to discover what women most wanted. And the answer turned out to be authority over their husbands."

"A noble desire," said Norah. "Actually, Wife of Bath is the only thing of Chaucer's I ever read, but it was enough to make me want to name a child after him."

"For that, Mom, I owe you great thanks. I do love my name," Chaucer said with a laugh. "Oh, and another thing about the Wife of Bath, she made no apologies for the pleasures of sex. That also went against the strictures of the church. I came across an apt comment about **The Canterbury Tales** by Havelock Ellis. Have you heard of him?"

"I've heard the name. Didn't he write about sex long before Dr. Kinsey?"

"Yes," Chaucer replied. "Ellis was a British physician, reformer, and writer who did extensive research into sexuality in the 19th century. At any rate, Ellis maintained that in the Prologue, Chaucer set the purpose of the pilgrimage as 'not primarily religious but biological, an impulse due to the first manifestation of spring.' That idea tickled me, that people didn't really go on pilgrimages to fulfill religious duties but because of, for lack of a better term, springtime restlessness. You know, with all that fresh sap running through their veins, they needed to get moving."

Norah nodded approvingly. Without conscious thought, she opened the Bible, which was still in her hand, to a book-marked place and peered at the text of Song of Solomon 3:4 that Chaucer had colored with a yellow highlighter. As if she were at a Poetry Society meeting, Norah read aloud, "I found him whom my soul loveth; I held him and would not let him go, until I had brought him unto my mother's house and into the chamber of her that conceived me." She peered into her daughter's eyes. "Hmm, that's pretty racy stuff. English majors may be interested in this, but you can be sure no preacher would ever have the balls to read it out loud to a congregation."

"Perhaps not, but non-religious authors will make sure that beautiful but neglected texts from books like the Song of Solomon will always be made known to people despite the puritanical attitudes of clergy," Chaucer said.

"That's good, but I hope this verse doesn't give *you* any ideas about bringing lovers into your mother's house…to you mother's bedroom chamber," Norah added. "Even in the name of women's rights, that would be a step too far, I think. Way too far."

"Not a chance of that ever happening," Chaucer said, looking directly at her mother. "I cited that passage in a paper on biblical influences in nineteenth century romantic literature."

Norah closed the book and placed it back on the shelf.

Chaucer breathed a sigh of relief that the envelope inside had not fallen out. To cover her reaction, she said, "You're still wounded from Grandma and Grandpa's religious fundamentalism, aren't you?"

"I suppose I am," Norah replied. "They were over-controlling with me. No games, no cards, no radio, no dancing. Dad's prayer at every meal always seemed to include some statement about how God is watching everything we do and is rarely pleased with what he sees. Anything even remotely related to sexuality clearly made God angry. And that included such evil vanities as lipstick and hair ribbons. And of course, dating was out of the question."

"You and dad were pretty controlling with Marlowe," Chaucer said. "She told me she felt smothered by you."

"That was more your dad than me, although I generally agreed with him," Norah said. "But it was not the same as with my parents. We never inflicted a voyeuristic angry God on any of you children. We let Marlowe go out on dates. It's just that we wanted to meet the young men before they went out alone. Marlowe was naïve and too beautiful for her own good. She needed protection."

"What about me?" Chaucer asked. "You didn't have those requirements when I started dating."

"Well, she's the firstborn. Parents are always stricter with firstborns. After that they loosen up a bit. Besides that, you're not naïve," Norah answered with a knowing inflection.

"And not beautiful, I suppose," Chaucer added.

"Apart from the red hair," Norah said with a now affectionate tone, "you are quite attractive. Unfortunately, your hair is not an asset. Although…maybe you could dye it."

"You never dyed your hair. Anyway, I've always thought of dying hair as phony," Chaucer responded. "I like my hair, color and all. It's who I am. And if it should suddenly turn green or even gray, so be it."

"Well, as I said before, it's your life," Norah said and departed with the dirty laundry.

As she later reflected on the exchange, Chaucer decided this had been the best one-on-one conversation with her mother she could remember ever having. She hoped it boded well for the future.

Three days later, Chaucer's mid-afternoon class was cancelled, and Natalie didn't have one then and was happy to leave campus early, so Chaucer arrived home in time to find her mother watching the Arizona Afternoon television program.

"I do like that Rex Fisher," said Norah. "He's so charming and full of wit."

"More like smarmy," said Chaucer. "I think he's a creep."

"I thought you liked him when he taught drama at West High. You got an A from him, if I recall correctly," Norah said.

"I *earned* that A," Chaucer said. "But he's still a slime ball as far as I'm concerned."

"What makes you say that?" Norah asked.

Chaucer hesitated and then thought that she may as well go ahead and shock her mother. "After first ascertaining that I was eighteen, he invited me to his house to enjoy a bit of wine with him, noting in the process that his wife was out of town. It was to be a kind of *audition* for his TV show."

"And what did you say to him?" Norah asked.

"I said I didn't drink. And the drinking age is twenty-one anyway," Chaucer replied. "So his asking my age was not relevant."

"It was the age of consent that he was concerned about," Norah said.

"Oh, I figured that out in about two seconds," Chaucer said. "He was being careful about that tiny matter of statutory rape."

"And did your being a teetotaler end his auditioning pursuit?" Norah asked.

"No, but I cut him off by saying I had too much homework," Chaucer said with a laugh.

"See, just as I told you before," Norah responded, "you're not naïve. And in light of your story, I guess Rex must be a bit of a letch after all to hit on a high school girl."

"Only a *bit?*" Chaucer asked.

"Well, your father could tell you plenty of stories about entertainers with zipper problems," Norah said. "It's an occupational hazard. So I guess that part's not surprising. The legendary casting couch and all that. But robbing the cradle, I'll admit, is way over the line. So I guess that does make Rex Fisher an official slime ball." Norah laughed. "And I give my daughter an A plus for so effectively turning him down."

"Thanks, Mom. Are you going to tell Dad about this?" Chaucer said.

"Of course," Norah replied. "He loves show biz gossip. And I think I'll still watch this show, too, because creeps can be so fascinating."

Throughout her freshman year at ASU, Chaucer repeatedly raised with her parents the subject of living on campus in a dormitory.

Commuting with Natalie was proving to be complicated, because the timing of their class schedules did not correspond on Tuesdays and Thursdays, and Natalie complained at having to get to the campus early on those days to accommodate Chaucer. Several times Chaucer was late to class as a result.

When her second semester grades revealed she had made straight A's for the year, Banky and Norah reluctantly agreed to put up the money for a dorm room and food plan for the rest of her time at ASU, on the condition that she would get a summer job to contribute toward her college costs.

The next day, Chaucer landed a job as an indoor waitress at Bob's Big Boy at Central and Thomas. She was grateful not to be assigned as a carhop, because even at night the summer temperatures often stayed above a hundred degrees, and rowdy boys from the privacy of their cars often treated carhops shabbily.

After a few circuits of Banky driving her to work and grudgingly picking her up again at the end of her shift, it became clear that transportation was a major frustration factor in the family. Bob's was too far to walk, and if she rode her bicycle, she would be drenched in sweat by the time she reported to work in late afternoon. Preparing mentally for an angry outburst, Chaucer asked her parents for a car.

"It doesn't have to be anything fancy," she said. "Just reliable transportation. If I buy the car, I won't be able to save any money toward my college costs."

As it happened, her parents took the request stoically. Banky was getting tired of being a chauffer and so conceded the point. He found an inexpensive five year-old Chevy II coupe for his middle daughter. The no frills compact car was white, with nothing optional inside except an AM radio. Chaucer was thrilled.

Late that summer, Chaucer's old boyfriend Chuck Wallace came into the restaurant alone near closing time, dressed in a U. S. Army uniform. He slipped into a turquoise naugahide booth and rested his folded hands on the tan Formica tabletop. When Chaucer approached him to take his order, she was startled to see him.

"What happened to college?" she asked, after he had ordered a side of fries and a cherry cream coke.

"My parents went through a nasty divorce, and one of the things they fought over was who would contribute how much to my college expenses," he explained. "I got so tired of it, I dropped out and enlisted. This way I'll get GI Bill benefits when I get out and can do college on my own."

"Very admirable," said Chaucer. "You look nice in khaki, by the way. And look, you've already got medals. That's impressive."

"Oh, the National Defense Medal. Everyone gets that for serving in a time of war," he said. "And this one is for qualifying as an expert sharpshooter."

"As I recall, you're an expert shooter with a camera, so why not with a gun. So where will you be stationed?" she asked. The restaurant was not crowded at the time, and she was able to linger a bit at the table.

"I have orders for Viet Nam," he said and noticed that Chaucer flinched slightly as he said it. "But one of the advantages of enlisting is that I got to choose my own specialty. I'm in the Signal Corps."

She left to turn in his order. Later when she returned with the food, he continued his story. "Because of my expertise with cameras, I drew a great MOS -Military Occupational Specialty. I'll probably be photographing and filming combat action and battle scenes. That will afford me a whole new realm of artistic possibilities, so it's really a continuation of my chosen occupation."

"It sounds dangerous," she said.

"Not nearly as dangerous as being a grunt," he replied. "Say, what are you doing after work. I can wait for you, if you don't have other plans."

For a moment she was tempted to go somewhere with him, but then shook her head and said, "Thanks, but I have to clean up when my shift is over, and my feet are already aching badly, and by then I'll be really worn out. I need to go home to bed."

"Can I come with you? I could rub your feet for you. Or other things. I have great hands, as you should remember."

She laughed in a pleased manner. "Are you that desperate to get laid before shipping off to war? Is that what this is about?"

"No!" he spat out immediately and paused. In response to her silence, he then sheepishly confessed, "Well, yeah, partly I guess."

"Well, I'm still living at home, and my parents would probably frown on my inviting a soldier to my bedroom," she said with a note of sarcasm.

"We could park somewhere," he suggested with hopeful expression. "I'm sure our old favorite spots are still there."

"It's been really nice seeing you again, Chuck. Let's leave it at that," she said.

When he left, she found a large tip on the table. As he approached the exit, she called to him and said, "Have a nice war, Chuck. Be safe."

He grinned and waved, saying, "I'll carry memories of you wherever I go."

At the end of the summer, her mother decreed that since Chaucer would be living in a dormitory on campus, she could not take the Chevy II to Tempe. Instead, her parents gave the car to Spenser to use during his senior year in high school.

CHAPTER 7:
EARTH MOTHER

I do not doubt the self I was
Was competent to me –
But something awkward in the fit –
Proves that – outgrown – I see –
                    Emily Dickinson

When Chaucer returned to school that fall, she moved into the much sought after McClintock dormitory. Being on campus all the time provided opportunities to participate in activities she had missed out on while she commuted. Her assigned roommate was an introverted young woman named Frieda Ackley, who was majoring in mathematics. Frieda was extremely studious and not interested in social activities. The rumor around the dorm was that her roommate from freshman year refused to be yoked with her again. Chaucer found Frieda so quiet and undemanding that it was almost like having a private room. She and Frieda got on splendidly.

The university sponsored a foreign film festival on Saturday evenings at the Lyceum. The first week of the festival, Chaucer saw *Les Parapluies de Cherbourg*, subtitled in English *The Umbrellas of Cherbourg*, and fell in love with the story and the star, Catherine Deneuve. Chaucer resonated with the plight of the seventeen year-old Genevieve. Her boyfriend Guy had been drafted, and on the night before he was shipped off to the war in Algeria, she had sex with him. The film reminded her of the pregnancy scare she had had when she and Chuck were going together, and it reinforced the wisdom of her decision not to make love to him before he flew off to Viet Nam. Intellectually, she was not concerned about getting pregnant, but at an emotional level, she felt the tragedy of Genevieve's life. When Genevieve capitulated to her mother's pressure and married a wealthy older man she did not love, tears flowed down Chaucer's face. She was awed by Michel Legrand's film score, and when she found a recording of "Watch What Happens," an American adaptation of a major melodic theme in the film sung by Ed Ames, she bought it and listened to it so many times that her exasperated and no longer acquiescent roommate forbade her to play it more than twice a day.

Chaucer developed a routine of spending Saturday mornings studying at the Hayden Library. It did not take her long to notice the regulars hunched over their habitual library table spots. A particular graduate student peaked her curiosity, and she felt drawn to him.

Though she did not know his name, something about the man resonated within her mind at a deep level, but she had no conscious awareness of what it was. It was not his long, light brown hair with sun bleached blond strands, although she found that attractive. Nor was it his penetrating blue eyes, which she found intriguing. Some hidden quality radiated from him, and she wanted to get to know him.

One Sunday morning just before dawn, she had a dream in which she met this mysterious student in midair outside the library while both of them were floating out of their bodies. The imagery stayed with her through the day, but Chaucer was not in the habit of telling her dreams to anyone and certainly not that dream.

The sensation of out-of-body floating, which she had experienced only once, was a thing she kept entirely to herself. But the idea that this attractive student was associated with this special sensation, made him all the more intriguing. Even if the connection is only in my imagination, she told herself, that's reason enough for trying to get to know him.

The following Saturday she made a point of taking an open chair at his table, sitting directly across from him. She tried to study but kept looking up, hoping to make eye contact with him, but he did not notice her. She thought he looked lost in another world, a sad world. He was so rapt in concentration on the book he was reading and jotting notes onto three-by-five cards that she hesitated to interrupt him to strike up a conversation.

When he reached down for his backpack, she thought this might be her chance, but without looking at anyone else, he placed it on the table and rummaged inside for what turned out to be more cards, and her eyes turned not to his face but to an identification tag on the front of the backpack. It looked like a calling card with either a first name or title blacked out. But she clearly saw his name: Cloud Morgan. Well, that's progress, she thought.

She waited patiently for an opening, but he stayed anchored in his seat, reading and making notes on cards.

At last, he looked up and stared in her direction, and for an instant she thought this was her chance, but then it seemed like he was looking right through her and literally did not see her sitting across the table staring at him. By the time she had formed her mouth to say hello, he had turned back to his book.

Eventually, Chaucer desperately needed to pee and got up to go to the restroom. As she walked away, she mused that very likely he would be undemonstrative even if she did succeed in attracting his attention, and so she dropped the idea of trying to make a connection. In any case, he was gone when she returned to the table.

Later that fall, Chaucer participated in several antiwar rallies sponsored by a group called University Students Against Rapacious Military Intervention. She had no inclination to join the organization but enjoyed hanging out on the fringes of the peace movement. Though she was clearly against the war in Indochina, she did not think that constituted being a pacifist. She suspected that many of her fellow students did not know whether they were for peace or against war, but to Chaucer, these were not the same thing.

USARMI was led by a charismatic student named Zebulon Cox, and thus the group was affectionately known as Cox's Army. Zebulon was the scion of a wealthy, socialite family. He flunked out of Stanford and enrolled at ASU to party and play, but instead he became radicalized by the conduct of the war in Viet Nam.

At one pre-rally meeting of USARMI that Chaucer attended, Zebulon began his address by saying, "To all you FBI agents or informers here tonight, we say welcome. Maybe we will be able to open your eyes to what true patriotism looks like."

He began by telling some of his personal story, as a young man growing up in the lap of privilege, and then launched into a history of the Indochinese war. "The French were kicked out of their colonial occupation of Viet Nam by the Japanese during World War II. At the end of the war, the French did not want a free and independent Viet Nam but lusted after re-occupying it. The most powerful nation in the world at that time was the United States of America and we could have stopped the tragedy before it started by saying no to French colonial ambitions. But the pantywaists at our State Department were afraid to stand up to the French and rolled over and let the Frogs start a war with Vietnamese nationalists.

"As a nation, the current war in Viet Nam is our own damned fault because our government supported the greedy French instead of the oppressed Vietnamese peasants yearning for freedom.

"You may ask, 'weren't the Vietnamese nationalists Communists?' The answer is mostly not. Ho Chi Minh used the Chinese Reds for sanctuary and leverage against the French, but he hated them. And if independence had come to Viet Nam after World War II, the country would have steered away from the influence of the detested Chinese."

The FBI agent in the audience thought to himself, "He's got a point there. This guy is doubly dangerous, because he makes sense and he appeals to patriotism and American ideals."

In November, an FBI agent named Milford Miller appeared at Chaucer's dormitory and asked to speak with her. When she came out to the lobby, she noticed that he was wearing a dark suit with white shirt and Navy blue tie. His spit-shined black dress shoes gleamed in the fluorescent light. Under his left arm he cradled a dark brown fedora.

Chaucer escorted him to a corner conversation pit. Upon sitting, he showed her his credentials and told her his name. "Thank you for giving me a little of your time," he began.

"What is this about?" she asked with real curiosity.

"Well, Miss Dickinson," he said, "do you know a man named Zebulon Cox?"

"Pretty much everybody on campus knows him," she said.

Agent Miller said, "Mr. Cox is under consideration for appointment to a Government advisory panel, and as a routine matter, I would like to ask you a few questions about his character and suitability." This was a lie, as the true purpose of the interview was related to a surveillance operation and investigation of Zebulon Cox and the USARMI organization that he led, which the FBI considered a subversive group.

"Ask away," Chaucer said.

"Mr. Cox has told us that he is the founder of an organization called University Students Against Rapacious Military Intervention. Are you aware of this organization?"

"Well," she said, "for months now stories about it have been splashed across the front pages of the *State Press*, which as a student here I read regularly, so I am certainly aware of the USARMI."

"Do you personally know Mr. Cox?" Miller continued.

"I've met him and had brief conversations with him," she answered.

"Have you participated in any of the events sponsored by the organization Mr. Cox leads?"

"It's a free country, isn't it?" Chaucer responded.

The agent ignored her rejoinder and said, "Just answer the question, please."

"Is this an interrogation?" Chaucer said. "Am I being investigated for anything?"

"No, ma'am," he said. "I'm just trying to establish how well you know Cox."

Chaucer resisted the temptation to make a penis joke. "I've never slept with him," she said dryly. "And since you did not answer my question about this being a free country, I'll just let your last question hang unrequited in the land of ambiguity."

"That's fine," the agent said a bit nonplussed because he did not understand what she had just said. He already knew, however, that she had attended USARMI activities, because he had photographs of her to prove it. "Now, as to Mr. Cox, would you describe him as a loyal American?"

"He loves his country more than the vast majority of citizens," Chaucer said. "His loyalty is not passive but courageously active. I see him as a patriot."

The agent made a small, disbelieving grimace as he wrote down her response and then continued in an indifferent voice, "Do you see him as a man of integrity?"

"Indeed, and a man of courage also," she replied.

"How would you describe his handling of sensitive information? Is he a man of discretion?"

"As far as I know," she said. "I've had no opportunities to be in either a discrete or discreet situation with him." She laughed but the agent kept a sober demeanor.

"Is he mature in his behavior?"

"Very much so," she said.

"And do you see him as a man of character?"

"A memorable character in his own right," Chaucer said with another chuckle. "Yes, sure, he's a man of character."

Agent Miller cleared his throat nervously and plunged into his next question. "Have you ever observed Mr. Cox exhibit any…homosexual mannerisms, tendencies, or behaviors?"

Now Chaucer produced a full-throated laugh. "Zebulon Cox is the most masculine, testosterone-laden man I've ever met. He's surrounded all the time by women ready to jump into bed with him at a nod. The stories are that he has nodded a lot."

The agent made a note on his tablet: "Subject displays excessive masculinity as possible cover-up for homosexual inclinations." He stood and said, "Thank you, Miss Dickinson. You have been very helpful."

Back at the FBI Field Office in Phoenix, Milford Miller made two reports, one for the subversive activities file on Zebulon Cox and the other for a newly opened file relating to the subversive activities of Chaucer Dickinson. In Chaucer's dossier Miller noted that Miss Dickinson should be considered a hostile subject, because she made fun of his questioning and had made the patently absurd assertion that Cox was a patriot.

<>   <>   <>

After the FBI interview, Chaucer decided that she preferred expressing her opposition to the war in Viet Nam is a less intense manner than that of Zebulon Cox's organization. It was not the implied intimidation by the Federal government that brought her to this view. Rather, the people attracted to USARMI seemed to her to be especially obsessed about efforts to end the war and ideologically unbending in their political views.

A particularly ardent coed, who had responded on multiple occasions to Zebulon's sexual invitations, was the catalyst for Chaucer to end her association with USARMI. The woman challenged Chaucer's apparent lack of zeal for peacemaking. "You're clearly not a dove, Chaucer. I don't know what kind of bird you are but you don't seem to have the heart for the peace movement."

Chaucer was momentarily stunned by the comment, wondering what had prompted it. Quickly, however, she recognized the truth in the charge. "No, I suppose I'm not *your* kind of dove, but I am genuinely troubled by the war," she replied.

Reflecting on the exchange later, Chaucer decided that she had never been a dove but a mockingbird, willing to try out other people's songs but in another sense of the word mocking, always a bit skeptical and suspicious.

Soon after she stopped attending USARMI activities, she was invited to a gathering of hippie peaceniks on campus. The hippies had no particular leader and tended toward spontaneous pacifism rather than intentional confrontation. This appealed to Chaucer much more than the dogmatism of Zebulon's followers.

Three students at the center of this group rented a house in a residential neighborhood south of Apache Boulevard, which they opened to fellow hippies for parties and for crashing if in need of a place to sleep. One of them was Sally Bloomsbury, who sat next to Chaucer in an anthropology class. When Chaucer asked Sally where she was going all dressed up in a rainbow skirt, tie-dyed tee shirt, and many beaded long-looped necklaces, Sally said, "There's a happening down at the ROTC drill field. Why don't you come along?"

"I'm not very colorfully dressed," said Chaucer.

"Doesn't matter," said Sally. "Come along and meet some really groovy folks."

A dozen or so people sat in the grass in the center of an oval track and passed around daisies and offered terse benedictions. Sally pressed a flower into Chaucer's hand and said, "Peace be with you, sister." Chaucer then gave the flower to the young shirtless man to her left and said, "Peace, man."

He replied, "Groovy. I'm Nick."

"Well then, Peace Nick," Chaucer said with a giggle. "I'm Chaucer."

Nick passed the flower to the woman on his left and accepted another one that was making its way around the circle in the opposite direction. Turning again to Chaucer, he said, "Here's some more peace, Chaucer. You're a groovy chick."

"I don't think anyone has ever said to me anything quite so eloquent," she replied with a chuckling lilt. She gave the daisy to Sally, saying, "Peace be with you too, sister."

A plump coed in a loose fitting denim dress stood and reeled around so that her tent-like garment flared out, revealing her pink thighs and white panties. "Make love not war," she chanted repeatedly as she whirled.

"We all know how loveable you are, Annie," said a young man clad in jeans and a tie-dyed tee shirt.

"Better to be horny than militaristic," Annie responded sassily.

"Time to go," said Sally. "Wanna come over to our pad, Chaucer?"

Chaucer walked the five blocks to the house with Sally. Shirtless Nick Shane and horny Annie Ware also came along. In the process, Chaucer learned that Nick and Annie were Sally's housemates.

The yard in front of the two-story wood-frame house was neat and well-trimmed. "We like to set a good example for the neighbors," Sally said as they passed through the wooden gate. "The landlord was a little leery of renting to students, but we promised we'd keep the place neat."

Once inside, however, Chaucer saw that the living room and kitchen had not received the same careful attention that the front lawn had. Dirty dishes and miscellaneous clutter were piled everywhere in both rooms.

"We keep the yard nice all the time, because we don't want any trouble," said Nick. "But we're more relaxed about the inside. We get into clean-up moods every so often, though."

A twenty-something man clad only in white underwear wandered out of a bedroom. He had a short shaggy beard and appeared to have just gotten out of bed. "Hey, how'd the happening go?" he said.

"Pretty cool," said Annie.

Chaucer assumed that someone would introduce her to the stranger, but no one did.

"I scored some fresh weed," the recently risen man said.

Nick, Sally, Annie, and the unnamed man wordlessly formed a circle on the living room carpet.

"Come on, Chaucer, have a seat," said Sally. She patted her hand on a place next to her on the rug.

Soon a generously packed joint circulated among them, which quickly provided Chaucer with a very pleasant high.

After a period of disjointed but seemingly profound conversation, Annie rose and pulled up no name by the arm. "Time to get laid," she said and led him into a bedroom.

"You interested, Chaucer?" Nick whispered into her ear.

"If Sally doesn't mind," she said.

"I'm cool with it," Sally said.

"Do you have protection?" Chaucer asked Nick.

"No, but I can pull out if you want," he said.

"Not good enough," said Chaucer. She reached into her purse and brought out a foil wrapped condom. "I'm pretty good at putting these things on. I think you'll enjoy the experience."

"I'm pretty good at turning women on," he said. "I think you'll enjoy the experience."

He did and she did.

On return visits to the hippie pad, Chaucer learned that the weed-scoring man with no name was not a student but someone who occasionally crashed at the house. A string of people arrived and departed at unscheduled times, and the permanent residents, that is those who were paying the rent, seemed to enjoy the parade of guests.

Chaucer became a regular, sometimes spending the night but most of the time returning to her dorm room. Since she often partook of the communal marijuana, she voluntarily contributed cash for the acquisition of new stashes, although she never directly purchased it herself.

People went about the house in their undies or even nude if they felt like it, and free love was the norm. Sally and Annie shared both a bedroom and partners, including, from time to time, one another. Chaucer, however, slept only with Nick when she stayed the night, although Nick was not exclusive when Chaucer was absent.

Chaucer's wardrobe underwent a change during this period. She eschewed beads and flowers but adopted flowing dresses in earthy beige and green tones, raw cotton peasant blouses, and denim skirts. She went about barefoot except for places where shoes were required, and then she wore open sandals.

Sally called her Earth Mother, and Chaucer decided she liked the epithet.

After months of regular marijuana use, Chaucer noticed that the drug made her hungry, and she had gotten into the habit of going to the kitchen to binge on whatever she could find there. Her weight crept upward, and she was on track toward becoming Annie's pleasingly plump body twin. But it did not seem to concern Nick, who assured Chaucer that he liked her just the way she was. By the end of her sophomore year, Chaucer had gained thirty pounds, and she felt dumpy.

"I've got to quit pot," she told Nick one night after an animated round of sex. "It makes me fat."

"I can dig your concern. It's cool," he said. "I've got something better that won't make you fat. Let's try it together."

"I'm not into hard drugs," Chaucer said warily.

"Me neither," said Nick. "But I've scored some acid. You won't get hooked on it, I promise you."

"OK," she said, "I admit that I'm curious about LSD. When should we do it?"

"Right now," he said.

Ten minutes later they were tripping into strange worlds within their respective minds. Chaucer lost awareness of Nick and crawled into a fetal position and focused her eyes on a semen stain on the sheet, imagining it as the surface of a planet in another universe. Mentally she wandered across the surface of the stain in search of intelligent life. But every creature she met was stupid or sad. Chaucer began to weep.

Debriefing their experiences the next morning, Nick explained that sometimes people have bad trips but at least she did not encounter anything frightening. "Give it another try," he cajoled. "Next time is bound to be better. I'm sure you have beautiful psychedelic potential inside your groovy brain."

Her next encounter with LSD proved to be gray, dull, and unproductive. She spent the entire time under its influence contemplating the weave of a blanket.

"Sorry, Nick, but this is not for me. My natural mind is far more colorful and awe-inspiring than with the aid of drugs," she said.

The next few days she felt depressed and irritable. Trying to shake the feeling, Chaucer took a long walk around downtown Tempe. This might also burn off a few calories, she thought as she strolled along a sidewalk. Then she saw a used book store and immediately gravitated toward it.

A bell tinkled as she pushed the door open. Once inside, she wandered through the shelves and found a paperback edition of **Norwegian Folktales** by Peter Christen Asbjornsen and Jorgen Moe. As she stood perusing the yellow-paged volume, she became aware that the shop smelled like vanilla, one of her favorite scents.

With the book of Norse folktales in hand, she stopped at an ice cream shop and ordered a large vanilla milk shake, which she sipped as she read a story about the Ash Lad. So much for burning off calories, she thought. At least the depression had lifted.

When the spring semester ended, Chaucer went home for the summer, returned to work at Bob's Big Boy, and began a diet to regain her pre-pot figure. She found it easy to burn off the calories bustling from table to table at the restaurant, and by July was back to her normal weight. She had enjoyed her time with Sally, Nick, and Annie, but was now indifferent to using drugs. She thought of it as something to check off her life experience list but not a viable lifestyle.

Spenser, who was now out of high school and had the summer ahead for cruising Central, did not want to share the car with her, but Banky and Norah begrudgingly ordered him either to take her to the restaurant and pick her up again after her shift or let her have the car on work days. Usually, he gave her the car and had a buddy pick him up to go out carousing. He had plenty of time for partying, because he did not have a job.

For something to do in the early afternoon before the start of her work shift, she dug out and read through her folder of juvenile short stories and then began writing new material. The old stories put her in a nostalgic mood. Her goal for the new work was not to produce carefully crafted narratives suitable for publishing but to let her mind communicate with the pen in her fingers without conscious control.

This, she thought, was a better way than crossword puzzles or solitaire to pass the time. She might even discover something about herself in the process.

CHAPTER 8:

ALLYS IN THE GROOVY GROVE

She ate a little bit, and said anxiously to herself,
'Which way? Which way?'
Lewis Carroll

Allys had stunningly beautiful long red hair, sky blue eyes, a pleasant face, and a keen intellect. Added to these assets, this day was her eighteenth birthday, so she had much to be happy about. Unfortunately, she was not happy and in no mood to celebrate. Her mother had made a calorie rich deep dark chocolate cake, but this only made the situation worse. Recently, it seems, Allys had indulged in food binging and had gained thirty pounds. Realistically, she was a bit tubby. Unrealistically, she felt enormously fat.

"What's the matter with you?" her mother asked. "A few more calories at this point won't make any difference. Enjoy the cake today and then you can go on a diet."

"Let me go out and walk off a few calories first," Allys said. She tried not to pout but was not sure she was successful at this endeavor.

As if on automatic pilot, Allys left the house and wandered in the direction of an orange grove that had once existed in her neighborhood. It had long since been bulldozed for the construction of houses, but Allys felt comforted as she meandered toward what had once been an oasis of fragrant green and orange and white.

When she arrived at the head of the asphalt street that now pierced the former grove, she was startled to discover that the street had turned into a dirt path that led into a stand of mature orange trees.

"This can't be!" she said aloud to herself.

But it was.

So she entered the grove and in no time at all found the spot where as a child she used to go when she wanted to be alone and speculate about the world and carry on conversations with the elemental spirits of the universe.

She sat in a clump of grass and reminisced about her painful yet beautiful childhood. Without thinking, she reached out and pulled a handful of purple berries from a nearby bush and popped them into her mouth.

"Mmm, these are sweet," she announced to the orange tree on her left. "Delicious, and much healthier than cake." The berries flowed easily down her esophagus.

Within seconds, her head started to swim and she nearly keeled over. Using an orange tree branch to steady and guide her, she lay down, hoping to regain a sense of balance. That seemed to work, so she closed her eyes and breathed deeply. In less than a minute she was fast asleep, or at least she thought she was asleep, for a bright and colorful dream filled her mind.

Allys's shoes melted off her feet, and her blouse and jeans split open and fell from her body. Her panties and bra evaporated too. Now her skin was rippling and changing shape and color. As the dream unfolded, Allys transformed from an overweight young woman into a slender bird –a gilded flicker, with a red patch on her head and beautiful golden wings.

Thus transfigured, the gilded Allys flew into the air and circled the grove, enjoying the splendid world of vegetation below. She flapped her wings for the sheer joy of sailing on the wind, rising up and swooping down, making a loud cackling noise as she flew.

"I wish I could do this forever," she thought on an upswing. But then on the downswing she thought, "No, not really. It would get dull after a while. But I wish I could do this again."

Without perceiving exactly how it happened, the effects of the purple berries suddenly wore off, and Allys found herself human again, lying on her back in the grass, completely naked. Her clothes were neatly folded in a pile under the orange tree. Being naked in this special place did not cause her anxiety, and she felt no fear that someone would tromp in and find her nude.

She examined her body, visually noting how unshapely and overweight she was. Her eyes lingered on areas of her anatomy that she was unhappy with. And yet -surely it must be an illusion- her body seemed a little more slender, her muscle tone slightly firmer than when she had entered the grove. A slight smile crossed her lips. "Groovy!" she said to herself.

Allys took her time dressing and when she buttoned her jeans, she realized that the jeans were no longer tight and maybe were even a tad loose. Once fully clad, she strolled in leisurely fashion back to her house. As soon as she left the grove, it transformed back into a housing development.

Allys was smiling as she entered the dining room. "I **will** have a **big** slice of birthday cake, Mom," she said. "Tomorrow I'll dine on vegetables and **berries** and begin working out, but today is a time to celebrate some wonderful memories."

CHAPTER 9:
PACIFIC OCEAN

I never saw a Moor –
I never saw the Sea –
Yet I know how the Heather looks
And what a Billow be.
Emily Dickinson

Chaucer enrolled in a course called the Bible as literature in the fall semester of her junior year. This was an upper division course, so she was initially surprised to find a freshman student sitting in the desk to her left.

Terp Person explained that she was in the honors program and because she had a double major in English and religion, her advisor allowed her into the course. Since Chaucer was also in the honors program and had taken junior and senior level classes in her first two years, this quickly dispelled the mystery.

As the semester unfolded, Chaucer and Terp fell into the habit of sitting next to each other and chatting before the habitually late professor bundled into the room with apologies for tardiness. Chaucer recognized Terp as a fellow intellectual and enjoyed conversing with the younger student, but was puzzled by Terp's interest in religion. One day Terp had told Chaucer that she was thinking about becoming a minister. This revelation created an emotional barrier in Chaucer's mind, and she became wary of pursuing a deeper friendship with Terp. Interest in religion was one thing but becoming clergy was another suspicious dimension altogether.

Chaucer had reached a firm understanding that she was a humanist, believing in the idea of God as universal energy and consciousness but not as a personal deity with a doctrinal agenda. She was fascinated by the Bible but could not fathom how churches could with any intellectual integrity derive the dogma they proclaimed from such a miscellany of stories, poetry, and mythology that formed the Bible. Her conclusion was that religious institutions in general did not exercise intellectual integrity. Thus normally astute people should be wary of people who wanted to become clergy.

Chaucer's negative feelings about clergy and the church were exacerbated by the experience of another member of this Bible as literature class. Audrey Humble, also a junior, was seduced by and carried on a brief affair with the campus minister, the Reverend Doctor Kirkegaard Trilby. When Trilby dumped her, Audrey turned to Chaucer for consolation.

Audrey and Chaucer had not been particularly close but they had been in many classes together during their time at ASU, and Audrey sensed she could trust Chaucer. One day after class, Audrey asked Chaucer to go for a walk with her, and in the course of their stroll toward a teashop on Mill Avenue, she confessed her seduction and rejection.

"That bastard!" said Chaucer with a combination of venom and revulsion. "How did he do it? What was his line?"

Audrey laughed tentatively at the way Chaucer had said bastard and took courage from Chaucer's question. "I'd been attending services at the Campus Ministry building, and helping out with the liturgy. He took me to dinner to thank me for volunteering and gave me a white rose. He told me he thought I'd make a great counseling assistant."

"A what?" said Chaucer.

"He wanted me to meet with him to help him with his pastoral counseling of troubled students. He said he thought I had great insights and could be a big help to him in understanding the minds of college students."

"Hmm," said Chaucer. "Let me guess. You met privately with him at night and talked about students' insecurities regarding sex."

"Yeah, I fell for his line, and your guess is pretty close. He threw in some existential angst about religion too, but mostly it was about how many students are having sex or obsessing about it."

"And then...?" Chaucer asked.

"And then one night at his apartment he plied me with wine and sweet talk and took me to bed," she said.

"And how did he end the affair?" Chaucer continued.

Audrey said, "He took me on what he called a Saturday-Sunday overnight spiritual retreat at a church camp near Prescott. It was fall, so no actual camping was going on there. The only person around was the camp manager who lived on the premises and who Kirk was good friends with and who let him use the facilities whenever he needed a break. So we got there and had lunch with the camp manager."

"And he was OK with Kirk bringing a coed to the camp?"

"*She* was perfectly OK with it. She gave me a big hug when Kirk introduced me and made a comment to Kirk about his improving standards. I wasn't sure exactly what that meant at the time, but now I think she was referring to me."

"Undoubtedly," said Chaucer.

"Anyway," Audrey continued, "the plan was we would go for walks in the woods and meditate. Which we did that afternoon. Then in a beautiful meadow, we made love. At the time I thought it was very romantic."

"But then?" Chaucer asked.

"But then we ended up at the camp manager's house, where we would spend the night. The cabins were too rustic for Kirk's taste. After dinner I began to get nervous about sleeping arrangements. I didn't know if Kirk was planning to share a bedroom with me, but I didn't want to do that in somebody else's house. So when Sue was in the kitchen, I asked him what the deal was."

Audrey paused in obvious embarrassment and Chaucer waited patiently for her to continue.

"He said there was only one bedroom in the house, so my options were to share a bed with Sue or sleep on a very lumpy couch," Audrey remarked.

"And where would he sleep?" Chaucer asked.

"That was going to be my next question," Audrey said, "but Sue came back into the dining room and said, 'I'm afraid there is only one bed in the entire house, but it's a king size, with plenty of room for three to sleep without rolling into one another.' Then Kirk laughed out loud and said, 'Unless they *want* to roll into each other.' And I said, 'What about getting beds from a cabin?' and Sue said, 'They're all full of bugs this time of year and would need to be fumigated.'"

"So right about then you were feeling trapped," Chaucer said.

"Exactly," said Audrey. "So Kirk said, 'It's up to you Audrey. Lumpy couch or luxurious bed. As for me, I can't resist a fine mattress.' I felt like he'd kicked me in the stomach. I cried myself to sleep on that couch, but about midnight I heard noises from the bedroom that sounded a lot like Kirk and Sue were having unrestrained sex."

"The real plan all along, of course, was for you to participate with them," Chaucer surmised.

"Yeah," Audrey said. "Kirk as much as told me so on the drive back to school. He said I had missed an opportunity for a life enhancing experience. But by then I wasn't talking to him. When I got out of his car I said, 'It's over.' And he just smiled and said, 'That's too bad because it could have been something really special.'"

Chaucer spent the rest of the day with Audrey, helping her get through the pain and embarrassment she felt about her involvement with the campus minister. Over the next few weeks, the two met regularly for lunch or coffee, and Audrey rose out of her depression.

"I've been thinking about letting the administration know about Trilby," Chaucer said one afternoon. "Are you willing to do that?"

Audrey inhaled in panic and spilled coffee on the table. "No, I couldn't do that. If my parents ever found out…"

"I don't see how they would, since you're legally an adult," Chaucer replied.

"They would," Audrey said. "They find out everything. They're very religious, and this would be devastating to them."

"So is Trilby," said Chaucer. "Very religious, I mean, if you define religious as regular participation in church. I'll bet your parents would be understanding and supportive once they got over the shock."

"You don't know my parents," Audrey said. "They would not understand and they would shun me."

"I'm sorry," Chaucer said. "But I don't find that behavior any more *religious* than Trilby's."

"Well, I don't think I could make this public," Audrey said. "I would be mortified. And he'd probably deny it. I don't have any proof. It would be my word against his. And if I named Sue as a witness in the whole sordid thing, she'd probably deny everything or put an innocent spin on it. I'm sure she would side with him and make me out to be a crazy, lovesick girl."

"Yeah, you're very likely right about Sue. Alright, I won't press you," Chaucer said. "I just wanted to raise the possibility."

Because of Audrey's fear, Chaucer did not tell anyone else about Kirk. Thus his secrets continued to be kept by others. Nevertheless, Chaucer seethed with anger at the wayward cleric

One afternoon in December 1970 while her roommate was away, Chaucer stretched out for a nap in her dorm room. With sunlight pouring in through the window and the heating system pumping warm air into the room, she was soon in a meditative state, somewhere between conscious awareness and deep sleep. In this circumstance, Chaucer had another episode of seeming to float out of her body while remaining firmly ensconced in bed. An aura that was acutely pleasant surrounded her body, and she believed that she was awake and not dreaming. Her mind told her she was traveling in another realm of existence beyond the mundane space of her dorm room. She was in a beautiful place with brightly colored walls in a five-sided room where her body reclined peacefully on a mat on the floor. She felt safe and without any fear. And suddenly she was back in her body on the twin bed in her rectangular dormitory room.

She felt dizzy when sitting up, but after a moment to regain her balance, she was energized and rested.

In the spring semester of 1971, Chaucer took a continuation of the Bible as literature course, and was pleased to see Terp also in the class. Despite her misgivings about Terp's interest in ordination, Chaucer was drawn to the intellectual in glasses.

In a pre-class conversation while waiting for the professor to appear, Terp mentioned that she regularly attended the campus ministry program. Chaucer had a strong urge to tell Terp about Audrey being seduced by Kirk Trilby as a friendly warning, but Audrey had renewed her plea that Chaucer not say anything about the episode to anyone, and so she held her tongue.

As Chaucer's twenty-first birthday drew near in April 1971, she began dating a psychology major who was a sports car aficionado. Ordinarily, Chaucer was wary of psychology majors because they tended to over-analyze everyone, but something about Gus Young's aw-shucks demeanor and engaging smile caused her to say yes when he asked her out.

Her birthday was less than a week away when they went out for the third time. This night they attended a John Denver concert at the Celebrity Theater in Phoenix. Afterward, as they walked through the parking lot toward Gus's red Austin-Healy 3000, he interrupted Chaucer cheerily singing "Leaving on a Jet Plane" to ask what else she wanted to do with the evening.

"Oh, I don't know," she said. "Surprise me."

"Well, as your birthday is coming up, we should do something special. Is there anything you've never done that you'd like to do?" he said.

"Anything?" she asked with an impish tone.

"Anything within the laws of physics and engineering –and my budget," he replied.

"I've never seen the ocean," she said. "I'd like to see the ocean for my birthday."

He made a quick mental calculation and said, "OK. Hop in. Let's go."

"Now?" she said. "I was thinking of closer to my actual birthday. Make a day trip or even an overnight out of it."

"No, we can do it right now," he said firmly. "Tomorrow is Sunday, so neither of us has classes. If we start out now we can be at the beach in Santa Monica in seven hours."

She laughed at the prospect of fourteen hours in a small, open sports car and said, "I have to tell you, Gus, I'm really impressed. Let's do it!"

When they stopped to fill the gas tank, she said, "Should we put the top up?"

"Can't," Gus explained. "The frame is broken. My brother promised to help me fix it, but he hasn't found the time yet."

The drive through the desert at night was enchantingly windblown. Traffic was sparse until Palm Springs and even then the flow of cars and trucks was light at three in the morning.

They arrived in Santa Monica before five. Gus parked the car in a lot overlooking the beach, and they walked barefoot to the ocean's edge and waded in.

"So, now you've seen the ocean and even put your feet in it," he announced. "Ready to go back?"

"Well, I can't really say I've seen the ocean. It's too dark to see much. I don't think it counts as seeing the ocean if I can't get a visual sense of its immensity," she said. "Although it is romantic in the dark."

"I guess we can stay till sunrise so you can see it properly," he said.

"Thank you," she replied. "In the meantime, I can make the wait worthwhile."

They returned to his car and began to kiss and fondle one another. There was no room in the roadster for more athletic sexual activities, so Chaucer offered him oral sex, which he gratefully accepted.

Seconds after the climax of that endeavor, a patrol car approached and flashed its lights on the backs of their heads. Gus was zipping his fly, and Chaucer was about to open the door to spit but thought better of it and swallowed instead. A police officer got out and walked toward the Austin-Healy with a flashlight shining alternately at Gus and Chaucer. "You better move on now, kids," the officer said.

"Thank you, sir," Gus said. "We'll be on our way immediately." He turned the key in the ignition.

Chaucer smiled innocently at the policeman and said, "My twenty-first birthday is coming up and I've never seen the ocean. Gus drove me here from Phoenix to see it and we're waiting for the sunrise."

The officer had already noted the Arizona license plate on the car and was in a good mood because his shift was nearly done. "Sun'll be up before long. Stay in the vehicle until then. You don't have to move now, but find another place if you stay on the beach more than an hour."

"Thank you," Gus and Chaucer said in unison.

At sunrise, they spent ten minutes on the beach and then headed back to Arizona.

On the way, Chaucer said, "The ocean is not as impressive as I imagined it would be."

"You don't really get the sense of it until you're in the middle of it and can see nothing but ocean in all directions," Gus said. "My dad was in the Navy, and that's how he describes it."

"Yes, that's what's missing," she said. "Until you have no visual options except ocean, until you leave land completely behind and have no reference but water and sky, you can't grasp how magnificent the sea must be."

Gus said, "The ocean is like the subconscious mind. It has immense power beneath the surface that can't be comprehended by looking at the surface. Imagine what it would be like to be fully aware of your subconscious mind."

"Here comes the analysis," Chaucer said to herself. "I expect it would be disorienting," she said aloud.

"To be sure," he said, "But it would provide an unprecedented sense of the complex depths of the oceanic human brain. It would be like sailing through a surreal wonderland."

"Wonderlands are surreal to begin with," said the English major to the Psychology major. "It's redundant to modify wonderland with surreal."

"An even more surreal than usual wonderland," he extemporized. "Like instead of reading a book, reading the mind of the author."

"Wow!" Chaucer said. "I'd love to be able to see the subconscious minds of great authors. Imagine going sailing into the oceans of brain cells that impel them to write masterpieces."

As Gus drove eastbound, the early morning sun gave him a headache, and just past Indio, his eyes glazed over and he nodded off for a few seconds. The car swerved onto the berm and back again into the lane.

This action wakened Chaucer from her drowsiness just as a semi passed them at seventy miles per hour causing the small car to swerve again in its wake. Now adrenaline pumped through her body and she said, "Maybe we should take a break and find a coffee shop."

"Too late for that," he said. "We should have stopped in Indio. There's nothing between here and Blythe. Besides, I'm fully awake now. We'll be fine."

Chaucer had doubts about his alertness, but she would watch him to make sure he stayed awake. Now another concern occurred to her. "With my red hair and fair skin, I burn easily," she said. "Do you have anything to protect me from the sun?"

"Always prepared," he replied with a grin. "In the glove box is a bandana."

She pulled out and examined the red and white checkered cloth. "Helpful but not big enough," she said. "I'll need to cover my face as well as hair. As we were simply going to a concert last night, I didn't dress for a drive across the desert. Do you have a hat tucked away somewhere in the trunk?"

"Sorry, that's all I have in the car," he answered defensively.

"Well, let's see what I can rig up," she said. Chaucer wrapped the bandana around her mouth and nose in the style of bandits in western movies. Then she unzipped her skirt and slipped it off over her legs. With the waistband across her forehead, she then draped the skirt over her head in the manner of an Indian war bonnet.

Gus glanced down at Chaucer's panties.

"Just keep your eyes on the road," she said. "And you damn well better obey the speed limit and do nothing to attract the attention of the Highway Patrol."

She put the skirt back on as they approached Blythe, where they stopped for refueling and lunch with multiple cups of coffee. On the road again, she removed it and reestablished her improvised sunscreen. They were slowed considerably by heavy traffic approaching Quartzite, as a caravan of snowbirds towing travel trailers blocked both lanes in the process of pre-summer decamping for northern climes. Traffic eased as many of the nomads exited northbound on State Route 95, and Gus was able to maneuver his Austin-Healy around the remaining slow vehicles and resume normal speed.

He was tempted to make up time lost in the congestion, but Chaucer looked at him and shook her head as he accelerated. He also knew that sports cars were prime targets for police scrutiny, and on this particular Sunday a speed trap had been set up near the Brenda Cutoff. Heeding Chaucer's admonition about the speed limit, he sailed through without difficulty.

"See!" Chaucer said as they watched a Lincoln Continental that had just passed them being pulled over. "Now you know, always listen to Chaucer about traffic."

"Thanks," Gus said. "You saved my ass."

Not until they reached the Mill Avenue Bridge across the Salt River into Tempe did she take off the bandana and shimmy into the skirt. Gus delivered Chaucer back to campus at four Sunday afternoon.

"Thanks for the wonderful adventure, Gus. I had a great time," she said before kissing him and getting out of his car in the parking lot. "Don't walk me to my dorm. I'm going straight to bed and you should too."

She slept until six o'clock Monday morning. During the night Chaucer dreamed of Alice traipsing around a more surreal Wonderland. The familiar characters were there in the dream but they were suffused with sexual energy, and guilt, and smoldering rage, and religious doubt, which they spoke about in dramatic soliloquies.

Chaucer and Gus continued to date the rest of the semester. When they went out to dinner on the last day of classes, Gus took her hand across the table and said, "Chaucer, I love you."

Her face went pale. She thought they had been having a compatibly good time together but had no clue that he was falling hard for her. She disengaged her hand. "This comes as a bit of a shock, Gus. I have a great deal of...affection for you. I enjoy being with you, but I can't use the word love for my feelings about you."

"A great deal of affection is a solid building block," he said confidently, apparently unfazed by her lack of reciprocation. "Someday you will use the word love about me. I know you will."

"Your optimism makes what I have to say all the more difficult," she added, "but I won't be able to spend any time with you over the summer. I have to work to earn money for school, and I will take as many hours working as I can get. There won't be time for social activities."

"I'll give you some money to make up for any hours of work you lose by going out with me," he said. "The more time you spend with me the more money I'll give you."

Chaucer bristled at this and snapped, "That would make me a whore!"

"No, no, I didn't mean it that way," he pleaded. "It's just...I wanted to find a way so you didn't have to work so much. The idea just popped out spontaneously. I didn't understand how it would seem to you."

"I don't understand how you can make A's in psychology classes and not see how an offer of money for companionship would be perceived," she said. She reached into her purse and extracted a ten-dollar bill. "Here's my half of the dinner tab."

As she left the restaurant, she looked back and saw that Gus was still at the table with a miserable look on his face. For a moment she was tempted to go back and make up with him but she resisted the urge and walked outside.

CHAPTER 10:
A NOVEL IDEA

There is no Frigate like a Book
To take us Lands away
Nor any Coursers like a Page
Of prancing Poetry –
                    Emily Dickinson

Bob's Big Boy took Chaucer on again as a waitress for the summer of 1971. As with the previous year, she competed with Spenser for use of the Chevy II, usually winning out, as her needs were more financially responsible than his. Many restaurant customers asked her for dates, but she said no to all of them. She met her extrovert needs by working in a busy restaurant and bantering with other employees in the kitchen during lulls in customer traffic.

As her senior year approached, she knew that she wanted to go to graduate school, and thus saving as much money as possible was her biggest goal. She asked for and got more hours and willingly worked shifts for other waitresses who wanted time off for socializing.

For emotional nurture Chaucer chose re-reading favorite novels and music. She decided to spend a little of her tip money each week on a record album to play in her bedroom, her only luxury. She started with Carole King's *Tapestry* album. "Will You Love Me Tomorrow" became her favorite cut from that album. The following week, she bought the self-titled *Elton John* album and listened to

"Your Song" over and over. After that, she picked up a Gordon Lightfoot album called **Sit Down Young Stranger** and meditated to its breakaway hit "If You Could Read My Mind." Chaucer liked that so much that she next chose another Lightfoot album, **Summer Side of Life**, containing the hit "Cotton Jenny."

Several weeks passed before her next musical acquisition, the Barbra Streisand album **Stoney End**, containing the Laura Nyro piece of that name. She thought she now had enough music to sustain her for the rest of the summer, but couldn't resist the soundtrack to **Midnight Cowboy** when it went on sale for half price. Thus she savored Nilsson's stellar performance of "Everybody's Talkin'."

Spenser wandered into her room one afternoon to find her curled up with Madeleine L'Engle's **A Wrinkle in Time**. "Hey, isn't that a kids' book? You already read that -years ago. Why are you reading it again?"

Chaucer looked up from the page and said, "This book appeals equally to youth and adult readers. As an adult, I get much more out of its deep substance."

"I don't waste my time reading things I've already read," Spenser said.

"It's no waste for me," she responded. "I read novels in search of light. I re-read them to enjoy those transcendent moments when my favorite characters are bathed in warm sunlight, metaphorically speaking. To re-read a favorite book is to bask in the sun."

When classes resumed in the fall, Chaucer once again gained time for dating and extracurricular activities. The first week back at school, a student in her twentieth century novels class asked her out. Baron Ulster was a cadet major in the campus Army ROTC program and was wearing his uniform at the time. Though she remained a peacenik, she admitted to herself that he looked quite handsome in starched khakis and aviator dark glasses. Tall and trim with blond crew cut hair, he exuded a boyish eagerness mixed with a dose of serious intellectual competence. The fact that he came from a family of long-time Arizona Democrats added to his appeal, and she chose not to resist his charm.

They dated throughout the semester, spending long hours talking about music. Chaucer's tales of her father's band enchanted Baron. His older brothers had put him on to the folk groups of the 50s and 60s, and he confessed a fondness for the Brothers Four.

"Among my very favorites are 'Green Fields' and 'The Green Leaves of Summer,'" he said. "And while we're on a green theme, the Anita Kerr Quartet recorded a beautiful song called 'Summer Green and Winter White.' Do you know it?"

"I know them all. They're all songs about death," Chaucer responded.

"Ah, but such lovely melodies," he said.

"Yeah, like Frost's lovely, dark and deep woods," she said. "Why so fascinated with death?"

"Being an idealist, I prefer to think of them as nostalgic," he explained with a charming shrug. "Besides, I'm minoring in geography, so songs about ecological issues appeal to me. And as a history major, songs about generational change also hit the spot."

Chaucer laughed and kissed him, making full use of her tongue. Though they found only a few occasions for making love, Chaucer found him fully satisfying.

When he took her to an art theater in Old Town Scottsdale to see a series of foreign films and then intelligently critiqued them afterward, she began to harbor tentative thoughts about Baron being someone she could marry. She found this prospect simultaneously exciting and frightening, not least because he told her he intended to be a career Army officer. Neither, however, had done more than hint about loving the other, and it felt easy to drift along in a relationship without expectations or promises.

"You're all spiffy in uniform or out," she told him one evening. "But very traditional in dress. What do you see in me with my hippie garb?"

"Hippie? Is that what you think you dress like?" he responded. "You don't look like a hippie. Your style is more...folksy...down-to-earth. I like your clean-cut look, with no jewelry or gaudy accessories. I see you as natural, not decorated. Certainly not excessively floral."

"Should I take that as a compliment?" she asked.

"All the way to the bank," he said. "Chaucer, I admire your style, your mind, and your healthy-looking body. You're the only woman I know who can keep up with me. You exude classiness."

"Well, I don't need to worry about lack of self-confidence in you, Baron. But I like to think of myself as spontaneous and open-minded," Chaucer said. "Those are hippie traits."

"Those traits are fair self-assessments," he said. "Your wit is spontaneous and your intellect is open-minded. But no one could work as hard as you to earn money for school and then to focus as deeply as you do on academic achievement and still qualify as a hippie. I just don't buy it."

"What about my support of the peace movement?" Chaucer asked with a note of defiance in her voice.

"I support the peace movement," Baron said calmly. "However, my concept of how to achieve genuine peace is different from yours. Genuine peace requires justice. You can't have justice without a realistic means of restraining psychopathic war criminals. Being pro-peace and anti-war are not synonymous."

"I've already figured that out," said Chaucer. "But since you're so astute about movies, let's look at the issue through that lens. Two war movies came out about the same time, *Patton* and *MASH*. Which of these do you like better?"

"Neither one," he replied. "Being a history major, I prefer another war film that came out last year, *Tora! Tora! Tora!*. It made a valiant attempt to follow history accurately. It certainly had the feel of authentic history. *Patton* was entertaining but essentially it's about an egomaniac general who was not a team player and who proved ultimately to be a failure as a leader. Not very satisfying. On the other hand, *MASH* was a thinly veiled swipe at the war in Viet Nam but failed the accuracy test. I just don't buy it. Those doctors could never have gotten away with that long hair. And that crowd scene in Seoul had people wearing the conical hats of Southeast Asian rice farmers. Give me a break!"

"I agree about *Patton*," she said. "I think of it as a portrait of an asshole as a middle-aged adolescent. I liked *MASH* at a *gut* level but hated the actors talking all at the same time and the demeaning way it treated women."

"Well on that point -about women- I'd give *MASH* points for realism," Baron said, "but not about the conduct of war."

"I found the patronizing of women more painful to watch than the scenes of blood and gore in the operating room," Chaucer said.

In early December, Baron took Chaucer to a campus drama production of Henrik Ibsen's *A Doll's House* at Grady Gammage Auditorium. All day, he had been toying with the idea of proposing to Chaucer and then quickly dousing the notion as premature. Perhaps he would simply say he was in love with her as the first step. At the same time, he found himself brooding about what he perceived to be Chaucer's attempts to exaggerate their differences. Maybe she's setting the stage for breaking up, he thought. The more he thought about that, the more likely it seemed.

The play starred a sophomore student named Dagmar Solbrent, who unbeknownst to Chaucer, was Terp Person's roommate. Dagmar inhabited the role of Nora Helmer with emotional depth and brilliant acting technique. She even managed a hint of a Norwegian accent to add verisimilitude to her performance.

Baron was smitten by the actress. Given the prospect that Chaucer was planning to end their relationship, he reasoned, it might be wise to make alternative arrangements. He made inquiries about where Dagmar was likely to be seen around campus. Armed with this information, he began loitering in areas where she might walk, and one afternoon near the Lyceum he got in step beside her and engaged her in chitchat. Once again, he appeared dashing in crisp uniform and aviator glasses. Before she reached her next class, Dagmar had agreed to a date with him.

Soon thereafter, in what he considered a prudent preemptive move, Baron ended the relationship with Chaucer and became Dagmar's regular beau. Taken by surprise, Chaucer was hurt and angry. Three weeks later, Dagmar deftly dumped Baron, and he crawled back to Chaucer full of abject apologies. If she had not previously experienced feelings that Baron could be the one to marry, she might have taken him back, for the sheer fun of critiquing films with him. But the thoughts of marriage to a military man also carried a measure of fear, and the scariest part was that she had come very close to telling him she loved him. Still mad at him, she used his breaking up as a rationale for telling him no when he sought to restart the relationship.

While home with her parents for the Christmas break, Chaucer played around with an idea to write a novel. The thought had originated at the dinner table one evening when Spenser reacted to a literary allusion that she made by saying, "Oh, why don't you go write a book instead of verbally flaunting your erudition."

"So, it's OK to flaunt my erudition in a book," she retorted, "but not orally?"

"Whatever," Spenser said. "Just as long as I don't have to hear it. You make me feel inadequate when you talk like that."

"And my writing a book wouldn't?" she responded with incredulity in her voice.

"Not at all," he said. "I'd probably **read** your book and tell all my friends that my **sister** wrote it. That'd make me feel good, actually."

"Spenser, I truly do not understand you," Chaucer replied with a pinch of frustration and a touch of affection.

That night, in the solitude of her bedroom, the notion of writing a book grew into a lengthy fantasy of social satire. She would use characters from various classic fairy tales as well as ***Alice's Adventures in Wonderland***. This would not, however, be a book for children, although she was certain in her mind that teenagers would be drawn to her literary vision.

In a rush, scenarios and characters bolted into consciousness from her inner mental recesses and she wrote furiously in a notebook, filling many pages with rapid scribbles. There would be talking animals, of course. She loved the Cheshire cat, but she would have a different feline. She quickly settled on a talking bobcat.

In a Victorian literature course that fall, she had become intrigued with Lewis Carroll, who in real life was Oxford math professor Charles Lutwidge Dodgson. Along with his literary efforts written on behalf of Alice Liddell, daughter of his college dean, Dodgson had an artistic avocation of taking photographs, specializing in children. A few of his models were boys, but most were little girls, among them Alice Liddell. Some of the children posed nude. She learned that in the imagination of nineteenth century England, nudes of pre-adolescent girls were thought of as innocent and not considered exploitative, and certainly not associated with child pornography. Her research into Carroll found no instances of his molesting any of the models, and their mothers were usually present when he took their pictures.

"Hmmm," Chaucer mused to herself half aloud. "In some ways the Victorians were less prudish than we are. Amazing."

Concerning the character *Alice*, Chaucer had long since wondered about the scene where Alice shrank when she drank the potion. It seemed logical to Chaucer that Alice's clothes would not have shrunk along with her body. The ingested liquid would not affect anything beyond her physical body, and thus Alice would have been naked when entering Wonderland. Chaucer imagined Alice blanketed by her own apparel, emerging from under the cover of her own giant panties. Therefore, to compensate for Lewis Carroll's faulty physics, or discreetly omitted detail, or Victorian literary repression, Chaucer decided to create a nude scene in the first chapter of her novel. She believed that the man who photographed the real Alice Liddell and wrote imaginative stories about her, and who took pictures of naked children, would not object to Chaucer's revision.

From the first moment of literary conception, Chaucer knew that she would use an updated version of the Allys from her juvenile short stories. For this new narrative, however, Allys would have a twin brother. Over the years she had changed Allys' hair color in a series of redactions, but now she determined that her resurrected Allys would have strawberry blonde hair, and her twin brother would also have this same shade of hair. Once settled on Alice-like twins as equal protagonists, the notion came to her to include Hansel and Gretel in the tale and make them twins as well.

Remembering her dream about Alice in the surreal wonderland of sexual tension and religious doubt following her visit to the ocean with Gus, she thought those elements should also be in the narrative. Thus to demonstrate this dynamic, her characters would have to be post-puberty adolescents. Following up on the notion from the shrinking episode in **Alice**, Chaucer decided that her Allys and the other teenage characters in the fantasy novel would all experience episodes of nudity. After sorting out possible ages for her two sets of twins, she concluded that fourteen was the perfect age, because secondary sex characteristics would be evident but, except for masturbation, it was an age not usually associated with sexual activity. Thus she could have the characters interact with one another without engaging in sex, yet also maintain sufficient narrative tension that they could do so at any moment if circumstances developed accordingly. As initially conceived, she did not expect that the teens would be sexually active, but she would keep an open mind about the prospect.

As a plot detail that she scribbled in her notebook, she would have them ingest a substance with magical properties, probably berries of some sort, but not to make them shrink. She also thought that characters in fiction generally and in fairy tales in particular rarely have to use the bathroom, and so she made an authorial judgment that **her** characters would have to stop periodically for calls of nature.

The prospect of writing a novel provided unexpected relief for Chaucer. Though still angry at Baron for deserting her in favor of a blonde, she missed him and grieved the loss of his company. Each night, as she was trying to fall asleep, her mind would grow full of angst about whether to take him back or forget him, and she tossed and turned in vexed perplexity. But since Spenser had given her the idea of writing a book, she concentrated on various aspects of that project as she settled in to sleep, and this blocked thoughts of Baron, enabling peaceful slumber.

Chaucer organized her notes during the week after Christmas, adding additional thoughts and details, and began writing the novel on January 1, 1972. Before returning to school, she had diligently produced an opening chapter. What she had not done, however, was to outline the flow and structure for the entire book. She had no idea how it would end or toward what goal the narrative would progress. Her imagination had created unusual characters that she cared about, but she had only a vague idea what actions they would be pursuing. That they would have strange adventures was clear in her mind, but beyond that she decided to let the story evolve naturally.

Once back in the crush of class work, however, the novel was soon set aside for more pressing academic deadlines, including applications for graduate school and financial assistance to make that possible. She was content now with Baron being part of her past. From time to time they encountered one another on campus and chatted amiably, including a pleasant half hour interpreting the lyrics of Don McLean's "American Pie." They disagreed about the reference to the widowed bride, with Baron guessing it was Jackie Kennedy while Chaucer was sure it was Buddy Holly's wife Maria Elena. He asked her to go to the Military Ball for old times' sake, and she accepted but made it clear this was out of friendship and not rekindling a romance. Since he would be leaving for active duty right after graduation, he agreed this was wise, although he still nursed a dream that someday he would win her back.

That spring of 1972, Chaucer graduated Magna cum Laude from Arizona State University and was accepted into a Master of Arts in English program at the University of Arizona in Tucson. A financial grant made this feasible, but she still needed to work over the summer to make enough money so that she could eat as well as study.

Based on her experience at Bob's Big Boy, she found a job as a waitress at Jordan's restaurant a half mile South of Bob's on Central Avenue. At Jordan's, she made a lot more in tips but also got frequent propositions from assorted businessmen, most of them married. Before the summer's end, she had become adept at turning them down with a combination of humor and flirting, which generated even bigger tips.

Spenser decided he wanted a motorcycle and badgered Norah and Banky into buying him one. Therefore, he didn't need the Chevy II at all, and reluctantly, they gave it to Chaucer to drive in Tucson while studying at the U of A.

In August, Helene came to town, having graduated from Berkeley with a pre-med major. She called Chaucer and they met for lunch at Bob's Big Boy. It felt odd for Chaucer to be sitting in a booth rather than hovering over it.

Helene told Chaucer that she was on her way to Harvard Medical School, which Chaucer thought impressive, but Helene's physical appearance seemed more noteworthy than her academic success. Her teeth, no longer bucked, had been fixed through orthodontia. Gone were the pigtails, which she had worn through high school, replaced by long, straight hair in the style of Mary Travers. She wore comfortably snug jeans and an oversized tee shirt with a picture of Charles Darwin on it.

"You look gorgeous in your collegiate duds," said Chaucer.

Helene laughed. "I live frugally and spend as little on clothing as possible. Looking good doesn't have to be expensive. Except for the orthodontia, but my parents covered that. I highly recommend orthodontia." She paused and peered at Chaucer. "Your front teeth aren't too badly misaligned. It shouldn't take very long to get them evened up. It would really improve your smile and shouldn't cost too much."

"I can't afford it," Chaucer said. "My parents wouldn't allow it when I was younger, but I don't think I'd do it now even if I could afford it. The lack of symmetry has grown on me. It adds a distinctive character to my features."

"Yes, it never did hamper your appeal with the boys," Helene said with a philosophical sigh.

Chaucer tried to think of a diplomatic way of asking Helene if she had been sexually active at Berkeley, and whimsically hit upon, "So did you succeed in seeing any weenies while away at college?"

"Oh yes, plenty," Helene answered with a grin. "Mostly in anatomy class…but also a few in the wild."

CHAPTER 11:
DISCOVERING TIMBERSCAPE

I know who I WAS when I got up
this morning, but I think
I must have been changed several times
since then.

Lewis Carroll

"They're both asleep," said fourteen year-old Allys to her twin brother Aylwyn. "Adults may need their afternoon naps, but I'm bored. Let's go exploring."

"Cool," said Aylwyn. He stood up from the sleeping bag he had been resting on while leafing through a guidebook to hikes in Central Arizona and pointed at a series of eerily spiral rock formations. "Let's check out those hoodoos over that way."

Though the heat of the day was at its afternoon peak, the mid-September weather was pleasant because an insistent breeze blew through the valley where Allys, Aylwyn, and their parents were camping in the Superstition Mountains east of Phoenix.

Aylwyn reached into the ice chest for a bottle of store-bought spring water and tossed it to his sister and then took one for himself. As they started walking up the trail, he said, "It's beautiful out here but kind of lonely. Part of me likes the solitude but another part would rather be in town hanging out with my friends."

"How many Saturday afternoons at the mall and movie

theater can you endure?" Allys said. "At least this is a major change of pace from our usual weekend fare."

"Yeah, you're right," Aylwyn said. "This is the real world and not some movie fantasy. But speaking of fantasy worlds, if you could have one power of a superhero, what would it be?"

"Hmmm," said Allys. "I think it would be flying. To soar weightless through the sky must feel wonderful. What about you?"

"I think it would be great to have x-ray vision," Aylwyn said. "Then I could see what people really looked like under their clothes."

"If you had actual x-ray vision," said Allys authoritatively, "all you'd be able to see would be their bones. I think it would be kind of creepy seeing everyone as skeletons."

"I hadn't thought of that," said Aylwyn. "I guess I'd want modified x-ray vision that could see only through fabric."

Allys laughed. "You're so predictable. But to be honest, that would be fun. Maybe we could swap our superpowers every once in a while."

"Yeah, twins with superpowers would naturally be able to switch with each other," Aylwyn said.

They continued walking along the trail paying more attention to their conversation than to their surroundings.

"If you could be any fairy tale character you wanted," Aylwyn continued, "who would it be?"

"That's easy," said Allys. "I'd want to be a fairy godmother. Strange and magical things happen **to** most fairy tale characters, but fairy godmothers actually **do** things, make things happen. Who would you be?"

"Along that same line," Aylwyn said, "I'd be a genii. Geniis can grant wishes and do all sorts of cool stuff. They make things happen."

Suddenly a jackrabbit bounded across the trail twenty feet in front of them, which made them look up and gape at it. The creature slowed down and stared back as if waiting for them to catch up. Without a word, they left the marked path and followed the jackrabbit into a ravine and over a wall of boulders. The long-eared creature was soon out of sight, but Aylwyn perceived a faint trail leading toward an escarpment bearing interesting hoodoos above it.

"Look, there's fresh rabbit scat," Aylwyn said. "Apparently jack paused long enough to mark the trail for us."

"A bush rustled over that way," said Allys. "Near the base of that cliff."

As they approached the rock wall, Allys spotted a cave about fifty feet up its side.

"I'd like to check that out," said Aylwyn, "but I don't see any way up to it."

Making a survey of the area, Allys said, "No, but if we climb that rock needle over there, we can see directly across into the cave. And it'll be a perfect spot for scanning the area for jackrabbits."

This is what they did, and once perched on the summit of the needle, they took a moment to orient themselves, as their parents had taught them.

"Look, Weaver's Needle is off that way," noted Allys.

"And the Peralta Trail runs down there," added Aylwyn. "Our camp is that way."

Satisfied with knowing exactly where they were, they turned to peer into the cave. That's when they felt the stone pillar sway, bending toward the cliff.

"Whoa!" yelled Aylwyn. "Allys, hang on!"

Before she could reply that she was indeed hanging on to her brother and planting her feet solidly against the curved surface of the stone seat, the column had reached the cliff face, its top parallel to the cave entrance. With a gentle tremor, the rock needle shook the twins free, depositing them into the mouth of the cavern.

"Oh wow!" Allys said as she stood and patted dirt from the backside of her jeans.

The needle snapped back to its original position, stranding them in the cave.

For a minute they stood in stunned silence, unable to make sense of what had taken place. This was beyond the laws of physics and possibly even beyond the conventions of religious miracles.

"What was that all about?" Allys eventually asked.

"I have no earthly idea," said Aylwyn. "But the good news is we can explore the cave now. The bad news is, we have no way of getting down without, at minimum, breaking a few bones."

"I suggest we yell for Mom and Dad," said Allys. "We haven't gone that far. They'll hear us for sure...and they'll find some way to rescue us."

"Good plan, Allys," said Aylwyn. "But if we have to be rescued, let's look around first, before we get chewed out for doing something dangerous."

"Yeah," Allys said, "and it might be hard to explain how we got up here. I doubt they'd believe the truth."

"Let's explore," Aylwyn said. "We might even find a rope or something in here we can use to get down. I'll bet Indians used this place as a hideout."

The cave was high enough for them to walk erect into its long tunnel. Strangely, the interior was dimly lighted farther into it than it should have been. This tempted them to keep going in deeper. After what seemed like five minutes of walking, they entered a large chamber with stone benches around its perimeter. Each twin selected one and stretched out to rest. The room gave off a faint glow, the source of which neither twin could ascertain. Drowsiness overcame them and their eyes closed despite each one trying to stay awake. With a start, they opened their eyes simultaneously, and saw that the room was completely dark.

"Aylwyn? Are you here?" Allys called out with a note of fear in her voice.

"I'm here," he said. "Although I'm not sure where here actually is."

Holding hands, they circled around the chamber feeling for the opening to the cave that would take them back to the entrance. They found nothing but solid rock.

"This is creepy," said Allys.

"We just need light," said Aylwyn. "All we can do is wait for the light to return."

After a prolonged period of silent anxiety, the twins fell asleep on their rock beds. At dawn, a faint glow of light entered the chamber. A shaft of sunlight beamed across their faces, wakening them from deep slumber.

"Look, Allys, there's the cave," said Aylwyn as his eyes filled with the light in the shaft. "I wonder why we couldn't find it last night?"

"I don't have the foggiest idea," Allys said, "but I think we'd better move our buns back to the entrance and start yelling for Mom and Dad. By now they've probably got rescue helicopters searching for us."

"Yeah," he said, "but first I have to pee desperately. I'm going over there and pee on that stalagmite."

"I'll find a private corner and pee too," she said.

As they proceeded through the cave, Aylwyn said, "This sort of looks familiar and sort of doesn't."

"I know what you mean," said Allys. "But we were going the other way yesterday, and things always look different coming or going."

A very bright disk at the entrance lured them confidently forward, but as they reached the end of the tunnel and looked out expectantly into the Superstition Mountain valley, they discovered they were not fifty feet up but at ground level.

"Uh oh, this is not the same tunnel we went into," said Allys.

"And this is not the Superstitions, either," said Aylwyn.

The twins peered into a strange, forested landscape of trees, bushes, and flowers at first sight unlike any they had ever encountered in real life, books, or movies. Mouths agape, they searched the scene with their eyes. As they became accustomed to the view, they began to recognize familiar vegetation. Here and there in the woods were ponderosa pines, sycamores, willows, cottonwoods, pecan, and orange trees. Everything, including rocks and boulders, had soft, impressionistic edges. There were more curves than angles in the forest. And the colors were more intense than the muted hues of Arizona, while also radiating impressions of being ancient.

"This looks like something out of a dream," said Allys. "But not a nightmare, more like a fantasy. A very old fantasy set in an antique world."

"It's like stepping into a fresh painting," Aylwyn added. "Everything's bright and glowing with red, purple, green, blue, and gold hues. I can almost feel a musical rhythm pulsing in the background. 'Magical Mystery Tour' popped into my head."

"I know what you mean," Allys responded. "The scene does cry out for a soundtrack of golden oldies, although I don't hear the Beatles. I sense something **really** old, like from the 19th century. Maybe the 'Peer Gynt Suite.'"

"Yeah, that fits, but I definitely don't want to meet any trolls around here," Aylwyn said. "Are you scared?"

"No," Allys said. "Maybe a bit anxious, but more excited than anything else."

Aylwyn took his sister's hand as they stepped out into the forest. The floor of grass felt firm and springy under their hiking boots.

"This is better than the track at school," said Aylwyn.

"Yeah," said Allys. "I bet I could take ten or fifteen seconds off my mile if I had this to run on."

"Me too," agreed her brother. Thinking of running made him realize he was thirsty and he reached for the water bottle he had been carrying and found that it was gone. "Do you have any water, Allys?"

Her bottle had also disappeared. "We'd better look for a spring or stream," she said.

No sooner had they taken a dozen steps than a pair of young people their age rushed up to them out of a copse of trees.

"Can you help us?" the girl with long blonde hair asked. "We are quite lost."

"Are you looking for the Superstition Mountains?" Aylwyn responded.

"Not any mountains," said the boy, who also had lengthy blond locks but not nearly as long as the girl. "We are searching for the forest that we were walking in."

"But you're in a forest right here," said Allys. A gust of wind blew her strawberry blonde locks across her face and she pushed it back with a hand. "This is very curious."

"But strangely fitting," said Aylwyn with the dawn of a joke registering in his mind. His hair was moderately short but the same shade as his sister's. He extended his hand to each of the strangers in turn. "My name is Aylwyn, and this is my twin sister Allys. We've just come here from that hole in the cliff behind us."

Taking the offered hand, the girl said, "I am called Gretel, and this is my twin brother Hansel."

Allys laughed. "Oh, now I get it! We're in a fairy tale."

"I did not know that fairies had tails," said Hansel. "And yet this is indeed a very strange place, so it should not surprise me if they do."

"No, no, a fairy tale is a story involving magic," explained Allys. "How long have you been here?"

"Only a few hours," Hansel replied. "We have made a modest exploration. You are the first people we have encountered. Where is this hole in the cliff you came through?"

"Right behind us," said Aylwyn. He turned and discovered that the cave had sealed itself. "Oh no, we're stuck now," he groaned.

"Well, we'll just have to find another way out; that's all there is to it," said Allys matter-of-factly.

Hansel was dressed in bibbed shorts and a long-sleeved white shirt. His leather shoes were crudely made, and he wore no socks. Gretel wore a long flax skirt and white peasant blouse, also without socks for her shoes.

"Your clothing is as strange as the fairy tales you spoke of," said Gretel to Aylwyn.

"It's pretty normal where we come from," he replied. "Jeans, tee shirt, tube socks and hiking boots. Not much fashion here."

Allys was dressed the same as Aylwyn, except her blue tee shirt had the words "Beam me up, Scotty" emblazoned across the front, while his read "It's life, Jim, but not as we know it."

"And what does it mean, beam me up, Scotty?" asked Gretel.

"It's from a TV show," said Allys. "A science fiction program about exploring outer space. Actually, it should say 'Scotty, beam me up' but somehow the quote got turned around in popular culture. The captain is asking Scotty to transport him from a planet back to his spaceship. TV is a kind of box people watch for entertainment."

"And what is outer space?" Hansel asked.

"The stars and planets," explained Allys. She pointed into the sky.

"So this show is also a fairy tale," said Gretel.

"Partly," said Aylwyn. "The stories are fiction, but humans have actually explored a little bit of space. A few years ago we sent men to the Moon. They walked around and then came back to earth."

"Incredible!" said Hansel. "This is a strange new world we have come to, Gretel. And what do the words on your shirt mean, Aylwyn?"

"Oh, it's just another catch phrase from the same TV show, **Star Trek**," Aylwyn answered. "It refers to the explorers finding strange living things in outer space. Or other intelligent beings that look nothing like we do. It's a way of telling us we're not the center of the universe."

"Similar to this place," said Gretel. "It is filled with living things but very unlike anything we have known in our world. And speaking of the unknown, please explain again what teevee show means."

"Well," said Aylwyn, "it's a box with a screen...a window on it which displays moving pictures and sounds and voices that tell a story. Everybody in our world watches it every day. It has news and weather reports too."

"A more pressing bit of information," said Allys, "apart from finding a way home, is locating water. Have you seen any?"

"Oh yes," said Hansel, "There is a river not too far in this direction." He pointed to the east.

Since they were all lost, the two sets of twins quickly decided to band together to find an exit out of the strange forest. But first, Hansel and Gretel led the way to the river to deal with their need for water.

Along the way they found bushes covered with colorful berries.

"We ate some of these a short while ago," Hansel said. "As of yet, we have not become ill. They are very tasty."

Each of the teenagers pulled fat and juicy red, blue, yellow, and purple berries from bushes as they walked along and popped them into their mouths. Soon they felt satisfyingly full, but still thirsty.

"How did you get here?" Allys asked the German twins.

Gretel said, "We were in the forest looking for a way back to our village on the Elbe River. We became lost. It grew dark, so we climbed into a cave for protection from the animals and fell asleep. A shaft of light awakened us and we followed in that direction and came out in this different forest."

"And did your cave disappear like ours did?" Aylwyn asked.

Gretel said, "No sooner had we stepped into the enchanted woods to look around than the light at the entrance to the cave went out and then the cave itself disappeared. It was right there where your cave was. I believe it must have been the same one."

"A cave that opens and closes whenever it wants to," said Aylwyn.

"OK, now I have another question," said Allys. "How come you two came here from Germany but speak perfect English? Better English than I speak, actually."

"Well," said Hansel in a serious tone, "I do not know the answer to your question. Prior to arriving here, neither of us could speak English, but as for me, somehow I **remember** how to do it."

Gretel said, "And now that I reflect upon it, I can also speak French and Norse, which I could not do before becoming lost in this place."

Hansel looked closely at his sister and said, "Yes, I too remember how to speak French and Norse, although I have never been to either land where they are spoken."

"Well, why can't we speak other languages?" Aylwyn asked Allys.

"Ah, but we can," said Allys. "*Wie gehts, Hansel und Gretel? Como esta usted? Ya'ah'tee?*"

"*Ach du liebe Zeit!*" said Aylwyn. "I remember too! We can now speak German, Spanish, and Navajo. Very cool!"

"Yes, yes, all very interesting," said Gretel. "But there is a great mystery surrounding **how** we are suddenly able to communicate. What have we done to bring this about?"

"My guess is that we have all gone through a magical tunnel that seals itself after anyone enters into this place," said Aylwyn. "In fantasy lands, magical things happen routinely. That would include everyone speaking the same language."

"Is there a law that decrees magic in such places?" asked Hansel.

"Indubitably," said Allys. "But it may also be something like the magic of American movies, where all the characters speak English even in foreign countries."

"What are American movies?" asked Gretel.

"Something like TV," said Aylwyn, "but on a bigger screen. We can tell you lots of movie stories, but first let's find water."

They walked a short distance pursuing a northeasterly course, unaware that they were moving away from the spring source of the Gymnarykum River that would allow them to return to their respective homes. The river, which they soon approached, followed a spiraling course throughout the Island of Gymnarykum.

Arriving at the grass-covered bank of the river, all four got down on their knees and bent their bodies to drink from the clear stream. The water tasted wonderful. Though neither too warm nor too chilly, the liquid was remarkably refreshing and after drinking their fill they splashed some on their faces.

By now the sun had risen high in the sky and they had grown warm and a little sweaty from the hike. Allys said, "This water feels so good on my face, that I'm tempted to go in for a swim and let it refresh my whole body."

"Don't just stand there being tempted," Aylwyn said. "Jump in. I'll be right behind you."

"Bathing appears to be our next task," said Hansel. "A good choice of activity."

Gretel looked wistfully at the water and imagined it flowing against her skin.

"Well," said Allys, "I'm ready to jump in, but afterward I

don't want to go traipsing through these woods in soaking wet clothes. I'm going back there and take a few things off."

Gretel followed Allys to a secluded spot behind a large shrub to disrobe while Aylwyn and Hansel went behind another one.

When Allys had removed her tee shirt, Gretel looked at her bra and asked, "What is that unusual garment strapped across your breast?"

"It's called a bra," Allys responded. "Women wear them in my world." She unsnapped it and handed it to Gretel for inspection.

"What is it for?" Gretel asked.

"Uh...well...it's to support your boobs, sort of. Although most women don't have breasts big enough to actually need the support. Mine certainly don't. And over the long run, bras actually undermine the muscle tone of your breasts. But nearly every woman wears them anyway. It's become a fashion necessity."

"I do not understand," said Gretel. "It looks uncomfortable. Why would you wear something uncomfortable that you do not need?"

"Well, I guess it's for status. It's a sign that I'm physically grown up," she said as she removed her jeans and panties.

"Very odd," said Gretel, who had finished undressing. "In my world that hair at the top of your legs would be a sign that you are a woman. That and the monthly flow of blood. I have been a woman for more than a year."

"Me too," said Allys. "For more than two years."

"What other uncomfortable apparel do women in your world wear?" Gretel asked.

"Well, uh, there are spiked high heels," said Allys. "They're sort of flimsy shoes with a really tall and thin back heel that make you tip forward and look ungainly. They're supposed to be high fashion, but I agree with my mother that no self-respecting woman would wear such instruments of torture."

"But some women *do* wear them, or else you would not have mentioned them," said Gretel.

"Yes," said Allys, "women who believe the sadistic men who tell them high heels make their legs look better. But they are deluded about that."

"Very strange," said Gretel.

The girls spread their garments across the tops of several bushes and ran giggling into the water just as the naked boys darted out from behind their shrub and jumped into the stream with loud whoops.

CHAPTER 12:
FEMINIST

I am a woman who has needs to speak
Or swell to bursting. How can I be meek
If we're as disputatious as he claims?
Geoffrey Chaucer

Buffeted by tractor trailer rigs passing her at 80 miles per hour on I-10 and tailgated by other semis whose drivers deemed her 75 in the right lane too slow, Chaucer made her way to Tucson in her flimsy Chevy II, arriving a week before classes started with a priority task of finding a place to live. She could not stay more than a few days in the cheap motel on Speedway. Following up on a bulletin board posting in the administration building, she called the number on an ad seeking a roommate to share a house off campus with four other graduate students.

With a sense of optimism, she accepted a room and a one-fifth share of the rent in a wood frame ranch house with five small bedrooms a few blocks north of Grant Road. Two of the students residing there were men, although it took Chaucer no time at all to see that their peculiar personalities eliminated any temptation to become sexually involved with either one.

As the semester unfolded, she discovered that her male roommates were inveterate slobs. When nagged about their habits, both shrugged it off, responding that it was the women's job to do

107

the housework. After too many occasions of cleaning up their messes in the kitchen and bathroom, in self-defense so that she could safely use the facilities of each room, she vowed to herself that she would never marry a slob. The first test of a prospective husband, she decided, would be his familiarity with neatness.

One of her female roommates, Gail Evans, came out to Chaucer as a lesbian. The athletically built Gail had long dark hair and broad shoulders. She was not publicly out but wanted her close friends and family to know. When she told Chaucer about her sexual orientation she added, "For the record, in case you might wonder about it, you're not my type. For one thing, you're too petite, but mostly, in spite of your evident disdain for your current male roommates, you simply like men too much."

"I think I'm average height and build," Chaucer said. "And I definitely do not wear petite sizes. But thank you for the compliment."

"That was no compliment," said Gail. "By my standards, you seem petite. I don't go for petite. Petite is a euphemism for scrawny."

Gail and Chaucer became good friends, often going together to movies and dinner at a favorite hole-in-the-wall Mexican restaurant in South Tucson. They appreciated each other's sense of humor.

In December, Chaucer and Gail became a duet, singing "You're So Vain" every time one of the slobby men came out of his bedroom. They did it so often that the men started calling them twin pains in the ass.

In the spring of 1973, influenced by Gail's confidently assertive personality, Chaucer became a self-conscious feminist. During a campus demonstration for equal rights for women, she burned a bra. It was an old one that she was planning to throw out. She attended the demonstration, wearing the bra without shoulder straps, so she could remove it efficiently to throw into the fire. This was all for show, because she had taken to going bra-less most of the time anyway. Otherwise she was dressed in jeans and a tee shirt with a picture of Anais Nin on it.

That evening, Chaucer went through the house picking up after the slobs and cursing under her breath about the irony of proclaiming women's liberation in the afternoon and cleaning up after male chauvinist pigs in the evening. She tossed assorted candy wrappers, beer cans, and newspapers in the trash, but on second thought pulled a two day-old *Arizona Daily Star* from the bin and settled into the couch to peruse it.

On an inside page the headline "**Arizona Soldier Killed in War**" caught her attention. Although she assumed she did not know any soldiers currently serving in Viet Nam, an intuitive sense pulled her to the article and she gasped when she read it.

"The Department of Defense has confirmed the death in combat of Second Lieutenant Baron Ulster, 23, of Casa Grande. He had been serving as a platoon leader in an undisclosed unit south of Saigon. Ulster was a 1972 graduate of Arizona State University."

There was more, but Chaucer could not continue. "What a waste!" she said aloud, thinking that he was bright and talented and could have done great things with his life. Looking about the messy room, she remembered how neat and organized Baron had been. Here's more irony, she reflected. I might be a widow now if he hadn't become smitten with that actress, Dagmar Solbrent. I should thank Dagmar for that small blessing. She began to cry, softly at first then in a torrent of tears.

Over the next few days, Chaucer could not get the death of Baron out of her mind. It seemed senseless to her, made all the more tragic because Baron chose the Army as his career and volunteered for combat duty. She remembered telling him he liked songs about death, and this thought sent chills through her body. In a used record store, she found two Brothers Four albums, which she played over and over, swept up in homesickness for a seemingly more innocent time.

Chaucer had been opposed to the war in Viet Nam since high school, but now it took on a more immediate and personal tenor in her mind. Thoughts of Chuck Wallace also surfaced. She had no idea where Chuck was but assumed he had survived his tour in the war zone, because she would have heard about it if he had been killed. Her mother, who obsessively read the obituaries, would have let her know. But, she wondered, had he been wounded?

On impulse, she telephoned Chuck's mother, who was still

living in the old house in Phoenix. Chaucer was relieved to learn that Chuck had been discharged from the Army in good health and was now enrolled at the University of Southern California.

During her first year at the U of A, Chaucer took two lovers, one each semester. Both men were generally attractive but mentally and emotionally damaged goods. This suited Chaucer, because she did not want entanglements with anyone she might fall in love with, but she did want her physical needs met.

Her first Tucson lover, Elver Newman, was tagged with the epithet Nudeman because he had been caught streaking by campus security and was thus featured on the front page of the ***Arizona Daily Star***. His only redeeming value, in Chaucer's estimation, was his great skill at cunnilingus. The second was Lance Lewdly, a drama major who was obsessed with his above average penis length. He sought continual admiration for it, but Chaucer was indifferent to his size. In a fit of pique, she told him she'd rather admire his brainy wit, but his wit was so much smaller than average. He sulked after she said this, and so she summarily dumped him.

Chaucer stayed in Tucson over the summer of 1973, having arranged a job at the University library, completing paperwork for the acquisition of books and tracking deliveries.

Soon after classes resumed in September, Chaucer's other female housemate, Jane Lithe, took up with a group practicing Wicca. After attending a full moon ceremony, in which everyone participated sky clad, she excitedly narrated the experience to Chaucer. "Oh it was *so* spiritual!" Jane enthused.

"It certainly sounds intriguing," Chaucer said in what she thought was a neutral voice, although she was indeed intellectually beguiled by the idea of Pagan worship.

"Oh, you simply have to go with me next time," Jane continued. "I won't take no for an answer. This would be perfect for someone with your open-minded sense of the spiritual nature of the earth."

So, Chaucer went with Jane to get a sense of what Wicca was about.

The service took place in an adobe house in South Tucson. In the living room, a pentagram was marked on the carpet with masking tape. The officiating priestess, Wanda Dovely, sat cross-legged at the apex or spirit point of the star. A male acolyte sat at the left (air) point and another male was positioned at the right (water) point. A female sat at the left (earth) point and another female at the right (fire) point.

All the other worshipers and visitors formed a circle around the pentacle, everyone present being equally nude.

"Tonight, we shall cast spells dedicated to ending the war in Viet Nam," Wanda the priestess said. "This is very difficult work, as the negative energy that controls war is very powerful. We may only succeed in making a small dent in the wall of rage that feeds that war, but even a small dent is better than giving up to despair.

"Hear now our invocation, the familiar words of sacred scripture recovered by Charles Godfrey Leland as published in *Aradia, or the Gospel of Witches*:

> *And as the sign that ye are truly free,*
> *Ye shall be naked in your rites, both men*
> *And women also: this shall last until*
> *The last of your oppressors shall be dead.*

"O Goddess and God of earth and spirit, animate our spells with your energy."

Priestess Wanda began to chant a series of statements relating to ending war and continued to do so for about ten minutes. When she stopped, she allowed silence to prevail for a minute and then instructed the other four sitting at star points to go out into the circle and select others to sit at their places. Having done so, the priestess engaged in another series of incantations. When she stopped, she ordered another round of changing places, and this time the woman sitting at the earth point selected Chaucer. Not wishing to disrupt the flow of the service, Chaucer gamely got up and sat at the star point.

When this third round of incantations was finished, the priestess instructed those sitting at the four points to return to the circle, and she spread herself supine over the pentacle, with her head resting on the spirit place, her right hand on air, her left hand on water, her right foot on earth and her left foot on fire.

"We shall now proceed to sealing the energy we have created this night through the ritual of sacred intercourse." She summoned the man who had sat on water during the first round of incantations. He approached on hands and knees and invoked the blessing of the Goddess and God upon the priestess.

Then he kissed the priestess all over her body, including breasts and vulva and sexually entered her. Following an interval of urgent undulation, the priestess announced that she had experienced orgasm. Her lover demonstrated his own experience of release by pulling out and spewing semen on Wanda's abdomen and breasts.

As a benediction, she said dramatically, "Rise and go now to thy home. Thou hast well deserved this grace."

When the ceremony was over, and while Chaucer and Jane were dressing, Chaucer said, "Whew! Nothing like prayers for peace in Viet Nam to make a girl good and horny."

"There are plenty of men here who would agree with you on that and be amenable to helping you satisfy that lustful energy. It's all to the good, contributing toward the power of the incantations for peace," Jane said.

"Maybe another time," said Chaucer. "I need to think about this duo-theistic God and Goddess doctrine. I can relate to one God being both female and male, but two separate Gods is a stretch for me."

Chaucer returned to the adobe house on other occasions, including a full moon ceremony and another at the winter solstice sunrise.

At the moon ceremony, Priestess Wanda again recited the words of Charles Godfrey Leland:

> *Once in the month, and when the moon is full,*
> *Ye shall assemble in some desert place,*
> *Or in a forest all together join*
> *To adore the potent spirit of your queen.*

"Let us now join together in a song sacred to our tradition," Wanda declared. As song sheets were distributed, she added, "Let us fill our hearts with love as we sing the marvelous hymn 'Moonglow.'"

Chaucer laughed silently, recognizing not a hymn but a standard that her father's dance band had played many times.

To conclude the service, Wanda again spread her naked body across the pentagram taped on the carpet and selected a male worshipper to have sex with her, to seal the prayers she had made. Before the eager man began his tactile attentions to her body, she said, "Our beloved Leland has written, 'every woman is at heart a witch.' I am the representative of woman, and you, who have been chosen this night, are the representative of all men, who are born to adore the witch essence of the sacred feminine. Make love to me." He did so with relish and passion.

The solstice sunrise service was noteworthy for Wanda leading the assembled worshipers in the George Harrison hymn, "Here Comes the Sun," although the freezing congregants came nowhere close to the sacred Beatles arrangement of the tune.

At another ceremony, everyone sat in concentric circles around Wanda. As before, all were naked. One lit candle was placed in front of Wanda and she ordered the lights to be turned off. After a lengthy invocation of the dual god and goddess, Wanda dramatically intoned, "Tonight we celebrate the sacred orgy. Gathering to meditate naked in the darkness symbolizes the body's metaphorical death and the laying aside of the demands of daily life. After an interval in the tomb of darkness, light will be restored and the sacred sex that follows our return to the light symbolizes regeneration and revival."

Chaucer had positioned herself in the outermost circle, and during the dark time, slipped out of the room and recovered her clothes. She decided that she was not opposed to group sex in principle and had no sense of immorality about it, but she did not know or like any of the men who were there. She did not want to have sex with someone she didn't know, and there was too little birth control in evidence. She knew condoms were in common use there but she didn't want to take any chances with that.

Later at the house, Jane asked why Chaucer had ducked out.

"I'm ovulating, and I didn't want to risk getting pregnant," Chaucer replied.

"Oh, how do you know? I never know when my fertile time is," said Jane.

Chaucer found Jane's comment incredible and thus let a little sarcasm into her voice when she said, "I can count. It's really not that hard. The tenth through the twentieth days from the start of my period is the time I'm most apt to get pregnant. When I'm actually ovulating, my sense of smell intensifies. It's a simple as that."

"I forget to count days and even when I do I get mixed up," said Jane. "It seems so complicated to me, and pretty often I feel a little menstrual pain in half the time of a regular cycle, and that just throws me totally off kilter."

"***Mittelschmerz***," said Chaucer.

"What?" said Jane.

"Middle pain. It means the pain that comes during the midcourse of your menstrual cycle," Chaucer explained. "It's a sign that you're ovulating."

"Oh, is that what that is? I thought it was a mini-menstruation," said Jane. "It's lucky I don't feel like doing it when I get that pain."

"Lucky indeed," said Chaucer with a suppressed smirk on her face.

Wanda Dovely was paranoid about FBI infiltration of her coven, not because of the unusual nature of the worship but because she was outspokenly anti-war. At ceremonies where the prayers were sealed with sex, she sometimes made a point of choosing a man she suspected might be an undercover agent, thus compromising him if he had sex with her or confirming her suspicions if he refused.

Sometimes in this strange world, however, paranoid people really are being targeted. In this case, though, the FBI informant was a woman, who was not an agent but a high-class call girl who was being paid well for attending the Wicca congregation. As her reports made their way to the FBI, her work turned into her pleasure, for she joined the coven and remained with it long after the FBI terminated her services.

The FBI maintained a lengthy subversive activities file on the priestess Wanda Dovely, and as a result of Chaucer's periodic attendance among the antiwar nature worshipers, the bureau's Chaucer Dickinson file also grew thicker.

Chaucer's Master of Arts in English was imminent, but what she would do with the degree was not entirely clear. As an undergraduate, she had deliberately reduced her future employability by refusing to take any education courses. She did not want to be tempted by financially secure offers to teach high school. Continuing to eschew education courses while working on a master's degree reinforced her intention not to teach elementary or secondary school.

Deciding what she would not do seemed easy to Chaucer. Now she had to make choices about what she would do. Teaching college felt like a good option. This meant going for a PhD, which held great appeal for her. But the competition for faculty positions in English was fierce. Perhaps a more useful and specialized career would offer greater promise. As the semester whittled away, Chaucer toyed with the idea of pursuing a doctorate in library science. She had loved libraries since childhood, and the prospect of getting paid for hanging about in libraries seemed deeply attractive.

In researching possible schools for a PhD in library science, Chaucer discovered that the University of Pittsburgh had a nationally respected library science department. Hedging her bet, she applied for admission to doctoral programs at Pitt in both English and library science. In the process, she learned that she would have to pursue a Master of Library Science from Pitt before embarking on the doctoral program there. This felt like a significant and costly delay, so she withdrew that application and continued to pursue acceptance into a PhD program in English at various universities around the country. Putting Pitt out of her mind, she was surprised to get a letter from that school offering her a grant and fellowship for doctoral work in English. She would be required to teach lower-level college courses to maintain her stipend, but there was enough money in the package to allow her to live frugally. None of the other applications had produced positive responses, so she quickly accepted.

After being conferred with a Master of Arts degree in May, Chaucer moved back to Phoenix temporarily, living with her parents for the summer, listening to their subtle grousing about the inconvenience of two grown children in the house. They bugged her about not getting a summer job, and so she signed up with a temp agency and went out on various vacation fill-in clerical jobs.

At dinner one night, Norah proposed that Chaucer pay room and board while living at home, since she was twenty-four and supposedly a career woman. Chaucer said she would think about it, but would need to save up cash to get an apartment and groceries when she arrived in Pittsburgh, adding that the money from the grant would not start until her program began in September. She had already decided, however, that she would never pay her parents for the privilege of enduring their criticism.

All summer, Chaucer daydreamed about life in the sophisticated East. She fantasized about weekend jaunts to Greenwich Village and Washington, D.C. Each day at home made her more anxious to get away to what she imagined was a far better place.

When it became clear to Norah that Chaucer was not going to offer even a token amount for room and board, she told Banky to take Chaucer's car back. The Chevy II was still registered in his name, and so he informed his daughter that she would have to give up the car when she left for Pitt. Thus Chaucer's expected means of transporting her things and herself to Pennsylvania evaporated.

Chaucer made a self-inventory and concluded that she was the product of a dysfunctional family, always being treated unfairly, as if she were a Cinderella in the house of wicked stepparents. The only way to avoid being dragged down by them, therefore, was to leave home and never come back. Forget finding Prince Charming, she told herself, and instead vowed to go into the world on her own to build her own castle.

A major part of the unhealthy dynamic in her family was that Spenser still lived at home, having flunked out of two colleges. Yet he remained the fair-haired boy. He occupied his time by playing occasional gigs with Banky but otherwise hung out with a group of drug addicts.

Chaucer recognized the signs of her brother's substance abuse, and one evening she took him aside and talked to him about getting into Narcotics Anonymous. In complete denial, Spenser flew at her in a rage. The next day, when Chaucer was out doing a temp job, he told his mother that Chaucer had been belittling him for not finishing college. To this point, he had convinced his parents that he had failed in school because he was suffering a phobic mental illness but was getting treatment from the psychologist father of a friend.

"Chaucer has no compassion," he told Norah, "and she always makes fun of me."

Norah suspected that Spenser was exaggerating but had a fair complaint. To maintain a fragile peace, however, she chose not to create a scene with her middle child.

Concomitantly, Chaucer brooded about telling her parents that Spenser was messing around with cocaine and who knew what else, but hesitated. She was not sure she had the courage to broach this subject, in part because inevitably Norah would ask her how she knew so much about drugs, and she would have to lie to her mother about her own drug use. As screwed up as the family was, Chaucer concluded, she didn't think it would aid her own recovery by telling her mother a huge lie. And she hoped that Spenser's anger about her confronting him was a sign that he knew he was in trouble and would seek help on his own.

To arrange transportation for her move to Pittsburgh, Chaucer went to the main office of Valborg Voyages Travel Agency at 20th Street and Camelback, where Ving Valborg, scion of the family-owned business, greeted her at the door and regally escorted her to a plush chair next to his desk. Once she was comfortably seated, Ving promised that he would take care of whatever travel needs she had.

"I'm moving to Pittsburgh," she said. "I'll need a one-way airline ticket for me and a means of shipping my personal things, including a ton of books, to my place once I get there."

"Hmmm," said Ving. "A lot of books. You must be going away to college. Am I right?"

"In a way," she said. "I'll be starting a PhD program at Pitt."

"No way!" said Ving. "You're far too young for such an advanced undertaking. You must be one of those child wonders who graduated from high school at twelve."

Chaucer laughed. "Thanks for the flattery, but I'm twenty-four."

"Well, you're certainly a well-preserved twenty-four," he joshed. "And now allow me to take care of you. The one-way ticket to Pittsburgh is a snap. I can even get you there without having to change planes in another airport. As for your things, I suggest shipping them by Greyhound. You can do it in stages if you like."

What Chaucer liked at that moment was Ving and his outrageous flirting, which he did with many women, young and old. He told her that his parents owned the agency, and he was the heir apparent whenever his father retired. He did not tell her that his older brother had previously worked for the business but left it to be independent from his over-controlling father. Chaucer felt comfortable around Ving, as well as confident that he would indeed take care of her needs. And his desk was neat and tidy.

"So, are you a native born Phoenician?" she asked him.

"I am," he said proudly. "Not one of those Midwestern transplants. And you?"

"Born here, too." She replied. "What high school?"

"Arcadia," he said with a note of pride.

"West," she said with equal pride.

"The high school question is the first thing one asks upon learning that someone was also born here," Ving said. "Being a true native creates an instant bond between people." He gave Chaucer a warm smile that almost felt to her like a kiss.

As a means of tuning out her family in her waning weeks in Phoenix, Chaucer devoted more time to her novel, which she had given the working title *The Timberscape of Memory*.

The new chapter she was outlining would reflect her experiences of communal nudity in priestess Wanda's coven but with an intentional tinge of innocence about it. Certainly there would be no sexual activity. She also decided to comment on all kinds of religious organizations and the sometimes-silly doctrines that undergird them.

She fantasized about how her characters would behave if they had grown up in happy families and had known that their parents loved them and wanted good things for them. Describing kids from a normal, well-functioning family, she realized, would be difficult, because she had little experience with such relationships. Even Helene's kindly parents were a little odd. However, the book was fantasy, she reasoned, so why not write about the parents she wished she had? In the end, she concluded that it was better to leave all the parents off stage and thus eliminated most of the exposition relating to her heroes' families.

That spring, "Mockingbird" recorded by Carly Simon and James Taylor had become a pop hit, and Chaucer liked it a lot. Since the song made her feel nostalgic for the good part of her childhood when she had watched mockingbirds with her mother and siblings, she decided she would also introduce mockingbirds into her novel.

By now a general structure for her narrative had settled in her mind. A vivid dream involving the Queen of Hearts from *Alice's Adventures in Wonderland* prompted the concept of building her story around four peculiar lands named for the four suits in a deck of cards. What would happen with her two sets of twins in each of those places she had no idea, but she felt confident that when the time came to create the characters to inhabit the lands of Hearts, Spades, Diamonds, and Clubs, and to conjure suitable plot action, she would be able to do so.

One afternoon while she was propped up in bed, deep in concentration jotting down thoughts about characters in a notebook, Spenser stuck his head in her bedroom door. "Hey Chaucy, what are you up to, looking all serious?"

"Just making notes," she replied dismissively.

"No, really, what are you up to?" he repeated. "I'm genuinely interested. You've been holed up in your room scribbling away for the longest time. Weeks maybe."

"If you must know," she said irritably, "I'm writing a novel. As I recall, you once suggested I do so rather than spout my erudition orally. That should make you happy."

"Oh yeah! Far out!" he said. "Am I in it?"

"Would you like to be?" she asked.

"Only if I'm a cool character," he said.

"Then no, you're not in it," she said coolly and threw a pillow at him. "Now scram. You're interrupting my thought processes."

He caught the pillow and tossed it back playfully. "OK, OK, I'll leave you alone. But what's it about?"

"Not this family," she replied. "It's a fantasy adventure set on a mythical island. And I would appreciate you not saying anything to Mom and Dad about it."

He put his finger to his lips and said, "Mum's the word."

"Seal up your lips and give no words but mum," she quoted.

"That's from Shakespeare, right?" he responded.

"Yes. *Henry the Sixth* part two," she replied.

"Mum is English for mom," Spenser said with an impish grin. "That means I can tell mom about your fantasy."

"In this context mum means silent, as you damn well know," she said. "Now get the hell out so I can concentrate on my work."

"I won't really tell anyone," he said. "But you know, you can be a real smart ass superior to everybody bitch sometimes."

"Fine. I'm a smart ass bitch," she snapped. "Just go!"

Spencer left the room, but her line of thought had been broken. With her heart racing, she tossed the notebook on the floor and stretched out on the bed to calm down.

CHAPTER 13:

BATHING IN THE GYMNARYKUM RIVER

Though he was now quite naked,
you must not think
that he was cold or unhappy.

J. M. Barrie

Aylwyn waded out until the water level reached his neck and then dove under. Stationing his feet on a large rock, he took in a mouthful of water and propelled himself up into the air, spewing water from his mouth as he broke the surface. This produced the laugh he was aiming for from the other three and began a sequence of splashing antics that all participated in to great comic effect. After the novelty of aquatic hilarity had worn down, they drifted and floated peaceably as they conversed.

"This is so great!" said Allys. "The water is not too cold but just right. Skinny-dipping is so much fun."

"And the water is so clean and clear," said Aylwyn. "If you stand still and don't swirl around, you can see your toes."

"And each other's as well," said Hansel.

"And not only toes," said Gretel. "Thus for the sake of modesty it behooves one to continue troubling the water." She made waves by swinging her arms in the river.

"Oh don't do that," said Aylwyn. "I'm enjoying the view."

"Well, I don't care who can see what," said Allys. "I think we're having a wonderful adventure. I just had a **déjà vu** experience, like we've all been here before. And there's a feeling that this river is washing us, like it's preparing us for something exciting ahead."

"Yeah, I feel that too, like we're getting scrubbed up for a party," said Aylwyn.

"And while we're preparing for what lies ahead," continued Allys, "we need to learn about each other. I'm sure we need to do that. Hansel and Gretel, what year was it when you went into the cave in the forest?"

She was expecting to hear a date from the European Middle Ages, but neither German could answer the question in a way that allowed Allys to make a linear connection with her own time.

"Years in our land are counted from the founding of villages," explained Hansel. "Our village of Zauberdorf was built by our grandparents' generation, so to us it is year forty-nine. Yet the age of our country is beyond the keeping of time."

Gretel asked, "And what year is it now for you two?"

Aylwyn said, "1971."

"Ach, that is very many years," Gretel responded. "This Village of Phoenix where you live must be very ancient indeed."

Allys said, "In a sense it is, having been the home of a previous Indian civilization. But we count the years from the birth of Jesus."

"And who is Geezuss?" Hansel asked.

"Since you come from Medieval Europe, I am surprised you've never heard of Jesus. He was a holy man who founded Christianity," said Aylwyn. "Christianity was the major religion of Europe in those days."

"Ach, yes of course, **Jesu**, the Christ," Hansel said. "But what do you mean by those days? We have not come from the past but from the present."

"I suppose you have," said Aylwyn. "But your present is different from the present of Allys and me."

"I have so many questions," Gretel said. "Is your village of Phoenix in India? Earlier you called your country

America, which is a strange name I have never heard before. Do you live on a mysterious new continent, such as Atlantis? And was the Christ the founder of Phoenix?"

"First things first," said Aylwyn. "Phoenix is not in India. The Indian civilization Allys mentioned refers to Western Indians from North America, not Eastern Indians from India. The name is a mistake that took hold. A European named Columbus sailed across the Atlantic Ocean to the continent we come from, but he thought he had landed in Asia and called the people who lived here...or there, because I'm not sure *where* we are now...Indians. Of course Columbus was wrong about nearly everything, so there you are.

"Second, North America is the continent at the western side of the Atlantic Ocean, in between Europe and Asia. South of North America is another continent called South America. As far as anyone knows, Atlantis does not exist and probably never has. And third, Jesus did not found Phoenix. The city's only about a hundred years old. Jesus lived in Israel, a small land on the Mediterranean Sea, about two thousand years ago." Aylwyn considered explaining that although they often referred to the area where they lived as Phoenix, they actually lived in an adjacent city called Tempe, but then quickly decided against adding further confusion.

"So, we are not in Europe now?" Hansel asked.

"To be honest, I'm not sure what continent we're on at the moment," said Aylwyn. "Allys and I came here from North America, and you and Gretel came here from Europe. Maybe we're not even on a continent. I suppose we *could* be on Atlantis or some island floating in the space-time continuum."

"An island in the what?" asked Gretel.

"That's something like the timeless land you come from," said Allys. "But judging by the line of cottonwood trees along the bank, I'd guess we're still in America."

"Time is not lacking in our land," said Gretel. "We measure time by hours and days and years. I do not approve your presumption that Zauberdorf is timeless."

"Forgive me," said Allys. "I meant that the time where you come from seems to be unconnected with the time where Aylwyn and I come from. In that context, I suppose Phoenix could be timeless."

"This is all very peculiar," said Hansel.

"I think that if any place is timeless, it's where we are right now," said Aylwyn.

The two sets of twins continued to talk about their lives in their respective homelands. Allys and Aylwyn revealed that they were born into a well-educated and financially comfortable family. Both parents were tenured professors at Arizona State University, with dad teaching English and mom biology.

Hansel and Gretel were modestly well off excepting that they were miserable at the present because of a famine in the region. Their father, a kindly man, was a blacksmith and their loving mother tended a now blighted vegetable garden near their home. Hansel and Gretel had decided on their own to go into the forest looking for nuts, mushrooms and other edibles to bring home, because their whole village had suffered a crop failure. Like Allys and Aylwyn, they had stolen off without permission and were certain their parents would be quite upset to find them missing.

Once the biographical basics had been exchanged, the Germans had more questions remaining than the Americans.

Gretel asked, "How can a woman be a university professor? I did not know that women were even allowed to study at university, much less teach."

"In our world, women can be and do anything they want, even serve as soldiers," said Allys. "This is true in Europe today as well as America."

Gretel shook her head. "No it is not. We come from Europe and we should know."

"Well, at a future time in Europe, women will be able to do anything they want," said Aylwyn.

Gretel sighed in wonderment at what developments lay ahead in her land.

Hansel turned to Aylwyn and said, "You spoke of Atlantis not existing, but I think you were being humorous. You must have been making a joke, for I think you must be from Atlantis."

"Why do you say that?" Aylwyn asked.

"While we were getting undressed," Hansel explained, "I

noticed your foreskin is missing. I have heard tales about men from the vanished continent of Atlantis whose religion required removing foreskins. I have never met anyone who came from Atlantis, but the stories about the place are vivid and strange. It must have been a hellish place to live. So I wonder if this may be a clue to your true identity."

"Circumcision is a common practice in America," Aylwyn said.

"Does America follow the sadistic religion of Atlantis?" Hansel continued.

"No, circumcision has nothing to do with religion," said Aylwyn. "It's supposedly done for hygiene reasons. Prevention of disease. But I suspect it may be more of a puritanical custom to desensitize penises, thereby decreasing general male horniness." He paused to reflect on what he had just said and added, "But I guess in that sense it **is** about religion, even though America is officially secular, with freedom of religion. And if decreasing sex urges is the goal, it's been a complete failure. There are hundreds of different religions in America, maybe thousands. I suppose there are people in America who worship Atlantis, but I don't think they're into removing foreskins."

Gretel had been following her brother's conversation and joined in. "Hundreds of religions! How do you know what to believe? In Zauberdorf, the people follow the religion the Dorfprinz tells them to follow. We used to worship the Three-Gods-in-One but the Dorfprinz changed his mind because of the preaching of a clever priest and now we must worship the One-God-in-Three. The villagers were very upset at first, but after a time they became used to the reversal, and no one would dream of challenging the fiat of the Dorfprinz. Most of them did not understand the difference anyway."

"Most of them secretly worship Wotan and Freya," said Hansel. "But publicly, they say whatever they are ordered to say."

Allys was bored with the talk of religion and turned to gaze at the vegetation along the riverbank. In the course of this survey, she noticed that their clothes draped on the bushes were now flapping in the breeze. "Look everyone," she said. "Our clothes are waving at us."

Hansel, Gretel, and Aylwyn momentarily followed Allys's direction, noting their flapping apparel and then returned to their conversation about religion.

"What's the difference between three-in-one and one-in-three?" Aylwyn asked.

"Burning at the stake if you worship the wrong one," said Hansel.

This got Allys's attention. "That's barbaric!" she said. "And I'm starting to turn into a prune, so I'm getting out."

"You still look human to me," said Gretel. "I see no emerging resemblance to a dried plum."

"It's a metaphor," said Aylwyn. "It means her skin is getting wrinkly from the water."

Allys waded toward the shore, visually searching for the bush with her clothing on it. But she could not locate it. "Hey! Our clothes are gone!" she shouted.

"The wind must have taken them," said Hansel.

The four scoured the area with their eyes until Aylwyn spotted their garments scattered on bushes on the opposite shore.

"This is very curious," Allys pronounced.

They all swam across the water and darted out onto the shore to retrieve their clothes, but just as they reached out for the garments a strong gust of wind picked them up and carried them away beyond sight.

"Well, I'm sure we'll find them eventually," said Allys with a shrug.

Gretel said, "So much for modesty. Hansel and I have accustomed ourselves to famine and other unpleasant circumstances. For the nonce, it seems we shall all have to accustom ourselves to nakedness as well."

"And yet going about naked in such a temperate and sunny climate," offered Aylwyn, "does not seem unpleasant at all."

"If I had to choose between not having any food and not having any clothes," said Hansel, "I would set aside my garments before my heart could render another heartbeat."

"The wind carried them in that direction," noted Aylwyn. "Let's head that way."

Soon they came upon a trodden path where the earth was a golden color and followed it for half an hour with no sign of their clothes. When they reached a sunny and pleasant glade, they stopped to rest. The trees were laced with leafy vines, and on the spur of the moment Allys pulled one down and made a wreath for her head. Soon the other three had also fashioned headwear from vines.

"You know," said Allys, "we could make garments out of leaves and vines, in case we can't find our clothes."

"That would feel itchy," said Aylwyn.

"No, it could be done and in no time you would become accustomed to the feel of it on your skin," said Gretel. "And yet, for the nonce, I quite enjoy the feel of sun and wind on my flesh. It is a virginal experience for me. I have never before exposed my entire body to the rays of the sun."

"First time for me too," said Aylwyn. "Besides, naked is more fun."

Hansel laughed. "And so we go forth with crowns of vegetation but no clothing."

And this they did.

As they continued on the path, in time they encountered a talking bobcat. They discovered the cat's linguistic skill when Gretel spotted it loping toward them and cried out, "What beast is that?"

Bobcat slowed down to a walk and continued toward them in a less enthusiastic manner. "I was of the opinion I was approaching friends who would be pleased to see me," the feline said. "And yet what response do I hear but a frightened question about my beastly identity. I assure you I am **not** a beast, yet I do feel somewhat emotionally hurt at being so categorized."

"I am so sorry," said Gretel. "I meant no harm. I used the term generically to indicate the being was not a human. Still, you did give me a fright at the rapidity of your approach."

"Upon second sight, you can easily recognize that I am a beautiful creature and not in the least scary," Bobcat said. "So now that you have offered apology, and I have implicitly accepted it, let us get on with developing a relationship."

"I am Allys, and this is my twin brother Aylwyn, and

these are the twins Hansel and Gretel," said Allys diplomatically. "Whom do we have the pleasure of meeting on this path?"

"Charmed," said Bobcat, as he offered a paw to each human in turn. "You may call me Bobcat. Please not Bob or Cat."

"Are others of your kind living here in the forest?" Hansel asked.

"Certainly," said Bobcat.

"And if we meet any of them, how shall we address them?" Gretel asked.

"In this land, every bobcat is named Bobcat," Bobcat explained. "Every mockingbird is named Mockingbird. Every jackrabbit is named Jackrabbit."

"Then how shall we tell them apart?" Gretel continued. "And how do they distinguish among themselves?"

"We are whoever we are in the moment," said Bobcat. "We know who we are. That is all that matters."

"What I would like to know," said Aylwyn "is **where** are we? What's the name of this place? And where is it in relation to North America and Europe?"

"As to where in relationship to North America or Europe or even Antarctica, I cannot say," Bobcat replied. "You have entered into the Timberscape of Memory and have swum across the Gymnarykum River." With a sweeping gesture of his front legs, Bobcat continued, "This place is affectionately called the Scape by some or Timmory by others. Many refer to it as Old Mem or Old Tom. Those who like short words simply say Tom. Nicknames for places are acceptable here but never for sentient beings."

"Is this a **real** place or only imaginary?" Allys asked.

"I fear that your use of the modifier **only** with regard to the imaginary betrays a level of immaturity," said Bobcat. "No matter, you will grow up in time and will better appreciate the interrelationship between real and imaginary."

"What I want to know is how do we get out?" asked Aylwyn.

Bobcat looked simultaneously unhappy and affirmed by the question. "I am sorry to say that this is the exact question

I anticipated from youngsters such as yourselves. Does it not occur to you that this is my home, and an evident desire to leave it may hurt my feelings of pride about my homeland? No, of course not. Youth does not think thusly."

"I meant no offense," said Aylwyn. "This is certainly an enchanting place, and we are having a wonderful adventure here. And yet, at some point, our parents will worry about us, and we would like to have knowledge of how to return for their benefit."

"Yes, we would love to stay in this beautiful forest, as your guests, but we want to be dutiful children and return home when it is good for us to go," said Gretel.

"Ah, yes yes, very nicely explained. Very diplomatic," said Bobcat. "You may not be as callow as my initial impression would indicate. So I shall say nothing of methods of departure and instead tell you something of where you have found yourselves. The great Island of Gymnarykum forms roughly a circle, consisting of four landed realms around the periphery, Hearts, Spades, Diamonds, and Clubs. Tom, that is the Timberscape of Memory, is the free and ungoverned region in the island's center."

"Until such time as we leave the island, we will need food and a place to stay," Gretel said. "Do you have any recommendations for us about accommodations?"

Bobcat said, "Choose any direction you fancy and walk. Eventually, if you walk straight enough and far enough, you will come to the ocean. Before then, unless you wander in a circle, you will come to another part of the river. When reaching the river, you will meet someone who can assist you about lodging.

"Which direction would be best?" asked Hansel.

"Alas, that is not my question," said Bobcat with the beginnings of a grin.

"Well then," said Allys, "is it alright for us to go about naked? Is that one of your questions? I don't mind being naked in front of animals but if we run into strange people, it could be embarrassing."

"Or they might not approve," offered Gretel.

Bobcat replied with impatience as if this question represented gross ignorance. "As you can see, I am naked, and I assure you it is quite proper for me to be so. Everyone knows that bobcats look silly in clothes."

"But what about people?" Allys continued.

"I see you are not to be dissuaded from belaboring the obvious," said Bobcat. "Do not ask me this again. Ask the woodswoman."

Hansel said, "Where shall we find her?"

Bobcat replied, "Stay on this path and do not take any forks. Stealing forks is frowned upon in the Timberscape." Bobcat chuckled in a self-satisfied way.

Gretel ignored the pathetic pun and pressed Bobcat, "But if the path divides into a fork, how will we know which tine represents the continuing path and which a new one?"

Aylwyn added, "Is it safe to assume that the path more traveled is the right one?"

"When in doubt, it is helpful to ask a jackrabbit," said Bobcat. "They know all sorts of arcane things. As to the one more traveled, it is never safe to assume that popular usage alone is an indicator of the true path. I fear you will be required to rely on intuition."

Aylwyn asked, "How come you can speak English or for that matter any language at all?"

"Oh happy day! This **is** my question. I am pleased that one among you has at last posed it," Bobcat said. "I eat language berries, just as you have, thus accounting for your multilingual abilities."

"Those multi-colored berries?" asked Hansel. "They are delicious and satisfying."

"And nutritious and edifying," said Bobcat.

The quartet walked east northeasterly, because the path, though now growing faint, led in that direction. Along the way, they picked and ate more berries, which satisfied their hunger. At length they met another human walking on the path toward them.

"Hullo," shouted Allys with a wave. "Are you the woodswoman?"

A broad-shouldered woman with narrow hips and silky black hair waved back. She too was naked.

"Aye, Cranna the woodswoman, at your service. And

you must be the four youths the birds have been twittering about."

"This place, this Timberscape is one wondrous astonishment after another," said Hansel. "I know of many woodsmen, but have never met a woodswoman. Are there more like you on this island?"

Cranna laughed delightedly. "In my humble opinion, I am unique, but woodspeople come in various types and sexes. I am a body who happens to enjoy rigorous outside work. And although it is not a criterion for the job, I joyfully claim the orientation of lesbian."

This was a word that neither Hansel nor Gretel knew in German but immediately understood its meaning in English.

"Another amazing discovery," said Gretel. "I have never before this moment heard of such a phenomenon, although, now that I think upon it, I have seen masculine women and feminine men in our village."

"Is there a male equivalent for lesbian?" Hansel wondered. "A morbian, perhaps?"

Cranna assured him there was. "But I must correct a conclusion drawn by your sister. Most homosexual people do not fit the stereotypes of male femininity or female masculinity. Unless they tell you, you won't know by looking. The men are called gay."

"Then they must be very happy," said Gretel.

"Not necessarily," said Cranna with a rueful voice.

Allys now addressed Cranna, "Bobcat told us to ask you about the etiquette of going about naked. Since you're nude, that suggests it's OK."

"Yes, it is quite appropriate, perhaps even normative to be nude in the Scape. But in the realms it is another matter. If you were going to a realm it would be prudent to have clothing available just in case. At present you are heading in the direction of the Realm of Clubs, which occupies the eastern quarter of the island. I myself am a refugee from the Realm of Diamonds to the south. I don't recommend going that way. Spades is to the west and Hearts north, but the closest realm is Clubs. Each is ruled jointly by a king and queen of varying temperaments."

"Is it a good thing to go into a realm?" Aylwyn asked.

"It may be a needful thing. A pathway home may begin there," Cranna answered. "But the day is beginning to turn to dusk and soon it will be too dark to travel. I will show you a gazebo where you can sleep tonight, but it is only for sojourners and you are not permitted to establish a camp there. You must leave before mid-morning."

Cranna led them to a circular structure a dozen paces off the pathway. Without the woodswoman they would never have seen it, however, for it was nestled inside a thick grove of trees. It was built of knotty pine and lined along its interior with padded benches that formed extended semicircles around its circumference except for the places where two doorways provided access.

"If it gets chilly in the night, there are quilts under the benches. In the morning you can tend to your personal needs in the woods and bathe in the creek," Cranna explained. "Then I suggest you be on your way to wherever it is you are going."

"But we don't know where we're going," Allys said.

"You will when you need to," said Cranna. "Good night and sleep well."

With that benediction, Cranna disappeared into the darkening forest.

The girls curled up on one bench with their heads almost touching and their feet at opposite ends, while the boys took the other bench with their feet almost touching and heads away from one another.

"We'd better get some sleep," Aylwyn said. "Who knows what we'll run into tomorrow?"

Their eyes closed almost immediately and they slept as if drugged, deep dreamless sleep. The morning sun awakened them almost simultaneously, and they set about their morning ablutions quickly and efficiently.

Aylwyn said, "It's been at least three days since I've pooped. I need to find a place to take a dump."

"Let me know if you find a good spot," said Allys.

Aylwn went off in search of a suitable location and soon called out so that the others could hear, "Hey! There's an outhouse here. A deluxe four-seater."

He made use of the facility and the other three in turns also emptied their bowels.

"The gossamer toilet paper is a nice touch," said Allys.

They returned to the gazebo after washing in a nearby creek, intent on making a travel plan. Upon entering it, they discovered a large platter of green, yellow, red, and blue fruits they had never seen before and something that looked like whole grain pound cake. Their mouths watered and they fell upon the food with gusto, discovering to their delight that everything was quite delicious.

Thus fortified and now agreed upon a plan, they set out on the generally eastward path. Before they had gone more than a hundred paces, Gretel cried out, "Ach! My wreath of vines! I left it at the gazebo."

"I'll make you another one," offered Aylwyn.

"Thank you, but I will run back and get it," she said. "Wait here. I shall be back in a trice."

When she reached the grove where they had slept, the gazebo was gone. There was no trace of it ever having been there. But lying in the grass at the place where she had laid her head the night before was her wreath. She picked it up and as she turned to catch up with her compatriots, she saw Aylwyn approaching.

"I thought I'd walk with you," he said. Seeing the tiara of vines in her hand, he added, "So you found it. But where's the gazebo?"

"It has disappeared," Gretel said with a note of wonder in her voice.

After carefully inspecting the site and ascertaining that the outhouse was also gone, he called out, "Allys! Hansel! Come quickly."

The shout proved unnecessary, for they too had walked back to the place and were similarly amazed at the mysterious development.

"The laws of physics are very different in the Timberscape," said Aylwyn. "We must therefore assume that nothing is as it appears."

"I wonder if that applies to the food we ate also?" Hansel mused.

"Well, I feel full and satisfied," said Allys. "But just the same, we should pay attention to our bodies to see if we lose weight. Then we'll know if the berries and such are imaginary."

"Not necessarily," said Aylwyn. "We might lose weight from eating healthier food and more exercise."

"Oh, right," said Allys. She glanced at the other set of twins whose bodies were quite lean. "But Hansel and Gretel here have been living through a famine, so they have no fat to shed."

"I think the food here must be real," Hansel said, "because it feels like I have gained a bit of weight since arriving in this place."

They resumed their hike and presently came again to the coiling river at a very wide point. There they encountered a naked ferryman, whose long brown hair was tied efficiently into a ponytail and whose name, they soon discovered, was Foxford. Foxford agreed to take them across the water, but they had no money for the fare.

"No matter," Foxford said. "Words are money here. The fare is a story from each pair of you."

Before embarking, Aylwyn asked Foxford if he knew why the gazebo and outhouse had disappeared.

"They are not built to last a long time," said Foxford. "All the structures in Old Mem are built to last only according to the needed use."

"Who builds them?" asked Allys.

"Various people and creatures," said Foxford. "All the outhouses, for example, are erected by a splendid fellow called the Mad Squatter. He makes them all shapes and sizes depending on anticipated use. How big was the one you found?"

"Four holes," said Hansel.

"There, you see," said Foxford. "Your outhouse was made with sufficient openings in anticipation of you four."

"But we did not all empty our bowels at the same time," said Gretel.

"Ah, but if the need had been great, you could have," said Foxford. "You see, the Mad Squatter is not really mad at all. Very crafty in my estimation."

"Never in my whole life have I pooped in a communal toilet," said Allys. "I'm used to having the bathroom to myself for stinky business. That's a thing a person does alone. The smells can be rather embarrassing."

"I would not mind sharing a four-seater," said Gretel. "It seems a much better method than the thunder buckets under our beds at home."

"In the Timberscape of Memory," said Foxford, "matters of bodily function are considered natural and do not require solitude and are not in the least embarrassing."

"That's good to know, but **why** did the outhouse and gazebo disappear?" asked Aylwyn again.

"Well, they won't be needed again for who knows how long, perhaps years. So what is the point of letting them stand there and decay?" Foxford explained.

"Will an outhouse appear every time I need to empty my bowels," Hansel asked.

"Sometimes other means will seem more expedient," said Foxford. "In the Scape, all such urges respond to cosmic riddles and natural rhythms."

"That's the weirdest thing I've heard all day," said Aylwyn. "Groovy, but weird."

They set out across the river.

Allys and Aylwyn told the ferryman about a magical land called Arizona inhabited by cowboys, Indians, and snowbirds, while Hansel and Gretel spun a yarn about an enchanted forest south of the Elbe River where witches and warlocks prowled about looking for unwary children to kidnap.

"They dress all in black but dance naked in circles in the moonlight and do silly things," Gretel said. "I have actually seen a witch, and she was not at all ugly like the stories tell but beautiful, with long golden hair."

"A handsome Warlock invited me to his house for candy," Hansel said. "But I was afraid to go because my parents told me that candy was addictive, and if I ate it even once, I would crave it forever and it would ruin my life."

As he paddled his raft, Foxford offered his story, that he was gay and a refugee from the Realm of Clubs, which they were moving toward.

"You will probably be safe in Clubs, as long as you are in heterosexual pairs. And I am sure from watching you that is the case. However, you will need to wear clothes once across the border into the Realm of Clubs. They won't appreciate the unclad human form."

"But our clothes have blown away with the wind," said Gretel. "Where can we get something to wear?"

"Not to worry," said Foxford.

When the ferry had landed at the far bank, Foxford summoned a gilded flicker and instructed it to fly off into the countryside in search of the missing garments. A few minutes later the flicker returned leading a group of mockingbirds carrying most of their clothes. They had found Hansel's bibbed shorts and shirt, Gretel's skirt and blouse, and Allys and Aylwyn's jeans and tee shirts. However, no under garments or footwear were found.

"They probably floated into the Realm of Diamonds, where scholars there will study them quite seriously and at great length," Foxford said.

Hansel stared with envy at Aylwyn's long pants, which he had never worn, and Gretel marveled that Allys wore pants the same as men.

"Well, hey, why don't we swap attire," Allys said. "It would be a hoot to wear a genuine medieval outfit."

This they did, amid great laughter.

"It feels odd to wear trousers," said Gretel. "But I confess that I like the sensation of cloth against my legs."

As they continued on their journey, a jackrabbit leapt onto the path in front of them, and they raced ahead to try to stop it and ask more about Clubs. Its pace was slow enough for them to track but not to overtake the long-eared creature. Then, as they reached the border between the Timberscape and Clubs, the jackrabbit zigged and zagged and disappeared back into the forest.

CHAPTER 14:
CHURCH PILLOW TALK

O Welaway! So sly are scholars old
That I know not what creed that I should hold.
Geoffrey Chaucer

Apart from a brief outing to Los Angeles while at ASU, Chaucer's arrival in Pittsburgh in the fall of 1974 marked the first time in her life she had been outside Arizona. The bus trip from the airport into the city amazed and confused her. To her desert-accustomed eyes, the countryside seemed lush and excessively green. She sensed this was what a rain forest must look like with all the trees and bushes crowded in upon one another.

Once through the Fort Pitt Tunnel and into the city, she had a hard time keeping track of the twisting route through downtown to the university. The street system was perplexing. From the Pitt campus, she oriented herself with a city map and felt somewhat confident about knowing where things were. However, forty-eight hours after arriving in Western Pennsylvania, Chaucer was convinced that the word system did not apply in any sense to the roads of Pittsburgh. Chaos was the operative word in her mind. It was one thing to see odd-angled roads on a map. It was an entirely different matter to walk them without getting lost.

She had grown up with the grid system of streets in Phoenix and Tucson and thus assumed that if two roads ran parallel, she could go from one to the other on a cross street. To her frustration, she learned that this assumption was not reliable in Pittsburgh, as this sometimes led to a third street that took her far afield from where she intended to go. Chaucer found herself cursing the random roads of Pittsburgh. Several times she felt like a rat in a perverted maze as she attempted to find her way back to her apartment after going forth in search of food and other provisions. Eventually, she learned to memorize routes, and intellectually she knew that the city had evolved from pre-industrial times, but emotionally, she harbored a sense that roadways in Western cities were far superior.

Chaucer leased an efficiency apartment in the Oakland neighborhood. Her books, clothing, kitchenware, and personal effects that she shipped prior to flying to Pittsburgh arrived in stages and she rejoiced to set up her first private, Chaucer-only home. Without a car, she was forced to make use of buses for a few weeks, which proved difficult to manage carrying two bags of groceries from the Giant Eagle. Providentially, a departing student offered to sell her his Vespa motor scooter at a bargain price, and she took his offer. Thus she was forced to learn to navigate the chaotic city streets. Once she mastered this task and found the streets familiar, she changed her mind about the superiority of the West and began to view the city as a crusty but charming character.

Chaucer's next-door neighbor in Oakland was also a graduate student at Pitt. One day she invited Chaucer to go to church with her. Chaucer politely declined, saying she was not a churchgoer. But the neighbor countered with the news that the Open Door Community was not a typical church and was in fact quite liberal. It attracted intellectuals from all over the city.

Since Chaucer wanted to get to know people in the multi-university area, especially the intelligentsia, her neighbor's description appealed to her curiosity. She decided to attend once to see what a quite liberal church looked like. She had no intention of trading in her humanist beliefs, but her previous experience with Wicca had been beneficially instructive to her, so learning about a Protestant congregation that catered to intellectuals would no doubt also provide information to round out her education.

The motto of the Open Door Community was "Recovering and Restoring the Roots of Christian Love and Grace." This group advertised itself as open to gays and lesbians and consistently advocated for all kinds of social justice. The pastor was Jenny Jaymark, a mid-thirties woman who was divorced from an abuser and re-married to the psychotherapist who helped her get out of the first marriage.

Jenny was slim-figured, with small breasts and a long face with widely spaced eyes, a nose that tapered to a square, and a wide mouth with full lips. Brown hair with bangs in the front capped her head. Her features, Chaucer thought, were unusual but they came together in a way that was beguiling and appealing to men and women alike.

Every Sunday the Open Door Community members sang the same congregational introit, joyfully proclaiming their genuinely inclusive welcome to anyone who entered the sanctuary. They sang their particular words to Bunessan, an old Gaelic melody. Chaucer recognized the tune as "Morning Has Broken." The piano arrangement the Open Door folks used followed exactly the Cat Stevens arrangement that Chaucer knew.

> *This congregation opens to all folk*
> *Whatever gender, whatever race.*
> *Orientations matter not to us.*
> *God welcomes every soul to this place.*

It took Chaucer no time at all to conclude that she liked the people of the congregation and was surprised to find that she was neither offended by nor in significant disagreement with the free-flowing theology of the sermons. Soon she fell into regular attendance at the services, enjoying the fellowship and unusually bright people she met there.

The second time she attended, the congregation sang "All Beautiful the March of Days" to a tune called Forest Green, and though she had never heard it before, Chaucer immediately loved it, thinking that her Pagan friends would probably like it too. Quick research on her part found that it was from an English folk melody, with a 1911 text by Frances Whitmarsh Wile.

All beautiful the march of days, as seasons come and go;

The hand that shaped the rose hath wrought the crystal of the snow;

Hath sent the hoary frost of heaven, the flowing waters sealed,

And laid a silent loveliness on hill and wood and field.

Through the activities of the Open Door Community, Chaucer became deeply involved in defense of gay rights. The ODC and Jenny Jaymark were under surveillance by the FBI because of their very public and strident gay rights advocacy, and so once more, reports were added to Chaucer's FBI file as a result of her participation with a purportedly subversive organization.

Despite the activities of the ODC, Chaucer was surprised to discover that the image of the fabled liberal East Coast she had grown up with was wrong. To her eyes, the people of Pittsburgh seemed provincial and much narrower in their views than the supposed rubes of Phoenix. She found the general population, including her English 101 undergraduates, clannish, ingrown, and suspicious of strangers and outsiders. ODC provided a distinct exception to this view.

During the fellowship time after worship on her third Sunday at the Open Door Community, a man with an air of comfortable erudition approached Chaucer with a plate of carrots and celery, which he offered to her.

"Would you accept this vegetable offering as a gesture of welcome to the community?" he said. "I saw you turn away from the table that was laden with cookies and brownies and thought this might be more suitable."

"Thank you," she said, taking the paper plate from his right hand with her left.

With his right hand now free, he extended it to Chaucer and said, "Skeffington Keck at your service. Semi-regular worshiper at the Open Door and professor of homiletics at the Seminary of the Western Frontier."

Taking his outstretched hand, she said, "Chaucer Dickinson,

grad student at Pitt, working on a PhD in English."

"Everyone calls me Skeff, even my students," said the professor.

"I take it you were named after Lewis Carroll's brother," Chaucer asserted.

"I am impressed," Skeff replied with a short bow. "You will do quite well in your studies here. My father thought Skeffington was a splendidly literary name. Alas, he had not anticipated the inevitable nickname that it cried out for. He never got over my adopting the abbreviated form of it, though it saved me from many schoolyard taunts."

"I take it then you are visiting from one of the Western states. I'm from Arizona. Where is your seminary?" Chaucer asked.

Skeff laughed. "It's right here in Pittsburgh. When the seminary was founded in the eighteenth century, Pittsburgh **was** the Western Frontier. The school fathers have never gotten around to changing the name to reflect the national expansion in the nineteenth century, much less the twentieth."

"Since you teach," Chaucer said, "perhaps you can shed some light on why the students here are so afraid of prepositions and infinitives in writing and speaking."

Skeff laughed. "I see you have encountered the distinctive language of Western Pennsylvania. I cannot tell you precisely why, but the peculiar usage may have resulted from a mixture of Scots and Eastern European speech patterns. I don't think it is a matter of fear."

"My theory, *apropos* of the outdated name of your school," Chaucer said, "is that the culture of this region is strongly oriented to the past rather than the present, and this is manifested in everyday speech. For example, my students stubbornly insist on using past participles where present participles are needed. I've repeatedly told them this is a linguistic problem that needs fixing, but they insist that it *rilly dahnt* need *fixed*."

Again he laughed and said, "You may be onto something." Being a practiced listener, the Reverend Doctor Skeffington Keck then skillfully coaxed Chaucer into talking at length about her personal life. Reflecting later on the meeting, Chaucer decided his attention to her words made her feel like she was the only one in the room.

Before Chaucer left the church that day, Pastor Jenny Jaymark approached her and said, "I'm so glad you've come back again this week. A word of...well, not warning exactly, but a heads-up about Skeff. He has three ex-wives to his credit and has a weakness for attractive women. Keep your eyes open."

"He has to be twenty years older than I," said Chaucer. "But he does have a quaint charm about him."

"Eyes open," said Pastor Jenny and patted Chaucer's hand in a motherly way.

In his mid-forties, Skeffington Keck was winsomely persuasive and suave. A former Marine officer, he stood six feet two inches tall and ramrod erect in posture, yet somehow this did not detract from an aura of approachability. His usual pattern was to target married women for his numerous sexual liaisons, and so his plan to seduce Chaucer was a departure for him, but one he eagerly sought.

Skeff's ordination was in the American Calvinist Church. In an early conversation, he explained to Chaucer, who was woefully ignorant of denominational history, that the American Calvinist Church was a sister denomination to the Presbyterians, having broken off from an antecedent Presbyterian synod in the eighteenth century. Seminary trained ministers were scarce in those days, so a Presbyterian group in Eastern Pennsylvania came up with the idea of sending elders into the western frontier to start congregations. If they became viable, they would then send out seminary graduates to take over. Strong objections arose within the institution, so proponents of the plan broke off and formed what became the ACC. The ACC did implement the plan, but it failed miserably. The elders who went into the frontier and built up congregations did not want to give them up to know-it-all young ministers. The elders, being older and worldly wise, changed the rules to get themselves ordained as clergy based on their practical experiences. So from the beginning, the ACC was involved with controversy and argument about doctrinal and ecclesiastical issues.

Chaucer waited until early December before joining Skeff in bed at his home. She found him an accomplished and considerate lover, but expressed amazement that a minister would fornicate. "I thought you ecclesiasts had hard rules about this kind of thing," she said. "Sex outside of marriage is sinful, and all that pious blather."

He replied, "The rules you refer to are ambiguous at best. The biblical model for male-female relationships includes multiple wives and concubines. The commandment against adultery only applies to having sex with the wives of other men, thus depriving them of exclusive use of their wives bodies. Historically, it has everything to do with property rights and nothing to do with sexual morality. Thus it cries out for modern reinterpretation, and modern reinterpretation obliges by providing room for consenting adults to play a bit."

"That's rather cynical, don't you think?" she said.

"No, that's realistic," he replied.

Reflecting later on the experience, Chaucer made a mental connection between Skeff and Kirk Trilby, the campus pastor at ASU. Somehow, Skeff's worldview seemed to explain the dynamics behind Trilby's behavior. Apparently, the campus pastor was not an anomaly but a piece of a larger pattern of clergy behavior.

Another time in bed during afterglow conversation, he told her about the various Seminary of the Western Frontier faculty members and local ministers who were currently engaged in sexual affairs. To Chaucer, there seemed to be a lot of them.

She responded by telling him about attending Wicca services. Her description of sacred sex caused him to become erect again. He said, "Heresy is such an effective aphrodisiac. It never fails to turn me on."

"Are you ready for another go?" she asked while stroking his growing member. They went again.

After the second set of orgasms for both, he said, "The unspoken rule in homiletics is to take the congregation to the edge of heresy and then pull back at the last minute. With your persuasive erotic heresy, my dear, I'm afraid there is no pulling back."

Chaucer said, "That sounds like a dishonest tease for the congregation. If you're going to flirt with heresy in your sermons, at least have the *cojones* to go all the way. Pulling back is the ecclesiastical equivalent of a woman giving a man blue balls or a man bringing a woman to the edge of orgasm and then stopping."

"No," he maintained. "It is a means for getting the sheep to think about other pastures without actually taking them there. If any of the brighter bench bunnies cross the boundary into more interesting theological places, they can claim that achievement for themselves, not because I led them there. I'm only priming their mental pumps."

"Spewing metaphors in the process," she said. "I presume it also provides you deniability if the conservatives accuse you of advocating what you teased them with."

Ignoring her remarks, he continued, "Preaching is an erotic art, as exciting as the **Kama Sutra**, but we can't have parishioners engaging in erotic contortions in the sanctuary. Since homiletics, the holy subject that I teach, is the art of blessed persuasion, we must find ways of inducing the flock to return week after week to *be* blessed. They won't return unless they are hooked into hearing more of the story. If preachers let the climactic details out too soon, people will be satiated and not bother to come back."

"Like because you have had two magnificent climaxes tonight, you won't bother to invite me back into your bed?" Chaucer teased.

"I take your point," he said. "Perhaps I should stop blathering and do something useful like tickling your back. Would you like that?"

She rolled over to give him unobstructed access to her aft side. "Tickle away!"

In the relationship between Chaucer and Skeff, it would be difficult to determine who was using whom. Both equally enjoyed the sexual release. Chaucer was not interested in marriage but very much liked the entrée Skeff provided her into the inner world of Pittsburgh, including introductions to corporate tycoons who served on the SWF board of directors. Desire for money and power was not her motivation, but rather she found herself fascinated by people who had both or who avidly sought them, as well as with learning the way things really worked behind the scenes.

In their lengthy after-sex conversations, Chaucer gained much inside information about the foibles and secrets of American

Calvinist clergy, including which ones had trouble with their zippers. She had no idea how this information would be useful but intuitively absorbed it all as fuel for future writing and teaching. She was astounded at the number of female church members who were having affairs with clergymen, if her seminary professor lover were to be believed, and thought it peculiar that so many ministers, including Skeff, had developed odd rationales for why adultery was acceptable behavior.

"Like the wedding at Cana," he explained to her, "sometimes in a marriage the wine simply runs out. One needs a fresh beverage from a new jar to recharge, so to speak. At a practical level, adultery can provide that finest wine that allows the marriage to renew and continue."

"Has that been your personal experience?" she asked. "How has that worked in your own life?"

"Let's just say that I have been involved in...uh...I am aware of situations where that was the outcome," he said, unsettled by the question.

"But Jesus never condoned adultery," Chaucer responded firmly.

"But he forgave it, my dear. Just accept the mellow metaphor," he said.

On a frigid February Friday in 1975, Chaucer visited Skeff at his office on the campus of the Seminary of the Western Frontier in Shadyside. That day, Fred Rogers, the Mr. Rogers of television, was on campus, visiting the daycare center, and Skeff offered to introduce Chaucer to him. Skeff explained that Fred was an ordained Presbyterian minister, having graduated from Pittsburgh Theological Seminary in East Liberty. Skeff had met Fred at one of Skeff's continuing education seminars on preaching.

"I told him that his low-key, non-theological preaching is far more effective than anything that has ever come out of my mouth," Skeff said to Chaucer.

When Mr. Rogers came by Skeff's office to chat, Skeff introduced Chaucer as a member of the Open Door Community, and Fred responded by saying that ODC was a wonderful congregation doing important work. Chaucer chose not to correct Skeff that she was not a member but only a regular visitor.

After Fred left, Chaucer said, "So, how many affairs has Mr. Rogers had?"

"None," Skeff exclaimed. "The man is a saint, a true saint."

"But you told me that most saints have rather checkered records when it comes to relationships. Saying someone is a saint is no indicator of marital fidelity. With all the tales of clergy sexual antics you've spun for me during pillow talk, I don't think I'll ever assume any minister is faithful." Thinking of Rex Fisher, she added, "And television people have a reputation for promiscuity."

"Fred McFeely Rogers is faithful to his lovely wife and he is a saint. He is the exception that tests the rule."

"Yes," said Chaucer. "I'm glad you said tests the rule rather than proves it. Most people don't understand that *prove* is an old English word that means to put to a test."

At their next session of pillow talk, Skeff said, "At present, four of my faculty colleagues are carrying on affairs. I don't count myself, of course, because I am merely fornicating and not committing adultery."

Chaucer gave him an accusatory look but said nothing.

He caught her intent, however, and said, "Not that I have never committed adultery. It's just that, at the moment, I am not. And my count did not include a female faculty member who is living in sin with a professor at Chatham College here in the Shadyside area. Neither is married, so it doesn't count as an affair. And truth be told, they would marry if the law allowed it."

Chaucer said, "I think a more appropriate name for your divinity school would be *semen*-ary."

"Don't think I haven't thought of that very name," he said. "But let me entertain you with a story about my involvement with pornography."

"Do tell," she said. "And while you're telling me, you can tickle my back."

"One of my dear friends is a defense attorney. Three years ago, he asked me to testify at the obscenity trial of a theater owner who had exhibited the film *Deep Throat*."

"Because, I imagine, you are expert at blessed persuasions or notorious for preaching from the *Kama Sutra*," Chaucer said.

"No, Miss Smarty Pants," he retorted. "Because he knew that I had taught classes on evaluating films for homiletical uses and would thus qualify as an expert witness. The fact that I am an ordained minister would also add credence to my testimony. I agreed to help him, and this required me to see the film. Two armed Allegheny County sheriff's deputies escorted me to a private screening of the film and sat grim-faced on either side of me while I watched and took notes."

"A vivid image," said Chaucer. "Deputies grimly watching a porn flick."

"They watched *me*," Skeff huffed.

"No doubt checking your crotch for unlawful bulges," she said.

"Believe me, it was not a context in which to become aroused," he said. "And frankly, the film wasn't all that sexy anyway. At any rate, in court I testified that the screenplay was sophomoric as art, but that it was clearly a satiric parody of the porn genre and therefore had redeeming social value. Unlike most porn films, it had a plot and character development. Linda Lovelace was a frustrated, non-orgasmic woman who went to a doctor and learned that her clitoris was in her throat. This was the guiding device that lent itself to puns and jokes. The dialog was tongue-in-cheek, I told the court. Its literary level was low but it had more artistic merit than a typical television situation comedy."

"It doesn't take much to surpass the artistic merit of a sit-com," she said.

Skeff asked, "Have you ever seen *Deep Throat?*"

"No," she said. "Actually, I have never seen any kind of porn film. And I'm curious about how you could be an expert, testifying that *Deep Throat* was a parody unless you had seen enough porn flicks to know."

"The Prosecuting Attorney wanted to know that very thing," he said. "I testified that as a wayward college student, I had viewed a number of stag films shown at fraternity house parties."

During yet another after-sex conversation, Chaucer asked Skeff, "Why do you insist on reinterpreting and explaining away Bible texts? Why don't you simply declare the Bible out-dated and non-authoritative?"

"What would be the fun in that?" he responded.

"Fun? We're talking about beliefs that negatively affect people's lives. It's not fun for the people in the pews to have their lives strangled by ancient superstitions and neuroses," she said.

"To the contrary," Skeff countered. "The people in the pews would not stand for it. If preachers told them the Bible was no longer authoritative, they'd rise and demand new preachers to tell them the Bible held them in thrall."

"Or they'd rebel and demand to know why the church has been projecting guilt on them all these years," Chaucer said. "And rightly so."

"No, they're like Lilliputians in *Gulliver's Travels*," he responded. "Lilliputians believed in a flat earth that would flip over at the resurrection. Thus they buried people head down so they would be heads up when the resurrection came. Jonathan Swift noted, 'The learned among them confess the absurdity of this doctrine, but the practice still continues, in compliance to the vulgar.' The vulgar folk in the pews won't listen to learned discourse." Snidely, he added, "Besides, what's the purpose of religion if not to control the morality of the laity?"

"Helping people to live healthy, empowering, and ethical lives," she said.

"That's OK for the intelligentsia," he said, "but not for the *hoi polloi*."

Chaucer replied, "If scientific evidence and documented historical facts are always trumped by the authority of scripture and doctrine, where's the integrity in religion? Maybe that's why so many religious leaders behave unethically. If science and history and demonstrable facts are worthless in the face of entrenched beliefs, then one does not need to worry about acting in ways that are harmful to people who pay attention to the facts. In church, facts don't matter."

"The Church is not a democracy," he said. "Rather it is a monarchical hierarchy. The priestly class, which is dominated by bloody Tories like me, creates the conventional beliefs and sets the rules, which are not put to popular vote. However, once accepted by the laity, they become exceedingly difficult to change."

"And of course, in the process, clergy make one set of rules for themselves and another set for everyone else," she added.

"As it was in the beginning, is now, and ever shall be, world without end, amen," the Reverend Doctor Keck recited with a smug smile.

"I thought God was supposed to do the creating," said Chaucer.

"With humans as co-creators," said Skeff. "God is a big-picture artist, who has left it to us to tend to the finishing details. Western society has left it to clergy to decide those details. Whatever our flaws, we take seriously our responsibility to order society."

"Seriously?" said Chaucer. "You make God into a mad impressionist artist who paints outside the lines and leaves it to the art students to clean up the mess."

"Yes," said Skeff thoughtfully, "that about sums it up."

"Well, if God is an artist who colors outside the lines," said Chaucer, "I think God must prefer people who color outside the lines over against than those who try to force everybody inside while doing what they like anyway."

"Touché!" said Skeff.

For months, Chaucer enjoyed Skeff's skillful attention to her body as well as her post-coital jabs at his doctrinal and ecclesiastical arrogance. But in time she grew weary of his narcissism and unhappy with his hypocritical ethics and disengaged from the relationship. Her timing was good for accomplishing the breakup smoothly, for he was ready for new flesh and had his eyes on the wife of a pastor recently arrived at a Squirrel Hill parish.

Chaucer decided to experiment with celibacy for her remaining time in Pittsburgh, devoting all her energy to her doctoral studies. She knew she would not have much time for socializing when she began work on her dissertation. To keep her body in shape, she took up jogging around the campus and her Oakland neighborhood and found that it helped with her intellectual and creative thinking as well. In a matter of weeks, her body cried out for a good run every day.

On a breezy day in March 1977, a drag queen nightclub singer using the stage name Marzipan entered a studio in Los Angeles and recorded a campy arrangement of Banky Dickinson's World War II novelty song "The Sally and Rose Comedy Shows." The music groove featured a heavy disco beat, and Marzipan's wailing falsetto on the chorus added an aura of mockery to the number. By June, the song had reached number one on the national pop charts, and Banky was in line for significant royalties.

Chaucer heard the song on the radio and in student hangouts around the Oakland District, and it made her remember how much her father had tried to ignore his novelty tune past when he had a dance band. Still, she thought, it must be gratifying to have one's work revived, even if in an over-the-top manner. Sensing that this might provide a chance to connect emotionally with at least one of her parents, and feeling a bout of nostalgia for the days when she listened to her dad's band practice, she wrote a note to him.

Dear Dad,

Your song is all over the airwaves in Pittsburgh, and I saw in the paper that it has been declared a gold record. Congratulations! I imagine the arrangement is not something you would have created, but I have become a minor celebrity on campus owing to the fact that my father wrote the "Sally and Rose" song. Though you never played that song in rehearsals at our house, I have fond memories of golden hours on the back porch listening to you practice the great standards in the fifties.

Love,
Chaucer

Banky was touched by Chaucer's note, all the more so since Spenser had not acknowledged his father's new-found celebrity, nor had Marlowe written about it. As a result of the cover recording, he had been featured in an article on the front page of the local section of the *Arizona Republic* and had enjoyed a boost in publicity. And yet it hurt him that his oldest and youngest children had ignored him.

Over the years he had often felt ashamed of his juvenile songwriting effort, although he experienced no compunction about accepting the royalties. Now a recent poll taken in Sun City ranked "The Sally and Rose Comedy Shows" among the top ten best songs of the World War II era. The music critic for the *Arizona Republic* called Marzipan's arrangement of the song a much-needed parody of the excesses of the disco era but raved about Banky's lyrics.

"Dickinson's words," the critic wrote, "are brilliant ironic satire. Each word counts. Not a syllable is wasted. He could have relied on the idioms of American jingoism prevalent at the time to make his musical point but instead chose spare and elegant satire to take down the crude Axis propaganda. Dickinson's way was more effective during that war, more essentially American, and this is why his song is a classic whose lyrics will transcend the musical arrangements of any era."

Overnight, Banky changed his attitude about novelty songs, at least *his* novelty songs. There is literary value to such works, he decided.

He replied to his middle daughter's note but could not help feeling suspicious that it was because of the royalties that Chaucer had written. She's having financial problems, he thought, and her letter is a subtle way of begging for money. Thus in reply he wrote:

Dear Chaucer,

Thanks for the congratulatory note. It has been fun being the subject of a temporary fit of nostalgia, although I have not seen a dime of royalty money from the cover. You sure are

right about the arrangement not being to my
liking. The whole thing has put me in the mood
to try some serious song writing. I have
discovered there are people out there who think
novelty numbers have literary merit. Who
knew? I hope you are doing well in your
studies. Not much else to report on around here.
Love, Dad

The remark about not seeing a dime in royalties was technically true but disingenuous. The check had not arrived, but the record company had advised him that he would receive a sizeable payment in July.

Nevertheless, it was true that his professional career had suffered a severe downturn in the early 70s. His band had fallen apart, in large part because he stubbornly refused to modernize his repertoire. Thus he was forced to play for studio recording sessions to make a modest living. The ignominious irony of this was that he had to perform music for these sessions that he would have refused to play with his band. As the opportunities for studio work were limited in Phoenix, he had to eat the expenses of getting to Los Angeles and Las Vegas for more work.

He managed an occasional nostalgia gig in Youngtown and Sun City, usually as a sub for another band member. Generally, he came home from such events in a foul mood, because he saw himself as a much better musician than the ones he was subbing for. The one professional area where he felt satisfied was playing in pit orchestras for traveling Broadway shows. Banky was getting by as a musician, but not prospering until his novelty song became a hit. Thus his leery feelings about Chaucer needing money arose from the context of his own financial vulnerability.

However, when the first of several large checks did arrive, Banky and Norah splurged on a trip to New York City to celebrate. Both of their daughters were then living in the East, Marlowe in Vermont and Chaucer in Pennsylvania, geographically close enough that visiting their parents in New York was reasonably possible. However, Norah made the decision not to let the girls know of their trip until it was over.

It fell to Spenser, who was still living at home, to send notes to his sisters to let them know that their parents were vacationing in the East.

CHAPTER 15:

SEARCHES, IMAGINARY AND REAL

You look as if you're searching for a hare,
For ever on the ground I see you stare!
Geoffrey Chaucer

Mired in work on her dissertation, at intervals during 1977, Chaucer relaxed and entertained herself by writing a little more of *The Timberscape of Memory*. Plot development gave her the toughest challenge. In her mind, she now thought of her four protagonists, Allys, Aylwyn, Hansel, and Gretel, as the quartet, and though she had determined that the quartet would journey first into the Realm of Clubs, she was stumped about what they would find there.

Digging into her vault of memory for ideas, she extracted her father's two decade old comments about playing dance gigs at country clubs around Phoenix and also her own experiences of being groped and propositioned when working as a waitress. These became the basis for the ethos of Clubs and the source of narrative details.

Wanting to put her own signature on more stock fairy tale characters, she conjured an alternative Cinderella who had a wicked stepbrother. Sexual sparks would fly between the two as they chased each other around the house. Chaucer struggled with a way to integrate these characters into the narrative. Eventually, she decided they did not add anything worthwhile to her story, and if ultimately she were going to include Cinderella in some way, it would be with a handsome prince. But for the present, she saw no useful place for Cinderella in her fantasy.

One Saturday night, when she was feeling satisfied from spending the day writing about Clubs, she went to bed with a tired but happy feeling. As she drifted off, she became aware that she was floating out of her body rather than entering into sleep. With pleasant surprise, she watched her body from the ceiling and felt unaccustomed affection for the woman she was. I look as innocent as a sleeping baby, she thought, but maybe that's because of the untroubled and almost blank expression on my face.

When she awoke the next morning, she composed a haiku to celebrate the experience.

Past my cranium
I float above my body
Free of tickling cells

During the last two years of the 1970s, Chaucer doubled down on her doctoral work. She gained approval of her dissertation subject. Before the preliminary submission, she would entitle it **Victorian Imaginary Worlds: Lewis Carroll, William Morris, and the Pre-Raphaelites**. She examined Pre-Raphaelite poetry, painting, and novels, as well as Lewis Carroll's writing and photography, William Morris's fantasy work, plus Edward Lear's verse and drawings. All of these creations, she argued, verbally and visually foreshadowed the twentieth century science fiction and fantasy genres.

On a weekend in 1979, Chaucer took a break from scholarly work and rode the train to Philadelphia where she changed railroads to get to New York City, Penn Station. Once in Manhattan, she successfully negotiated the subway by herself, arriving at the theater district to see a Broadway play –any play that she could get a ticket for, she decided philosophically. She had been told by friends in Pittsburgh that she would be unlikely to get a same-day ticket in New York for any of the really good shows. Just being in the New

York theater district was enough of a thrill, so she prepared herself to take whatever she could get. Because she wanted only one, Chaucer was able to get a discounted ticket at the TKTS booth in Times Square for a musical she had hoped to see.

She thoroughly enjoyed watching **Annie** at the Alvin Theater and longed to do it again, not by herself next time but with someone she loved. The greatest impact of **Annie** was that it pleasantly reminded her of reading ***Little Orphan Annie and the Gila Monster Gang*** as a child. This was welcome nostalgia. But the play also brought to the surface memories of her own personal struggles with emotionally absent parents. She was not an orphan but there had been times when she had felt like one.

As approval of her dissertation reached the final stages in the early spring of 1980, Chaucer began searching for a teaching position in a college or university anywhere in the country, but focusing more attention on the mountain and coastal West. In due course, she received a pile of rejection letters but reached the interview stage with the sectarian Peaceful Shepherd College in Central Pennsylvania, a school associated with the Christian pacifist tradition, the Re-Reformed Brothers of Jesus.

Prior to the telephone interview, the search committee had sent her a colorful, glossy brochure about Peaceful Shepherd that used the word **new** a dozen or more times in its promotion of the college. Nothing in the brochure provided a clue as to the school's theology or denominational association. This was by design so as to recruit students who were not churchgoers and then evangelize them once enrolled. The underlying thought was that it was much easier to convince and convert captive audiences.

In the telephone conference call with the search committee, the subject of her personal religious beliefs did not arise. A search committee member alluded to Chaucer's Curriculum Vitae in which she had noted her work on children's literature and the ways that adults also enjoy the stories and appreciate the values in this literature. This is what had attracted the committee to her application. They assumed that she was studying such works as Louisa May Allcott's ***Little Women*** and C. S. Lewis's ***Chronicles of Narnia*** and that Chaucer was searching for G-rated values.

When she visited the campus for the face-to-face interview, she expected to encounter a Quaker-like openness to matters of religion. That notion was soon proven wrong. Before any actual questions were exchanged, the committee chairperson advised Chaucer that all faculty contracts contained a provision that teachers were not permitted to teach anything contrary to the doctrine of the conservative denomination that financially supported the college. Additionally, all teachers must subscribe to a set of fundamental Christian doctrines.

"We assume you've done your homework about who we are," the chairperson said, "and thus have come prepared to subscribe if the position is offered to you."

Chaucer had done a cursory accreditation review but had not researched the theological stance of the school and now felt embarrassed and ambushed. "I was under the impression that employers were not allowed to discriminate on the basis of religion," she said with as much polish as she could muster.

"This is not a matter of discrimination but of doctrinal integrity," said the chairperson. "But for your edification, churches and religious institutions are legally permitted to make employment decisions on the basis of religious beliefs."

"Well, in that case," Chaucer said as she rose from her chair, "You *really* don't want me on your faculty. Thank you for your time." She left the room without another word.

The following week, she had a telephone interview with a small liberal arts college in Idaho. While Chaucer waited on the line to be connected with the search committee members gathered around a speakerphone, the secretary who set up the call expressed frustration with that task.

"Are there difficult technical bugs involved?" Chaucer asked simply to pass the time.

"It's not that," the secretary replied. "The phones are the easy part. I shouldn't say this, but it's been hard to get women to agree to be interviewed. Thanks for doing this. Now I won't have to do it again."

"Why is it so hard?" Chaucer asked, now intrigued.

"Well, the committee has to interview at least one woman to satisfy the equal opportunity requirement," the secretary explained.

"Which means they are not serious about me," Chaucer said.

"You never know," the secretary said. "Lightning could strike. You could wow them into hiring a woman."

"That surprises me, because there are other women on the faculty," Chaucer said.

"Not in the English department," the secretary said.

At that moment the chair buzzed that they were ready for the interview, and Chaucer was connected with the all-male search committee. In the event, she did not wow them but did enjoy provoking a few defensive comments about institutional misogyny.

A few weeks later, an invitation came from Anasazi College in Sedona to interview for a position as assistant professor of English. This greatly excited her, and she did not need to do any homework on the ethos of the school, because she had once applied to it for undergraduate admittance. This is the one I want, she decided.

For the on-campus interview, in April 1980, Chaucer wrapped her long red hair in a bun at the back of her head and wore a stylishly cut gray suit to convey a no-nonsense professional air. She had practiced projecting as much gravitas as possible, even experimenting with lowering her voice, but in the end decided to be her normal self, except for the hairstyle and attire.

Although not the chair, the key member of the Anasazi search committee was associate professor of history Cloud Morgan. He had made no enemies among faculty or administration during the three years he had taught at the school, and he was therefore sought after to serve on various committees where partisan agendas might come into play. Hiring new professors was one such area.

When Chaucer shook hands with him, a strong memory of her out-of-body experiences washed through her consciousness. It felt to her as if the physical contact with Cloud had elicited the remembrance and she wondered why. As a student at ASU, she had a similar reaction in Cloud's presence but that did not come to mind on this occasion. Nevertheless, she clearly remembered watching him at the library table at ASU and blushed at the image of her foolish behavior.

The being Chaucer called Riff, quite apart from any involvement in her life, had in the past participated telepathically and surreptitiously in search committee interviews at Anasazi College. Riff considered mentally observing Chaucer's interview in order to add a favorable suggestion or two into the mind of a committee member. But seeing that Cloud would be present, the mysterious entity decided there was no need to monitor this particular event.

During the course of the interview, Cloud commented, "Looking here at your educational history, I see that our times at ASU overlapped. But you were an undergraduate in a different department, so it's not likely that we met."

This provided the opportunity for Chaucer to say, "Actually, I remember you. We sometimes sat at the same study table in the library on Saturdays but I don't think you noticed me." She thought but did not say that she remembered him as appearing to be grieving.

Cloud said, "Now that you mention the library, you do trigger a vague aura of recollection. However, in those days I was too busy feeling sorry for myself to pay attention to coeds no matter how attractive. I was lost inside myself until I met Terp."

She wanted to explore with Cloud the reasons for his introspection and lostness, but kept the conversation safe. "I knew a student named Terp," Chaucer said. "A tall brunette with glasses and a graceful way of walking into a classroom. Brains and looks."

"Yes, that's Terp," said Cloud with a smile and a gleam in his eyes. "I married her."

"You're both very lucky," she said.

Based on the results of their previous reference checks, the search committee had ranked Chaucer as their top candidate. As the interview wound down, a clear consensus developed to offer her the position. Chaucer quickly accepted.

The chair of the search committee, physics professor Astrid Oslo, escorted Chaucer to the office of Magnus Bergen, the college president.

On the way, to make small talk, Chaucer said, "I was accepted for admittance to Anasazi in my senior year in high school, but my parents couldn't afford it, so I ended up at my third choice, ASU. It feels like poetic justice to be joining the faculty here."

"What was your second choice?" Dr. Oslo asked

Chaucer flushed. "Anasazi. At the time my first choice was Prescott College, which had also accepted me, but it was a real toss-up between Prescott and Anasazi. I would have been thrilled with either."

"What tipped the balance toward Prescott College?" Astrid asked.

"The town of Prescott has a deeper history than Sedona," Chaucer said. "Prescott has an aura of Old Arizona."

"Sedona has an aura too," said Astrid with a chuckle, "but mystic rather than historic. I assume you are aware of the New Age ethos that permeates this place."

Chaucer nodded with a slight smile. "It's ironic that mystical things, which are usually associated with phenomena from the past, should be called New Age."

"Faculty and students alike are known to mock the New Age persona of Sedona by calling the college Vortex U," Astrid continued. "However, some of our students take it seriously, and you can count on probing questions from them to ferret out your thoughts about New Age beliefs."

Chaucer truthfully said, "I am more interested in scientific humanism than science fiction religion." Sensing that the physics professor would not approve, she did not mention that she had experienced mystical phenomena and as a result maintained an open mind about such things.

Chaucer's comment pleased Astrid, and she immediately began thinking of the new professor as a potential ally in faculty disputes.

Magnus Bergen stood six feet tall in a relaxed posture. The term athletic would not be used to describe his frame, but he jogged regularly and his mid-forties belly was flat. Blond hair, blue eyes, and classic Nordic facial features revealed his Scandinavian genetic heritage. The college president greeted Chaucer in a smooth, diplomatic manner and offered what seemed to be genuine congratulations for her appointment.

Chaucer's first impression was that Magnus was slightly stuffy and aloof but kindly, and not manipulative or ego-driven. She was inclined to like him as she might a favorite uncle.

For his part, Magnus took note of Chaucer's pretty face and nicely proportioned body, but on the basis of her hairstyle, he projected upon her a repressed personality. She's probably a feminist suspicious of males, he mentally judged. He had already reviewed her resume, writing samples, and references and was satisfied with her academic credentials.

"I hope you will quickly feel at home here, Dr. Dickinson," he said as Astrid escorted Chaucer from the president's office.

Chaucer turned back toward Magnus and said, "I'm not a doctor quite yet. The conferral is still a month away."

"A mere technicality," he said. "The approval of your fine dissertation says it all."

The prim hairdo and business suit had proven successful in the interview, and so she decided to wear a bun when she began teaching classes in the fall. This affectation would last until reading week at the end of the first semester. By then she was so comfortable in the role of college professor, rather than lowly graduate student instructor, that she let her hair down and dressed in casual clothes to administer final exams. Thereafter she resorted to garb more suited to the literati. A stone colored corduroy jacket with patched sleeves became her signature piece.

Magnus left his office at noon and strolled to the president's residence at the far end of the campus. He was in the habit of eating lunch at home two or three days a week. This day he put a bowl of leftover vegetable soup in the microwave while he made a cheddar cheese sandwich.

As the oven beeped, Janett entered the kitchen wearing an elegant gray suit with a single strand of perfectly matched pearls around her neck. "Did you leave any of that soup?" she asked.

"There's plenty more in the fridge," he said. "You look very nice. Which of your many board meetings are you going to this afternoon?"

She removed the container of soup from the refrigerator and said, "I have the Community Arts Council at two. It's a frustrating meeting, because the secretary inveterately calls me Janet. Somehow, he can't bring himself to say Ja-*nett*. But I can't very well nag him about it, because he makes a five-figure contribution to the council every year. I would never hear the end of it from the rest of the board if I alienated him. Alas, I have to be there, because I chair the deuced thing."

Though she would never reveal this to anyone, including her husband, Janett had received her name from her ill-educated mother, who had never seen the name Jeanette in written form but liked the sound of it. She simply spelled it the way she heard it. Janett was in the habit of telling people that her mother had been fond of distinctive orthography. As for her own feelings, Janett liked the name because the double "t" at the end made it strong. She had asserted in conversation many times over the years that a final "e" made names look girlish and frilly, although never knowingly in the presence of someone with a final "e" in her name.

"Any other commitments after that?" Magnus inquired.

"I have the Library Auxiliary this evening, so we'll need to have an early dinner," she said. "And just in case it has slipped your mind, Bud Pflinders and his trophy wife are coming to dinner here on Friday."

"No problem about tonight," he replied. "And I haven't forgotten about Bud. And for the record, I don't think it's a good idea to be snide about the spouse of the president of the College Board of Regents. She's only a couple of years younger than he is."

"I won't be snide on Friday, as you well know," Janett said. "I'm just getting it out of my system now. And she may be close to him in age, but she's at least five dress sizes smaller than his ex. I think that qualifies as a trophy for the old coot."

"You don't have anything to worry about in the size department," Magnus said.

"Thank you, dear. You always were an astute diplomat," she replied.

The microwave beeped and she removed her soup from it and sat at the kitchen table with her husband. She dipped her spoon into the bowl and made a careful circle with it, moving the utensil across the surface of the soup away from her and then in an arc toward her mouth.

"There's something I want to run by you," Magnus said as she noiselessly took nourishment. "Stanford wants to administer the Myers-Briggs Type Indicator to all the faculty. He thinks faculty meetings will run more smoothly if we all know each other's personality types. Extrovert or introvert, that sort of thing. What do you think?"

She rolled her eyes in mockery. "I would be suspicious of any proposal from Stanford R. Shock, esteemed professor of psychology, who refuses to respond to anyone who calls him Stan and who obsessively insists that his middle initial be included any time his name appears in print," she said.

"You mean like the way you bristle when anyone calls you Janet?" Magnus said.

"That's different and you know it," she replied. "In my case it is a matter of correct pronunciation. His is an affectation of vanity. At any rate, my advice, since you asked for it, is to be wary of probing personal quizzes that result in facile taxonomizing of people. Psychologists are notorious control freaks and love to pigeonhole one another."

"The MBTI is well-tested and not at all facile in its typology," said Magnus. "It's an accurate instrument. But I take your point about Stanford."

"Just keep him well boxed in," Janett said.

"In other news," he said to change the subject, "we acquired a new professor for the English department this morning. She's a newly minted PhD from Pitt."

"What is she like?" Janett asked.

"Very bright," he said. "Interested in nineteenth century British literature. She wears her hair in a bun."

"Oh, one of those," she said. "Well, I'm sure the committee made a good choice."

"Yes, one of those," Magnus said with a sigh. "But of course at Anasazi we don't discriminate against feminists, even Victorian ones."

"Absolutely not!" Janett said "Or you'd have the president's wife to answer to."

That afternoon, Chaucer turned on the television in her motel room for audio-visual company as she packed for the Sky Harbor shuttle.

She switched channels to the Arizona Afternoon program, thinking it would be interesting to observe how Rex Fisher was aging. But Rex was no longer host of the show.

"My God!" she blurted out to the room. "That's Dagmar Solbrent! She's certainly come a long way since stealing my boyfriend at ASU." But Dagmar had not initiated anything with Baron, she thought. That episode was entirely his doing. She wondered if Dagmar knew Baron Ulster was dead. "Well, thanks again, Dagmar, for being so alluring. You well may have saved me from widowhood," she said to the screen.

CHAPTER 16:
IN THE REALM OF CLUBS

*Sometimes I've believed as many as
six impossible things before breakfast.*
Lewis Carroll

After catching their breaths, they crossed the border into Clubs. Miles of carefully trimmed oleander hedges and cultivated grape fields marked the boundary. Before advancing more than a hundred yards, the quartet saw security guards in golf carts moving rapidly toward them. In short order they were apprehended, and without being allowed to ask any questions were taken directly to the court of King Laveltino and Queen Modessa.

As they approached Clubtown, they noticed that the streets and parks were littered with beer, wine, and liquor bottles, and party paraphernalia.

"Is it always this messy in Clubs?" Allys asked.

The guard driving the cart she was in said, "Don't be stupid. The Holiday of the Realm was yesterday. It always takes a few days to clean up properly from celebrating our independence."

"Independence from what?" Aylwyn asked.

"Looks like you're just as stupid as your sister here," said the guard, and she would say no more.

The guards drove their carts through a golf course to the palace, where the four were marched to the throne room of the king and queen. They were made to stand at attention as the king, in a red polo shirt, white Bermuda shorts, green knee socks, and leather golf shoes, and the queen in a short white sports skirt, coral pink sleeveless blouse, plaid knee socks and leather golf shoes, entered the room and sat upon their side-by-side thrones.

Looking with a sneer at the clothes of the intruders, King Laveltino spoke. "Have you urchins come to our realm in search of work? I suppose you have, because we in Clubs suffer periodic streams of people from other less prosperous realms who cross our border in search of jobs."

Aylwyn said, "We have come in search of answers, your majesty."

"Answers?" Queen Modessa said. "We don't give answers here. You must earn your way in Clubs through honest labor."

"And our wages are more than fair," said the king proudly, "considering the unsophisticated backgrounds of most of our laborers."

Modessa visually assessed the four, mentally noting their trim and healthy bodies. They will look sharp in servant uniforms, she thought. She turned to a courtier and said, "Go to the clubhouse and tell the manager he now has two more strapping boys and two fetching girls at his disposal for suitable employment."

The courtier departed immediately.

"What is that they have entangled in their hair, my dear?" Laveltino asked the queen.

"It looks like crowns made out of...what is that?...twigs? Oh how dreadful!"

"Our wreaths are made of vines, your majesty," said Gretel. "We had such fun making them."

"Utter impertinence!" said Modessa. "Peasants do not wear crowns. Off with their crowns!" she bellowed. Immediately, four guards leapt forward and yanked the wreaths from their heads.

Though the only value of the wreaths was sentimental, the act of removal felt like an assault to each of the teenagers. The Realm of Clubs did not appear to be a friendly place at all.

The king then instructed a guard to escort the intruders to the servant's quarters. This turned out to be a dormitory for domestics, waitresses, gardeners, and valets situated two blocks from the country club.

When the palace guard escorted them into the lobby of the dormitory, the quartet observed a blonde young woman and a burly older man playing what appeared to be a strange game of tag, circling back and forth around a desk.

"Bet ya can't touch my fanny," said the blonde woman with a laugh.

"Bet I can," said the burly man as he lunged and joyfully swatted her petite rump and darted away giggling.

"Ooh, bet I can do that to you," the woman said and sprinted the opposite way around the desk and smacked his behind with both hands.

"Pardon me, Goldilocks and Papa Bear," said the guard, "but I've brought four new servants to be housed here."

"Oh, all right," said Papa Bear with a disappointed air. "There never seems to be any time for fun anymore. You lot, come here so we can have a look at you."

Showing no embarrassment at having been caught playing erotic tag, Goldilocks said, "We are superintendents of the servant house. You must obey all the rules and do everything we say. Do you understand?"

"I understand your words," said Allys, "but since we have no earthly idea what the rules are, obeying them could be a problem."

"And if you tell us to do something beyond our physical or intellectual ability, that would also be problematic," added Aylwyn.

"Where did these smart-mouths come from?" Papa Bear asked the guard. "They're not your typical border-crossers."

"They wandered in across the Scape frontier," said the guard.

"Ah, wild ones," said Goldilocks. "That explains a lot. Well, we know how to handle weirdoes from the Scape. See here you wiseacres, I'll have you know Papa Bear is a retired boxer, and he can beat you to a pulp without breathing hard if he feels like it."

"Yeah, but I'm gentle as a lamb with servants who do their jobs and keep quiet," Papa Bear added with a leer.

Goldilocks took the girls to the female ward while Papa Bear led the boys to the male ward. Hansel and Aylwyn would share a barracks-like room with eighteen other boys, and Gretel and Allys would share an equally Spartan room with eighteen other girls.

After being assigned bunk beds, the four were summoned back to the superintendents' office. There, Goldilocks and Papa Bear gave them their assignments. Hansel and Aylwyn were given suits of livery and told they would be parking golf carts, which was the only form of personal transportation in the realm, and also stock the club kitchens and bars with food, ice, and beverages. Gretel and Allys were handed skimpy French maid costumes with miniskirts and tiny white aprons and low-cut blouses and assigned to the country club restaurant and bar as waitresses.

Returning briefly to their wards, each of them stowed their original clothing in footlockers at the end of their bunks and donned their servant outfits. Once more lined up in front of the dormitory superintendents, the quartet awaited an escort to their workstations.

"Take my advice, Gretel, and shave your legs and armpits," Papa Bear snorted.

"I have never done such a thing in my life," Gretel replied indignantly.

"Yeah, it shows. Just a word to the wise if you wanna go places," Papa Bear said.

Ignoring her partner's shaving advice, Goldilocks said to the four of them, "Now, before reporting to work, I have very good news. Your room and board here in Clubs is essentially free. That is, the cost of feeding, clothing, and housing you will be deducted from your pay but in fairness, it will never exceed your actual wages. Because of our progressive laws, you can't go into debt while living in Clubs."

"How much money will we have left over at the end of a typical week?" Allys asked.

"That depends. Unless you have put in major overtime," said Papa Bear, "there won't be anything left over after all the reasonable deductions have been made. But that's only fair. If you should manage to put in, let's say, eighty hours in a given week, you will clear about enough to buy an ice cream cone at the river front park. That's always a great treat for hardworking servants."

Goldilocks added in a cheerful voice, "And you will have one day off each week. A whole day with nothing to do but rest. Are there any other questions?"

Aylwyn spoke up. "The guard who drove us to the palace said that yesterday was Independence Day. But she didn't say independence from what. Can you explain?"

"She can but she may not," Papa Bear said.

"But then again, I may," Goldilocks said. "Yes, I think I shall. It is an inspiring story. So long ago that the date has been lost in the mists of antiquity, the Realm of Clubs declared its independence on the day of the autumnal equinox. We have been free ever since."

"But independence from what?" Allys asked.

"Why, from the rest of the island," said Papa Bear in a huff of exasperation. "Are you stupid?"

"Had anyone treated you badly?" asked Hansel. "Was there an evil king or queen that made your lives miserable?"

"Or were you being taxed without representation?" Allys added.

"No one treated us at all," said Goldilocks. "That was the problem."

"And so you fought a war for independence because you were being left alone?" said Aylwyn with a note of incredulity in his voice.

"That makes no sense at all," said Gretel.

"Apparently they are stupid," said Goldilocks. "We did **not** fight a war. That would be stupid. Let me explain, **children**. The Island of Gymnarykum existed for many ages as an unincorporated paradise. You can imagine how unmanageable such a state can be. Very boring. Very uncompetitive. So on an auspicious equinox day, Clubs declared its independence, and no one challenged our right to do so. The other realms eventually followed suit. Spades will say that they went first, but that's a lie. Now be done with your foolish questions. The guard will show you to your assigned stations. Be sure to remember the way back, because guards have more important things to do than to escort servants to and from work."

Relaxing in the dormitory common room a week later, after a long day at work, the four gathered in a corner to talk.

"So far, I haven't learned anything useful in Clubs," Allys said. "Nothing to help us get home, that is. What about the rest of you?"

"Agreed," said Aylwyn. "But I think the people of this realm are aptly named. About all they do is socialize, and they seem especially snobbish about it."

"Yet they always wear sports clothes and golf shoes everywhere," said Allys.

"After serving them more liquor than I care to think about," said Gretel, "my view is that they enjoy getting inebriated and cheating at golf and then complaining about everyone else cheating at golf. That behavior gives us no useful insights."

"And they seem addicted to wagering," said Hansel. "They bet on the outcomes of every sport in the realm, particularly boxing. Nothing for us there either."

"They are rather demanding," said Gretel, "but the other servants are nice."

"Yes, but the servants are not native Clubbers. They've all come here from somewhere else," said Aylwyn. "Maybe we can learn things from them."

"Well, Club men are male chauvinist pigs," said Allys. "And so in solidarity with Gretel, even though there are razors in the bathroom, I'm not going to shave any more."

"A pleasingly natural decision," said Hansel. "Good for you!"

At a gala country club event, Gretel was assigned to the table of an odd-looking couple. The manager told her they were very distinguished persons who required special care and respect. Their attire was not unusual in any way, thought Gretel, but both the man and the woman wore their jet-black hair in bangs covering their foreheads.

"Who exactly are they?" Gretel asked.

"They are Deckle and Eckle, the Chief Religion Officers of the Church of Orthodox Conventionalism," the manager said in a hushed tone.

"And is it that office which makes them distinguished?" Gretel said.

"Are you stupid?" the manager replied in a huff. "Of course that makes them distinguished. The COOC is the national church of Clubs, and that makes Deckle and Eckle a major power couple in our realm. Now I don't want any mistakes with those two. Do exactly what they want."

"Yes, sir," Gretel said obediently.

Gretel tended efficiently to every demand the chief religion officers made about their meal and drinks, and both Deckle and Eckle were impressed at how swiftly and accurately she produced the intricately specific orders they made for food and beverages.

When the power couple was relaxing with cheesecake and port near the end of the evening, Deckle said to Gretel, "Tell me my dear, have you ever been to a COOC service?"

"No, sir," Gretel answered. "I'm new here and have not had the opportunity."

"And have you come here to the Realm of Clubs all by yourself?" Eckle asked sympathetically.

"Oh, no ma'am," Gretel replied. "I'm here with my twin brother Hansel and dear friends Allys and Aylwyn."

"Well," said Deckle, "you must come to one of our services as my personal guest. How about next Sunday?"

"Thank you, sir," Gretel said. "But I must work all day Sunday."

"When is your day off?" asked Eckle.

"It varies," said Gretel. "Whenever the manager tells me it is."

"Well, I shall see to it that you have a day off next Tuesday, and your brother and friends as well," said Deckle. "Eckle and I will treat you to a church picnic."

And so it was arranged. And as the event unfolded, the

quartet found to their great surprise that they were the only guests at the picnic. Without knowing it, they had become the focus of an ecclesiastical experiment.

For many months, leading COOC clerics had been debating whether it was advisable to proselytize non-citizens of Clubs. Increasing numbers of native born church members were opting for golf on Sunday mornings instead of sitting in pews and listening to sermons. Church bureaucrats were embroiled in plots to increase worship attendance. The Chief Religion Officers were of the progressive opinion that foreign servants were people too and should be allowed to join congregations as apprentice members without vote. They had been looking for likely prospects to test the matter.

Thus on a sunny Tuesday afternoon, Deckle and Eckle filled the four foreign teenagers with rich foods and evangelized them about the benefits and beliefs of the Church of Orthodox Conventionalism.

"Our church has eleven holy books," Eckle explained. "Each one reveals a completely different holy aspect of God, and, of course, each is literally true."

"We use a simple mnemonic to remember the name of each holy book," Deckle added. "JAW PLUG JIVE. The books are named **Judge**, **Accountant**, **Warrior**, **Pacifist**, **Lover**, **Unapproachable**, **Gracious**, **Jealous**, **Indifferent**, **Vindictive**, and the last revelation, my personal favorite, the book of **Enthusiastic**."

Aylwyn said, "Meaning no disrespect, but how can all eleven books be literally true if they are contradictory about the nature of God?"

"Tut tut, my boy," replied Deckle. "You're a bright lad. I would have thought the answer was self-evident to someone like you."

"I'm sorry, sir, but it's not," Aylwyn said.

"Well," said Deckle with a sigh, "It is a mystery of God, a profound mystery that lies in the heavenly realm of truth beyond logic or reason."

"Oh, of course," said Allys with a hint of sarcasm. "That's so obvious. Why didn't we think of that?"

The Chief Religion Officers suggested a walk around the

grounds to clear their minds after being stuffed with picnic food.

They strolled beside a large pond and watched golfers try to hit balls over it. Many golf balls fell into the water.

Hansel spotted a sign nearby that said in bold letters: **No Walking on Water**. He turned to the clergy couple and asked about the sign. "Can people here actually walk on water?"

"Only witches and warlocks," said Deckle. "And they are known to cheat at golf. With their magic, they can get around sand and water traps."

"That's why anyone who cheats at golf is automatically suspected of witchcraft," added Eckle, "and punished if proven."

"Proven to have cheated or proven to be a witch or warlock?" asked Allys.

"Either," said Deckle. "One is as bad as the other."

"How do you prove witchcraft?" asked Gretel.

"We have a foolproof test for them," explained Eckle. "Suspects are thrown into deep water with their hands tied. If they rise to the surface and walk on water, they are automatically proven to be witch or warlock."

"So, if they sink," said Hansel, "They are thereby proven innocent."

"Oh no," said Deckle. "We Clubs are not that stupid. Sinking witches or warlocks may be allowing themselves to sink to get away with witchery. If they sink, they are still watched closely for signs of cheating at golf."

"What if they drown?" said Aylwyn.

"We make every effort to save them," said Eckle. "That is, after they start to inhale water. If they perish before our efforts are successful, we take that as the will of God. We save more than we lose."

"What if the ones you rescue do not play golf?" asked Gretel.

Eckle answered with a sneer at Gretel's stupidity. "Everybody plays golf! Not playing golf is ipso facto suspicious behavior."

Allys said, "We don't play golf."

"Servants don't count," said Deckle dismissively.

"Does that mean that servants can't be witches or warlocks?" asked Aylwyn.

A look of fear spread across the faces of Eckle and Deckle. The thought that a servant could be capable of witchcraft had never before occurred to them, but now that it had, they became troubled and shooed the four away to discuss this development.

When the four got back to their dormitory, they saw Goldilocks and Papa Bear chasing each other around the desk.

"So, where have you lot been?" Papa Bear asked as they sought to get past the superintendents without notice.

"Yeah, you have guilty looks smeared all over your faces," added Goldilocks.

"Guilty is the last thing we look like," said Allys.

"We've just come from a picnic with Eckle and Deckle," Gretel explained. "They have been teaching us about the religion of Clubs."

"You'll want to watch out for that pair," Papa Bear said. "They think that servants belong in church rather than at work. That's pretty radical religion in my book."

"Well, you can relax, because their teaching wasn't very convincing," said Aylwyn.

"I'll tell you all you need to know about religion," Goldilocks said. "As long as you put on a good front, it doesn't matter what happens inside your brain. Just pretend to go along with the boring things the preachers say and do whatever you like."

"Great!" said Allys. "Does that mean we can skip work and pretend to go to church on Sunday?"

"Definitely not! Servants don't count," said Papa Bear. Turning to Goldilocks he added, "I told you we've got to keep an eye on these smart alecks from the Scape."

The quartet sauntered off to the common room to relax. As they left the office area, Papa Bear came up behind Goldilocks and cupped his hands over her breasts. "Guess who?" he called suggestively.

<><><>

Deckle and Eckle had a seven year-old daughter named Xie, who was such a brat that they had difficulty finding teenagers willing to baby-sit for them when they were attending to terribly important church duties or enjoying themselves at the country club. As a result, the clergy couple engaged Goldilocks and Papa Bear to watch the little girl from time to time. The servant dorm managers charged exorbitant fees for the extra work, but Deckle and Eckle decided the cost was worth the respite and charged it to their expense accounts. Goldilocks and Papa Bear alternated evenings sitting with Xie. When Goldilocks was on duty, she kept the child calm by telling her lewd gossip about various Club people. Papa Bear quickly discerned that Xie had an exhibitionist streak, and in no time he had convinced the girl to pose nude for photographs. At the end of each photo session, Papa Bear would tickle the still naked Xie all over her body, while remaining clad himself.

After three months in Clubs, Aylwyn asked Papa Bear if the weather ever changed in the realm. It had stayed the same pleasantly warm temperature the entire time they had been there.

Papa Bear huffed and said, "Of course it changes. Are you stupid? You've been here a whole quarter. Haven't you noticed that the daily high temperature has dipped by half a degree each month? By the time you've been here six months, the late afternoon temperature will be a full three degrees cooler than when you arrived. Then, of course, it will begin to rise again by the same interval."

"Is it that way throughout the entire island?" Aylwyn asked.

"As far as I know," Papa Bear answered, "but I've heard tales that the variance is greater in the north and south. The changes in ambient temperature may be fifty percent greater on the warm side in Hearts and fifty percent greater on the cool side in Diamonds."

Before the quartet had time to reflect on the fact, another three months passed and all the talk among Clubs was the spring equinox celebration, which was an occasion for lavish partying and exchanging outlandish gifts. Hansel and Aylwyn were ordered to dress up in elf costumes while Gretel and Allys donned fairy attire. At a huge feast, they distributed wrapped boxes and holiday stockings to country club members. Back in their dorm at the end of the evening, the four exchanged leftover stockings they had salvaged. The socks were stuffed with golf tees, score pads, gum, and assorted candies.

Chewing a chocolate ball, Aylwyn mumbled, "At least the candy's not bad."

A few weeks later, Papa Bear entered the girl's sleeping area unannounced and selected ten girls for a special assignment, Allys and Gretel among the chosen. He told them that there was an annual event at the club where men choose lingerie to buy for their wives, girlfriends, and mistresses. But in order to see the items properly, they need to be modeled. The servants Papa Bear named were to model sexy lingerie from a famous boutique called Cecil's Secret See-throughs.

"I don't want to do that," Allys declared.

"You don't have a choice," Papa Bear said.

"I'd rather go naked," Allys exclaimed.

"You can't do that," Papa Bear said. "It's against the rules. The club would be fined if you did that."

"What would happen to a model if she removed her lingerie while modeling it?" Gretel asked coyly.

"As I said, the club would be given a large fine," Papa Bear answered.

"But what about the girl who did it?" Gretel continued.

Ruefully, Papa Bear said, "She would be reassigned to other duties. Very unpleasant duties, such as scrubbing pots in the kitchen. It would not be a kind fate."

"I, for one, would enjoy being reassigned to the kitchen," Allys said. "That would be better than getting pinched on the fanny by drunken golfers."

"I as well," Gretel said. "If you make Allys and me do this, we will remove our clothes in front of everyone, the club will be fined, and we'll tell them it was your idea."

"I shall talk to Goldilocks about this," Papa Bear said. "You may be sent to the kitchen anyway. But now I've decided I don't want you for this special duty. You pair are too hairy anyway. Did I mention that you get extra pay for it? Too bad. You lose."

"No, I think we just won," Allys replied.

The only available kitchen job was inventory clerk. Allys and Gretel were issued drab unisex pants and shirts for their new work in which they took deliveries of food, ice, and beverages, and in the process had regular contact with Aylwyn and Hansel. Months of dull routine dragged by until the anniversary of their servitude in Clubs approached.

During the autumnal equinox Holiday of the Realm, which marked the independence of Clubs, by tradition nearly all the citizens got totally sloshed. Because of the increased need for servers, Allys and Gretel were given back their waitress outfits and returned to the floor of the restaurant.

The quartet took advantage of the inebriated revelry to slip away after the girls had served an excessive amount of liquor to the country club manager. In the deserted dormitory, they quickly changed into their original clothes and found them very snug. Since they had last worn them, the boys had grown a few inches in height and their chests were beginning to fill out. The girls' breasts had grown also, and their hips were starting to widen. They too had grown in height. With more important things to worry about than tight clothing, they rushed out into the night.

Hansel and Aylwyn stopped a golf cart driven by a drunken reveler and pulled him out and rolled him under a tree, where they propped him up with his back to the trunk. Commandeering the cart, the boys swung back and picked up the girls to make a dash for the border.

As they cruised along the road beside the golf course, with Hansel driving, a tall, gangly valet ran after them and jumped on to the back of the cart. "Take me with you!" he ordered and then pleaded, "Please take me with you."

Gretel was about to pry his hands off the bars and push him off when Allys stopped her and asked the young man why.

"My home is in the Timberscape," he answered. "I was kidnapped by Club thugs when I accidentally ventured over the border."

"I know this guy," said Aylwyn. "Your name is Morey, right?"

"Yes, Morey Tarot," he said.

The cart continued on its inland course.

"Why did they kidnap you?" asked Gretel.

"Because I'm a Fool," said Morey.

"Well, aren't we all," said Allys.

"No, I mean a real Fool, a Jester from a tarot deck."

"You don't look like a card," said Aylwyn. "You look perfectly human."

"A lot you know," said Morey with a huff of exasperation. "You may be as witless as the Clubs."

"There is a lot we do not know," agreed Gretel, "but we are **not** as witless as the Clubs."

"I beg your pardon," Morey said. "That was foolish of me. I was only being true to my nature."

Hansel turned his head back toward the hitchhiking passenger while continuing to press the accelerator and more or less steer the cart. "Well are you or are you not a card?"

The cart swerved precipitously and Aylwyn nearly fell out. "Watch the wheel!" he screamed.

With the vehicle now back on a straight path, Morey began to explain himself. "For centuries, hundreds of live human Tarots have resided in a village called Tarot Mesa in the Timberscape of Memory. We are not cards but real people. I am of the clan of Major Arcana and descended from a long proud line of Jesters. I was out exploring one afternoon and must have wandered a bit too close to the border with the Realm of Clubs, because a rowdy band of golfers saw me and ran at me and grabbed me and took me forcibly to their country club. They laughed among themselves and said I was exactly what they needed for their game that night."

"What game?" asked Gretel.

"Poker," replied Morey. "They were having a huge poker tournament using a deck of human cards. But they had lost their joker, and they mistook me for a common joker. They have no discernment! Hah! A Tarot Jester mistaken for an ordinary poker joker. The very idea!"

"OK, calm down," said Allys. "We'll take you with us. Just hang on."

"Bless you, dear lady," said Morey. "I am ever so anxious to reunite with the maiden I love."

"How long have you been captive in Clubs?" asked Aylwyn.

"Three long years," said Morey.

"Maybe the maiden has given you up for dead and found another love," said Allys. "We'll get you home, but don't get your hopes up too much."

"All I have is hope," said Morey. "And I'm fool enough to believe she has waited for me to return. Her name is Stella…"

"And she is from the Star lineage," Allys interrupted.

"Indeed," said Morey. "And as with all Stars, she has not worn a stitch of clothing her entire life."

"Then it is fortunate she lives in the Timberscape," said Hansel.

They reached the border without incident and abandoned the cart before running across into the uncultivated forest. Once safely inside, the quintet made a quick hike to the river at which point the quartet decided to follow its bank southward.

Morey said, "I shall depart from you now and travel to Tarot Mesa. Thank you ever so much for rescuing me. Farewell wise and generous friends."

With Morey gone, Aylwyn remembered how uncomfortable he was in his tight clothes and said so out loud.

"Me too," said Allys. "Let's take them off."

This they did.

As they made their way toward what they believed was the center of the Timberscape, they come across a thatched roof cottage with a yard enclosed by a fence of tall sunflowers. Sitting in lawn chairs in front of the cottage were an old couple, male and female, both diminutive in size and with white hair. Their skin was aquamarine and they were dressed alike in black conical hats and blue and tan saddle oxford shoes and nothing else. Their auras felt safe and friendly to the four.

"Hello," shouted Allys from a distance while waving her arm. As the quartet entered the yard, she continued, "We've just escaped from Clubs and need help finding the center of the Scape."

"We can help you there," cackled the female genially. "Witches and warlocks are deft at directions."

"Are you a witch?" asked Gretel.

"Indeed. Flowerina at your service."

"And I am a warlock," said the male. "Sunny, equally at your service. As it happens, we've been expecting you. We provide overnight accommodations for wandering pilgrims and refugees from the realms."

"It does not appear that your cottage has room for four more people," said Hansel.

"You will change that view momentarily," said Flowerina. She waved a wand in the air and a second story appeared on top of the thatched roof, perched at a precarious angle although quite still. "Sturdy as the Rock of Remembrance," she continued.

"What's that? Asked Gretel.

"It's a giant boulder in the middle of the Gymnarykum River," said Sunny. "It's known for its sturdiness."

"I gathered that," said Hansel. "Where along the course of the river does it stand?"

"That's hard to say," said Flowerina. "You see, it moves around a bit depending on its mood."

Hansel started to protest that this was not a sign of sturdiness but thought better of antagonizing people who were helping them and thus held his tongue.

The four teenagers stepped forward and introduced themselves.

"Welcome to Greenwitch Village," said Sunny. "This region of Timmory is a community for retired witches and warlocks. We so much enjoy the occasional visits from young people, although you must be at least a hundred and fifty to be a permanent resident here. The senior wizards don't like the noisy centenarian crowd."

"I almost forgot," Flowerina said. "You will need your own bathroom. Ours is rather small." She waved her wand again and another room appeared at a right angle to the upstairs bedroom. "When you get inside, you will find that despite external appearance, everything will be properly oriented."

They entered the small house and discovered that it was spacious and upon climbing the stairs to the added rooms found that they were perfectly level.

Sunny followed the four upstairs and said, "Do you prefer shower or bath tub?"

In unison, Allys and Aylwyn said, "Shower," while Hansel and Gretel answered, "Tub." Sunny waved his wand and when they peeked into the large bathroom, they saw a modern walk-in shower and a full-sized bathtub on legs shaped like giant cat paws.

Over a delicious dinner of vegetable soup, sourdough bread, green salad, and chocolate cake, the four chatted amiably with Flowerina and Sunny.

"Have you spent any time in the Realm of Clubs?" Gretel asked the couple.

"We've flown over it the odd time or two," said Sunny. "But it's not a congenial land for people of color."

Flowerina giggled. "We've talked about gathering a battalion of covens and establishing a colony there, as a way to integrate Clubs by the force of numbers, but every witch and warlock we know has better things to do with their time. Still, it's a lovely thought to imagine."

"We teach occasional courses at the University of Hearts," said Sunny, "but otherwise enjoy the pleasant ambience of the Timberscape of Memory."

"There's a university on Gymnarykum?" Aylwyn responded.

"Indeed, a fine old institution," said Flowerina. "There is much to surprise the newcomer on this fair island."

"Too bad we won't be staying long enough to see it," said Allys. "You said you were good at providing directions. We need to find the cave we came in through."

"All in good time," said Sunny. "You've all had a stressful day. Get a good night's sleep. We'll talk about directions tomorrow."

In the morning, over breakfast, Sunny and Flowerina described the island with such verbal intricacy that none of the four could follow their descriptions or absorb all the details.

"The first thing you will encounter on the green path," Sunny explained as they were about to depart, "is the meadow where the pine tree with two trunks used to be. Bear right on the khaki colored trail. Be sure not to go on the tan trail."

"Is there a tree stump or something to identify the spot?" asked Hansel.

"No stump. It's a large meadow. It's covered with grass," said Flowerina. "Everybody knows the spot."

"Once on the khaki trail, you will pass a field of oak trees. Keep going past it," Sunny continued.

"How can we distinguish between khaki and tan?" asked Allys.

"Easy," said Flowerina. "One is the color of a khaki shirt and the other is the color of a tan shirt."

"Which one comes first?" Hansel asked.

"You will reach them at the same time," said Sunny. "But you can tell them apart because they diverge in different directions. The one veers to the left and the other to the right."

"Do we do anything when we pass the oak trees?" Gretel asked.

"Yes," said Flowerina. "It is important when you get beyond them that you keep hiking in whatever direction is available to you."

"Will we be in danger there?" asked Aylwyn.

"You are never in danger in the Timberscape of Memory," said Sunny. "You may be lost, you may be bewildered, you may be awed, but danger is not part of the Scape."

"Then why is it important that we keep hiking at that place?" Gretel asked.

"If you stop going, you will not get to your destination," said Flowerina with a smirk.

When they were finally shooed out of the yard on their way, each one had a different concept of where they needed to go. But they all agreed that finding and following the river was their best bet.

They passed through several meadows but found no paths that looked tan or khaki. Somehow the river eluded them. While walking along in search of it, they met a coyote, who, they were not surprised to discover, spoke fluent English and whose name was Coyote.

"Well," Coyote said in answer to their question about finding the cave, "You might learn what you need to know about locating the cave and getting home in the Realm of Diamonds."

"How about an alternative source?" Allys asked.

"I am sorry, but I know of none," Coyote replied.

Remembering Cranna's warning, they were apprehensive about venturing into Diamonds, but having no better plan, they started walking dispiritedly on the path toward that realm that Coyote pointed out to them. After a hundred or so paces, they stopped to reconsider the wisdom of taking the word of a coyote. Agreeing that it was foolish to do so, they turned around to head toward what they believed to be the center of the Timberscape of Memory.

"OK, so what exactly is our plan?" Aylwyn asked.

"I guess we wander inland, as best we can discern it," Allys said.

"We should be on the alert for sources of information to compare with what Coyote told us," Gretel added.

"Human preferably," said Hansel. "But we should listen to whatever animal we encounter who speaks an intelligible language."

Just then, a jackrabbit appeared before them on the trail and darted past them mumbling words about business opportunities. They gave chase but it remained enticingly ahead of them going first one direction then another. Before they knew where they had gone, the border with Diamonds loomed before them.

All four at once shouted for the creature to stop so they could talk, but it merely looked over its shoulder and shouted, "I'm late for an important business lunch."

They rested for a while and talked it over.

"I guess going to Diamonds is our fate," Hansel said.

The others agreed. Before taking the fateful steps across the border, however, they donned their outgrown clothes and then walked arm in arm into the unknown realm.

CHAPTER 17:
VING, ENGLAND, AND VORTEX

I dwell in possibility –
A fairer house than Prose –
More numerous of Windows –
Superior – for Doors –
Emily Dickinson

Feeling flush and confident with a doctoral degree and a position teaching at a progressive liberal arts college, Chaucer decided the summer of 1980 was the perfect time to make a literary tour of England. She had lived so frugally on her stipend, that she had been able to save a little money, all of which she would now completely deplete on airfare. Brimming with financial optimism arising from having a full time professional position, she would charge the rest of the costs on a credit card and pay it off at leisure.

She called her travel agent, Ving Valborg, long distance from Pittsburgh to arrange her return to Arizona. Her parents' house would be a way station until she secured a place in Sedona. Once back in Phoenix, she instructed Ving to outline an English itinerary for her, laying out a series of possibilities to explore.

Ving outdid himself in planning the perfect trip for Chaucer. The first thing he insisted on was taking Chaucer to lunch so he could learn more about her interests. "I am an artist with the travel package," he told her. "In order to create a superlative itinerary, I need to know personal things about the traveler." He had known her for six years, although not well. Now they were spending hours together working on this trip, and as a result, he began to cast his eyes on her as a potential mate.

When he presented her with the finished itinerary, he said, "Oh, Chaucer, I am so jealous of you going on this trip. I truly wish I could go along and chase the ghosts of Oscar Wilde and Aubrey Beardsley through elegant London salons and drawing rooms."

"You're the agent with the magic guide books," she said with an infectious laugh. "I'd love to take you along if you can make it happen."

"Alas and alack," he said. "I just returned from a fam trip to France and need to stay put in the agency for a while."

"One of those free familiarization junkets that travel agents enjoy? Where all did you go?" she asked.

"Mostly around Paris," he replied. "I shouldn't say this but after a while Paris can become tedious. So another agent and I managed to slip away for two glorious days at Cap d'Agde on the Mediterranean coast."

"I'd love to see the Riviera," Chaucer said.

"Oh, the Cap is much better," Ving said. Sensing that Chaucer would not be offended, he added, "They have a village at the Cap where everyone runs around naked for everything -grocery shopping, dining at restaurants, the beach. The whole town! In French it's called **Village Naturiste**, but Americans call it Naked City. It's marvelous. All those gorgeous naked bodies! Even the old codger I went with was impressed with the unadorned beauty of the place. But they're very strict about the rules. They go ballistic if anyone wears skimpy or suggestive clothing. Complete nudity is **required** in the village."

Chaucer grinned. "And you, Ving, being a responsible and law-abiding citizen, naturally complied with the requirement."

Now he grinned and nodded. "Naturally."

"You couldn't hire me as a temporary agent, could you?" she said. "This England trip is tapping out my personal finances and then some, but I'd have a hard time saying no to an expenses paid fam trip to a Mediterranean beach in France." With a wink she added, "Particularly a sojourn in Naked City."

"If 'twere within my power, fair princess, I would grant your wish," he replied with a wave of an invisible wand. "I am a master artist composing travel venues, but alas, as a magician I am but an apprentice. What I could do is revise your British itinerary to include a day at an English nudist resort. There's a place called Fiveacres Country Club at Bricket Wood, not far from London in Hertfordshire. I've heard they also host a witches' coven there. That might be fun to see."

Chaucer found his campy Renaissance Faire speech annoying, but enjoyed his flirting and was intrigued not only by his knowledge of exotic places but more so with his interest in Oscar Wilde and Aubrey Beardsley. "I may cross paths with the ghosts of your boys on my search among the haunts of Lewis Carroll and the Pre-Raphaelites, and if I do, I'll bring you souvenirs. Thanks anyway, but I'll pass on the coven."

"I so much envy you the experience. I adore the Pre-Raphaelites," he said. "I majored in art history in my first go at college. But as fate would have it, I ended up with a more useful degree in business administration."

"What happened?" she asked.

"I started out at UC Santa Cruz in its first year of classes. At the end of my sophomore year, I was drafted," he explained.

"Unless your grades were atrocious, you could have gotten an educational deferment," Chaucer said.

"No, my grades were pretty good," he replied. "My dad thought I should go in the Army. He's a World War II vet and thought it would be character building. So, to please him, I did not ask for a deferment. Then, when I got out of the Army, I enrolled at ASU and switched majors. I wanted to be prepared to take over the family business."

"It sounds like you haven't lost your interest in art, though," she said.

"Indeed not," he said. "And I want a full report on your hobnobbing among the literati and artists of Britain."

She laughed. "That's the least I can do for all your efforts."

<><><>

Chaucer wished she had someone to go with her on the trip, but she had lost track of her friends at ASU and the U of A, and none was that close to her anyway. She tried to think of anyone (excluding her family of origin) with the money and time to go along. The only name that came to mind was Skeff, but she immediately nixed that idea.

The excursion proved to be a lonely one. She stayed in a small hotel near Hyde Park, amazed at how tiny her room was. She pursued the usual Central London tourist things and took the bus to Oxford to visit Christ College and the touch-points of Lewis Carroll's career there.

Her morning runs took her past the Peter Pan statue in Kensington Gardens and she wondered how she might weave an allusion to the play (and not the Disney cartoon) into her novel. She admitted to herself that she had been enchanted with Disney's *Peter Pan* as a child, but now she had become a snob about preferring original works and was therefore skeptical of anything redone by Walt Disney. All the more so since she had read Richard Schickel's deconstructing biography *The Disney Version* in graduate school.

During the cool-down walk after a particularly vigorous run, she reflected on the idiosyncrasies of J. M. Barrie. Applying her academic expertise in exegeting fantasy literature, she decided that the character Peter Pan was an extension of the author, an amoral pied piper luring children away from their families. Peter was little more than a child villain. The real heroine of the play, she thought, was Wendy. "I don't think Barrie intended it that way," she mused aloud to herself, "but once again a female comes to the rescue to redeem males from their inability to handle responsibility."

Glancing up from her meditation as she walked along Bayswater Road, she noticed a sign on a building at the corner of Leinster Terrace that indicated that Barrie had once made his residence there. "You bastard!" she mumbled to herself. "Living right across the street from a park full of gullible children. How convenient!"

In a second-hand bookshop on Charing Cross Road, she bought a pre-WW II edition of *Peter and Wendy*, Barrie's 1911 novelisation of his play, intending to compare how Barrie portrayed Wendy and Peter in this format. In addition, she picked up an 1886 facsimile of Lewis Carroll's original manuscript of *Alice's*

Adventures Under Ground, illustrated by the author and precursor to ***Alice's Adventures in Wonderland***.

She also visited museums and saw dozens of Pre-Raphaelite paintings, thus mentally enhancing images that had instructed her doctoral studies but that she had heretofore seen only in prints. At the British Museum shop she bought an inexpensive book of Aubrey Beardsley black ink drawings for Ving.

Remembering her father's initial negative reaction to the Beatles, which he had since tempered, Chaucer decided to visit Abbey Road to see the famous zebra crossing in front of the recording studio where the Beatles had done such inspiring work. She took the tube, transferring from the Central to the Bakerloo line and got off at the Maida Vale station. From there she wandered through St. John's Wood to Abbey Road, where she quickly found the crossing as well as many other Beatles pilgrims. Dodging the automobile traffic speeding through the intersection, she ran across with two other tourists. A German man with a potbelly and three cameras hanging from his neck offered to use her camera to snap her making the iconic trip, and she gratefully accepted. Later, when she had the roll of film developed, she found that she was one of a quartet of crossers in her photo, which pleased her greatly.

On the bus trip to Stonehenge, she flirted with the attractive tour guide who was not wearing a wedding ring, but when he tactfully mentioned his wife in one of the stories he told to the tour group, she stopped. Across the aisle from Chaucer on the coach was a young woman close to her age, so she struck up a conversation during a lull, thinking she might make a new friend to pal around with the rest of the trip. But all this woman wanted to talk about was how small and inferior British bathrooms were compared with American ones. Not being able to talk intelligently with anyone about the things she was seeing *as* she was seeing them frustrated her.

On her penultimate night in London, she unexpectedly floated out of her body and for the first time, she left her room and floated to the park and mentally chastised the Peter Pan statue. There really ought to be a Wendy statue across the path to keep an eye on this one, she thought. When she returned to her body, she concluded that this out-of-body experience was an especially marvelous form of wide-awake dreaming.

Before leaving, although it was not on her itinerary, Chaucer used a day scheduled for shopping in London to make a trip to East Anglia to visit Summerhill, the experimental elementary and secondary school founded by A. S. Neill in the 1920s. Since she would be teaching at a non-traditional school, she thought it important to see a historically successful example and was delighted to discover that Summerhill was located on a road called Westward Ho, for this reminded her of the historic Westward Ho Hotel in Phoenix. She had always liked that name and felt it epitomized the open and pioneering ethos of Phoenix.

Summerhill, she knew, was run democratically by students and teachers alike, following the philosophy of its founder that schools should fit the child rather than force children into educational structures that may not fit them individually. The founding educational principle is "Freedom, not license." Students are free to decide which lessons to attend if any. Neill believed that children needed to live their own lives rather than the lives proscribed by anxious parents or know-it-all teachers. Through frequent school meetings, students and staff share equally in decisions about how to live as a community. In some years, they have adopted a rule that nudity around the campus and even in classrooms is acceptable. Neill favored a secular education, finding little redeeming value in institutional Christian culture. He once wryly noted, "A child is closer to God in masturbation than in repenting."

Chaucer smiled at the irony that C. S. Lewis had satirized Summerhill in his **Chronicles of Narnia**, by inventing a school called Experiment House. Lewis did not like coeducational schools but preferred institutions that provided religious education as part of the curriculum and used corporal punishment to discipline students. Lewis made his fictional Summerhill a place of student bullies, conveniently overlooking the effective way students at the real Summerhill dealt with bullying behavior. By advocating corporal punishment, Lewis was favoring a school where the teachers were bullies. Chaucer decided that C. S. Lewis was greatly overrated as a writer and hopelessly trapped in the nineteenth century. He was looking backward in his writing while Lewis Carroll was looking forward.

<><><>

When Chaucer returned to Arizona, Ving interpreted the gift of Beardsley prints she brought him as a sign of romantic interest, and so he began a campaign to woo her. For his part, Ving found Chaucer charming and suitably attractive but was further motivated by paternal pressure to marry rather than remain a "perpetual bachelor." His father did not know his sexual orientation, and since Ving hoped to take control of the agency when his dad retired, it behooved him to find a bride. Taking over the business most assuredly would not happen if his dad knew he was gay.

Ving was tall, well-built, slender midsection, well-groomed, immaculately coiffed blond hair, and dressed in the latest casually elegant fashion. Chaucer teased him that he dressed and looked better than she did, and he did not protest.

When Chaucer began work at Anasazi College, an FBI researcher made a note of the event in her case file, noting that she was now teaching at the progressive experimental college that the Bureau considered a hotbed of notoriously subversive activity. Other faculty members there were also persons of interest to the Bureau.

After her first day teaching, Cloud Morgan dropped by her office to see how Chaucer was settling in.

"Very well," she said. "Apparently students here like to test new professors with the get the teacher to say a particular word game. I'm sure you know it. Where they ask strings of leading questions to get you to say a word they've decided upon."

Cloud laughed. "I know it well. My first lecture they tried to get me to say hump. At first I thought the questions seemed odd, and a little later I realized they were contrived, and by the time someone was talking about whales, which had absolutely nothing to do with Taoism, I knew their game. I'm afraid I sorely disappointed them. When the class was over, I went to the chalkboard and wrote H-U-M-P in large block letters and acted out zipping my mouth shut. What was your word? Did they succeed?"

"I had played that game too often as a student to let them get away with it," Chaucer said. "My word was cock, and I used every synonym for a male chicken and priming a gun that I could think of. They quickly figured out I was on to them. But I didn't have the presence of mind to write the word on the board. That was brilliant."

"Other than that, how are your classes going?" he asked.

"I'm enjoying my fairly large introduction to American literature class more than I expected I would. Students here seem so much more open to novel ideas than those I taught at Pitt. And I am absolutely rejoicing in my independent study of D. H. Lawrence."

"I wrote a paper on **Lady Chatterley's Lover** for a twentieth century novels course at ASU," Cloud said. "If I had known then that Lawrence was impotent when he wrote it, I would have read the book very differently. And of course, I had no idea that his wife had engaged in multiple affairs. It's a mark of his genius that he could write such elegantly erotic sex scenes while being painfully aware of his own spouse's infidelity. At the time I was very naïve not only about sex but about human relationships in general."

"He was dying of tuberculosis and was mentally ill at the time," said Chaucer.

"I haven't had the heart to reread **Lady Chatterley** in the wisdom of middle age," Cloud said. "I want to retain those golden images of Connie and Mellors in the rain, and I'm afraid that would all evaporate a second time through."

"No doubt," said Chaucer. "Everyone's existential pain is much more obvious in second and third readings."

"Glendon Swarthout taught the course that I did my **Lady Chatterley** paper for. It was great being taught literature by a man who had published several novels, even lightweight fare like **Where the Boys Are**. Did you ever study with him?" Cloud said.

"Unfortunately, he was gone by the time I got to ASU," Chaucer replied. "He left academia to devote full time to writing. My favorite of his books was published while you and I were still there at ASU, though −**Bless the Beasts and Children.** It made a wonderful movie too."

"I wasn't aware that he had left the university," said Cloud. "Of course, I wasn't aware of much outside my narrow field of study in those days."

"Well, it's all turned out for the best," said Chaucer. "Thanks for stopping by to check on me. I love teaching here."

"If there's anything I can help with, please let me know," he said as he left.

Ving continued to press his suit throughout the fall, pursuing both a romantic agenda and a business one.

"If we could get together a group of students, alumni, and faculty from Anasazi College for a trip to England," Ving proposed to Chaucer, "you could go for free as group leader. You'd make a great leader for literary excursions in the British isles."

"I've only been there once, and that was as a tourist," Chaucer replied.

"But you know a lot about the country and its traditions," Ving countered. "You're a natural for this kind of business."

"Speaking of natural," she said, "I'd rather have you escort me on a tour of the naturist village at Cap d'Agde. Tell you what, if you take me there so we can run around naked on the beach, then I'll lead a tour group of literary Anglophiles to Britain."

"Very tempting," he said. "I'll see what I can do about arranging something. In the meantime, ask around and see if anyone at Anasazi is interested in England."

Neither followed through on their parts of the deal, but at Thanksgiving, Ving spent the day with Chaucer in Sedona. They ate an early dinner at a restaurant and took a stroll around town to work off the excess food. During the walk, she raised the subject of his military service.

"I was a payroll clerk," he said. "Good training for running a business."

"Did you get overseas?" she asked.

"I did," he answered. "But it was not quite as character building as my dad imagined it would be."

"Viet Nam?"

"Yes," he said. "I worked at the headquarters of the 9th Infantry Division at Bear Cat. I was a clerk not a shoot 'em up type."

Thinking of Chuck and Baron, she said, "Did you win any medals?"

"Well, I was what they call chair-borne, working at a desk. I don't really like to talk about it, though."

"What was so detrimental to your character?" she pressed.

"OK, let's get this over with," he said. "I had a traumatic experience. I was in a two-vehicle convoy heading up Highway 15 to Long Binh for supplies, and the jeep ahead of mine hit a land mine. The two men in that jeep were badly hurt, and I was struck in the left shoulder by a couple of metal fragments and was bleeding all over the place. Somehow, I managed to get the two men in the lead jeep into mine and drove like a maniac the rest of the way to Long Binh to get them medical treatment. The whole way I kept praying there were no more mines in the road. They both lived and got golden tickets home. My wound wasn't severe enough, so I finished my tour, but it scared the hell out of me every time after that I had to drive to Long Binh."

"But you did drive there anyway," she said.

"I had to," he explained. "It was part of my job."

"I see," she said soberly. "So you have a Purple Heart. My dad has one."

"My dad does too, and he said he was proud of me for being a man, for being brave. That's what he thinks of as character. But I didn't feel brave at all." Ving paused and shook his head ruefully. "Of course I couldn't tell my dad I was scared. But I got something out of it that he doesn't have, something that in his eyes makes me worthy to take over the business. They gave me a Bronze Star for saving the lives of those two men. I'm not a hero, but if thinking so helps my dad love me, I'll take it."

Chaucer stopped and faced Ving, pulling him into an embrace. "Thank you for telling me this, for revealing a part of your soul."

In her apartment that evening, they made love and then snuggled together to watch *The Sound of Music* on television.

Chaucer was feeling a glow from the accumulated blessings of their time together. She could not remember ever having this much affectionate fun in a single day. And Ving revealing his war experience, willing to be so open and vulnerable, made him powerfully attractive to her. Thus she was in a receptive mood when Ving sought to take the relationship a major step further.

"Chaucer, will you marry me?" Ving said as the von Trapp family was climbing the mountain toward freedom in Switzerland.

Because she was feeling so pleasantly snug at that moment, and because she had turned thirty the previous April, and because she had gone alone on her trip to England, and also because there was no one at Anasazi who looked remotely promising for a relationship, she was open to his entreaty. "What a perfect ending to the day," she said. "I can't think of any reason to say no."

"Then say yes," Ving said with a gleeful rise in his voice.

"Then yes," she said, and they fell into a laughing embrace.

"Would sometime during the break between semesters in January work for a wedding date?" he asked.

"That seems a little soon," she said, "but it would allow time for a brief honeymoon. However, there's an issue we need to settle first. I'll marry you, but I won't change my last name to Valborg. I want to keep Dickinson."

"I have no problem with that stipulation," he replied.

Having heard that he was a part-time minister at some alternative church in the area, Chaucer approached Cloud and asked about his ordination status.

He said, "Terp and I serve as co-pastors at the Sedona Natural Christian Church. She's full-time and I'm part-time. Both of us hold ordination in that denomination, although Terp was originally ordained by the American Calvinist Church. She left it because of intolerant developments there." Cloud went on to explain the naturist ethos and practice of the NCC.

"I'm attracted to counter-cultural spirituality," Chaucer said, "but for now I'm not interested in getting involved in church per se. For a brief time while at the U of A, I attended a Wicca church, where the people worshiped nude. But it didn't offer much intellectual depth. And I know something of the dark side of American Calvinists, too. In Pittsburgh I was in a brief relationship with an ACC seminary professor. He was very skilled at disillusioning graduate students."

Cloud said, "We don't do magic in our denomination, but we

don't shun those who profess to do so. And we're more into disrobing than disillusioning. You and Terp might enjoy swapping tales of the dark side of Calvinism some time. At any rate, we practice a sort of Christian humanism in our church."

"That appeals to me," Chaucer said. "While at Pitt, I attended a congregation called the Open Door Community, which was fully inclusive and particularly welcoming to homosexuals. I tend to think of myself now as not only a humanist but also an aesthetic Christian. I appreciate some aspects of liturgy and a great deal of church music. But I'm really not ready to immerse myself in a spiritual community at the moment."

"There is an opportune time for everything," Cloud said. "It's not good to rush spiritual endeavors."

"Wise words," Chaucer said. "By the way, is your church connected with the nudist church in New River? I just thought of that. In high school, I used to go for picnics near a nudist church in that area."

"It is indeed," said Cloud. "That's my home church, although I wasn't attending it at the time you were in high school."

"So I wouldn't have met you if I had visited back then," she said with a sigh. "At any rate, my motivation for asking you about your ordination concerns my personal life. I'm engaged to Ving Valborg, and we need someone to officiate at our wedding."

"I suspected that's where you were going with your question," Cloud said.

"It will be a very informal ceremony," she added. "We've reserved the campus chapel for a date in early January. Would you consider officiating?"

The chapel at Anasazi College had been endowed by grocery store magnate Eddie Chen and bore the formal name The Yu Wei and Lee Nan Chen Memorial Interfaith Chapel and Meditation Center. It was a circular building made from local stone and known informally as Chen Chapel.

"If the day is clear on my calendar, and if you and Ving will meet with me for pre-marital counseling, I would be honored to do your wedding," Cloud replied.

"Wonderful! Thank you," Chaucer said. "In a way, it feels strange to be asking you to do this."

"Strange, how?" he asked.

"Thinking about my being interested in you at ASU," she answered. "I stalked your study table at the library, but you ignored me. What if you hadn't ignored me? What if we had...dated?"

Cloud laughed. "Even if I had noticed you and we developed a relationship, in the end, your extraversion would have scared me away."

"You're right, of course," she said. "I feel very comfortable as your friend, but wouldn't want to spoil that with romantic trappings."

They set a date for the first pre-marital counseling session.

"By the way," Chaucer said, "I should have mentioned this earlier. Ving is not traditionally religious and he especially does not want any syrupy Jesus or Trinitarian language in our wedding service. He's OK with mentioning God but not a lot of pious doctrinal stuff or sentimental goo. Is that a problem?"

"No problem at all," said Cloud.

In the midst of all the activities swirling through her life, classroom responsibilities and wedding plans, Chaucer carved out blocks of time to work on her novel. I need to do this for my own sanity, she rationalized.

Acting on an intuitive sense that it would provide her ideas for the next chapter, she dug out the copy of **Peter and Wendy** that she had bought in London. Taking notes as she habitually did with anything she read, Chaucer scribbled down Barrie's description of Peter Pan's home which resonated with her own creation of the Timberscape: "Neverland is always more or less an island, with astonishing splashes of colour here and there." His image of unsteady fairies climbing over Peter Pan's sleeping body "on their way home from an orgy" also caught her attention and with a sly smile was added to her notes.

Though she was looking for useful tidbits about the relationship between Wendy and Peter, it was Wendy's mother, Mrs. Darling, who caused Chaucer to pause with dismay. Barrie wrote that Mrs. Darling first learned about Peter Pan while "tidying up her children's minds." Mary Darling was in the habit of traveling through her children's minds while they were sleeping and editing their thoughts. This notion of maternal invasion of privacy appalled Chaucer, and she shuddered at the idea of her own mother having access to her private inner world and being able to alter what she found there.

"That's as bad as that creepy 'Santa Claus Is Coming to Town,'" she said aloud to the walls of her office. Mentally, she reviewed the song lyrics until arriving at the lines about the jolly old man watching you sleep and knowing if you've been bad or good. Since childhood, she had interpreted the popular Christmas song as a heavy-handed way of scaring children into behaving. "It's a form of child abuse, but Barrie is even worse," she announced to her desk. "He is a sadist, intent on terrorizing children, and not with threats of some external and distant Santa Claus God substitute who judges their secrets but by their very own mothers' prying into their fragile psyches."

Reinforced in her negative view of J. M. Barrie, she came away from the book determined to include Peter Pan and Wendy characters in her own work but not with Wendy playing mother to Peter. Rather, she would transform them into potentially romantic equals.

Her progress was thwarted for a week by the news of the assassination of John Lennon on December 8, 1980. This so traumatized her that she was unable to concentrate on her fiction and barely kept up with her students. But when she shed her grief and regained focus, she found writing to be a comforting retreat from painful events.

Subconsciously, she was also thematically influenced by an aversion to Ving's sense of style. He always knew what was in vogue and what made a sophisticated fashion statement. Chaucer was inclined toward timeless classic designs and was equally happy wearing jeans and a sweatshirt. She had been attracted by his neatness in dress and meticulous appearance, so this was not what tickled her mind beneath the level of consciousness. Rather it was that he was so aware of what was hip and what was simply gauche. She did not care what was in style and thought that buying current fashions was a waste of time and money.

CHAPTER 18:

IN THE REALM OF DIAMONDS

And now the bird threw down to her a dress which was more splendid and magnificent than any she had yet had, and the slippers were golden.

Jacob and Wilhelm Grimm

Red carpet extended as far as they could see along the border of Diamonds, not running into the realm but parallel to the boundary line. Still in pursuit of the jackrabbit, the four teenagers let go of one another's hands and proceeded warily across an open field.

The jackrabbit remained in view for a mile or so, although every time they sped up, the jackrabbit did the same. And then the creature disappeared without a trace. They rushed up to the spot where it had been a moment before and were immediately surrounded by a pack of horse-mounted lawmen.

"Halt in the name of the Fashion Police!" an officer in a crisp baby blue uniform demanded.

As they were completely encircled, the command seemed unnecessary. However, apart from staring intently at the four captives, no one said anything further. Then two horses moved aside to make room for a horse-drawn carriage carrying a tasseled and epaulet-bedecked man wearing a coral uniform.

"I am Inspector Labellust of the Fashion Police of the Realm of Diamonds," the pink suited man said imperiously.

Wrinkling his nose in disgust, he continued, "And who on earth might you tatterdemalions be?"

Allys replied, "We came from the Timberscape. We were chasing after a jackrabbit and accidentally strayed across the border."

"Yes," added Hansel, "and we apologize for the intrusion and will turn around immediately and run back where we came from."

"You will do no such thing!" Labellust said. "Justice must be done for your serious infractions, not least of which are your shabby and ill-fitting clothes. Officers, bind them and take them to the Royal Court!"

Each was handcuffed and the four were then forced into a small wooden cart attached to the back of the inspector's carriage. Four hours later, they were removed from the cart and paraded through the city of Diamondville to the hoots and catcalls of gawkers. The parched and hungry prisoners were then escorted into the castle courtroom and made to stand at attention before King Rustabar and Queen Quartzita.

No hearing or trial occurred. The royal pair simply gazed in silence at the sweaty and uncomfortably dressed quartet. Based only on their appearance, two minutes later Rustabar and Quartzita pronounced them guilty of multiple violations of the Comprehensive Dress Code, the Statute of Acceptable Style, and the Felonious Fashion Law.

"There is no doubt of your guilt," said the queen. "The only issue is the appropriate punishment."

"Summon the Royal Phrenologist," the king ordered.

A dozen feet scurried from the room in a clatter of heels on tile. Shortly they returned accompanied by a grim-looking, spidery man wearing an ivory turban and dressed in a mauve suit.

"Ah, Facet, we are in need of your expertise," Rustabar said pleasantly.

Facet gazed at the four with a sneer of disgust and without a word pulled rubber gloves over his long, thin fingers. He then began to fondle Gretel's head for about thirty seconds. From there he proceeded to do the same to Allys, and then to Hansel and to Aylwyn.

Looking up adoringly to Quartzita and Rustabar, Facet announced, "Your majesties, I can aver with full confidence that all four are in possession of a common skull shape and thus they belong to the lowbrow obsequious archetype. They will make wonderful servants."

"Splendid!" said Rustabar.

"Do we have a proper posting for them?" inquired Quartzita.

"Yes, your majesty," Facet said. "Tweedledumdum and Tweedledeedee have made inquiries about needing new servants for their wedding business. The last two they employed were lured away by a baker to work as wedding cake models."

"Can they use all four?" Rustabar asked. "It would be convenient to make disposition of all four cases at once."

"Your majesty, they have requested only two, but as these four are fashion criminals, and thus won't be paid, I believe my good friends Deedee and Dumdum will be able to make appropriate use of the lot," Facet said obsequiously.

"So ordered!" shouted Rustabar and banged on the table with a gem-encrusted gavel.

The four were immediately trundled off to the wedding shop of Tweedledumdum and Tweedledeedee, a married couple who looked very much alike except that he had a belly and she had an enormous bosom. Thus they fit together quite nicely when embracing face-to-face. The shop was attached to a wedding chapel with a large residential area in the back and upstairs.

"To the showers immediately!" Tweedledeedee proclaimed when she saw her newly indentured employees.

This seemed an appealing prospect to the quartet. They were led to a large bathroom, where they disrobed and took turns under the spray of water, shampooing their hair and washing their bodies. Retrieving their unfashionable apparel, they were shown to a common bedroom containing two beds that the four would have to share.

Allys said, "Would it possible to bring in two more beds? We are, after all, four instead of the two you were expecting."

"We'll see what we can do," said Tweedledumdum. "In

the meantime, get dressed in the uniforms hanging in the closet and report to me in the showroom."

They stored their old clothes in a dresser and donned servant uniforms. The girls were now clad as English maids, with white hose, plain cotton skirts with bibs over starched white blouses and the boys as English livery servants, clad in white hose, red knee pants, and starched white dress shirts under red vests.

When they reported to their new employers, Tweedledeedee told Hansel and Aylwyn to go to the storage closet and select two mattresses for their bedroom.

"Unfortunately, we have no more bed frames, but you can place these on the floor. They will do nicely, I believe."

This they did, and the boys then volunteered to sleep on the floor mattresses so the girls could have the beds.

Their work days were soon filled with a variety of tasks, including running off to pick up items at other shops, cleaning the chapel and other venues after weddings, setting up rooms for receptions, and hauling returned rented tuxedos and gowns to the dry cleaners. In between chores, they listened as Tweedledumdum and Tweedledeedee offered haughty opinions about the uncultured couples they extracted small fortunes from for manipulating their nuptials.

Everywhere they went on their errands, the four saw shoppers and shopkeepers alike bedecked in the latest fashions, jewelry and accessories. They also encountered other servants, who wore traditional service garb with no extra ornamentation.

One day when there was a lull between tasks, the quartet was treated to Tweedledumdum and Tweedledeedee carrying on at length about a new law the king and queen were considering proclaiming. It would allow marriage between any two people regardless of sex.

"Rustabar and Quartzita think such a decision would make them look urbane and suave," said Tweedledumdum. "It would become the monarchy."

"Well, yes it would be the fashionable thing to do," offered Tweedledeedee. "But it all seems so...unseemly."

"The very idea is disgusting," said Tweedledumdum. "Just imagine. Who, my dear, would wear the veil, the jewelry, the tiara, and so on. Surely they would not both wear tuxedos or both wear gowns. It's quite upsetting."

"I agree that would be a major fashion faux pas," Tweedledeedee replied. "Have they no shame? I don't care if gays pair up with one another. They have that right no matter how inelegant it looks. But a **wedding**? Give me a break!"

Allys could not resist butting in to the conversation. "I think it's only fair to let people who are born homosexual make formal ties with partners just like everybody else. They have a right to marry the person of their choice."

"What does **fairness** have to do with fashion?" Tweedledeedee responded. "It may be fair to let those kind of people live together but as for getting married, it simply doesn't **look** right. No, there would be simply too many fashion clashes."

"What if they got married naked?" Hansel asked.

"Perish the thought! That would put us out of business," Tweedledumdum said.

"No it wouldn't," Aylwyn said. "They couldn't be your customers anyway if they weren't allowed to marry. If they married without clothes, they would not be breaking any fashion laws, and you can't lose a customer you never had. The effect on your business would be neutral."

"Not really," Tweedledumdum said. "If gays have nudist weddings, in no time at all straights would see that as a new fashion statement, and then our gown and tuxedo business would go bankrupt. No, it just won't do."

"What if they got married in fours?" Gretel suggested. "Two men in tuxes, marrying each other and two women in gowns marrying each other. It would all balance out. Surely that would **look** right."

Tweedledeedee was intrigued. "Hmmm. That might be the answer. Yes, that would definitely be very good for our business. I'll talk to Facet and have him suggest a rider to the proclamation requiring homosexuals to marry in fashionable foursomes."

"Now that you put it in the proper context," Tweedledumdum said, "I see that Rustabar and Quartzita are indeed enlightened monarchs worthy of our support on this issue of economic justice."

The following day, the king and queen announced that because of concerns raised by the Royal Revenue and Tithing Bureau, they would be delaying indefinitely a decision on gay marriage. When Quartzita and Rustabar recognized that married homosexual couples would be entitled to the same tax breaks as heterosexual couples, they deemed it prudent to reconsider the matter.

"Once again the royal pair has shown a lack of moral fortitude," Tweedledumdum commented at the dinner table.

"Yes, I am so disappointed in them," said Tweedledeedee.

A young married couple named Dis and Ria operated a flower shop where singly or in pairs Allys, Gretel, Hansel, and Aylwyn often went to pick up arrangements for weddings. The dark-skinned couple took a liking to the four and let them hang out at their place, taking extended breaks and chatting. One day Ria told Allys that their business was not doing well, and if things did not improve she feared they would go bankrupt.

Time passed slowly for the quartet, filled with weeks of cleaning up the wedding chapel and reception hall where Tweedledumdum and Tweedledeedee conducted much of their business. Their bedroom, just upstairs from the reception hall and event kitchen, was used by bridal parties for changing, so the twins often had to vacate their only personal space.

Nevertheless, Tweedledumdum and Tweedledeedee repeatedly told them that as common criminals they should be grateful for a roof over their heads and fine food to eat.

"The last servants we employed were hauled off to work in dungarees on a pig farm because they were ungrateful," said Tweedledumdum. "Imagine the disgrace of having to go out in public wearing dungarees."

"I thought they became wedding cake models," said Allys.

"Never you mind what happened to **them**," said Tweedledeedee. "It'll be the pig sties for you bunch of louts if your attitudes don't improve."

After yet another harangue about gratitude, Allys, Hansel, Aylwyn, and Gretel huddled in their room and discussed escaping from Diamonds.

"But the fashion police are everywhere on foot and horseback, and they would probably pick us up and bring us back here," said Gretel.

"More likely we'd end up in dungarees," said Aylwyn with a subdued laugh. "Actually, I think I'd rather feed the pigs."

"Let's develop a plan," said Allys.

They brainstormed ideas for several days, but before they had put together anything substantial, Tweedledumdum told them they had been contracted to do a wedding at a resort on the beach, overlooking the Universal Sea.

"You four will be taken along as the clean up crew," he said.

"I would like to see the Universal Sea," said Hansel later. "Let us not escape until after this job."

The sea was clear turquoise blue with gentle waves and tropical fragrance. Nothing but water was visible as far as the eye could see. The beach consisted of fine white sand. All four servants thought it was a spectacularly beautiful setting for an outdoor wedding. They soon learned, however, that the ceremony would not take place next to the sea. The bride and groom had chosen to exchange their vows on the deck of the concrete swimming pool, three hundred yards inland, where the natural wonders would not distract the guests from the fashion finery of the wedding party.

Fastened to the fence around the pool was a large sign that read:

NO SPLASHING
Be considerate of Hair Styles
and Make-up of Others.

"Why would anyone want to be married on a cement slab by an artificial pool rather than in the sand on the beach of the enchanting ocean?" Gretel said to her companions.

"Good question," said Aylwyn.

"Are you stupid?" rang out a familiar but out of place voice. "I see you four are still as clueless as ever."

Standing at the gated entrance to the pool was a security guard in a stylish navy blue uniform with gold epaulets.

"Papa Bear!" cried Allys. "What are you doing here?"

"I could ask the same about the pack of you," Papa Bear responded.

"Oh, the job opportunities are so much better here," Aylwyn quipped.

"I'll give the same answer then," said Papa Bear. "I fancied working in uniform. Like it?" He pirouetted daintily to show off his apparel.

"Is Goldilocks here too?" Gretel asked.

"Still in Clubs. She's taken up with a mud wrestler," Papa Bear said grumpily.

"Well, we have work to do," said Hansel. "It was...good...to see you again."

"Yeah, seeing you has been a real trip down memory lane," added Allys.

They passed through the gate and began their set-up tasks. When the service was over, and after the servants had finished cleaning the wedding space, they had nothing to do until the reception in the resort ballroom ended, when they would begin the major cleanup drudgery at that venue.

Taking advantage of their free time, the four slipped down to the shore and swam naked in the salt water. Then they sat on the beach, burrowing their feet in the sand and enjoyed the elements. Hearing the music fade in the reception hall, they reluctantly put on their servant uniforms and returned to their duties.

On the trip back to Diamondville, Allys told her employers that they had met a security guard they had known when they lived in Clubs.

"Oh, Papa Bear," said Tweedledeedee. "Yes, we know all about him."

"Why is he here in Diamonds?" asked Gretel.

"Got his butt into a bit of trouble in Clubs," said Tweedledumdum with a lecherous grin. "It seems he had been in the habit of taking nude photos of the underage daughter of some high muckety-mucks in that loony church they have up there. The parents walked in on the scene and caught him with his big paws fondling the little girl. He ran for it and escaped into Diamonds by the skin of his teeth."

"And how does that qualify him to be a security guard here?" Allys asked with accusatory anger in her voice.

"He looks good in a uniform," explained Tweedledeedee with a knowing shrug.

"Speaking of uniforms," Aylwyn said, "I've never seen any ministers or priests in robes and stoles and whatever get-up they wear at any of the weddings we've worked at. Is there a church in Diamonds?"

"Certainly," Tweedledumdum responded. "But it's rather low key. We don't draw attention to it. And we do have priests but they are not allowed to wear distinctive garb. It simply would not do for a cleric officiating at a wedding to upstage the bride with colorful robes and stoles."

"Do people go to church?" Gretel asked.

"Usually four times a year for the holiday services," Tweedledeedee explained. "Our holy days are Epiphany, Lent, Eastmas, and Westmas. Many Diamonds go to church on those dates to show off their devotion to fashion, but others quietly observe these holidays at home."

"We celebrate Epiphany and Lent in our village in Germany," said Hansel. "But what are Eastmas and Westmas?"

"Well, I very much doubt that a village in the sticks of wherever it is you come from would observe Epiphany and Lent in the elegant way we do here in Diamonds. They are holy seasons for the unveiling of new fashions," said Tweedledumdum. "Epiphany is when hemlines are raised and more cleavage exposed on women's dresses and the cuffs on men's slacks disappear. At Lent, the hemlines lengthen, cleavage is covered up, and cuffs reappear. Of course there are other decorative changes as well. It's all very solemn."

"And Eastmas and Westmas?" Allys asked.

"They are more festive," said Tweedledeedee. "At

Eastmas we honor one of our well-established fashion designers whose old styles are temporarily resurrected to be in again. We celebrate with retro parties. Westmas is the time to recognize a new breakthrough designer by gift-wrapping the latest styles and putting them under the Westmas tree to impress family and friends."

"It's good that the church in Diamonds stands for something truly important," Aylwyn deadpanned. "What is the name of this holy institution?"

"Our church is called the Tastefully Understated Religious Diamonds Society," said Tweedledumdum with boastful pride in his voice.

Silence prevailed for a time as the four reflected on the church name. Then Aylwyn laughed out loud as a light dawned in his head. "You don't by any chance have punchbowls on your Communion tables do you?"

"How did you know that?" asked Tweedledeedee in astonishment.

"Just a lucky guess," Aylwyn replied.

A year after chasing a jackrabbit into Diamonds, the four still had no feasible escape plan, but they were so fed up with Tweedledumdum and Tweedledeedee that they decided to test what would happen if they simply walked away and did not return. Being captured and sent to the pig farm seemed a reasonable risk. One afternoon when their employers were engrossed in a wicked croquet game with the king and queen, they retrieved their old clothes from the dresser and in broad daylight, still wearing their servant attire, set out through Diamondville on foot. To their surprise, the fashion police ignored them, assuming they were running errands.

Their pathway out of town passed the shop of Ria and Dis, and Ria saw them walking intently by. She ran out and asked them where they were going.

Hansel put a finger to his lips and then whispered, "Hush please. We do not want the Fashion Police to be suspicious."

"You're running away to the Scape, aren't you?" Ria whispered back.

"Yes," said Gretel truthfully.

"Take us with you," Ria said impetuously. "The Finance Police will be coming to close our doors tomorrow. Let us run away with you."

"Quickly then," said Allys.

Ria ran inside to tell her husband. They had been planning to flee anyway and had already packed their bags. Having heard frightening stories about the Timberscape, they thought they would try their luck with Clubs. But these four young ones had come from the Scape and knew how to get around there. It was an opportunity too timely to ignore.

The six walked on into the late evening. Overnight, they hid in an arbor to sleep. By midmorning the next day, the uniforms of the four were sweaty and grass stained, and the work clothes of Ria and Dis were also soiled.

Apart from being tired and dirty, they reached the border without incident.

"What burns me up," said Aylwyn, "Is that we could have done this months ago. No one did anything to stop us."

"Well, we're glad you didn't leave then, because we wouldn't have gone with you," said Ria. "Your timing was providential for us. Thank you for guiding us here."

"Now that we're here, we need to wash and put on clean clothes," Dis added.

Allys said, "It's better to go naked in the Timberscape. We'll head for the river where we can bathe."

"Well, you're the experts," said Dis. "We'll follow your lead."

"I would like to dispose of these servant outfits," said Gretel.

"I have an idea for that," said Hansel.

Following his plan, all six disrobed and then used fallen tree branches and dried grass to make scarecrows out of their servant and shopkeeper clothes. They propped up the scarecrows inside the border, facing inward as a warning to anyone from the Timberscape thinking about crossing into Diamonds.

Carrying but not wearing their old clothes, the four began hiking into the interior, along with the unclad Ria and Dis, who were toting small suitcases. They proceeded northward, in search of the river, where they would bathe and plan their next steps. But before they reached water, they were stopped by a mockingbird.

"Welcome, Diamond shopkeepers," said the bird. "The Timberscape of Memory welcomes refugees from the realms, and there is an orientation center nearby where you can be cared for until we find a home for you. I will show you the way."

Eagerly, Ria and Dis accepted the offer.

"Should we go too?" Aylwyn asked.

"No," said the mockingbird. "Go to the river. You'll find what you need there."

The four said goodbye to the two and continued on their way.

When they reached the river, they ate berries, washed their clothes, spread them out on rocks to dry, and then jumped in to bathe. While in the water, they carried on a whimsical conversation about which clothes each should wear when they had dried.

"I'd like to try on Hansel's clothes," said Allys.

"In that case, I wouldn't mind trying on Gretel's skirt, at least for a while," said Aylwyn a bit sheepishly.

"The thought of getting into Aylwyn's pants has a great deal of appeal to me," opined Gretel with a flirtatious laugh.

"That leaves Allys' things for me to wear," said Hansel, ignoring his sister's behavior. "But is it proper to wear items intended for the other sex?"

"The only issue is one of fit," said Allys. "Much of the everyday clothing in our world is essentially unisex in style, but with tailoring allowances for the different shapes of male and female bodies."

They climbed out of the river and sunbathed to dry their bodies and then took turns donning each other's apparel and laughing at the misfits due to their body shapes and sizes. All of them had grown more, and all the garments were too small for everyone.

"Apparently these shrank in the wash," said Allys.

"No," said Aylwyn, "we've all grown. They are unwearable now."

"You're right. I can tell my boobs have gotten bigger," said Allys.

"Big enough to require wearing a bra?" asked Gretel.

Allys laughed. "I'd say I've grown to a B-cup. But I know better now. Over the long term, wearing a bra will lead to weakening muscle tone and strength. That's one fashion item I won't need to waste money on in the future."

"We do not need any of these things here anyway," said Hansel.

"But we **will** need them to get home," said Aylwyn. "Let's hang on to them."

They agreed to proceed without clothing, putting all their things in a bundle that they took turns carrying. Continuing north toward the center of the island, they soon encountered Coyote again.

"Hello friends. I have been expecting you," said the erudite canine.

"Have you now? Well, I have to tell you that we did not discover anything about how to get home in the Realm of Diamonds," Hansel said. "You lied to us."

"I did not lie," Coyote replied calmly. "You learned far more than you now realize. Next you will discover an important piece of the puzzle in Spades."

"But we've already lost two years and have nothing to show for it," Allys said.

"I tell you with certainty, you will not reach your true home without sojourning first in the Realm of Spades," Coyote said.

"And when we return," Gretel said with angry accusation in her voice, "you will tell us we have to go to Hearts, will you not?"

"I assure you I will say no such thing," Coyote averred.

With heads bowed in discouragement, they turned west toward Spades, with the unspoken assumption that a jackrabbit would appear again to lure them into a new realm, but no such event happened. Presently, they came upon a thick forest of cottonwood trees and stopped to discuss whether to go around or through it.

"Through is shorter and we may find something interesting in there," said Gretel.

They entered the trees and within a minute spotted a naked boy leaping from one tree limb to another.

Hansel cried out, "Hello! Who are you?"

The boy stopped as if caught in the act of doing something bad and then continued leaping across boughs in an attempt to get away, shouting, "You'll not catch me!" But his words interrupted his coordination and he missed his intended branch and fell to the ground. The four rushed up to him.

A naked girl approached also on tree limbs and cried, "Pieter? Are you hurt?"

"Wendlich, run and hide. There are strangers here, and they've captured me!" Pieter shouted.

"We won't harm you," said Allys. "We are as caught as you are. Maybe more so."

The girl dropped to the ground next to the four. "I'm not afraid of you," she announced boastfully.

"And you have no need to be," said Aylwyn.

An introductory conversation revealed that the boy and girl were eleven years old and lived in a tree house nearby. When shown the place, the four were dutifully impressed with the architecture of the arboreal abode.

Hansel, Gretel, Allys, and Aylwyn explained that they were stranded on the island and had been searching for a way home.

The girl said, "I am Wendlich Liebchen and this is Pieter Faunus."

Pieter added, "We would like to escape too."

"How did you get here?" Gretel asked.

"A mean warlock cast a spell on us and sent us here to live forever as eleven year- olds," Wendlich explained.

Allys asked, "How long have you been here?"

"About five years, we think," Wendlich said.

"And why did the warlock put a spell on you?" Aylwyn asked.

"It is an embarrassing story," Pieter said, his face reddening.

"As we are all naked, and five years ago we were the same age as you were when you came here, there is nothing to be embarrassed about," said Hansel.

In thoughtful silence, Wendlich considered whether to tell the story and the idea came to her that doing so might help them find a way to break the spell. "It's worth a try," she said to Pieter. "Tell them the tale."

Pieter settled himself comfortably on a limb and began. "We were living in a village near the Elbe River, as next-door neighbors. One Saturday afternoon, Wendlich and I stole away into the forest to play make-believe games, as we had often done over the years. On this particular day we decided to play a game called physician and nurse."

"Oh, I know that game," said Allys. "We call it playing doctor."

"Or sometimes just 'You show me yours and I'll show you mine," said Aylwyn.

"You have played it?" Wendlich asked.

"Not with each other," said Allys. "We're brother and sister, so we've seen each other's bodies lots of times."

"Since you are not shocked, I will continue the tale," said Pieter. "We took our clothes off and were touching each other in ticklish places, when a warlock with a long beard and a wooden wand stepped into the hidden place where we were playing, and he said, 'What are you children doing?'"

"It was obvious what we were doing," said Wendlich. "He was a stupid warlock, and I told him so."

"That made the warlock angry, and he yelled that he would punish us for disrespect," said Pieter. "He lifted his wand and put us under an enchantment."

"I shall never forget his words, although I do not know what they mean," said Wendlich. "The spell was **Prepubescentia aeternia**. Just before he pronounced the spell, he laughed and said, we would be eleven years old forever and would never have pubic hair and my breasts would never grow and Pieter's organ would never grow."

"He said we would be perpetual innocent virgins," said Pieter. "And then poof! We appeared here in this forest and have not aged a day since then."

"You sound older than eleven," said Allys, "even if your bodies are that age."

"I think we have grown older in our minds," said Pieter. "And we feel more grown up than when we arrived. But as you can see, we are still children."

"Can you help us?" Wendlich asked.

"We are in search of knowledge to help us get home," said Aylwyn. "We will try to find answers for you, too. If we find anything that will help you, we will return and let you know."

"You might seek out help from Flowerina and Sunny," said Gretel. "They are a witch and warlock living over toward the border with Clubs. They were awfully friendly when we visited them."

"But a bit confusing with their directions," said Allys.

"Oh we know Flo and Sun," said Pieter. "They tried to undo the spell, but they found that it was a particularly difficult kind that could only be reversed by a non-wizard."

"That's diabolical!" said Hansel. "How would someone who is not magical know how to do magic?"

"There is a way," said Wendlich. "Flo and Sun explained that to us. Somewhere on this island is a learned doctor who knows the right words to free us, but we have no idea where. So we ask everyone we meet to help us."

"Could an animal do it?" asked Allys.

"No, it must be a human being," said Pieter.

"We'll be on the lookout for anyone who might qualify to help you," Aylwyn said. "If we discover anything useful, I promise we'll come back."

"Oh, please do," said Wendlich with a vulnerable quaver in her voice.

The four journeyed on toward the border with Spades.

As they neared the frontier with the black-suited realm, Hansel said, "I suppose we should get dressed before entering, but these clothes no longer fit us."

"Maybe we could stretch them," said Allys.

"They're already stretched as far as they can go," said Aylwyn.

At that moment, a mockingbird flew in and alit on a berry bush and said, "Perhaps I can be of assistance." The mockingbird whistled a summoning call and a flock of mockingbirds flew in and carried off the quartet's clothes.

"How will that help?" asked Gretel.

"You will see," said the bird. A few minutes later, the birds flew back with the same clothes now enlarged to fit them.

"How did they do that?" Aylwyn asked.

"Most things in the Timberscape are wonderfully elastic," said Mockingbird. "One need only know where the stretching and bending energy flows in the air as vigorously as the water in the river."

"Can you show us such places?" Gretel asked.

"When you can transform yourself into an avian creature," said Mockingbird, "I will gladly point out such vortices."

"In other words, we shouldn't hold our breath," said Allys.

"Certainly not," said Mockingbird. "Breathing is a vital activity."

Aylwyn sighed noisily. "Well, kids, let's get this over with. We have the realm of the trump cards ahead. Let's find out what instructive mischief awaits us there."

CHAPTER 19:
CONFESSION AND COMFORT FOOD

Owing to divergent disposition,
Each falls at the other's elevation.
Geoffrey Chaucer

Three days before their initial pre-marital counseling session with Cloud, Ving nervously told Chaucer that his conscience was bothering him and he had something he needed to confess.

"That sounds ominous," Chaucer said as she set down her glass of wine. "OK, I'm listening."

"I'm not going to draw this out. I'll just say it," he stammered. "I am...bisexual."

Chaucer's face went blank. This was not a total surprise, but the confirmation of her suspicion wielded a great deal more impact than she had imagined it would. "Thank you for telling me this now rather than after we are married. I'm not shocked. I suppose that thought has been in the back of my mind from the first time we met."

"But I want you to know," Ving said earnestly, "that I choose to spend the rest of my life with you. I may be attracted to both sexes, but you are the one I am most drawn to, the one I want to be with. Straight men typically find many women attractive but usually settle down with only one. I happen to find men as appealing as women, but it's the same principle. I want to be monogamous with **you**."

Despite the serious confessional nature of the conversation, Chaucer burst into laughter. "Now that's a genuinely novel marriage proposal," she said. "I want to be monogamous with you. How terrifically nerdy. I love it."

"I take it then that you're not angry," said Ving tentatively.

Based on her gay rights advocacy in Pittsburgh, Chaucer was inclined to dismiss his confession as having no significant relevance for her. She believed Ving was truly bisexual. This did not make any difference, she told herself. It is character and not sexual orientation that makes some people prone to wander and others true to their vows.

"I'm not angry," she said. "As long as we're faithful to one another, Ving, it simply doesn't matter at all. I have a liberal view of sex when it comes to single people. Singles can have as many willing partners as they like, as far as I'm concerned. But once a marriage commitment has been made, exclusivity is the rule. I really believe that, and I hope you do too."

"Only you," Ving said and then sighed heavily. "Well, that was easier than I thought it would be. Do I really sound like a nerd?"

"Some day the world will be ruled by nerds," she said. "Consider it a compliment. For the record, though, you don't look like a nerd but you sometimes talk like one."

"Oh how dreadful," he said. "I must brush up on hip vocabulary."

"If I'm the one you want to impress," she said, "I much prefer nerdspeak to hipster any day of the week. And here's a tip that will get you a long way. Literary allusions make me horny."

"Call me Ishmael," Ving said, reciting the first three words of Herman Melville's **Moby Dick**.

"Ooh, what wonderful foreplay," she responded. "Associations with a huge white sperm whale can lead to wonderfully erotic imaginings."

"It's the first thing that popped into my head," he said. "I don't know what Sigmund Freud would make of that, but it opens an ocean of possibilities."

"Good one. Keep going, seaman," she said with an encouraging laugh. "What else can you spout?"

"The name Moby Dick sounds like a nineteenth century sexually transmitted disease, don't you think?" he said.

"Bad move, sailor. The humor is certainly nerdish," Chaucer responded. "That's a plus, but STDs are a huge turnoff."

"Sorry," he said. "I won't raise the subject again."

At the first pre-marital counseling session, Cloud put them both at ease about his religious views. "I'm not theologically orthodox, and I won't impose any doctrinal requirements on you with regard to vows or wording of prayers."

"That's good to know," said Ving.

Intuitively, however, Cloud sensed that sexuality issues needed to be discussed. "Let's jump into a more important area," he said. "Have the two of you had any in depth conversations about sex? For example, have you talked about your past sex histories with one another?"

Chaucer's immediate mental reaction was not about the many lovers she had known but that somehow Cloud knew about Ving's bisexuality.

Ving's first thought was that Cloud suspected he was gay. Ving was right. Given his recent confession to his fiancée, Ving decided to answer directly with the same information he had given to Chaucer. "We've talked about my bi-sexuality, if that's what you're getting at."

"I see," said Cloud. "And have you discussed in depth the relevance of this orientation on the unfolding of your lives together?"

"We've talked about it a little," Chaucer said. "Personally, I don't see that it has any particular significance."

"And why is that?" Cloud asked.

For a moment Chaucer was stumped. Why did she minimize its importance? "Well, uh, that is, uh," she stammered. And then she found her voice. "Well, I've been involved in gay rights issues for years, so I'm comfortable with people of various sexual orientations. People are people regardless of whom they love. And the thing is, I happen to be straight and have never had homosexual relations, but I admit I *am* curious about sexual relations with a woman, so I guess I could be borderline bisexual too."

Ving quickly but carefully added, "I have had sex with both male and female partners and have truly enjoyed both." What he left unsaid was that the only female had been Chaucer and he fantasized about men during intercourse with her.

Cloud said, "I harbor no negative feelings about bisexuality, or for that matter, homosexuality. I know several bisexuals, involved in both same and opposite sex relationships. And the ones who are married took a long time before making that commitment. So let me throw out an idea. Seeing how your wedding will be a low-key affair with few guests, what's to stop you from postponing the ceremony and simply live together for a year or so? What's the rush?"

"Wouldn't the college have a problem with that?" Chaucer asked. "Don't they want their faculty members to live conventional lives?"

"The college wouldn't care a fig," said Cloud. "And it's none of their business."

"Perhaps," Chaucer said. "Ving, what do you think?"

To Cloud's surprise, Ving strongly opposed the idea of living together. For him it was the marriage and not the relationship that would provide him the paternal approval he sought, although this thought went unspoken.

"I have dreamed of being married for a long time," Ving said. "And as it happens, I'm in love with Chaucer. I don't see any value in waiting, especially since we're both past the big 3-0."

Chaucer asked Cloud, "Is this an issue over which you would refuse to officiate?"

"Assuming overall compatibility, I would not refuse to marry you over this matter in isolation," Cloud replied. "But I still don't see the need for haste."

"We've known each other seven years," Ving said. "I see no reason to delay."

Cloud administered the Taylor-Johnson Temperament Analysis to them individually and compared their responses about their self-perceptions and their perceptions of one another. He found that they were remarkably compatible in the key behavioral areas and that both had answered the questions honestly.

During their last counseling session, Chaucer mentioned that Ving was a Viet Nam veteran. In the inevitable ensuing conversation about Army life, Ving and Cloud learned that their tours in Viet Nam had overlapped, and Cloud had briefly served in the same division as Ving, although at a different base. Thus a bond of respect grew between the two men. Chaucer was pleased at this development but also felt excluded by it.

On schedule, the marriage took place in Chen Chapel. Cloud officiated at the brief and simple service, with Terp acting as a witness and Chaucer's faculty colleagues Bookman Donne and Emily Congo as well as Prasada and Darshan Pratyaksha attending as guests. No one from Ving's or Chaucer's family of origin was present. Marlowe had eloped in Vermont, so there was no Dickinson tradition of big weddings, and Banky and Norah were grateful for not having to expend any money for the occasion.

The barefoot bride wore jeans and a puffy sleeved off-white peasant blouse, a fringed red hippie vest, colorful beads and flowers in her hair. The groom also wore jeans, although his were ironed and neatly creased. He sported an expensive purple silk shirt and suede sports coat. On his feet were loafers with no socks.

Chaucer enjoyed the nostalgic feeling of her hippie days and the counter-cultural daring of a wedding in denim. As she processed up the aisle, she mentally contrasted the fastidious fashion addiction of the people of Diamonds with the author of their story. She hoped that she and Ving could have a carefree, bohemian life together filled with travel adventures and many quirky friends.

In polite but uncomfortable visits for all the parties, Ving and Chaucer introduced their new spouses to their parents in Phoenix. The Valborgs had nothing against Chaucer, and the Dickinsons harbored no negative feelings about Ving. Rather, the discomfort arose because neither set of in-laws had previously met their respective new daughter-in-law and son-in-law.

After the introductions, Chaucer and Ving continued on their way to Sky Harbor Airport for a four-day honeymoon trip to New York City, where they had tickets for the Peter Schaffer play *Amadeus*. Remembering her solo visit to Manhattan to see *Annie*, Chaucer was thrilled to explore the Theater District hand in hand with her husband.

<><><>

Since Chaucer was working in a tenure track position at Anasazi and would not give it up to move back to Phoenix, Ving opened a branch of the travel agency in Sedona. Doing so fit his father's plan to expand the agency statewide, so the transition went smoothly.

With remarkable ease, she settled in at Anasazi, especially enjoying leading independent studies with wonderfully motivated students. In occasional spare time at her campus office, she continued to work on her fairy tale. Before her first year had ended, Chaucer developed a following among women students as well as a few men who also found in her lectures something of star quality.

Ving enjoyed running a branch of the family business out from under the watchful eye of his father and soon built an extensive client list.

However, he continued to fantasize about men while having sex with Chaucer.

For her part, Chaucer was experienced sexually and appreciated sex aimed at orgasm. She regularly achieved her desired climaxes with her husband but never seemed to connect with Ving at a deeper level that she longed to experience. For her, soul sharing, revealing one's depths, was sexually stimulating. But Ving resisted talking about his inner life. She had felt more intimate with men she was sleeping with without intention on either part to form a lasting relationship. On a day-to-day level, they worked well together but passion was somehow lacking on both sides, and long before their first anniversary both found excuses not to make love.

To compensate, Chaucer began eating more, especially comfort food, and gained twenty pounds in a few months. When her clothes were no longer wearable and she was forced to buy new things too often, she decided that drastic action was necessary. The first step was to resume daily jogging, which she had abandoned since moving back to Arizona. Next, she enrolled in a yoga class offered by the college.

Getting control of her diet was the hardest part. Ice cream with chocolate sauce had to go. Chocolate chip cookies had to go. These were temporary concessions, she told herself. And when she reached a point where she could reintroduce them into her menu, she would set limits. No more would she eat a quart of ice cream at one sitting or munch an entire bag of cookies in one evening while reading.

She adopted a Vegan diet, but quickly became impatient with the time and effort required to insure she took in the needed protein. She then shifted to a modified vegetarian diet that included yogurt, low fat cheese, and fish. This worked for her, and she gradually slimmed down. But the underlying dissatisfaction with her marriage remained, although she never spoke of it to Ving or to anyone else.

Ving faithfully accompanied Chaucer to the round of parties given by various Anasazi faculty members, but inevitably they split up and socialized separately as soon as they arrived. At a Christmas party, Ving drank more than his usual carefully measured intake of alcohol, and Chaucer, too, exceeded her two-drink maximum.

As the evening wound down, Chaucer and Ving happened to cross paths while changing conversation groups, and Ving bent his mouth to her ear and whispered, "I'm being good, darling. See, I've been hanging out with the girls all night."

As soon as the words were out of his mouth, he realized even through the fog of alcohol that he had said too much.

Though tipsy, Chaucer clearly heard Ving's words, but when she considered what they revealed, she convinced herself that he had not really said what she heard. He had really said something about being good at having a whirl. Of course, that made no sense, but since he was drunk, nothing he said would.

Bookman Donne, Chaucer's colleague in the English department, took note of Chaucer's condition as well as that of her husband. Gently placing a hand on her shoulder, Bookman said, "Would you and Ving like a ride home, Chaucer? Not being a drinker, I'm used to the designated driver role."

"Thanks, Bookman," she responded through a slight mental fog. "I'm pretty sure we walked over, since our place is only six blocks from here. I suspect the fresh air is what we're really going to need. But thanks anyway."

When Ving and Chaucer left the party, they discovered that a light snow had begun drifting down, and the streets were slick. Neither had suitable shoes for such conditions. Bookman and Emily had departed at the same time and watched as Ving slipped on the sidewalk and Chaucer barely kept him from falling on his back.

Bookman pulled his car beside the alcohol-impaired couple, and

Emily rolled down the window and said, "No arguing now. Get in the car both of you."

Chaucer and Ving gratefully complied.

The next day, neither spouse mentioned Ving's words about being good by socializing with the girls. Indeed, nothing was ever said about this subject by either one. Chaucer simply put the comment out of her mind, while Ving briefly worried about what Chaucer must be thinking. But he had other more problematic things to worry about, so this incident was soon forgotten.

As a couple, they remained outwardly harmonious, with Ving making a greater effort than Chaucer to act like the marriage was healthy and sound. Chronic bouts of constipation, so intense that even visits to the campus library brought no relief, left Chaucer on the verge of grouchiness much of the time. This made pretending to be amicable hard work for her. The situation was aggravated by Ving's offhand comment describing constipation as a female psychoneurosis.

Chaucer glared at him and spat out, "Martin Luther, the **male** chauvinist pig!"

"What's that non-sequitur supposed to mean?" he responded, perplexed.

Through clenched teeth she said, "Martin Luther was notorious for his constipation. Ergo, constipation is a gender neutral affliction."

"Point taken,' he said. "Still, I tend to think of clergy as a separate gender."

When not tending to her academic responsibilities, Chaucer buried herself in her fairy tale. Rather than write anything new, however, she repeatedly rewrote the early chapters, at times spending hours trying to find exactly the right word in a particular sentence. This was a genuinely engrossing task, although she devoted more energy to it than was needed. The major benefit was that it ate up time that she otherwise would have spent interacting with Ving pretending to be happy.

Introducing Cinderella into the narrative remained an elusive goal, and she struggled with how to do that in a way that was congruent with the plot. In her mind, Cinderella represented the girlhood desire of traditional culture that was very different from the adventuresome heroines she preferred. Cinderella was the passive and compliant one whose happy ending came about because of outside intervention. But there must be a place for such an important symbol in a book that explored subconscious realms through fantasy characters, she thought. Surely she could transform Cinderella's passivity.

Her most recent idea was to have Cinderella meet the Ash Lad, her soot-covered counterpart from Norse fairy tales. The Ash Lad was the small one left at home to tend the fire while the older brothers were out doing manly things. But in the end, it was the Ash Lad who became the family hero. He was a David, who saved the day not by slingshot or other weapon but by wit and superior intelligence. Chaucer considered making Cinderella and the Ash Lad twins who had been separated at birth but who were reunited in the Timberscape. Though they would be attracted to each other, being siblings would leave the way clear for a handsome prince to fall in love with Cinderella and a beautiful princess to share her father's kingdom with the Ash Lad.

Twisting these characters every which way in her mind, she found no satisfying narrative. "Ah well," she sighed. "It looks like there's no room in the book for Cinderella or the Ash Lad." But that was only a minor disappointment.

Chaucer returned to reworking what she had already produced years earlier, devoting a week to the references to *Star Trek* in the first chapter. One moment she thought it would be better to replace these with allusions to more contemporary fantasy material, and the next she preferred leaving them in. Ultimately, she kept them. She also deleted and then reinstated the conversation about what year it was for the German and American twins.

CHAPTER 20:
BLOOD WORK

There is a Fitting – a Dismay –
A Fitting – a Despair –
'Tis harder knowing it is Due
Than knowing it is Here.
Emily Dickinson

Married life drifted from 1982 into 1983 without overt confrontation of the mutual unhappiness simmering beneath the surface. Since he seldom had sex with Chaucer, Ving engaged in multiple affairs with men, each one typically lasting a few weeks. But the idea of a long-term relationship intrigued him, and he considered proposing a ***ménage a trois*** to his wife.

One evening when they were sitting at opposite ends of the couch reading, he decided the time was at hand. "I remember you commenting in a pre-marital counseling session that you were curious about having sex with a woman," he said. "Do you still feel that way?"

She was startled by the question but also intrigued. "Intellectually, I guess so. Writers are always interested in new experiences."

"Have you ever done a threesome?" he continued.

"You mean with two men at the same time?" she said. "No."

"Well, to be honest," he said, "our sex life is rather tepid, and I've been trying to think of things that might spice it up."

"Yes, it is rather blah, and I suppose it's time we had a talk about that," she responded.

Feeling that the conversation was moving in a productive direction, Ving said, "I wonder if we should experiment with threesomes? If that's something you'd consider, I think you should have the first choice -either another woman or a man. It would be fun watching you make love to a woman and also to make love to you while a man is doing me."

"That sounds like a foursome," Chaucer said.

"The ultimate bi thrill," he said. "But that's not what I meant. I was talking about you and me and one other person of your choosing. Then the next time it would be of my choosing."

Chaucer was titillated by the thought but when faced with a direct proposal felt extreme reluctance to try it with real people. Fantasizing was one thing, but actually doing it quite another. "It's something to consider. One day we should talk about it some more. The truth is, at present I don't know anyone at all of either sex that I'd want to experiment with." She thought but did not say that at that particular moment this reluctance to experiment included her husband. "At any rate, I really need to get this book finished before class tomorrow."

She reopened her book to return to reading, but Ving reached over and closed it.

"Now it's your turn to be honest," he said. "Do you have any moral reservations about three-way sex?"

"Hypothetically, such things are perfectly acceptable among consenting adults," she said. "It depends on the people and situation and their personal ethics about marriage."

"And your personal ethic is?" he asked.

"In need of scrutiny. I need to do some serious thinking about it," she replied noncommittally.

Two weeks later, Ving raised the subject again over dinner.

"I'm still thinking about it," she said. "Please give me time."

Suspicions about Ving's sexual orientation roamed through her consciousness from time to time. Her intuition said her husband was not bisexual but gay. She did not want to deal with what her intuition told her, however, so she buried such thoughts whenever they arose.

He developed the habit of being late for any plans they made to meet at a restaurant for dinner or lunch or for a concert. He was always profusely apologetic but the behavior continued. Frequently, there were unaccounted for gaps of time between leaving his office and getting home. But Chaucer could not summon the energy or courage to question him about where he had been.

And then for Christmas, Ving bought Chaucer an expensive, and for him out of character, diamond necklace as a guilt offering, without confessing anything that he should be guilty about. It was a beautiful piece, and intuitively she knew what it represented, but she would not let her mind acknowledge the reality of his infidelity.

By the next day, however, the tension in her mind was so intense that she was willing to risk a showdown. Ving, of course, was ready to confess that he had lied about being bisexual. Thus began their marital separation.

Fearing AIDS, Chaucer made an appointment with her gynecologist. She had not yet found a physician in Sedona, so this entailed a trip to Phoenix to the doctor she had visited over the years, since getting a prescription for birth control pills while in college. The doctor explained that there was no blood test for AIDS yet, but he examined her for signs and symptoms and found none. Given her personal circumstances, he recommended she be checked for a range of other sexually transmitted diseases and she agreed.

The nurse who drew blood for the tests seemed strange to Chaucer, wearing unisex scrubs and with a hairstyle that could be either male or female. Chaucer was not sure which, but had a pleasant feeling about the person. While the nurse, Kelly Fife, was updating Chaucer's medical history, she told Kelly the reason for the blood work. Kelly was sympathetic, and even more so after Chaucer talked about her involvement with homosexual civil rights activities in Pittsburgh and then marrying Ving, believing he was bisexual.

Chaucer thanked Kelly for being such a good listener and spontaneously said, "Some time when I'm in Phoenix, I'd like to have coffee with you, Kelly, to talk more. I feel so much better after chatting with you."

Kelly smiled and nodded but did not say anything.

For the first time in years, during the waiting period for lab results, Chaucer engaged in conversation with Riff. Riff had initiated the interchange, although Chaucer thought that Riff had simply popped out of her subconscious because of her distress. Riff was supportive and encouraging, telling Chaucer that all would be well.

Still, in great anxiety she waited for test results through the New Years Eve and New Years Day holidays. Never before had she been as pessimistic about the prospects for a new year as she felt on this January first.

As a result of her depressed mood, the news of January 2, 1984 would be long remembered by Chaucer. At 9:00 a.m. she telephoned the doctor's office.

The receptionist said, "Laboratory reports should be delivered by eleven, and the doctor will review them this afternoon. We will call you by five p.m."

Chaucer paced for a few minutes before deciding she did not want to wait all day. "I bet Kelly will tell me the results if I drive down there," she said to herself. Not only that, but the time behind the wheel will give me something to do, she thought. She arrived at the medical suite at 11:45 and asked to speak with Kelly. Her supposition had been correct.

Kelly led her into an unoccupied examination room and pulled out her chart. "The tests are negative," she said and then smiled. "No indications of any STD."

Chaucer breathed a long sigh of relief. "The drive back to Sedona will be much easier than the trip down."

Influenced by a suggestion from Riff, Kelly said, "I'm about to take a lunch break. Before you head back, are you interested in getting a bite together so we can chat?" Kelly had in fact brought a lunch, which was in the refrigerator, but on a supposed whim she decided to test Chaucer's previous comment about talking more over coffee.

They went to a restaurant and ordered lunch.

Feeling intuitively that she could trust Chaucer, and unknowingly encouraged by Riff, Kelly said, "I know you're curious, so I'll just tell you. I am intersex. Do you know the term?"

"Yes," said Chaucer, fascinated by the news. "It's what we used to call hermaphrodite."

"Right," said Kelly, "and I have chosen to remain faithful to both my genders, not preferring one over the other."

"It must be very hard to form relationships with the…opposite sex," Chaucer said. "What exactly would be the opposite sex?"

Kelly laughed. "That *is* the problem. I've thought about putting a personal ad in the paper, but I can't think of a way to do so honestly. It would have to say 'Hermaphrodite seeks same or adventuresome bisexual.' Even if a paper would print it, I fear the responses would be from really kinky types. And apart from my double anatomy, I'm really quite conventional."

"But you managed to get your RN," Chaucer said. "Did you have any hassles along the way with that?"

"Not really," Kelly said. "My guidance counselor thought nursing was the best career I could choose. All of the faculty at ASU were great about everything, and I had no trouble finding the perfect job. The medical practice here has intersex and pseudointersex patients, so the doctor values me as an important asset. The only area where I feel unsupported is in finding a faith community."

"They're not so accepting?" Chaucer said.

"Right. Even liberal congregations seem uncomfortable with my open identity," Kelly replied. "But I take comfort from the biblical affirmation of people like me."

"Where is that found?" Chaucer asked.

"It's implied," Kelly said. "Isaiah 60:16. 'Thou shalt suck the breasts of kings.' Suckable breasts would by definition make them intersexual kings. The context is the people being amply fed. Even if it's metaphorical, though, not only are we acknowledged by the Bible but included among those who occupy the highest levels of society."

"I must remember that," Chaucer said and jotted down the scriptural reference on a napkin that she tucked into her purse.

Chaucer and Kelly would become friends, meeting periodically for movies and dinner. No sexual energy existed between them, and both were happy with that, although much of their conversation centered on the longing for soul-mates each one had felt.

Once back home on the day she had lunch with Kelly, Chaucer whooped and danced for joy and went out for a calorie-rich, chocolate fudge sundae, rationalizing that she would resume her healthy diet the next day. Returning to her house, she watched *Casablanca* on television and wept throughout the film. The next morning, it came to her that in the absence of a blood test, she could not completely rule out having the AIDS virus. Probably not, she told herself, but with no definitive way of knowing, her worry resumed.

Beginning in April 1984, people at risk for HIV infection marked their calendars with the date they passed or failed the newly developed blood test for AIDS. Chaucer passed. Without knowing she had been tested, Ving also had blood work done, so that he could reassure Chaucer if she ever began to wonder about AIDS. The result was negative, as he was sure it would be, because he had been careful and always took precautions. He telephoned Chaucer to let her know, just in case she had been worrying, that he was clean of all known sexually transmitted diseases, including what he called the big one.

"I'm grateful for the gesture and the information, Ving," she said, "but as it happens, I beat you to the phlebotomist."

For the 1984 spring semester, Chaucer led an independent study on vocabulary changes in the English language. Two first-year coeds, Vera Toll and Terra Birtles, petitioned for the course, and during their years at Anasazi, they would become Chaucer Dickinson groupies.

"Among the words and phrases that have changed meaning over time," Chaucer said at the first meeting with Vera and Terra, "are some that were originally innocuous and ordinary that became offensive to later generations. Words relating to sex and race provide many examples. Let these words by Geoffrey Chaucer from *Troilus and Cressida* be your guide for this independent study." She opened a book and read:

Take heed that in the forms of speech come change
Through centuries, and words that long ago
Were well esteemed, seem foolish now and strange,
And yet time and again they spoke them so.

Professor Dickinson also offered a course on George Orwell's **1984** at the start of that year, which was over-subscribed, and a larger venue had to be found for her lectures. Each student was required to write a paper on what they thought Orwell got right and what he got wrong.

News of Chaucer's separation from Ving and impending divorce circulated quickly among the faculty. She was embarrassed by the failure of the marriage and for a while avoided contact with Cloud, because he had diplomatically tried to get Ving and her to take more time before getting married.

Cloud stopped by her office one day and said, "I've noticed what appears to be avoidance of me, and I want to check in with you to see if my perception is accurate."

Chaucer took a deep breath and said, "You've caught me. It's been hard to face the man who tried to warn me about Ving."

"You have nothing to be embarrassed about," Cloud said. "I certainly don't think less of you because the marriage didn't work out. Actually, I think both you and Ving are fine people. I had no crystal ball about your marriage. And I especially esteem your teaching ability and intellect and would like to maintain a collegial relationship with you."

"You can read me like a book," Chaucer said. "How do you do that?"

"Simple," he said. "I don't bury my intuition."

"Again, you know me too well. That's exactly what I'd been doing in the marriage," Chaucer said. "However, I won't make that mistake again. Is there anything you don't know?"

He thought of something he suspected but did not know. His intuition radiated a sense that Chaucer had either already had an out-of-body experience or was a prime candidate for inducing one. Still, he said nothing about this, because floating was an intimate subject, and he sensed the time was not right to inquire about it. Instead, Cloud saw an opening to shift the conversation in a way to get Chaucer out of herself and he took it. "Well, I've plumbed the mysteries of the human psyche, but one enigma remains. Why do slow drivers always speed up when they're about to be passed?"

"Oh, I know that one," Chaucer said with a smile. "They're working out their passive-aggression. They're passive when they block traffic and outright aggressive when they speed up to make it harder to pass. They make people pay to pass them."

"I guessed that it had something to do with human competitiveness," Cloud said. "But you'd think a slow driver would be happy to be rid of people riding their bumpers."

"You miss the point," Chaucer said authoritatively. "They're not happy either way, but with frustrated drivers tailgating them, at least they're in control."

"You're a wise woman, Chaucer. You've made my day," he said.

After this meeting with Cloud, Chaucer felt much better, and her depression began to lift, but a good measure of repressed anger remained in her psyche, which she channeled into her views on politics.

Over the summer, Chaucer chiefly occupied herself with her novel, making changes in its tone as a result of her encounter with the possibility of AIDS, as well as the jingoistic sentiment of the nation during the Reagan administration. She believed an ethos of aggressive imperialism ran through the American populace, abetted by Ronald Reagan, and this influenced her words as she wrote more of her fairy tale.

CHAPTER 21:

IN THE REALM OF SPADES

"But I don't want to go among mad people,"
said Alice.

"Oh, you can't help that," said the cat. "We're
all mad here."

Lewis Carroll

Iron spikes adorned the top of the concrete block wall that spanned the border between the Realm of Spades and the Timberscape of Memory. Hansel, Gretel, Aylwyn and Allys walked along the outside of the wall until they found a rusted iron gate. Aylwyn reached through the bars and tugged hard on the corroded ancient lock and it popped open. He then pushed on the gate, causing it to swing free with a loud creaking noise.

"Anyone within a mile of here is bound to hear our entrance," said Allys.

"The sooner we are found, the sooner we will know the situation in this realm," said Gretel.

When they had gone about a quarter mile into Spades, a panel truck with the word DOGCATCHER painted on the side approached at a rapid speed and skidded to a stop in front of them. A hulking man with pistols in twin holsters stepped from the vehicle.

"I am Deputy Sheriff Ymir, and I demand to know what you rabble are doing in this fair and free land."

"We are earthlings who landed in the Timberscape," said Aylwyn with a hint of insolence in his voice, "and a hyper-intelligent being there suggested we ought to visit Spades to learn the importance of trump cards."

Ymir had no idea what an earthling was, but he was sure it was not a good thing to be. "What are your names?"

They recited their names one at a time.

"You have strange accents, and you're dressed funny too," Ymir announced, "so I'm going to run you in." He pulled a revolver from a holster and ordered them into the back of the panel truck.

After a long bumpy ride over a rutted road, the prisoners arrived at Spade City. The deputy escorted them into a nearly bare room with gray walls and pushed them along toward a metal desk with a bored clerk sitting behind it.

"I netted a pack of illegal aliens," the deputy announced roughly.

Without looking up, the deputy sighed and said, "Name and land of origin."

Allys said, "I'm Snow White from Fairyland."

Now the clerk looked up. "Try again, sweetheart. I **know** Snow White personally and you ain't her."

"Oh, alright then, I'm Allys from Arizona," she said.

"A likely story, but it'll do for the moment," the clerk said. "Next."

"I'm Aylwyn from Arizona."

The clerk made an entry on a page.

Hansel and Gretel gave their names but claimed the Timberscape as their homeland. This caused the clerk to snort. "I thought so," he said. "Just what we need, more lunatics from the Scape to fill our jail."

The four were summarily thrown into the Pink and Green Pavilion, a prison made of gingerbread fortified with pig iron, where a score of young men were lounging around in lacy pink underwear and see-through peignoirs, while an equal number of women were clad in olive drab boxer shorts and camouflage hunting vests.

Before they could inquire about the strange apparel of the prisoners, however, they were taken from the jail to stand trial before King Burpeedo and Queen Steeper. As they were escorted to the court, they passed a pond with a sign in front that read: **NO ICE SKATING**.

Allys asked the guard, "Does it get cold enough here for the water to freeze?"

"Not in my lifetime," replied the guard. "Not in the lifetime of my parents or grandparents either."

"Then why post a sign prohibiting ice skating?" asked Aylwyn.

"Well," said the guard, who had never to that moment considered the sense of the sign, "you never know what may happen meteorologically. It's good to be prepared. Our laws anticipate all possible pleasures."

"Does anyone in Spades own ice skates?" asked Hansel.

"Watch your mouth," the guard said.

"I shall need a mirror to do that," said Hansel.

"All of you stop asking questions! Questions only get you in trouble," said the now irritated guard.

By this time they had reached the courtroom.

A jury of two people sat in a raised section on the left side of the room. According to the nameplates in front of them, the jurors were Snow White and Prince Charming. While waiting for the trial to begin, Snow continuously flounced her hair and gazed at her red painted fingernails. Prince Charming stood and sprayed his chair with furniture polish and wiped it with a white cloth. Then he pulled a bottle of liquid soap out of his tote bag and washed his hands. He repeated this cleansing ritual several times before the entrance of the queen and king put a stop to his rising and sitting.

"What sly crime are these rabble charged with?" Queen Steeper asked the guard.

"I do not know, your majesty," the guard replied.

"No matter, no matter," said King Burpeedo. "It is fully obvious they are odd."

"Certainly," said the queen. "Has the jury duly reached a verdict?"

"But we haven't been tried yet," cried Allys.

"Hush, you strumpet," said the king. "We do everything

carefully in order in the Ancient and Honorable Realm of Spades. Jury, what say you?"

Prince Charming stood and announced, "We have a verdict, your majesties. By a unanimous vote we find the defendants guilty of the crime of being odd."

"How is being odd a crime?" Aylwyn shouted.

"Perhaps we should have considered an additional count of being ignorant," said Prince, "But we are not bloodthirsty people."

"For your information, young whippersnapper," said the king, "odd means not native to the Realm of Spades and having the unmitigated gall to cross our stately border. And now to the jury, do you have a recommendation as to punishment?"

"We have, your majesties. We recommend exposure."

Queen Steeper said, "We think that is a punishment too laxly imposed."

"Since you appear to have strange definitions of what words mean," Allys said, "what exactly is exposure in Spades?"

King Burpeedo answered the question. "It means exposing you to a deadly disease. If you contract the disease and die, it means you were innocent enough to be susceptible. Although not being native-born Spades, you are innately guilty of impurity, so there is no damage to the realm if you do die. However, if you resist the disease, it proves you are magicians and must therefore be put to death."

"And how could that be considered too lax?" Aylwyn asked sarcastically.

Queen Steeper fielded this one. "No one suffers inherently in exposure. If you get the disease you'll die within days. If you don't, you'll be executed because you've been exposed to it and might infect someone else. It's all over within a fortnight. Not long enough for an enjoyable period of suffering. Certainly not long enough for a life of remorse. It's all done very humanely, as you can see."

"Guard, take their silly clothes and accordingly issue them prison garb while we consider what punishment to inflict," said the king.

The four were ordered to undress and when they were naked, a bailiff took their clothes away. For a time they stood before the court in the buff, until the bailiff returned and issued lacy pink panties and peignoirs to Aylwyn and Hansel and olive drab boxers and hunting vests to Allys and Gretel.

"You may be wondering why these particular items of prisoner apparel," said the king. "I greatly enjoy telling the story behind this. You see, I did graduate study on the nature of criminals. I discovered that there is a criminal class in which men suffer from an excess of maleness and women suffer an excess of femininity. Thus, to be reformed, prisoners need to integrate their animus/anima yin/yang manly/womanly elements. My brilliant solution is to dress prisoners in the clothing of the other sex. If given enough time in incarceration, this method inevitably leads to reform of hardened criminals."

"Your majesties," said Allys, "these finely made clothes must represent a great deal of money to the realm, and the price of feeding your prisoners must also weigh dearly on your treasury. We would gladly accept banishment to the wilds of the Timberscape and save you the costly upkeep of our unworthy selves."

"Yes, gladly," added Hansel.

"Hmmm," said Queen Steeper. "I am certainly amazed at this performance. These criminals may be on the path to reformation already. My dear, did you hear what the girl so cunningly said? And the boy repeated a word of it."

"Indubitably, my sweet," King Burpeedo said excitedly.

"Yes," said Aylwyn. "We wouldn't want to cause you any undue expense on our account."

"Perhaps," said the king, "we could suitably expose them and let them madly run into the river. Then we could learn if the legend is true that inside the bounds of the Scape the Gymnarykum River has healing properties."

"Yes dear one," said Steeper, "but then we would have to quickly send in a squad of deputies to capture them to see if they live or die. That place is unmistakably dangerous, and even brave deputies fear to go into the Scape. They may be torn to pieces by savage beasts. If they reach the Scape we would probably never capture them again."

"I kindly take your point," said Burpeedo. "And now that I think on it, this other boy has spoken illy and not well."

"Yet two did," offered the queen. "I think a lenient sentence would be orderly."

"Very well, darling," said Burpeedo. "Instead of the typically imposed life sentence for your heinous crimes, you are happily sentenced to indefinite incarceration."

Gretel asked, "What did Aylwyn say so badly and Allys and Hansel say well?"

"Three of them are very likely on the path to reformation," noted the queen. Then she addressed the four. "You must understand that King Burpccdo, brilliantly trained scholar that he is, has discovered the underlying symbology in the seemingly common adverb. Words that end in LY proclaim the union of male and female principles."

"Yes, yes," said Burpeedo beaming at his cleverness. "You see, the L is a symbol of the male phallus, and the Y is a symbol of the female delta. It is the erotic genius of our Spade language to grandly proclaim the unity of male and female in everyday speech. Unwittingly, three of you used LY words in your speech. I encourage you to use as many adverbs as you can think of, because this will surely speed your reformation and shorten your prison terms."

"Regally spoken and brilliantly conceived, your majesty," said Aylwyn. "How quickly may we expect this reformation to occur?"

"Now there's a sign of real progress," the king said to the queen. Addressing the four, the king proclaimed, "I am pleased to inform you that your transformation from odd criminals to normality may rapidly occur in under ten years, if you are lucky and apply yourselves diligently."

They were taken to a communal cell where two people were already held. In the process of introductions, the quartet learned that the prisoners they were now living with were Tovah and Ollam, who, it turned out, had connections with people the four had met in the Timberscape. Tovah was the lover and partner of Cranna the woodswoman, and Ollam enjoyed the same relationship with Foxford the ferryman.

The next morning, the four were put to work mixing and kneading gingerbread and pig iron dough for repairing prison walls, the same detail Tovah and Ollam were assigned to.

Ollam asked the four about their sham trial, and in the course of the conversation he said, "Among the prisoners, Queen Steeper is called the wicked witch of the Southwest. Burpeedo is the drag king."

"That's comforting to know," said Allys. "They were going to shoot us up with some deadly disease. It was only because we accidentally used adverbs that we got off with indefinite incarceration."

"At least you weren't sent to the pig iron mines," said Tovah. "That's something to be thankful for."

"The pig iron mines?" Gretel asked.

"That's where they assign the hard core criminals," explained Ollam. "The prisoners spend all day crawling through dirt with magnets extracting little specks of iron. It's really hard and grimy work."

"As you can imagine, pig iron mining is rough on lacy garments, so they make the prisoners work nude," Tovah added.

"I don't understand this thing about men in women's lace and women in men's boxers," Aylwyn said. "If you want men and women to become more like each other, rather than accentuate the differences, it would seem better to put everyone in unisex clothing, that way they could see how much they are alike. None of this makes sense."

"Well, now you've hit on the key point of life in Spades," said Ollam. "Anything that makes sense is automatically rejected as subversive."

Prisoners were fed breakfast and supper only. The food was bland, barely nourishing, and not enough, so everyone lost weight. On Saturdays, they were not fed at all but only given water. Aylwyn said philosophically, "Once you've learned to go about without clothing and live off berries and nuts in the wild, you become truly confident about survival. You know you can suffer and survive. You know you can take risks and come through. We will not be in prison forever."

A weekly routine was soon apparent. Each Saturday, all the prisoners were herded into a dark, metal room for a communal shower. Water sprayed from showerheads in the ceiling, while the guards, male and female, watched and laughed. Inmates were handed new underwear after the shower.

Each Sunday morning, all prisoners were taken from their cells to attend church in the prison chapel, a large tent called the Black Pavilion. Following the service they were herded to the mess hall for a meal that would break their Saturday fast.

The officiating clergyperson was a tall, severe-looking man named Tookie-Maledict. Rather than religious garb, however, he was attired in military fatigues and combat boots. His waist was girded with a web belt from which a bayonet hung on one side and a pair of handcuffs on the other.

Because there were new convicts in need of indoctrination, at the end of the first church service that the four attended, Tookie-Maledict explained, "In all the universe, there is one truly holy book, which is the Spade Bible. Other realms claim to have holy scriptures, but they are deluded. All they really have are compilations of superstitions.

"Wisely, the sacred pages of the Spade Bible lay out a harsh regimen for daily living. Pleasure is a thing to be postponed until the next life. If we behave properly in this world, however, we will have infinite pleasure in heaven. In heaven, each man will have his choice of seven virginal lovely wives and each woman will have seven obedient handsome husbands."

Unable to constrain herself, Allys blurted out, "But that's mathematically impossible! Unless, that is, there's a lot of overlap, with people married to multiple other people at the same time."

Tookie-Maledict glared at Allys and thundered, "It is not impossible! How impertinent! It is simply a matter of God's arithmetic. None of a man's seven wives will be married to anyone else but that man and none of a woman's seven husbands will be married to anyone else but that woman."

Following the lead of Allys, Gretel said, "That means that a majority of men, no matter how well-behaved they have been, will not have the choice of seven wives but will themselves be one of seven husbands and vice versa for most women."

Tookie-Maledict went red in the face and growled, "Only Spades go to heaven. No other suits will be saved. The extra spouses will come from the other suits and free souls and jokers."

Now it was Hansel's turn to speak. "If only Spades go to heaven, then the other suits, who by definition cannot go to heaven, but who nonetheless serve as wives and husbands, will not be available for the pleasure of the dead Spades. Either that or suits other than Spades will go to heaven."

"Or dead Spades will have to leave heaven to visit their spouses," Aylwyn added.

"Rubbish and nonsense!" Tookie-Maledict said. "The omniscient and omnipotent God will make it work by magic. You vermin do know about magic, I presume, since you have magically appeared in this realm."

"How can God possibly be both all knowing and all powerful?" Aylwyn asked.

"Because he is!" Tookie-Maledict shouted.

"But those things are mutually exclusive," Aylwyn averred. "An omniscient God would know everything that will happen in the future. If God knows what will happen, then God is not able to change any of what God has already decided will come to pass, and is therefore not omnipotent. An all powerful God would be free to change anything that is yet to happen, but thus cannot be omniscient, because God cannot know in advance what God may decide to change later on."

"Yeah, Reverend, explain that away, if you can," Allys said.

"Here's my explanation, you gaggle of oddities. Your impertinence will cost all of you an indefinite extension of your indefinite prison terms," a red-faced Tookie-Maledict declared through clenched teeth. "Nevertheless, the good news is that in Spades, you have the freedom to be both impertinent and odd. This is a liberty-loving land. Of course, one must pay the consequences of one's actions. Freedom is not free."

Ollam laughed and said, "It is a distinct honor, O Most

Reverend Tookie-Maledict, to be impertinent in the presence of such an unprepossessing personage as yourself. An indefinite extension of something that is already indefinite is an achievement many have sought but few have attained."

Allys added, "If we're not going to heaven anyway, because we're not Spades, why should we obey your stupid rules? What's in it for us?"

"Because," Tookie-Maledict said with a broad grin on his otherwise brooding face, "Spades are in charge, and it gives us immense pleasure to force you to do what we want."

"But according to your own rules, you're not supposed to have pleasure," said Aylwyn.

"Our God grants us this kind of joy because he loves us," the cleric replied.

"Hypocrisy is the most cowardly form of evil, and among the lowest for all that," said Tovah.

"Is there a name for people who think that liberty means the freedom to impose their religious views on everybody else?" asked Allys.

"Indeed," said Tookie-Maledict. "Spades, the master race."

Returning from a detail to deliver gingerbread and pig iron panels to a repair crew, Allys saw a bailiff carrying a skirt and blouse into a large storage room near the mess hall. She paused long enough to see the bailiff hurry out of the room with boxer shorts and hunting vest. When the court official was out of sight, she ducked into the room and discovered that this was the repository for the prisoners' personal clothes as well as a supply facility for standard prison garb. She slipped out just before the bailiff returned to lock the room.

Months passed with the unwavering routine of work, showers, fasting, and church. At night in their common cell, Ollam, Tovah, and the four teenagers plotted and planned for an escape, but no suitable opportunity arose. They knew, however, that security tended to be lax in the interval between the Sunday church service and lunch.

On a Sunday close to the anniversary of their capture, the four along with Ollam and Tovah dawdled in the sanctuary after worship to test the security system. Tookie-Maledict had left immediately, and the guards were so busy talking to one another that they did not notice six prisoners were not in the line to be escorted to the mess hall.

When no one could be seen in the long hallway, the six made their way along the corridor. If spotted, they would tell the truth, that they had lingered in the sanctuary. Untruthfully, they would add that they had been engaged in earnest prayer. Beyond that, they had no plan, but as they strode down the hallway, they passed the door of the clothing storage room.

Allys whispered, "Look, the lock is open." She peeked inside and saw no one there and motioned for the others to follow. As quietly as they could, they opened and closed many drawers until they found the garments belonging to all six of them.

"Should we take these back to our cell?" Hansel whispered.

"I think this is a sign," said Tovah. "I think we should run for it."

"We won't get a better chance for a long time," Ollam said.

Holding their clothes, they tiptoed out of the building and ran through a conveniently open delivery gate.

"See, this is another sign," Tovah said.

Once out of the jail yard, they sprinted into the nearby woods and kept going. After ten minutes, they heard the barking of bloodhounds and knew that their absence had been discovered.

"Take off your prison things and hang them high in trees," Aylwyn said. "The hounds will go right for that stuff."

This they did, and a few minutes later the hounds circled and barked at the empty garments while the guards tried to catch up. This gave the escapees time to run into a creek and wade in rapid steps along its shallow side far downstream from the posse and dogs.

Eventually, they came out of the water on the opposite side of the creek from the search party, but they were disoriented and did not know which way led to the Timberscape.

"I suspect the creek runs into the Gymnarykum, but that's only a guess," said Ollam. "And if it does, that won't help us. To get back to the Scape we'll need to go overland, because the Gymnarykum at Spades City leads only north to Hearts and South to Diamonds."

"Look," said Allys, "there are three paths over there, all perpendicular to the creek. My sense is they lead inland."

"Which one leads us to safety?" asked Hansel. "Right, center, or left?"

"My intuition says left," Aylwyn said.

Without taking time to weigh the matter, they started out on the leftmost trail. Once completely hidden by trees, they stopped to don their old clothes, because wearing them left their hands free.

Soon they heard thrashing in a cluster of bushes ahead of them. They froze, expecting to see guards emerge to capture them, but instead, the noise came from a jackrabbit mumbling about the humiliation of having his American Express Card rejected at a fine establishment. The long-eared creature set off in a different direction, and Tovah said, "Yet another sign."

The six followed the jackrabbit along a secondary path that led into an area of rolling hills, which providentially provided them cover against being seen by a search party. There they decided to rest and watch the arc of the sun to orient themselves.

After discerning which way was east, they set out hiking in that direction. In two hours they had made it through the hills and came to a broad, arid plain.

"I remember this," said Ollam. "There's no place to hide between here and the Scape. But we have no choice. We have to cross these open miles."

"That will be dangerous," said Gretel. "We will certainly be seen by a search party. Is there no other way?"

Still hidden in a field of boulders, they scoured the countryside and spotted several hovercraft carrying deputies soaring over the plain looking for the escapees.

"It looks like we'll have to do it at night," Aylwyn said.

"Darkness is disorienting. There is the danger of wandering in circles at night," Gretel said.

"Or getting totally lost in a dark cave," Allys quipped.

"Or a forest," added Hansel ruefully.

"We could wander in circles even in the daylight," offered Tovah. "There don't seem to be any landmarks to guide us, and at night we won't have the sun for orientation. But what choice do we have?"

"In any case, we will not get far without water," said Hansel.

They spent the rest of the daylight looking for a source of water. Toward dusk they found a well enclosed in a barbed wire fence. Using rocks, they pulled the wire apart enough to climb inside. A water bucket was perched on the stone ledge of the well, and they lowered it on its rope until they heard a splash. Raising the wooden vessel, they drank their fills.

"Imagine you are a camel," said Allys, "and drink more than you need for now. We may not get another chance at water until we get to the Timberscape."

"Yeah, but it's certain we'll need to pee long before that," said Aylwyn.

"That's a plus," said Allys with a laugh. "We can mark our territory as we go along."

As night fell, they drank and drank, and when their stomachs were fuller than they had ever been, they forced down additional mouthfuls. Then they left the protection of the hills and trekked across the barely visible plain. They took note of the location of the quarter moon to orient themselves to the east, knowing that the moon would move across the sky as they walked across the expanse of dried grass.

They proceeded at a steady pace, pausing periodically to relieve their bladders, until the early light of dawn teased their eyes. Now they were heading straight into the sunrise, which made it difficult to look straight ahead but nevertheless encouraged them. No sign of the Timberscape was evident, and they were surrounded by flat land, but the direction of their movement was due east. At least they had not been going in a circle.

This was all to the good. Yet they were still on the plain in clear daylight, and now airborne scouts could see them easily. Their walking pace increased and no one had any desire to stop for urination. About two miles from the border, they first spotted trees in the distance. An unvoiced shout of hooray rose from the fleeing group. The plain was Spades territory but the trees were within the Timberscape. They knew they were close but were still dangerously exposed.

"Oh crap!" Aylwyn said. "We're going to have to get over a spiked concrete wall at the border, unless there's a gate in sight."

"Even if there is a gate, it may be locked," added Allys. "We can't count on a rusted lock this time. Getting past the wall may be the most treacherous part of our escape."

"We'll just have to deal with it when we get there. We have no other choice," said Tovah.

"We have to get there first," said Ollam. "Let's keep moving!"

Their pace quickened even more, but when they had covered half the distance to the trees, a squad of hovercraft approached from the west.

"They're far enough away, we could get there before they catch us. Let's make a run for it," said Aylwyn.

Instinctively, the Arizona twins stood up to run. Both ran cross-country track at school and knew they could cover the required distance at a healthy speed. But none of the others was a practiced runner. And they would need to stay together so that no one could be separated from the group and picked off by the deputies.

Ollam motioned them down and whispered, "Stop. Our movement will attract their attention. They are like animals looking for prey. They are attracted to movement and can travel five miles faster than we can go one."

For a moment no one spoke. Then Allys said, "This may sound stupid, but if we take off our clothes, our skin will blend in with the colors of the yellowed grass and tan earth."

"It's not stupid; it's brilliant," said Ollam.

With no further discussion, they disrobed and spread out, perching prone upon wide clumps of wheat-toned grass with their clothes hidden beneath their bodies. There they remained as still as possible. A few minutes later, a pair of hovercraft floated directly over them and Allys, whose idea this had been, suddenly felt perilously exposed and foolish. They are sure to see us sprawled out in plain sight, she thought.

Aylwyn's thoughts were not on the overhead danger. Rather, he was acutely aware that his bladder felt ready to burst, and he was tempted to relieve himself as he lay there. There would be no need to move to do this. But the act would soak his clothes. For some reason, not wetting his clothes seemed important enough to him that he held on a bit longer.

At that particular moment, the spotters in the search planes were not looking downward where the naked escapees lay but were scanning the scattered rocks and trees along the border where they assumed the escapees would hide. Seeing nothing and detecting no movement in the area, the airships moved on, turning north to search a different part of the border region.

Then a jackrabbit appeared out of a hole in the ground and without a word bounded due east toward the Timberscape. The six quickly rose from their places, grabbed their clothes, and loped after the rodent, who was heading toward an open gate.

As he ran, Aylwyn lost control of his bladder and let loose a strong stream of urine that sprayed right and left in alternating rhythm with his steps. A generous amount of the yellow liquid splashed against his legs.

All of them reached the Timberscape in minutes, panting and gasping at the stitches in their sides -but free.

Gretel noticed Aylwyn's legs. "That is more than sweat on your thighs and knees, Aylwyn."

"Yeah, well I decided to combine fleeing and peeing," he replied. "But I was going so fast that I ran into my own stream."

"You were marking out your territory on the Spades plain," Allys said.

"No," Aylwyn responded. "It was more a matter of acting out a gesture about what I thought of Spades."

"Piss on the whole realm," said Tovah. "I think that's a great idea. Anyone care to join me?" She tossed her bundle of clothing aside, turned and strode out of the forest back onto the plain. A hovercraft was gliding toward the spot where the group had escaped through the gate, but Tovah did not flinch from its approach. She stood with hands on her head and her legs apart, laughing as she too urinated on Spades territory.

Ollam, Gretel, Hansel, and Allys quickly formed a line at intervals beside Tovah and also made liquid gestures of contempt while maintaining eye contact with the infuriated searchers staring out the windows of the descending aircraft. Aylwyn had nothing left to add, so he turned and bent over and mooned the deputies.

As the hovercraft landing gear touched ground, the gesturing sextet sprinted back into the Timberscape, laughing all the way. They could hear frustrated curses from the posse of would be apprehenders. One particularly loud voice shouted, "How dare they desecrate the pure soil of the Realm of Spades!"

"Do you think they might run in after us?" Gretel asked Tovah. "We are not that far from them, and we have no weapons."

"They won't set foot even an inch inside the Scape," Tovah answered. "The Scape would play creepy games with their minds, like force them to do self-inventories. That scares them more than the threat of violent resistance."

Once satisfied of their safety, Tovah and Ollam decided to strike out on their own in search of their lovers. They hugged the four and expressed gratitude and eternal friendship.

"I am quite certain we will meet again," Tovah said.

"Me too," said Ollam.

The four then continued eastward toward the center of the island.

"Well, so far we haven't seen Coyote," Aylwyn remarked.

"Let's hope we don't and that instead we find an exit to return home," said Allys.

Eventually they came to the river, and as they were all sweaty, grimy, and in the case of Aylwyn peed-upon, dove in to bathe. They threw their clothes in also to wash them.

"I believe this river does have healing properties," said Allys. "I feel like it's washing away the fear and stench of Spades."

"I feel rejuvenated," said Hansel. "Good enough perhaps to make the Scape my home forever."

"Do not say that," Gretel replied. "This place is very pleasant and attractive and it would be too easy to fall prey to its charms and linger for decades, but we must return home to our parents."

Ruefully, Allys said, "I just remembered Pieter and Wendlich. We didn't find out anything that will help them."

"We were so wrapped up in own troubles that we didn't even ask anyone about how to lift enchantments. I'll bet one of the other prisoners knew, but none of us thought to ask," Aylwyn said.

"We shall have to make inquiries here in the Scape," said Hansel. "We will ask the next person or animal we meet." This made them feel less guilty.

While they were drying their clothes on rocks and lolling in the gentle sun, Buzzard circled down to them and Allys asked about Coyote. "We've been expecting that rascal."

"Coyote is up north near the border with Hearts," Buzzard said.

"Well, we don't **really** want to see him," said Aylwyn. "Whenever he tells us where to go it always leads to trouble."

Buzzard replied, "As **she** promised, **she** won't do that anymore. But I will. You need to visit Hearts, for there you will learn the lore of the Spring of Memory."

"We want to go home," Allys said. "We've spent three years on this island."

"Yes, I know, but the way out is through Hearts," Buzzard said.

With exasperation in her voice, Gretel said, "Why did not someone tell us this before? We could have gone directly to Hearts in the beginning and long since now we would have been home."

"To the contrary," Buzzard said. "You would not have known what you now know if you had gone directly to

Hearts. You would still be in Hearts today if you had gone there prematurely."

"Oh why must everyone here be so cryptic and uncooperative?" Allys moaned.

"I don't know what you mean," Buzzard said.

"Jackrabbits can be very useful but they won't stop to talk to us," Allys replied.

"And coyotes keep us going in circles," Aylwyn added.

"Answers to our questions are vague and confusing," Hansel said.

"In my experience, coyotes and jackrabbits are downright direct and plain spoken," said Buzzard, "especially as compared with roadrunners. Now if you want cryptic and uncooperative, try engaging with a roadrunner."

"But we don't want those things," Allys said. "And we haven't met any roadrunners."

"Roadrunners don't eat language berries," Buzzard continued in erudite fashion, "so they can't speak to humans. All they do is cluck, crow, coo, and bark. One simply can't do anything with them at all...except coyotes. Coyotes and roadrunners have a symbiotic relationship, protecting one another."

"No beep beep, huh?" said Aylwyn. "I guess the Road Runner and Coyote cartoons must be Looney Tunes." He laughed at his joke but no one else did.

"Now who's being cryptic and confusing?" Buzzard said. "Beep beep, indeed! What nonsense!"

"Say, Buzzard, do you know how to lift enchantments?" Hansel asked. "Our friends Pieter and Wendlich would also like to go home, to a village near to mine."

"Only humans can undo the spells made by other humans," said Buzzard. "But you may learn something about that in the Realm of Hearts."

With heavy sighs they trudged north toward Hearts, with their now dry clothing wrapped in a bundle that they took turns carrying.

CHAPTER 22:
MAGNUS

Such Guilt – to love Thee – most!
Doom it beyond the Rest –
                                    Emily Dickinson

"**Divorce**, I think, is most painful the day after it becomes final," Chaucer said to Cloud on a chilly early spring day in 1984.

"You may be onto something," Cloud responded.

"As much as Ving and I were emotional ships passing in the night," she continued, "it was nice having someone around the house. This legal document represents a kind of death."

"Aptly expressed," said Cloud.

"But I'm not mourning Ving so much as the loss of being married," she said. "I desperately want to be in a relationship, to be snugly settled into a household with a brilliant, kind man. I'm smart enough, though, to know that my very neediness argues against developing another relationship any time soon. My judgment about men is impaired, and I was in denial about Ving for so long, that a period of hibernation is in order."

"Very wise," said Cloud.

"Intellectually, I know this about myself, but I also know that I am crazy with desire to have an attractive, erudite man in my life."

"A little intellectual horniness is quite normal," Cloud said.

"The thing is, that very desire scares me, because it makes me vulnerable to the entreaties of the first attractive, literate, straight male who notices me," she said. "And with my luck, he's likely to be a narcissistic control freak."

"You're smarter than that now," Cloud said.

"I've fantasized about you," Chaucer confessed.

"I'm flattered," Cloud said.

"But you don't have to worry about that," she said. "Upon reflection, it would never work, because you are married to the perfect mate for you, and also because of your intuition and insight. I would never have any private thoughts around you."

Now Cloud laughed. "Would you mind if I told Terp that bit about private thoughts. She would find it deliciously astute and ironic."

"Go ahead," said Chaucer. "And thanks for your listening ear. I feel so much better," Chaucer said as she rose to depart his office for her own.

In the months that followed, Chaucer retreated into a shell, and in time came to appreciate the healing qualities of solitude.

However, her intentional foray into celibacy was tested that spring. Teller Zurich, a student in her class on American Transcendental writers, developed a crush on her. After class one day, utilizing his winsome smile and aw shucks persona, Teller invited his professor to play Thoreau with him in a family cabin near Strawberry.

Though feeling vulnerable and needy, Chaucer had the presence of mind to rebuff him sternly. "Come back when you have a PhD, Teller." Nevertheless, that evening she fantasized about what it would be like to make love to a randy, lovesick college student.

The following week, he gave it another try, tempting her with a hot tub where they could relax. This time Chaucer chuckled while firmly turning him down. He interpreted the laughter as her being interested and thus tried yet again the next time the class met. At that point, she put on a stern façade and leveled with him, saying, "My career would be ruined if I breached professional ethics by getting involved with a student. It's never going to happen, Teller. Please stop badgering me. And if you persist, you will find it increasingly difficult to register for the independent studies you want."

Teller's face fell into a pained frown. With sudden recognition that he had been harassing a professor, a wave of remorse washed over him.

Chaucer noticed the change in his expression and in compassion loosened the rigor of her physiognomy. "As I said, nothing will ever develop between us, but I can't tell you not to fantasize about it."

Teller's face brightened again. "You're way too late on that score," he said with a wide grin.

Early in the fall semester, Magnus Bergen summoned Chaucer to his office. The college president often invited faculty members to meet with him this way, particularly those with personal problems. As Chaucer entered his suite, the sociology professor, whose daughter had recently been diagnosed with leukemia, was leaving the president's private study.

"I appreciate your concern," the sociologist said. "It's very kind of you to care."

"I really mean it," said Magnus with a catch in his voice and a gentle pat on the professor's shoulder. The compassion was real. What he had gone through with his own child saturated his mind, and his usual emotional equilibrium was reeling.

Chaucer took a chair across from the president's secretary to wait, but without returning to his office, Magnus strode over to her and a little too cheerfully said, "Right on time, Chaucer. Please come in." Once she was comfortably seated on the sofa across from his desk, he said, "I worry about faculty members who have difficult burdens to carry. I wish I could magically make all their problems and pain go away. How are you doing, Chaucer? I can't do magic, but I'd like to be a dear friend if that would help. All you have to do is say the word."

Chaucer looked across at Magnus and a surge of affection for the earnest administrator rushed through her mind. With a voice laden with vulnerability she said, "Thanks, Magnus. I could really use a friend right now."

Chaucer stood, as did Magnus a second later. He stepped around his desk, and without premeditation, they were in one another's arms, kissing passionately. It seemed so natural and right to her, as if she had been yearning for this man for a long time, but she knew that she was acting spontaneously.

When at last they stopped kissing and let their arms fall to their sides, neither spoke for a quarter of a minute. Then Magnus said, "We'd better sit and talk about this."

As he joined her on the sofa, Chaucer experienced a sense that Riff was with her, encouraging her to talk. Consequently, she opened up and allowed emotionally painful words to flow from her mouth, holding nothing back. She had never been so honest and revealing, not even in her counseling sessions with Cloud. However, she said nothing to Magnus about the presence of Riff.

When it was his turn to speak openly, he said, "Usually I am quite reticent about my personal life, but it feels like a guardian angel is encouraging me to let it all hang loose."

This caused Chaucer to break out in goose bumps.

"A minor chord of dissatisfaction has been humming through my life for years," he continued. "Most of the time I don't even hear it, but the unhappiness it represents is always with me. But when you said you could really use a friend, the timbre of your voice overrode the sad song in my mind. Out of the blue, I felt an overwhelming desire for you that I did not know was in me."

Before leaving, Chaucer kissed Magnus once more and said, "When can we meet again?"

"I'll call you this evening to arrange something," he said. "Will that be alright?"

"Yes, I'll stay off the phone awaiting your call."

It was well into the lunch hour when she departed, so the outer office was empty. Magnus was grateful that his secretary was not present to observe his face at that moment.

Magnus was the first married man Chaucer had ever been involved with, and that night as she waited for him to sneak in a call, she felt guilty about it. She knew firsthand what it was like to be cheated on and experienced great compassion for Janett. From her years in

Pittsburgh, she also knew how common adultery was among academics and clergy. To assuage her conscience, she told herself that Magnus initiated the kissing when he knew she was vulnerable. On further reflection, however, she admitted to herself that she wanted him to hold her and kiss her and perhaps she had conveyed that message to him non-verbally. She rationalized the situation as a relief from the pain of having been cheated on. "Everybody does it," she said aloud to the room. "I guess I'm no better than anybody else. That is, if I take this any further. It's not too late to stop it before anyone gets hurt."

Just then the phone rang, and she knew before she answered that she would not stop. She wanted Magnus like she had never wanted any man before.

Early in the affair, Magnus found a way to see Chaucer in public and interact with her in the normal academic way of the campus. He sat in on her class in Code-switching and macaronic language. When the dozen surprised students saw the college president at a desk, he told them he had decided to sit in on classes periodically to get a sense of the professors' teaching styles and learn new things into the bargain. He was also interested in the phenomena of language. It was not to evaluate Chaucer but only to get to know her better. Chaucer blushed at this last remark, but the students were looking at Magnus and did not notice.

"Code-switching," Chaucer explained, "refers to two or more people fluent in two languages using elements of both in their verbal exchanges. It may also refer to mixed languages, such as Spanglish. Macaronic language relates to texts that contain a mixture of languages, including bi-lingual puns."

"Does macaronic language extend to single words that use roots from two different languages?" Magnus asked.

"Those are called hybrid words," she said. "Were you thinking of any particular examples?"

"Well," he said, "bigamy comes from the Latin *bis*, meaning twice and the Greek *gamos*, meaning wedlock."

"Yes," she said. "And homosexual is made up of the Greek *'omos*, meaning same and the Latin *sexus*, meaning gender."

At the end of the class, he commented out loud that the lecture was so interesting he might have to come back for more.

Chaucer frowned. She had enjoyed him observing her teaching techniques and his excellent questions, but she realized it would look suspicious if he continued to attend her lectures. Someone was bound to notice how his eyes lit up when she spoke, she thought.

Magnus noticed her facial expression and knew at once that he had made a foolish error. Afterward, he felt so guilty about his explanation that he was routinely sitting in on faculty classes that he visited one of Cloud's history lectures and a political science seminar done by Prasada Pratyaksha to add credibility to his assertion.

Then it was Chaucer's turn to risk seeing him in a public setting. Ducking into his office one day while his secretary was on her lunch hour, Chaucer brought Magnus a poem she had written soon after Ving left her. "It's called Repentance," she said, and read aloud:

Certain psychic wounds derived of loving
Never can be healed without surrendering
The dream that love produced.
And so I turn for balm to the aesthetics
Of my room, my sheltered cell, and tend
To the interior of my battered soul
And acquiesce to solitary sleep.

Magnus' eyes moistened, and he said, "I want to protect you from any more pain. If it weren't for the possibility of someone walking in on us, I would enfold you in my arms and rock you gently back and forth the whole afternoon."

"I've experienced catharsis simply from sharing this with you," she said. "It feels so liberating to reveal my depths to someone who understands."

"Ah, but I don't want you to acquiesce to sleeping alone," he whispered.

<><><>

Chaucer drove to the Village of Oak Creek and rented a motel room for the night. She told the clerk it was for her brother and his wife who were coming to visit, knowing that it was a lie and that Spenser was not even married. Since she used her own name and credit card, however, she felt some explanation was needed. Driving back to her office at the college with two room keys in her purse, she felt sleazy for the dishonesty but energized by the prospect of an evening with Magnus. Unfortunately, it would be an early night, because he had to get home before Janett became suspicious. Supposedly he would be having a few drinks with a potential new regent who was visiting a relative in the Village of Oak Creek.

He arrived, noticeably nervous, a few minutes after she did. Once in the room, he pulled her into an embrace and held her as he sought to calm down. When he loosened his hold, Chaucer began to sniff at his hair. Moving her nose to his neck, she inhaled his odor, and then moved to his armpit. His scent was appealing, exciting, she thought. Magnus was simultaneously bemused and perplexed, never having had a woman do that to him.

"I...I used deodorant," he said apologetically. "Has it worn off? I'm a bit uneasy about...about meeting like this. Maybe that's making me sweat too much."

"Hush," she chided. "It's not your deodorant that turns me on. It's your authentic smell. I wanted to know your true fragrance."

"Do I pass the smell test?" he asked.

She licked his neck, and he let out a surprised giggle.

"Oh yes, and the taste test too," she replied. "I'm not wearing any perfume, so you can examine me with your nose and tongue...if that holds any interest for you."

They quickly undressed to take their explorations to more advanced levels. Their lovemaking in that rented room was more satisfying than either had known for many years, although he was quiet during what were manifestly the most passionate moments of their coupling. Chaucer was thrilled to experience that intimate connection that had been missing in her relations with Ving.

Nestled into Magnus' side enjoying the afterglow of sex, Chaucer said, "I really don't know much about your earlier life. What did you do before you strayed into the minefield of college administration?"

"I taught a little," he said, "but mostly I've worked as an

administrator or executive in one venue or another."

She tickled his side playfully and said, "You're holding back. What did you teach? What is your PhD field?"

"Library science," he whispered. He waited for her to laugh or to express disbelief.

"Wow! Really?" she said with enthusiasm. "That's cool. I had no idea you are a librarian. They're my favorite kind of people."

Magnus grinned. He had never received such a response before.

"What's your dissertation about?" she continued.

"The title is ***Comparative Acquisition Conflict Paradigms Among Public, Private Secular, and Private Sectarian College and University Libraries***. I'm afraid it makes for rather dull reading."

"It sounds fascinating," Chaucer said with genuine interest. "The summer I worked in the library at the U of A, I did paperwork for acquisitions, and I picked up on some minor faculty squabbles about selection priorities. I suppose it's inevitable there would be conflict over buying books for college libraries. Is conflict normative? Tell me all about it."

"Well," he said, "nearly all libraries of academic institutions have to prioritize purchases. But the real battles occur over the specific titles to be acquired. When it comes to choice of books, sectarian schools tend to be hierarchically controlled. Librarians have less discretion in the selection process. Doctrinal considerations are involved. Some of these schools exclude books that conflict with their creeds. Or they include heretical works for purposes of deconstructing them and shelve them in separate evil books sections.

"But public and secular schools have their own conflicts over title acquisition. One of the reasons I switched from library administration to general college administration is that I noticed that the dynamics of buying books are not much different from the dynamics of hiring professors."

"This is a truly fascinating subject," Chaucer said.

Magnus laughed. "You're having me on."

"No, really," she said. "I have always loved libraries. I experience a pleasurably sensate response every time I go into a library."

"I do too," he said.

"You may think me strange," she continued, "but the idea of studying libraries seems...erotic. Imagining you not as a college president but as a librarian turns me on." She reach down and began to stroke his penis. "Would you like to do it again?"

Though it was the first time in his life that he had engaged in intercourse more than once in any given day, he quickly reached the necessary stiffness and entered into an extended round of lovemaking with Chaucer, in which she reached orgasm twice.

Before leaving the motel room, Magnus showered to wash away the scent of Chaucer and the fragrance of their sexual activities. They had not imbibed any alcoholic beverages during their tryst, but after kissing Chaucer goodbye, he pulled a mini bottle of scotch from his briefcase and gargled with it, being careful not to swallow any, and then spit it into the sink.

By the spring of 1985, Magnus Bergen's life was a mess, and in his hour of need, he turned for help to part-time professor Cloud Morgan. Magnus sat in the Kennedy rocker in Cloud's church office, rocking nervously. "I turned fifty a few months ago, Cloud, and received a major spiritual crisis for a birthday present. I need help dealing with it."

"Would you like to talk with our spiritual director? Tallis is excellent at helping intellectuals sort through such crises," Cloud said.

"Thank you, no," said Magnus. "I need to talk with someone I know well and trust completely, and you're the only one who qualifies on both counts. I recognize that you are very busy, but I'm prepared to impose on our friendship and place myself entirely at your mercy."

"Take as much time as you need, Magnus," Cloud said.

"To start with, I believe in God," Magnus said, "but I'm something of a Deist, not comfortable with dogmatic religion, especially moralistic religion. Now I'm having second thoughts."

"Toward atheism or a more personal God?" asked Cloud.

"Toward a God of judgment," said Magnus.

"I see," said Cloud. "And who is the person who has engendered this change?"

"Am I that transparent?" asked Magnus. "How did you know

I'm involved with someone? Have rumors been circulating around campus?"

"No rumors, Magnus. But a spiritual crisis at a change of decades in which guilt enters the picture usually points to an extramarital affair," Cloud responded. "Besides that, you've lost weight and look more trim. That's a definite giveaway."

"Can you guess who?" Bergen asked.

Cloud mentally scanned a roster of Anasazi faculty members. He considered several women whose marriages he knew to be troubled. There was Astrid Oslo, who held Norwegian ancestry in common with Magnus. Her finely chiseled Scandinavian features and accessible intellectualism could be rather alluring. Somehow he could not envision Astrid getting involved with Magnus. As he continued his survey, none seemed likely until he reached Chaucer Dickinson, whereupon his mental stylus stopped. Though Magnus was fifteen years older than Chaucer, Cloud saw immediately that the college president was exactly the kind of man she would fall for. And if she did, he had no doubt that Magnus would be equally dazzled by her brilliant mind and her long red hair and radiant blue eyes.

"Chaucer," Cloud said with quiet confidence.

Magnus blushed. "I love her more than I can bear. Janett found out yesterday. I foolishly left a love letter from Chaucer in a place where Janett could find it. Now she's threatening to go to the regents to get me fired unless I end the relationship immediately. She said she'll fight to keep me and doesn't care whether or not she fights fairly."

"Foolishness apart," Cloud said, "is it possible at some level you wanted Janett to find the letter?"

"Why would I want to bring this grief on all three of us?" Magnus asked.

"Why indeed?" Cloud countered. "How else did you plan to resolve the tension?"

"I suppose you're right, Cloud. Secretly I did want Janett to find out and I couldn't bring myself to tell her face-to-face. I suppose I knew at the time I stuck the letter in a coat pocket that Janett would be searching for items to send to the drycleaners," Magnus confessed.

"Would you like me to refer you and Janett to a marriage counselor?" Cloud asked. "I know several excellent ones."

"No," blurted Magnus. "At least not now. I'm not clear what I want to do or what I should do. I have no idea of right or wrong at this moment. I know that I love Janett and I love Chaucer and I pretty much despise myself."

"What about your position with the college?" asked Cloud.

"The regents could make things uncomfortable for me, and it would be incredibly embarrassing with the student body and faculty. But even if I were fired as president, I would remain as a tenured professor. Until adultery becomes a felony, my employment position is secure. And now that I think about it, the president of the regents is in his second marriage, which informally began before his first had ended. So…"

"So you can cross that matter off your worry list, and we can focus on complex love relationships and spiritual confusion," Cloud concluded. "Just start talking, Magnus, and I'll interject questions from time to time."

"About what?" Magnus asked.

"About the first thing that pops into your mind," said Cloud.

"Chaucer," said Magnus. "My mind is full of her. And thoughts of her spill over into every cell of my body. I am smitten. I am inebriated with love for her. She occupies my attention all the time. I can't get any work done because I dream about her when we're apart, and nothing else exists when we're together. Even when I think about other things, like the college, Janett, or even God, it is in relationship to Chaucer. My body aches in remembrance of her image and in recognition of her presence."

"And when was the last time you felt that way about a woman?" Cloud asked.

"Never until now," Magnus said. "Janett fell in love with me and I loved her in return. I still do, but I have never felt such obsessive passion for her as I do for Chaucer."

"Have there been any other extramarital relationships?" Cloud asked.

"Not really," said Bergen.

"Not really means maybe yes," noted Cloud.

"Well, there was a woman in my PhD program whom I fancied a lot. Janett and I had been married about a year. I saw this woman frequently at the library, and I fantasized about having a relationship with her, but I never said a word to her about my feelings, and nothing happened."

"But you remember her still. How often have you fantasized about her over the years?" Cloud asked.

"Truthfully? Thousands of times," Magnus confessed.

"What did she look like?"

"Medium height, dark complexion, black hair, brooding brown eyes. She was of Middle Eastern ancestry. Pretty much the opposite of my Scandinavian blondness," said Magnus.

"Nothing at all like Chaucer then," said Cloud. "At least physically. How would you compare her with Chaucer intellectually and in personality?"

"Both are brilliant intellectuals. Strong women with a touch of tragedy about them. That's what makes them vulnerable and approachable. I guess the melancholy nature is what hooked me with both women. One very quiet and the other outgoing."

"Chaucer must be the outgoing one. How did the affair with Chaucer begin?" asked Cloud.

"A few months after her husband left her, I invited her to my office to see how she was doing. This is something I've routinely done with faculty members of both sexes when they have gone through difficulties. I certainly had no intention of becoming emotionally involved with her. At any rate, she sat across the desk from me and I said, 'How are you doing, Chaucer? If I can be a friend to you let me know.' And she said, 'Thanks, Magnus. I could really use a friend right now.' I don't know what happened. There was something in the way she said it that took hold of me. I stepped around my desk, she stood and faced me, and the next thing I knew we were holding each other and kissing more passionately than Janett and I had ever done.

"It was as simple as that. Over the next few weeks we talked about our lives, inner and outer, at a level of intimacy that was new for me. The more we shared, the stronger the bond between us grew. Chaucer knows more about me than any other person on earth, and for some strange reason, she loves me anyway."

"Tell me about your love for Janett," said Cloud.

"She's the perfect first lady," Magnus replied. "A great hostess, elegant, literate, great behind-the-scenes advisor. She really watches out for me. Very protective. I don't think I would have become a college president without her. Janett's been a wife and the sister I never had all wrapped in one package. She's been very loyal to me, and I owe that same loyalty to her. Now I have failed her on that score. I'm really in her debt because of my infidelity."

"OK, I have an outline of your human relationships," said Cloud. "Now tell me about your love for God."

"I thought for certain you were going to ask me about sex," said Magnus.

"That would not be a particularly relevant subject at the moment, with the scent of Chaucer still clinging to your body and the memory of her embrace filling your mind."

"How did you...uh...never mind," said Magnus. While his eyes focused on Cloud, a deep memory replayed in his consciousness. He and Chaucer were making love. This was their second meeting at a motel, this time along I-40 near Bellemont. She had already reached orgasm and sensed that he was getting close to release but he had been prudently quiet, as he had been the first time they had intercourse.

"Oh, Magnus, come loudly," she breathed into his ear.

"I've been told it's unseemly to shout while coming," he whispered. "And we're in a motel. People in the next room might hear." His climactic trajectory waned slightly.

"They don't know who the hell you are," she said. "And it turns me on to hear a man respond with full lustful vocalization. It might even turn on the people in the next room. You'd be doing them a favor."

"Well, in that case..." He began to moan his pleasure with each stroke, and during ejaculation he produced a slightly modulated shout, "Yes, yes, oh yes, ooooh yes!"

This brought Chaucer to a second climax.

During the cuddling time afterward, Chaucer said, "It was Janett who told you making noise was unseemly, wasn't it?"

"Yes," he confessed.

"Well, you don't have to be seemly with me," she said.

"So I gather," he said. "By the way, was your pun on **Magna cum Laude** intentional? Magnus come loudly indeed!"

"Absolutely," she said. "There's nothing like a good pun to enhance the ecstasy."

"Enhanced ecstasy, huh? Maybe that's what Lewis Carroll was critiquing with his poem 'The Three Voices.' Do you know it?" He then recited from the poem's second voice:

"The Good and Great must ever shun
That reckless and abandoned one
Who stoops to perpetrate a pun."

"I think the second voice in that poem was a person not to the liking of dear and punful Lewis. He was making ironic fun of himself," Chaucer noted and then began to caress his face. "And it tickles me that you not only know that obscure work but that you have memorized a portion of it. Magnus, you magnify my soul."

Cloud recognized that part of Magnus' mind was elsewhere and paused a few seconds before speaking. "What I want to know," he said in a slightly raised voice, "is whether you love God enough to give up *both* Janett and Chaucer."

Magnus' attention was now on Cloud and the question stunned him. "Both?" he gasped.

"That's right," said Cloud. "Do you love God enough to become a monk and never see either of them again?"

"God no!" Magnus exclaimed. "I couldn't live without... without..." The college president began to weep. Soon his chest pulsed uncontrollably with sobbing.

Cloud remained silent, placing a hand on Magnus' shoulder.

As the tears slowed and the shuddering subsided, Magnus whispered, "God forgive me. I don't love you that much. To be honest, God, I'm not sure I love you at all."

"Good," said Cloud. "At least that much is clear. We've got a place to start. And for the record, Magnus, billions of people on this planet love God even less than you do, people whose deeds express contempt for God, so you'll have to get in a long line to wait your turn at condemnation. That's why grace is so much more efficient."

"Are you letting me off the hook that easily?" Magnus asked.

"Not at all," said Cloud. "You still have to come to terms with the pain you've created. You can't escape the earthly consequences of your actions. In addition to resolving your romantic triangle, you need to discover what you truly believe about God and all those eternal questions."

"What am I going to do?" Magnus moaned. "I need to get right with the elemental forces of the universe but I can't even summon the strength of mind to make a simple decision about the future of my marriage. I'm teetering in a state of irresolution."

"You want it simple then? Would you like me to take care of that for you?" Cloud asked, as if he were a mortician offering help to a bereaved client.

"Would you? Oh yes, Cloud. I'd be so relieved. Please, tell me what I need to do," Magnus pleaded.

"What I'm asking," said Cloud, "is whether you want me to make an irrevocable choice on your behalf. Janett or Chaucer...or neither. Whatever I decide will be your fate forever. Ready? Alright then, let it be quick and simple. I pronounce that from this moment onward and for the rest of your natural life you shall..."

"No! Wait!" Magnus shouted. "I may be confused, but I've got to take some responsibility for this mess. If I'm going to be miserable for the rest of my life, I want it to be because of my own foolishness and not because somebody else told me what to do."

"Very wise, but are you determined to be miserable?" Cloud asked.

"At this point," Magnus replied, "I can't imagine being happy staying with Janett if it means never seeing Chaucer again, and I yet I know that life with Chaucer without Janett would be filled with painful recriminations. And I'd miss Janett's bedtime comments on the galaxy we live in. I'm damned if I do and damned if I don't."

"Hmmm," said Cloud.

"I wish there were a way that they would agree to a ***ménage a trois***," Magnus whispered. He had fantasized about the three of them living together, with Janett and Chaucer having separate bedrooms that he alternated between.

"Even if they did," Cloud responded in matter-of-fact voice, "such arrangements are notoriously unstable and brief among highly educated people. You'll search the literature in vain for a truly successful one." He knew that Ving had proposed something similar to Chaucer and was sure she would find it objectionable if Magnus were to do so also. But he would not reveal this or anything else he had learned in a confidential counseling session.

At once Magnus realized that he would inevitably spend more time in Chaucer's room than in Janett's, and this would surely lead to severe conflict.

"Thanks for bringing me back to earth," Magnus said.

"You know, of course, that I would never make that kind of decision for you," said Cloud.

"I know," said Magnus. "You were helping me to clarify things. Thank you for not being judgmental."

"It would be premature to offer moralistic conclusions, Magnus, but if you were sleeping with a student, you would have experienced my judgmental side," said Cloud. "Now here's a homework assignment for you. I want you to spend at least half an hour a day for the next week in prayer or meditation, imagining what your life would be like with neither Janett nor Chaucer. How would events unfold for you in such a circumstance?"

"Alright," Magnus said without enthusiasm. "I'd also like to start attending church again. I haven't done so since high school. Is there a mainline church in the area you could recommend? You understand I'd come to your church if it weren't for the nudity."

"Our church is officially CO -clothing optional," said Cloud. "Many worshipers stay dressed."

"It's not that I'm a prude or anything," said Magnus, "but even if I stayed dressed, naked people would be all around mc, and if the parents of our students found out I was consorting with…"

"I should think you had more immediate concerns about what parents may find out," Cloud said testily. He paused and added, "Forgive me for being defensive at your expense. But you've touched upon a subject Terp, Malama, and I have been discussing for some time. A lot of people who would otherwise be interested in our church find nudity a stumbling block. Some of them, for medical or other good reasons, will never be comfortable being nude themselves or being around people who are. We've decided to experiment with a contemporary service where everyone is clothed, including the pastors."

"That would interest me," said Magnus.

"This will be a major departure from our traditional service," continued Cloud. "The pastors will wear preaching robes. We'll do the service in the chapel and block off access to the naturist areas of the facility. The liturgy and sermons will be the same as the traditional services, but we'll have a quartet instead of the whole choir, and there will be more solo anthems. We call it metaphorical naturism."

"OK," said Magnus. "What time is your metaphorical contemporary service?" The thought of going to church slightly alleviated his sense of guilt, as if this were a first step on a path of atonement, and he left Cloud's office with relief showing in his face.

Feeling a glow from her involvement with Magnus, but not able to be with him very much, Chaucer devoted time to a new chapter of *The Timberscape of Memory*. A detail from Cinderella teased her mind much as a related detail had done years before when she imagined Alice shrinking out of her dress when she drank a potion. She mentally pictured the coach transforming back into a pumpkin and deduced that Cinderella's gown would likewise disappear at the stroke of midnight. If she did not have her ragged dress on underneath, when the gown disappeared she would be naked. Oh, well, she thought, fairy tales are not meant to be logical. But now she had a hook for introducing Cinderella into the narrative. As she pondered the possibilities, a solution came to mind about how to add Cinderella and the handsome prince into her story.

The inaugural clothing required service attracted thirty people, among them Magnus Bergen, who came alone. While greeting people before the service, Cloud wore spit shined black dress shoes, charcoal gray slacks, a blue oxford cloth shirt and red silk tie. He then donned a black preaching robe before pronouncing the call to worship. Malama and Terp were not present, as the three co-pastors had decided to rotate leadership of this service in the interest of preserving personal energy.

Magnus wore a Navy blue suit, white shirt, and a maroon and blue power tie that first Sunday, while all of the other worshipers were dressed more casually. Jeans and tee shirts were common attire among male and female visitors, and a few younger women wore shorts and tank tops. No skirts or dresses were in evidence, although several women wore white slacks and long sleeved blouses with pastel prints. Apart from Magnus and Cloud only one other man wore a tie, a western string bola tie with a silver clasp in the shape of a jackalope, the mythical offspring of an antelope and a jackrabbit.

In a later conversation with Cloud, Magnus confessed that attendance in worship had helped him better understand the emotional context of his life and his need for spiritual guidance. He would return faithfully every Sunday, but never again wearing a suit. His church uniform evolved into khaki slacks and a polo shirt. His triangulated situation, however, was far from resolution.

CHAPTER 23:
IN THE REALM OF HEARTS

The king said, "If you are forsaken by all the world, yet I will not forsake you."
Jacob and Wilhelm Grimm

Flower gardens in long rows marked the boundary of the Realm of Hearts. Happy people were strolling through the gardens admiring the beauty of nature when Hansel, Gretel, Allys, and Aylwyn entered Hearts. Having become so used to going about naked, they forgot to dress before entering. Nevertheless, the pilgrims were welcomed as returning prodigals. Numerous citizens spontaneously removed their own shirts and blouses and offered them to the four.

"It's kind of you to offer, but we have clothing," said Allys. She pointed to the bundle that Hansel was carrying. "It simply escaped our minds to stop and put them on."

"Yes, yes, Scapers are like that," said a kindly old woman. "It's alright, my dears. We've seen stark naked rascals from the Scape dart in here to pick a snapdragon or chrysanthemum from one of our gardens and scamper right back again. Something must happen to your perception when you live in Old Mem. Imagine forgetting you are naked!"

Hansel distributed the now threadbare garments and they dressed while garden visitors watched. As they were donning their clothes, a rosy red convertible limousine noiselessly pulled up and the visitors were invited to go for a ride in the back seat.

"Sit up so people can see you," the driver instructed. "And if people wave, it's only polite to wave back. My name is Carlos."

The four introduced themselves in turn.

"Where are you all from?" Carlos asked.

Hansel and Gretel said Germany, while Allys and Aylwyn said Arizona.

"Arizona!" cried Carlos. "Me too. Morenci. My family has worked in the copper mines for generations."

"How did you get **here**?" Aylwyn asked. "Were you in the Superstition Mountains by any chance?"

"Superstitions?" Carlos said. "Nah, I was in the Central Highlands of Viet Nam and working out of the Plei Me Special Forces Camp. We'd found a cave, and being from a family of miners, I was always the one to check out tunnels and caves. But I had a funny feeling about this one. Bad vibes, real danger. It was like I could smell violent rage inside. But it was my job to go in, so I did. I was easing through the cave as quiet as possible and heard voices up ahead jabbering in Vietnamese and coming toward me fast. I thought about turning and running for the entrance, but didn't like the idea of getting shot in the back. Luckily, just then I found a side tunnel and stepped into it instead. A dozen or so meters further on I saw a light and headed that way. You can probably guess what happened next."

"You came out of the cave into the Timberscape," said Gretel. "And then it sealed up."

"Exactly!" Carlos said. "And my weapon and web belt with canteen and tools had disappeared. I had 'em when I was in that cave but they were gone when I stepped into the forest. It didn't take long to figure out I wasn't in Kontum Province any more. I wandered about for an hour or so, hoping I didn't need my weapon, until I met a talking Bobcat. She could tell from my uniform that I was a soldier, and she told me I needed to be in Hearts and I should take the north path to Hearts right away. And I did, after stopping at the river a while for rest and refreshment."

"Did anything odd happen to your clothes while you were in the Scape?" Hansel inquired.

"Funny you should ask about that," Carlos said. "When I found the river, I laid down to get a drink and then decided I needed a bath, so I jumped in clothes and all. In the water, my uniform turned pure white. Like all the color had been bleached out, but there wasn't any acid in the water. It was good to drink and my skin was OK. So I climbed out and took off my duds and hung them on bushes to dry. Then a big wind came up and blew them away. I never did find them, but the people of Hearts gave me new clothes when I got here."

"Do you ever think about going home to Morenci?" Allys asked.

"I like it here," Carlos replied. "People treat me with respect. Before I went to Nam, I was determined not to be a miner when I got back, even open pit. And since arriving here, I've decided that I'm never going inside another cave or tunnel for the rest of my life. Besides that, the Army's probably listed me as MIA, presumed dead."

Carlos drove the four to Heart Center to meet King Kenilworth and Queen Kensinga.

"It feels like being in a New Year's Day parade," said Aylwyn as they waved at the citizens of Hearts lined up along the road.

"This is certainly a much better reception than we received in any of the other realms," noted Gretel.

"What's the catch?" whispered Allys. "There has to be a catch. Maybe we're being softened up for a ghastly trap."

"On the other hand," reasoned, Hansel, "perhaps the people of Hearts really do have kind hearts."

"We'll know soon enough," said Aylwyn.

"Soon would be good," said Allys. "My arm is getting tired."

Shortly thereafter, they were politely ushered into the throne room of the rulers of the Realm of Hearts, King Kenilworth and Queen Kensinga, who received them as long lost family.

"Sojourners from the Timberscape of Memory are always welcome here," said the king heartily.

"If it pleases you, we shall have the Royal Tailor mend your garments," said the queen. "Or you may select new things from our textile treasury...or both. Both would be best, I think."

"That is very kind, your majesty," said Gretel.

At the close of the audience, they were taken to the apparel room, where they undressed and gave their clothes to a Royal Aide. They were then given purple robes to wear while they wandered through racks of new clothing from the Storehouse of the Realm, from which they were invited to take whatever they wanted. Hansel and Aylwyn selected khaki trousers and sky blue polo shirts. Gretel and Allys chose the same items but cut for female shapes. They all chose matching sandals for their feet.

"The people of Hearts do not wear undergarments," explained the aide, "so there are none here for you to choose from."

"Why not?" asked Aylwyn.

At that moment, Queen Kensinga entered the room. "I've just come to check up on how our guests are faring," she said.

"Splendidly, your majesty," said Allys. "But we were just inquiring about the absence of undergarments in Hearts. It also seems to be that way in the Timberscape."

"Ah, yes, but no outer garments as well, in the Scape, I am told," Kensinga said with a merry glint in her eyes. "As to our custom, we have heard many sordid tales about the rulers of Spades forcing people to wear humiliating undergarments, and the people in Clubs look upon such apparel merely as objects for seduction. The residents of Diamonds, meanwhile, spend exorbitant sums of money on lingerie just to be fashionable. Some go bankrupt, I am told. Considering all that, the Governing Council of Hearts decided we could do without them altogether to avoid those traps."

"But what if someone **wanted** to wear panties, or a teddy, or tidy whities, or whatever?" Allys asked. "Would they be punished for donning undies?"

"First, no true red-hearted Heart would **want** to do something so socially insensitive," the queen explained.

"Second, if anyone did have such a desire, the necessary items would have to be imported from elsewhere, since they are not made here. Imports are inordinately expensive. Refugees from other realms are free to wear whatever they bring with them, of course. But they all end up tossing their knickers into the rag bin soon enough."

"Well, we didn't bring any with us," said Aylwyn. "So that's not an issue."

"In answer to your second question, Allys," Queen Kensinga continued, "no one would be punished for wearing socially insensitive garments. Our standards are subject to the consciences of our citizens. Years ago we had a visitor from one of the alternative realms beyond Gymnarykum who insisted on wearing boxer shorts as an *outer* garment, and no one molested her for doing so, but many felt compassion for her."

Next, Gretel, Allys, Hansel, and Aylwyn were escorted to a comfortable room to be quizzed about their career goals and talents by Parzival, the Royal Guidance Counselor. As a result of this interview, all four were enrolled in the University of Hearts to study for whatever careers they set their hearts on.

A placid, clear blue lake bordered the university campus to the south. Signs posted along the shore proclaimed: ENJOY THE WATER. The campus buildings were rustic palaces, with comfortable wood-paneled classrooms and individual oak desks with padded seats for each student.

The newly enrolled Hansel, Gretel, Allys, and Aylwyn were housed in a dormitory suite, with the girls sharing a room on one side and the boys on the other. A kitchen and common area separated the suites. Their mended clothes were soon delivered and stowed for the duration.

After settling in, they gathered in the common room to debrief. "Carlos was sent to Hearts first thing," Allys said. "But we were shuffled through the other realms before being sent here. Why?"

"I have been wondering the same thing," said Hansel. "It does not seem fair. There must be a reason, but I have no idea what it could be."

Nor did Gretel and Aylwyn.

<><><>

The Omniform Reverend Spalpeen, who served as chaplain to the university, dropped by to visit them their second day on campus. From him they found out that the mascot of the University of Hearts was the Martyr.

They also learned that the people of Hearts believed all religions shared some piece of truth, however small, and that Hearts tolerated diversity, even when the diverse beliefs were inherently inhuman or dangerous. As a result, over the centuries many Hearts had become martyrs because they routinely turned their other cheeks to Spades. Their matron saint was Xenodocha, who was trod upon and executed by an early Spade queen, Usurpa. Hearts experienced great pride that Xenodocha would not give Usurpa the pleasure of criticizing or questioning her most outlandish doctrinal statements, some of which the queen made up just to shock Xenodocha and elicit a challenge.

"If we Hearts have a fault in our ethos," Spalpeen said, "it is that we tend to be overly optimistic. Our hearts have been broken many times by people from other realms who are less kind, generous, or gracious. No one in Gymnarykum is more romantic than any Heart you may meet anywhere in the realm."

"Have people from Hearts had love affairs with people of other realms?" asked Allys. "Broken hearts would seem to imply that."

"From time to time," said Spalpeen. "Usually this happens when a refugee from another realm comes here through the Scape. Typically, a Heart will care for the pitiable creature and fall in love with her or him, only to discover that our notion of what that means is not shared by everyone."

"In Zauberdorf, belonging to a church is determined by what you believe," said Hansel. "You have to assent to certain doctrines to be a member. May I presume that is the case with the Hearts church?"

"No, not with Hearts," replied Spalpeen. "Belonging in Clubs is dependent on behavior. In Diamonds it is how one dresses. In Spades, belonging is a matter of ancestry. But in Hearts, belonging is determined by love -by what or whom one loves. That you love and are in turn loved is the qualifier.

And since Hearts love nearly everyone, you four are already accepted -if you wish it. No one is ever forced to belong."

All four registered for the same university classes: Yoga, Magical Enchantments, History and Mythology of Gymnarykum, Boons and Blessings, Astral Projection, Self-Validation and Managing Relationships, plus a required language course called Subtle Irony, Intellectual Satire, and Paronomasia as Literature.

The yoga professors were a brother and sister named Jack and Jill, who had suffered serious injuries in a fall down a hill when they were young but were now fully recovered, due in large part to the healing qualities of yoga. Since the yogis were twins, they formed affectionate attachments to the two sibling dyads who were now their students.

When they lectured on the philosophy of yoga, Jack and Jill sat on mats in the lotus posture. When they spoke about the medical science of yoga, they did so while standing on their heads. Otherwise, they were busy demonstrating positions and assisting students to assume them as well as to breathe properly.

Professor Nudimmut taught the class on magical enchantments, including a variety of techniques for undoing spells and curses made by evil beings.

"You must be the learned doctor Pieter and Wendlich spoke about who knows the right words that could help them," said Aylwyn.

"I have never heard of Pieter and Wendlich," said Nudimmut. "Are they under an enchantment of some kind?"

"They are perpetual children living in the Timberscape," Gretel explained. "An evil warlock did that to them."

"Yes, we want to help them break the spell," said Aylwyn. "Would you be willing to travel to the Scape to do that for them? We can guide you there."

"I never venture into the Timberscape," the professor said. "My calling is to empower others to do that. Perhaps you may learn something in my class that would prove useful for aiding your friends."

"Fair enough," said Allys.

"Incidentally, virtually all the dark spells that victims living in the Scape suffer from have been cast by creatures from alternate universes," the professor explained. "The native born of Gymnarykum are either too fearful, ignorant, or kind to do such things."

"So we have noticed," said Hansel.

Astral Projection was a practicum led by Professor Jove in which the students learned how their conscious mental perceptions could travel about without moving their bodies.

"This is a basic skill that most residents of Hearts are able to perform before they leave their teenage years," Jove explained. "It has may uses and is an especially good means of conserving energy."

Aylwyn, however, decided its major value was as a safe method to spy on people without leaving home.

In the early weeks of the course, only Allys was successfully able to free her mind from her body, travel to another building on campus, and correctly identify the item Jove had placed there.

"It's a painting of you, professor," Allys reported after returning to her body.

"By Jove, you've done it!" the professor exclaimed.

Eventually, the others also mastered this art.

Professor Sennet was a strikingly beautiful woman who had been born male but who had gone through a long process to switch her gender. The quartet learned this from a student named Max, who quietly informed them of this fact the first day of class while other students were filing in.

"Well, she obviously made the right choice," said Aylwyn. "I can't imagine her as a man. She's just so...natural as a woman."

"The people of Hearts agree with you on that," Max replied. "She's really smart and well respected throughout the realm."

"I wonder what King Burpeedo would think of Professor Sennet?" Gretel said. "He seems to be very interested in crossing sexual identities."

"Oh, he wouldn't like her at all," Allys said. "She's a talented, productive member of society. That's not where his heart is at all. He gets off on criminals in forced drag. Authentic self-expression is anathema to Burpeedo."

Their conversation ended when the professor stood to address the class.

"I recognize that this is a required course that you must take regardless of your interest in the subject," Sennet announced. "Some of you would prefer to be in a different course at the moment. Nevertheless, I expect your full attention. There will be no slapstick antics in this classroom."

Max chose that instant to rise slightly and shove a whoopee cushion under his rump and sit down heavily upon it, producing a loud and recognizably crude sound. Most of the students in the room were native born Hearts and thus too polite to laugh. Aylwyn started to guffaw but stifled it.

Without missing a beat, Sennet remarked, "Max here has just completed my course in onomatopoeia. Thank you for the demonstration, Max, but we will be moving on to more refined subjects now. Paronomasia, class, is undisputedly the highest form of literature, and I wish you to appreciate the nobility of its art. By the end of this course, if you have paid attention, you will be able to recognize irony in its most subtle narrative emanations and identify satirical references in typical political speeches.

"The key to success," Sennet continued with a stony expression, "is to maintain an open mind and not be afraid of unexpected humor that may leap at you from hidden places among crowds of words."

"This is my kind of subject," Aylwyn whispered. "I'll be sure to cop an A in it."

In their study of history with Professor Noricum, the four learned about the source spring of Gymnarykum, sometimes called the Golden Mind by religious pilgrims.

"It is a thin place that people from other parallel worlds occasionally migrate to," Noricum remarked. "But everyone who has tried to control it or use it for personal gain has disappeared, never to return. Once upon a time, a German man named Jacob Waltz, who was prospecting for gold in Arizona, came into the Timberscape through a cave in the Superstition Mountains. Upon reaching the spring, he was so enamored of it that he believed its waters could produce giant crops. In order to test his theory, he built a homestead nearby and dug a canal to divert spring water into his field. But though his field was downhill from the spring, when he released the gate, the water would not flow out. He stepped into the water to investigate the problem and promptly disappeared."

"We know about Jacob Waltz," said Aylwyn. "In Arizona he's known as the Lost Dutchman."

"Indeed," the professor said. "And this episode served to reinforce the ancient wisdom of the four realms to leave not only the spring but also the entire center region of the island wild and ungoverned."

"Very interesting," said Hansel.

"Here is a historical footnote that Allys and Aylwyn in particular should also find interesting," Professor Noricum continued. "When he was expelled from the Timberscape, over the homesteading fiasco, Jacob Waltz reappeared in the parallel universe called Arizona. Many years later, on his deathbed, Jacob told a friend about the spring called the Golden Mind. This friend, however, thought the delirious man was talking about a lost gold mine that presumably he had discovered in a cave in the Superstition Mountains. He was referring, of course, to the spring of Gymnarykum in the Timberscape of Memory, also known as the Spring of Memory. This is why no one in that parallel reality has ever found a lost gold mine in the Superstition Mountains. All those gold seekers have been looking for the wrong thing in the wrong universe."

"Far out!" said Aylwyn.

"Indeed!" said Noricum.

In a mythology lecture a few weeks later, Noricum spoke about a legendary set of twins who loomed large in the prehistory of Gymnarykum. The brother twin was Wander and the sister was Vogel. Islanders commonly believed that Wander and Vogel were able to travel in both directions to and from Gymnarykum. Legend had it that they had entered and left multiple times to many different worlds and were widely expected to return at any time, signaling the beginning of the end of time.

"Wander and Vogel are German names," said Allys. "So could it be possible that Hansel and Gretel are really Wander and Vogel?"

Gretel said, "Do not be silly. We are not masquerading as people we most certainly are not."

"Well," said the professor with a knowing smile, "many people in the realm are excited by the possibility that you, Gretel, and your twin brother are indeed Vogel and Wander returning to usher in a golden era of peace and prosperity. Of course, in Spades, they believe it will be to begin a rapturous era of war and damnation in which they will be allowed to witness everyone but themselves being tortured for their sins. However, there is a puzzling complication with your particular appearance at this time, as you German twins arrived with a set of American twins."

"Double the trouble, double the fun," said Aylwyn.

"Yes, but there is a part of the legend I have not yet mentioned," Noricum continued. "Each time they return, the Wander and Vogel twins use different names and do not remember that they have been here before."

"It seems more likely," said Hansel, "that various twins have sojourned here from time to time and the residents have made the incorrect assumption that they were reincarnations of previous twins."

"That is certainly a possibility," admitted Noricum. "Nevertheless, you can rely upon our psychohistory scholars wanting to study our new German twins along with their anomalous American companions. Reincarnation or not, you four may well represent a novel blessing to this realm...or, dare I say it, to the entire island."

"Speaking of the entire island," said Allys, "when we were in Clubs, we were told that Clubs was the first realm to declare independence. Is that true?"

"The chronology of the evolution of the realms is a matter of intense scholarly dispute," Noricum replied. "Dating the order of secession is one area that is particularly problematic. Clubs and Spades both claim to be the first realm. What is known is that at one time in the far distant past the Timberscape extended throughout all Gymnarykum.

"Scholars champion their own theories about which separation came when. My view is that Clubs was indeed first to separate from Old Mem. I base this on their tendency toward dense obstinacy. When it comes to destroying unity, the ignorant are apt to lead the way. Other colleagues apply the same reasoning to the primacy of Spades. The only thing known for certain about establishing realms is that Hearts was the last to let go of the Timberscape, and that occurred long after the other three were well established."

Boons and Blessings was taught by a man of short stature but with a large head and thick neck perched on improbably narrow shoulders. Though Doctor Rumpelstiltskin would be the first to admit his unusual appearance, he was a brilliant scholar and much admired among university colleagues. His course of study was methods of helping people in need.

"I have heard tales about you," Gretel said the first day in class.

"No doubt all of them bad," said Professor Rumpelstiltskin.

"Yes," said Hansel. "They say you are a kidnapper and even worse."

"Those fairy tales represent a calumny upon my good name," Rumpelstiltskin replied. "Germany in those days was rife with antidiminutivism. This is why I am a refugee from that land and now a proud citizen of the Realm of Hearts. The truth is that a tall but rather foolish man bragged that his daughter knew how to spin gold from straw. When put to the test, he panicked and sought my help. Of course, I did not know how to turn straw into gold. The idea is absurd. It cannot be done."

"Then why would he seek you out?" asked Gretel.

"He was a fool," said the professor. "What I **could** do, and was renowned for, is to enhance the riches within the human mind –the golden cells of the life of the mind."

"Did you try to help the girl?" Allys inquired.

"I tried to help her father," said Rumpelstiltskin. "Alas, he was a rather oafish sort. I offered to go to the king and explain that the father had misspoken, but that the young maiden was indeed a person of golden kindness and had a beautiful personality."

"I'll bet the man loved that idea," said Aylwyn sarcastically.

"As it happened, he did not," said the professor. "But what happened next has been covered up, replaced by a cockamamie story about my demanding the girl's first born child unless she could guess my real name. Pure fantasy. Never happened."

"What really happened?" Allys asked.

"The maiden was pregnant by her loutish father, and he was desperate to get her married off soon before the pregnancy became apparent. His effort failed, however, and soon the whole village knew she was with child. So this man blamed me for impregnating his daughter. Since antidiminutivism was rampant throughout the country at that time, people believed that I had forced myself on this girl. She was considerably taller and stronger than I, so that idea lacked merit. But people believed it anyway. I had to run for my life."

"How did you get here?" Gretel asked.

"I ran into the forest and hid in a cave," Rumpelstiltskin said. "In the morning, I sought to leave, but when I exited where I thought I had entered, I found myself in the Timberscape of Memory. Soon thereafter, with the encouragement and assistance of a kind coyote, I migrated to Hearts. But enough of my biography. The purpose of our study is to develop your skills at helping others. We shall begin with mental exercises to enhance attitudes of compassion."

The diminutive professor then hypnotized his students and spoke suggestions into their receptive minds that they truly cared for the underprivileged.

Cinderella and Prince Handsome, both dressed in elegant simplicity, jointly taught the Self-Validation and Managing Relationships course. To begin the first class, Cinderella told the story of how she and Prince Handsome met, and the prince joined in the narration at various points. The tale was traditional for the start of this particular course, and Cinderella and Prince Handsome never tired of telling it.

"I was slaving away cleaning up after my wicked stepmother and stepsisters," Cinderella said. She explained about the ball in honor of the returning prince and how she wanted to go but was told no by her stepmother. "I was out in the garden crying and feeling sorry for myself when a kindly old lady stepped in and told me she was my Fairy Godmother. You can imagine how shocked I was, but even more so when she told me she would help me go to the ball. She proposed using magic, but, of course, we all know that the magic is really inside our hearts."

Prince Handsome acted out the part of Fairy Godmother. "Now, Cinderella dear, you simply cannot go to the ball all grimy and sweaty. You need to be scrubbed up. Before we make you a suitable gown, you will have to take a shower."

"What is a shower?" Cinderella asked.

"It is a kind of bath, but the water pours over you from above," Fairy Godmother said. She made a shower appear and said, "Now get out of those ragged, stinky clothes and let's get you cleaned up."

"Well, I was good at following orders," Cinderella said. "I complied and got into the shower, where I used soap and shampoo to good effect, scrubbing up quite nicely. 'This is like bathing in a waterfall,' I said."

"Only with hot water," said the prince in his Fairy Godmother voice.

"Fairy Godmother provided me a towel and used her wand to dry and style my hair," Cinderella continued. "She then produced –out of thin air- a beautiful gown and jewelry and glass slippers. Next came a coach made from a pumpkin and horses from mice."

"As Cinderella started out for the ball in the pumpkin coach," Prince Handsome said, "Fairy Godmother called out, 'Now remember, dear, **everything** will disappear at midnight. Be sure to be back here before then.'"

"I waved an acknowledgment," Cinderella said, "but I did not believe her words. At the ball I met the prince, who, in my humble opinion, was immediately captivated by my aura of sensuous spirituality."

"So true," said Prince Handsome. "I was dumbstruck by her."

"We danced for a while and then he invited me to go for a walk outside," Cinderella said. "The time flew by with neither of us aware of it. We were holding hands and talking. It felt so natural. Then, as the clock tower began tolling I looked up and saw that it was only seconds away from midnight, and I remembered what Fairy Godmother had told me. I looked in the lane where my coach was parked and saw it fading from view."

"She gasped very loudly," said the prince.

"Then I realized that my gown was disintegrating," Cinderella said. "By the time the clock had struck nine times, I was completely naked and the prince had definitely noticed. Now wipe that grin off your face, darling."

"I stared agape at her beautiful body," Prince Handsome said. "Her breasts, legs, and delta enraptured me. She turned and loped away and I so enjoyed the sight of her athletic movements that I stood transfixed until I realized she was disappearing. Not disappearing in the way her clothes did, but vanishing from sight. At any rate, now I gave chase but could not find her.

"The next day, her face and body filled my dreams, and I determined to search the entire realm for her. I also wondered why her clothes disappeared and decided this was a heavenly sign. For months, I personally visited every house in every town and village in the realm. One day I arrived at the house of the Wicked Stepmother and when I set eyes on the stepsisters, I dismissed them immediately and was about to leave when I heard a noise upstairs."

"It was caused by Fairy Godmother turning over a chair," said Cinderella. "I did not know the bloke was there."

"Naturally, I asked if anyone else was in the house," Prince Handsome continued. 'Only Cinderella,' said Wicked Stepmother. 'I guarantee she is not your type.' Let me have a look anyway, I said. Cinderella was summoned and when she appeared, I positively bellowed, 'You are the one! Why did you run away?' I must confess that I thought but did not say aloud that I knew why but did not expect her to reveal to these women that her clothes had disappeared."

Now Cinderella took up the narration. "I looked directly

into his eyes and said, 'My Fairy Godmother set a curfew of midnight and the consequence of breaking curfew was –well, you know what it was.'"

"And then I said, 'Come to the castle with me. We need to talk,'" the prince added.

"I looked down at my raggedy frock and said, 'I'm not dressed properly for the palace,'" Cinderella noted.

"We'll stop at a dress shop on the way," the prince proclaimed.

"So, we left and stopped at a stylish boutique en route, and I picked out an elegant dress and changed into it," Cinderella said.

"So now we are at the castle," Prince Handsome said, becoming animated. "Picture it. We are in a drawing room, and Cinderella is standing there in an elegant and very pricey gown. I got down on my knees and proposed."

"To be more specific, he proposed marriage," said Cinderella. "Men are known to propose many things other than marriage. At any rate, I said, 'In the interest of parity, it is only fair that I should see you naked before answering such an important question. For all I know, you may have warts all over your body.' Without a word, he stood up, disrobed, turned around slowly so I could see for myself. Clearly he had no warts and was as muscularly thin as I. He got back down on his knees and said, 'Cinderella, will you marry me?'"

"And then," the prince said, "She removed her dress and other garments and got down on her knees facing me and said, 'Consider this a yes,' and we kissed passionately."

"Did this happen in Hearts?" Gretel asked. "It does not seem like something that would happen here."

"Very astute, Gretel," said Cinderella. "No, this happened in a far off land called Burgundy."

"Then how did you get to Gymnarykum?" inquired Hansel.

Prince Handsome replied, "One day Cinderella and I were having a look at underground parts of the palace where I had not been allowed to go when I was young, and we happened upon an ancient tapestry depicting an enchanted forest with four birds in the corners and one in the center. At the top were a bluebird and dodo and in the bottom corners were a peacock and a vulture, with a hoopoe in the center. As a child, I had heard servants whisper about a legendary secret tunnel entered only through an avian forest that led to a magical island, and on impulse I pulled the tapestry aside and found such a passage. Naturally, we decided to explore it."

"And came out in the Timberscape," said Cinderella. "And the rest is history."

Cinderella began the unit on the philosophy of sexuality by saying, "My husband has a cute story he likes to tell about sex and conception."

Prince Handsome cleared his throat and began to narrate: "Once upon a time, there was a pious sperm cell who fervently believed that the only acceptable purpose of sex was procreation. And he very much wanted to participate in a conception. Therefore he swam laps to build up his endurance, so that when the chance came, he would be able to swim faster than the other sperm in his ejaculation group, thus ensuring that he would be able to fertilize an ovum.

"Well, the day finally arrived when our pious sperm was caught up in an orgasm, and because he had diligently prepared for the event, he easily out-swam the other sperm cells. As he approached the exit of his home urethra, he watched carefully for the vagina into which he would continue to swim. But there was no dark tunnel. From his penis tip perch, all he saw was an expanse of cottony white. This caused our pious sperm much agitation, and in anger, he reversed his direction and swam against the stream, crying out to the other cells now coming toward him, "Go back! Go back! It's only a wet dream!"

Following the nervous laughter from the students, Cinderella, said, "Despite his preparation and intention, our little sperm cell was spewed out onto a bed sheet and died childless. This common occurrence is an apt introduction to the many natural expressions and uses of sexual activity in addition to procreation."

A vigorous discussion ensued concerning the ultimate destinies of trillions of ejaculated sperm cells and sloughed off ova that never find each other. "The search for an answer to this question was the key factor in the emergence of existential philosophy in the last century," Cinderella added as a historical footnote.

Jack and Jill took their yoga class, including the quartet, to the beach at the place where the Gymnarykum River flowed into the Universal Sea. They spent the day at the beach doing yoga and meditating and swimming in the salt water. All the beaches along the shore of Hearts were clothing optional, and everyone did their stretches and swimming nude.

One of the students in this class was a fifteen year-old prodigy named Kyp, who was slim, with black hair, olive skin and blue eyes. She told Allys that for most of her life she had carried an inner conviction that she was the reincarnation of another soul. The young woman longed to discover the identity of who she was before her birth as Kyp.

"How could you do that?" Allys asked.

"I would have to go to the Timberscape and bathe in the Spring of Memory," said Kyp. "Doing that will elicit memories of any previous incarnations a person has known. I truly intend to go there someday."

At the end of a year studying at the university, the four were tempted to stay in Hearts and find careers there. It was clearly the best realm on the island. But they missed home and wanted to see their parents again. In addition, they did not appreciate the cult of martyrdom that characterized the spirituality of that realm.

In a devotional service one Sunday morning, they heard the famous "Parable of the Spade in the Woods" and found it troubling. The preacher stepped up to the lectern, opened the holy book to the pertinent passage and read:

A citizen of Spades wandered into a deep forest and in time became quite lost. "No matter," said the citizen, "because wherever I am is the center of the universe." A citizen of Hearts, who knew the forest well, followed the citizen of Spades and offered to lead the lost one back home. The Spade said, "I am not lost, but you may accompany me on my journey home." The Heart agreed. The citizen of Spades then wandered even farther into the forest, becoming even more lost. Eventually, the Spade led the Heart to a dark place where no fruit, nuts, or berries grew and no water flowed. The Spade was now too confused to determine which way to go, either forward or backward and decided to sit and do nothing. The citizen of Hearts stayed with the Spade, until both perished from starvation.

"This is the ideal toward which all true Hearts must strive," intoned the cleric with great passion. "When you lay down your life for another, you demonstrate great spiritual maturity."

As they were leaving the sanctuary, Aylwyn said, "I understand caring for the needy, and I can see the value in leading even an egotistical citizen of Spades to safety, but it beats me how abetting someone's stupidity shows spiritual maturity."

"Especially when doing it endangers one's own life," agreed Hansel.

Beyond their concerns about the religion of Hearts, the four were nostalgic for the Timberscape. The island's surreal center had an aura about it that felt like home, despite the fact that they had spent nearly all of their time on Gymnarykum in the four realms. Whenever speaking the word **home** all four were unclear in their minds whether this meant Arizona and Germany or the Timberscape of Memory. They also felt a commitment to look for Pieter and Wendlich to try to undo their enchantment with some of the magic reversal spells they had learned at the University of Hearts. As well, they were curious about what had happened with Morey and Ria and Dis.

Allys said, "An extended holiday to visit the Timberscape would help us in making decisions about our futures. We need to find a way to go home, wherever that is."

"Yes," said Hansel, "but I think we should consult with King Kenilworth and Queen Kensinga before we depart. Once we leave here, it is distinctly possible we will never return."

"And we should thank the royal couple for their hospitality and care," said Gretel.

Aylwyn sought a royal audience, which was soon granted.

Kensinga and Kenilworth were sympathetic to the quartet's desire to undo the enchantments of Pieter and Wendlich and their quests for their home countries. The royal couple expressed hope that, in the Timberscape, the four would find the vision to adopt Gymnarykum as their new homeland.

"Many find it congenial to be in essence dual citizens of Hearts and Old Mem," Kenilworth noted with an encouraging smile. He was concerned that these gifted twins would soon be lost to Hearts forever, but giving them a hard sell to stay would push them away faster.

Next, they visited Kyp to say they were returning to the Timberscape and asked if she wanted to go along. Kyp said yes and the quartet became a quintet.

CHAPTER 24:
VERMONT

He said, "What love has done to me!
It binds my heart, no joke.
By God I dreamt all night," said he,
"An Elf-Queen should my mistress be
And sleep beneath my cloak."
Geoffrey Chaucer

Craving a period of distance to give her emotions a rest, Chaucer decided it would be good to spend the summer with her sister in Vermont. Time apart might also help Magnus sort out his irresolution, she thought. When she called Marlowe about visiting, she confessed that her life was in turmoil and she needed a temporary refuge.

Marlowe and Grant Archer lived in a well-insulated, four-bedroom red brick house in Bennington with thirteen year-old son Harrow and nine year-old daughter Millay. Marlowe was surprised to get Chaucer's call, because to that date the only family member who had sought sanctuary with her in New England had been her chronically troubled brother, Spenser. Marlowe had been under the impression that Chaucer was the model among the Dickinson siblings for having her life together. The Dickinson sisters had much to catch up on when Chaucer arrived.

"The last I heard, you had married a travel agent," Marlowe said when they found some privacy for honest conversation. "What happened?"

Chaucer told Marlowe about Ving, the divorce, and her affair with Magnus.

"Well, I'm not one to cast stones," Marlowe said. "I guess I'm the stable one right now, but it wasn't always so. I've never had a chance to unload my guilt on anyone, so I guess the cost of your sojourn here is to be my therapist."

"I always thought you were the normal one," Chaucer said. "And I admired you for getting as far away from our parents as possible."

"That I did," Marlowe said. "But I overreacted to their overprotective smothering. I went wild when I got to Middlebury. I was into drugs and sex in a big way. Grant was my sweetest lover but by no means the only one, even after we started going together.

"Is that why you didn't come home for the summer holidays?" Chaucer asked.

"Right," Marlowe said. "I didn't think I could disguise the wild woman I had become and didn't want the hassle of dealing with Mom and Dad. So I made excuses about summer jobs, invitations to visit classmates in the East, and that sort of thing.

"After graduation, Grant and I went to live in a hippie commune in Northern New York. It was fun for a few months, running around like naked free spirits in the woods, but then it turned into a struggle to survive the winter in a drafty old house with inadequate heating. But we all held together and helped each other cope through that first winter. Shared pain bonded us in good will. In the spring, things started to unravel. Members who had been into groovy love were getting irritable. Money was a continuing problem. There never seemed to be enough for food because so much of the shared revenue of the commune was used for marijuana. No other drugs were tolerated, except the occasional supply of LSD that a visitor bequeathed to the founder and self-proclaimed autocrat of the commune, Penrick Uriel. He had been so cool at the beginning, but within a year he was becoming erratic and threw tantrums at unexpected times for no discernible reason.

"We were there from June 1970 to September 1971. When I got pregnant, we used that as an excuse to leave, and so Grant and I married and moved to Bennington. We became respectable here, developing a food co-op and becoming successful merchants and environmentalists."

"It sounds like everything worked out well," Chaucer interjected.

"There was a major complication," Marlowe continued. "During my first pregnancy, I was not completely sure Grant was the father. The odds were that he was but the baby could have been by Amos Isaacs, a fellow Midd student who came to stay at the commune for a few weeks in the summer of 1971. Grant had not objected to my having sex with Amos, because he was going into the woods with a giggly teenager named Epha Hare. She was very rabbit-like with her sexuality. The commune considered both flings groovy, and both soon ended due to passion flameout."

"Amos Isaacs the Republican Pennsylvania Congressman?" Chaucer asked with interest.

"The very same," said Marlowe. "He came from a megabucks coal industry family. His father wisely let him run wild during college but after a few years reeled him back into the fold."

"That sounds like what the Amish call rumspringa," said Chaucer, "although the Amish let their young men sow their oats as teenagers."

"Same principle," said Marlowe. "For a time I thought I would end up married to Amos, but the thought of all that money and the restrictive power that goes with it frightened me."

"Do you know who Harrow's biological father is?" Chaucer asked.

"The good news is that by the time Harrow was two months old, I knew for certain that Grant had contributed his genes to the baby boy. This brought me such a sense of relief that I vowed to carry on a normal and conventional lifestyle. No more drugs, certainly no sleeping around, and no more hippie style casual nudity."

Chaucer spent her summer leisure working on her novel as well as writing poetry and letters to Magnus. Her goal with the fantasy tale was to wrap it up, but nothing she wrote in pursuit of that goal satisfied her. Several drafts of the conclusion were ripped up and thrown in the trash. She also decided that due to its relative brevity, she would henceforth think of it as a novella.

Much more satisfying were the things she produced for her lover. In the first letter she penned to Magnus she wrote in part:

You may write to me as much as you like, care of Marlowe Archer at the address I gave you. For two reasons, I request, <u>please</u>, that you not telephone unless there is a dire situation. First, there are children in the house who would no doubt enjoy overhearing their aunt trying to be circumspect while talking to her lover, whom she misses acutely. Second, I don't think I could hear your voice without weeping, and this would be sure to draw attention from whomever might be in the house at the time. That said, I love you and am impatient to hear your voice, to see your eyes, to feel your touch, to taste your mouth, to be surrounded by your smell, which makes you Magnus and makes me love you.

Vermont is my favorite place in the East, much more congenial than Pennsylvania. Adding to the charm is that my sister and brother-in-law are former hippies now into ecological pursuits, although otherwise disappointingly prim and proper.

In Magnus' reply he wrote:

I have told you only the bare information that Kit died at age three. It is a subject that I have great difficulty speaking of in person. But through the enforced distance of a letter, I feel better able to let you know how devastating his death was to me - and Janett as well. If you and I are to have any future together, you need to know about this. Cystic Fibrosis is a genetic disease, and both Janett and I are carriers.

Long before Kit left us, we were terrified of having any other children, and even now, I would never take the chance of fathering a child. That, of course, is why I have been such a fanatic about your birth control methods. I don't want to appear clinical, but my greatest fear is contributing to the birth of another child like Kit.

Chaucer wrote back:

I do not want children, because I know that I would smother them with love to compensate for the lack of love I felt as a child. The first time you told me about Kit, I wanted to make love to you so passionately that it would make your pain and grief go away. Making love to you is unlike anything I have ever experienced because it is like making love to a part of myself.

Earlier today I was mentally reliving the time Janett was out of town and we spent the night in a motel room in Flagstaff, because you didn't want to park your car at my place overnight and didn't want to be seen riding in my car near the campus. I think of it as the night that we could keep till dawn. My fondest memory of that time, after much laughter and sex without having to watch the clock, came as we were getting ready for bed. It was such a very domestic scene. You brushed my hair, and I cherished every pleasant stroke.

Magnus responded:

I have kept a file with every note and letter you have heretofore written to me and now look forward to adding more. The file is in a very secure place in my campus office, but I am amazed at my growing brazenness about you, beginning last spring with the first time I arranged a tryst. I have always been such a careful and prudent man, and now I feel positively foolhardy to confess feeling a sense of invisibility when I was traveling somewhere to meet you. I know that is self-delusion, but the feeling was so powerful. And no *one saw or caught us, except for Janett finding a love note in my coat pocket. That, of course, was a classic example of carelessness on my part.*

Chaucer wrote to Magnus:

Your letter brought back to me a particularly acute memory. I showed you the incomplete manuscript of Timberscape one afternoon at my apartment. Apropos of the sense of invisibility you wrote about, you were getting braver and decided to chance being there, although you did park two blocks away. At any rate, I had never shown any of this to anyone, even Ving. Ving knew I was writing something but was not sufficiently curious to ask about reading it. You asked right away if you could read my unfinished and unedited work. I hesitated until that day you brazenly came to my place.

Before I let you read it, I revealed something about my writing methodology. I told you that for years I had struggled with an outline for the whole book but eventually produced one. Since then, however, the characters had taken over the writing. They tell me what words to type, and if I think of something they don't like, they let me know and rebel until I write what they whisper in my head. I feared you might think me absolutely loony, but I felt like taking the risk.

When you said that description gave you goose bumps, and that you believed many gifted writers experienced the same thing, I wanted to make love to you most exquisitely. But what I remember vividly is the sight of you sitting up beside me in bed, naked and with the pages of my manuscript resting on your pubic hair. As you finished a page, you flipped it over onto the bedspread with your left hand.

All the while, I was looking for some sign from you that you liked what you were reading. You were clearly engrossed but said nothing, and I was so impatient for feedback. Then a few pages from the end, you took my left hand in your right and gently squeezed it. And tears of relief fell down my face.

When you turned over the last page, you looked into my wet eyes and said, "All I want to do now is make love to the talented writer who created this amazing and imaginative world." And did you ever! I had at least three orgasms.

Magnus wrote:

To quote J. M. Barrie, "What a delicious book you are, and how I wish I had written you! With every word you say, something within me is shouting." With your extensive knowledge of fantasy fiction, you may know the source of the quote, but in case you don't, it's from an obscure work called Tommy and Grizel. I happened upon it by accident years ago, and as a librarian, I found it very appealing. It came to mind today while rereading your accumulated correspondence. You are indeed a delicious book, dear one.

I am breathless with longing for you. I want to run and romp and make love to you. I want to take you with me all over the world to those special places which have taken hold of my heart in ways no one else knows. I want you to see what I see, and smell what I smell, and taste what I taste, and touch what I touch. I want you to know what I'm thinking and how I'm feeling. Then I want to switch it all and be you.

This letter from Magnus inspired Chaucer to write a poem, which she sent to him:

SWITCHING IT ALL

Celebrating life, I have rejoiced when you were deep within

My chamber, entered into pleasant conversations with your skin,

Savoring the tastes of flesh and fluids — these the finest foods

My mouth has ever known. I've listened to your moods

And musings eager to discern whatever depths of mind

You might reveal, and you have given of them freely, signed

Your name with flair to every sentence, every stroke of tongue.

The delicate, delicious, fragrant melodies you've sung

Have opened inner gates in me, releasing clear

And corresponding songs, and though you are not seer,

You've made me want to tell your intellect and intuition

Every need and seed I own. Love, let us nurture to fruition

All these tantalizing hints that we may

someday be

Inside each other, feeling, tasting, touching, smelling, flawlessly

In tune, our bodies rocking gently, lost in perfect pitch

And understanding all at once how we can wholly switch,

With only silent glances, back and forth, as often as we choose,

Our egos and our bodies swirled in ever-changing hues.

Magnus wrote:

An ache of awe infuses every nerve cell in my body when I imagine the green and transcendental place you're staying this summer. I long to see the place. I've never been to Vermont and want to visit. Especially because you are there, I burn to visit Bennington. Realistically, however, I recognize the imprudence and near impossibility of showing up on your sister's porch.

Janett is using all her wiles (except sex) to get me back into line and to behave like a proper college president. I have to confess that I feel incredibly guilty for cheating on her. She and I have been through a great deal together, including the loss of a child, and one cannot easily dismiss those "until death us do part" values.

There is a sense in which a death, that of Kit, has long since split asunder the bond between Janett and me, but when I use that tragedy as a rationalization for divorce, I feel like a sewer rat. The truth is, I was fully satisfied to stay in a lackluster marriage with Janett until that day I fell in love with you.

Chaucer replied:

I too have been meditating on the all too present subject of adultery and remembered a line from Donne that seems to beg for understanding of that sin. Being truly in love can, or at least <u>feels</u>, like a defensible answer to the charge of infidelity. I know what it feels like to be betrayed by a spouse, but now I'm abetting marital cheating, or more accurately, a guilty party to it. But my soul continues to protest its innocence. Can souls as well as minds be in denial? Here for your perusal is my literary response to our situation.

INFIDELITY

"For Godsake hold your tongue, and let me love."

John Donne

For Godsake I'm alive with being touched and felt,

And filled with laughing health in every cell.

Your naked self and mine have joined in passioned joy,

Creating something exquisite to sense.

So how can this be wrong, the seventh

And the tenth commandments notwithstanding?

How can love that heals be so condemned?

Why then are forbidden acts the very ones

That bless most deeply, kiss the soul?

Why, if this be wrong, do I feel whole?

Magnus replied with a note indicating that he resonated with the sentiment and the questions in her poem. She sent a letter in return reiterating how much she missed him, mind and body, and that his words flooded her with good feelings. She wrote that she felt deeply loved and was thrilled by his literate and profound thoughts and feelings and then added:

The deepest secret of our relationship is not the wonderful sex. I think that most people, even injured parties, understand the lure of forbidden sex. They may not approve and may feel deeply hurt and betrayed, but they recognize the power of the physical attraction. That affairs involve passionate sex should be no surprise to anybody. What you and I must hide most securely are the quaking words we share, words that tumble from protected vaults in our minds, words that we write on paper or speak aloud to one another. These must remain concealed from all but us, for they are naked, honest, raw, and binding, and therefore far too blinding for any forsaken spouse to endure.

Near the end of the summer hiatus Magnus wrote:

This is a painful matter, but I feel it prudent to raise the question about whether we should avoid meeting once you get back to Sedona. I still need time to assess the prospect of leaving Janett, and of course I want to do it in the most humane way possible. I freely admit to being fearful of the huge mess Janett could cause if I directly opposed her demands for reconciliation. I have yet to figure out the best strategic way to extricate myself from the marriage. And no matter how that eventuates, it would be exceedingly difficult to have an open relationship with you while a divorce is in progress. In any case, for the time being I think it best that we not meet anywhere in private.

Chaucer sent him two sentences in reply:

I will respect your wish for more time to work out the situation with Janett and hereby acknowledge the reality that we should not be seen together in the mean time. I promise to avoid trysts but will not promise to stop writing you notes, letters, and poems.

Marlowe and Grant took Millay with them to work at the co-op. The plan had been to take both children, but at the last minute Harrow remembered he had made a commitment to mow the grass and trim the shrubs for an elderly widow down the street. So he marched off in a different direction when the four Archers left the house.

Chaucer had been meditating over a cup of herbal tea when they departed. She spent the morning making more notes for her fantasy novella, so that it was approaching noon by the time she headed to the bathroom for a shower. Thinking she would have the house to herself for most of the day, she left the bathroom door open to keep the mirror from steaming up.

While she was relishing the flow of water over her body, Harrow returned home drenched in sweat and grime from his lawn work. He left his sneakers on the back porch and threw his tee shirt and socks into a laundry room hamper. Still wearing cutoff jeans, he went to his bedroom to get a clean pair of underwear and khaki shorts.

Thinking about how refreshing a shower would feel, Harrow walked into the bathroom as Chaucer was bending down to dry her calves. Each was startled to see the other.

"Oh, excuse me," Harrow said, with his adolescent voice uncontrollably changing to soprano on the last word. "I didn't know anyone was here."

Chaucer stood and wrapped the towel around her but mentally noted that in the interval it took to cover up, Harrow could not help but stare at her nakedness. Her mind registered an image of her quartet in the Timberscape, just a year older than her nephew, encountering nude adults who were not ashamed of their bodies. She said, "You've never seen a real live naked woman before, have you Harrow?"

Harrow's voice squeaked as he replied, "Not since I was a baby. I saw Mom naked then but don't remember much."

"I'll wager you've seen pictures, though," she said.

Harrow blushed.

"It's nothing to be embarrassed about. I'd be more concerned about you if you hadn't. Well, here, have a good look." She removed the towel, dropped it to the floor, and slowly turned in a circle. "You can look," she said sternly, "but don't you dare touch."

He gazed at her body for some moments, ultimately focusing his eyes on her delta, and then said, "You have red hair down there too. Mom's is blonde."

"You remember more than you think," she said with a wry smile. "And yes, I am a natural redhead."

"Mom and Dad have a picture album from their days in the commune," Harrow added. "There are some photos of naked people in it. You know, sitting around in a circle, dancing in the meadow, having a picnic, swimming in the lake. Things like that. Mom and Dad are in some of the pictures."

"Hmmm, I'd be interested in checking it out," she said. "I put in a bit of time among the hippies myself, but I never lived in a commune."

A panicked look spread across Harrow's face. "They don't know I've seen it. They keep it stowed away in their bedroom closet. I only found it by accident when Mom sent me in there to get a bag of old clothes to donate to charity. I snuck back later and leafed through it. They'd be furious if they knew. Mom's almost a prude now."

"OK, don't worry. I'll keep your secret safe," she said.

"Thank you, Aunt Chaucer. I won't tell anyone about this either, but I'll always remember it. You're beautiful," he said solemnly.

"In the mean time, you've got grass and twigs all over you, and you're sweaty and stinky," she said. "You'd better get out of those pants and into the shower, pronto."

His mouth fell open and he stammered, "Do you want to see me naked too?"

She picked up the towel and hung it up on the peg that Marlowe had assigned her. Each family member had a specified place to hang towels, and Chaucer had inherited the one that Spenser had used on the several occasions when he had sought sanctuary with his oldest sibling. "No offense, Harrow, but I've seen my share of naked boys – young men, that is. I know what a penis looks like. I'll go now and you can have the bathroom to yourself."

"Mine's different from most," he blurted out with a note of pride. "I'm not circumcised. Mom and Dad thought circumcision was unnatural when I was born and wouldn't let the doctor cut me."

"Yes, I imagine their counter-cultural world-view would extend to the barbarity of cutting foreskins," she replied. "Or what the Apostle Paul called mutilation of the flesh. And now that you mention it, I haven't seen that many intact penises. Care to show off?"

Now feeling more comfortable in his naked aunt's presence, Harrow unzipped his shorts and slid out of his briefs, revealing his natural organ of average size for his age.

"Oh yes," Chaucer said. "Yes, very nice. You are in possession of a very attractive penis, Harrow. Use it well." With that, she left the room.

CHAPTER 25:
LIMERICKS AND COMING OUT

Wild Nights – Wild Nights!
Were I with thee
Wild Nights should be
Our luxury!

Emily Dickinson

When classes resumed at Anasazi College, in September 1985, Magnus remained confused about his marital situation. He did have a clearer idea of what he believed about God, and he acknowledged to himself, and to Cloud in a counseling session, that he bore a strong responsibility to resolve the triangular relationship. How he could or would accomplish that resolution, however, he had no idea.

In the course of their summer correspondence, Magnus had written that they should not meet privately when Chaucer returned from Vermont, and she had agreed, but there was no way to keep from seeing one another as daily life unfolded on campus. Each of them flushed with desire at these ordinary events that put them together in the same public place, and both struggled to achieve a studied indifference to one another on those occasions. Neither proved to be a good actor in this regard, but as it happened, most people present were not good observers of body language and facial gestures, thus suspicions and rumors about them did not materialize. Only Cloud noticed that Magnus and Chaucer could not keep from darting their eyes at each other during faculty meetings.

Though it represented great struggles of their wills, the two did manage to avoid trysts. Both knew that such meetings would lead inevitably to passionate physical behavior and increase the odds that they would be found out. Whatever delicate act Magnus was engaged in to finesse Janett toward accepting a separation would be blown apart by news of a campus scandal, which would spread like a forest fire throughout the community.

Their written exchanges continued, nevertheless, and these notes served as substitutionary expressions of their highly charged feelings. It felt to both of them much like a continuation of their summer correspondence, except that now they could see one another face-to-face, and be close enough to inhale each other's body scents, and feel the pulsing of amorous energy across a room.

Chaucer's erotic limericks, in particular, filled Magnus with longing for her touch, and, ironically, his accounts about attending church and his subsequent theological musings had a similar effect on her. She burned with desire to curl up in his arms and talk intimately about spiritual things.

Forgoing her usually lighthearted epistles, Chaucer spent an entire evening writing a letter in which she posited to Magnus that Janett going public about the affair might not be a bad thing. There would be an initial explosion of negative publicity, but people would soon get inured to it and bored by it. Resolution of Magnus' dilemma would certainly be accelerated. Concomitantly, if his secretary or a faculty member should catch Magnus and her ardently kissing in his office, and the matter became public that way, the same result would occur. After reading this letter a dozen times, she tore it up, fearing that Magnus would interpret it as a high-pressure sales job that would turn him against her. Either that or it would scare him permanently back into Janett's arms.

At the start of a faculty meeting, with most participants present but the session not yet convened, Chaucer innocently handed Magnus a request form for additional funding for a proposed independent study involving travel to Phoenix. He quickly scanned through the pages and blushed when he turned to the last page and read a handwritten limerick based on an erotic episode the previous spring:

I gave you climax with my tongue.

Such orgasmic tremors were flung

From the tips of your toes

To the end of your nose

It felt like *my* bell had been rung.

All through the meeting, he was distracted with thoughts of that particular encounter, which had been extremely risky but all the more exciting because of it. She had engaged in oral sex with him in a wooded area in Oak Creek Canyon behind a tourist lodge. But now in the midst of a room full of scholars and administrators, risky erotic behavior did not feel exciting. Yet his longing for Chaucer had never been more acute. His mind was now clear that he wanted out of his marriage, but he saw no way forward to accomplish that goal.

Near the end of September she sent him:

GINSENG IN THE DARK

The sun is unrevealed, but soon, too soon

Its light will penetrate the eastern panes.

This hour of night it seems ungentle

Switching on the kitchen chandelier,

So tea is brewed in pre-dawn dark.

Ritual proceeds by touch: an unsmooth mug

Is lifted from its certain place, the steaming

Water is decanted, powder poured and stirred,

The spoon is licked and set aside.

I slip into the lotus posture, and my hands

Caress the common cup, excited by its secondary warmth.

And as I sip the steeping drug-laced tea

My heart and loins awake and ache for unspent nights

And for an unforgotten lover.

Magnus mailed a response to her home address:

Dearest Chaucer,

My lover is also unforgotten, and my loins ache for her - for you. My mind is filled with images of you through sleepless nights of longing. How I hate the pain that you are enduring on my account. Please forgive me.

Janett has told me she is now available to serve my sexual needs, but I am impotent in her presence. Having sex with her at this point would feel like a complete capitulation. It would signify a return to the marriage and a renunciation of my love for you. Nevertheless, she is exhibiting supreme patience waiting for my emotional return to her, and she has not said a single thing to indicate openness to a separation. I remain alert, however, to any opportunity to ease her toward accepting the inevitability of divorce. One fine day, I am certain, a chink in her armor will appear, and I will be ready to fill it with the painful truth that I must leave her.

Chaucer left a note in his campus mailbox:

> My God, did she really phrase it that
> way? Available to serve your sexual needs? I
> would have said I want your body. I want to
> feel you inside me. As a matter of fact, I do.

Chaucer's note made Magnus feel momentarily defensive about
Janett. After all, they had been married twenty-seven years, he thought.
And his wife was fully justified in being furious with him and
therefore cutting him off from physical intimacy for a time. Janett
had not always been so clinical about sex, but he had wounded her
affectionate nature, so her emotional distance was understandable.
However, he would reveal none of that to Chaucer. In reply, Magnus
handed Chaucer a folded three-by-five card as they passed on the
sidewalk in front of the Administration building:

> Those were her exact words. I prefer yours.

Ving was emotionally torn by guilt and self-loathing about deceiving
Chaucer. He realized that he still loved her, but not as a wife. He and
Crandall had a long conversation about this, and Crandall told him
to go see Chaucer to clear the air. Taking a page from the Alcoholics
Anonymous Twelve-Step program, Ving went to Chaucer to make
amends.

Meanwhile, Chaucer had come to recognize that Ving had been -
and still was- under enormous social pressure to be something he
was not. Society was trying to force him to be dishonest, and he had
caved in to that pressure by marrying her. She had already forgiven
him in her mind long before he came to her and asked for
forgiveness in person. She missed his friendship.

When they met, Chaucer spoke again about her fears about
AIDS. "For a few days I was in a serious panic. But an unexpected

blessing came from it, because I made a new friend -a nurse at my gynecologist's office- when I rushed down there to have blood drawn."

"How stupid of me not to have seen that you would be afraid. Any rational person *would* be afraid of that," he said. "I sincerely apologize for not telling you that I had been fastidious about taking precautions. I had blood tests multiple times and was always clean. I was as obsessive about that as you were about birth control. But at the time, it never occurred to me that you would get yourself tested."

Feeling empowered by this talk with his ex-wife, Ving then went to his parents to tell them he was gay, although his mom already knew. For the occasion, however, she pretended that she had not known. Ving believed his father would have a hard time processing the news but was surprised by how quickly and decisively the patriarch of the family responded.

Van Valborg was apoplectic. "I don't know what perverted urges led you to adopt that so-called lifestyle," Van declared with venom, "but it certainly did not come from me or my side of the family." He turned toward Verna with an accusatory glare and then looked directly into his son's eyes. "There is only one way to deal with your disgraceful behavior, Ving. You're fired! I want the keys to the Sedona office by tomorrow at noon."

Van then sought out Ving's older brother Vic to go to Sedona to manage the branch office that Ving had established, but Vic refused, appalled at his father's behavior. Unwilling to reconsider his rapid and harsh judgment, Van transferred Polly Ellice, his best Phoenix agent, to Sedona to run the shop.

Ving opened his own agency down the block, calling it Exotic Journeys, and ninety percent of his clients went with him rather than stay at the old Valborg Voyages agency. Polly, the new agent, tried hard but could not make a go of the business. Van then made the tough business decision to close the branch. Polly, however, liked Sedona and did not want to make another household move so soon after relocating from Phoenix. Ving rescued her by offering her a position in his new agency.

Polly was plump, mid-forties, never married and had given up on relationships with men, because the only ones who pursued her were, in her mind, either control freaks or losers. In Sedona, she joined a New Age congregation called the Crystal Chapel, led by Sacred Lens Athena Helicon. There, Polly enjoyed worshiping by means of crystals, incense, chimes, meditation, and ethereal music. Polly flourished as a person by exploring her inner life with other unconventional people. She found wholeness and lost a great deal of weight amidst the crystals and aromas.

Ving soon initiated thematic dress at the agency. Two or three days a week, he and Polly came to work clothed in various costumes and regalia of exotic places tourists wanted to visit. Their clients loved it.

CHAPTER 26:
THE CRUSADE

You can by pious claim declare a place
A mile across in twenty feet of space.
Let's see if this place has sufficient size
Or make more room by speech, as is your guise.
Geoffrey Chaucer

Fundamentalist Christians participated in a picket against the Sedona Natural Christian Church in early September 1985. Their goal, driven by the firm belief that the naturists were blasphemous and evil heretics trying to recreate Eden in Arizona, was to force the naturist congregation out of the area. Since one of the NCC pastors was also on the faculty at Anasazi, the college was inevitably drawn into the protest, which became a sustained siege.

At five past twelve, the receptionist rang the college president and said, "Dr. Bergen, I think you will want to take this call. Duffy Davar is on the line." He was a reporter for the Verde Valley Intelligencer.

At ten past twelve, Duffy was seated in an overstuffed chair in Magnus Bergen's office ready for an exclusive interview. Magnus acknowledged that some of his faculty members attended the Sedona NCC but to his knowledge, no students did.

"Religion is a private matter," Magnus said, "so I will not divulge the names of people who practice this or any other religion. I

311

will neither confirm nor deny any of the names on your list, except for Cloud Morgan, who as one of the pastors of the Sedona Natural Christian Church is a well-known leading citizen of this town."

In the course of the interview, Magnus made several statements that later appeared in print and produced an angry outburst from an unexpected quarter.

"To the charge that the Natural Christians are heretics, I say if their church is not part of your particular tradition, you have no basis for judging their orthodoxy. Anyone can critique, compare, and contrast various theologies and prefer one over others, but only the followers of a particular tradition have the right to decide the parameters that constitute heresy. Heresy is an internal affair and not the business of observers from other traditions. The bottom line is that the charges brought against the Natural Christian Church from certain other Christian organizations are completely bogus," Magnus said. "They have done nothing illegal and have a constitutional right to practice their religion according to their beliefs. To some eyes they may seem immodest, but they are not in any way immoral. The protesters, on the other hand, remind me of a line from Byron. They 'hope to merit heaven by making earth a hell.'"

The source of the negative reaction was not members of the Board of Regents, who were secretly pleased to see Magnus take a strong stand on something. As to the matter of religious freedom, the regents recognized that he was right and thus should be supported. It was Janett.

In an effort at placating his wife soon after she had discovered his affair with Chaucer, Magnus had suggested they go together for marital counseling. Janett had adamantly refused.

"There is no need for counseling," she huffed, "because the issue is crystal clear. You strayed, and you need to return to the fold. I forgive you, Magnus, so all we need to do is resume the marriage and I'll never say another word about your infidelity."

"Well then, let's go to church together," he suggested.

"Going to church is only one step removed from marriage counseling," she replied icily, "and I won't fall for it, dear. You may be confused, but I assure you I am not. I don't need psychobabble mumbo jumbo to explain away your midlife wandering, and I don't need theological mumbo jumbo either."

Janett was angry when Magnus started going to church by himself but considered it a small price to pay for his apparent return to their marriage. If he had chosen to attend a prestigious mainline church, it would have been better than the embarrassing NCC, but he would soon grow tired of it, she reasoned. But when she read his defense of the nudist church in the Verde Valley Intelligencer, she was livid.

All through the morning, Janett stewed over the newspaper article. As the hours passed, she nursed a sense that having now publicly defended the outrageous behavior of one faculty member, her husband would likely do the same for other professors who peddled their crackpot ideas through journals, seminars, and protest marches. His next tilt at a windmill, she decided, would probably be to support Dr. Shock's ridiculous anti-circumcision crusade. She had long since regarded the psychology professor as a lunatic obsessed with penises. What's the big deal about clipping off a bit of unsightly foreskin? Yes, Magnus was enamored of that idiot Shock, she noted mentally. That will be his next misstep. And after that? Hadn't someone in the religion department made waves speculating about the lost descendents of Jesus? Or was it the lost tribe of Israel? She couldn't remember which. But the notion that Magnus would now be unable to refrain from championing weird and embarrassing causes took hold in her mind. The man was hopeless.

"How dare you defend that crackpot church at the risk of your career!" she screamed at him when he walked in the door for lunch. "After all the years I've given to mold and shape your career, after all my efforts to make something of you, to cover up for your social clumsiness, you thank me by doing something incredibly idiotic! Had it not been for my *devoted* efforts, you'd still be stuck as a lowly librarian at some second-rate cow college."

"And be contented with it," he whispered. "I love libraries." Now she had pushed too far. He was ready to fight back.

"Why be a Norwegian peasant, Magnus? Why not live up to your great name and be a Viking *chief?*" she answered in exasperation.

"Peasants don't love books," he replied. "And it is the *literature* of the Vikings that has survived, Janett, not their leaders."

"You're a hopeless second-rater," she said with a dramatic sigh.

"Well, you're a hopeless social climber," he countered. "You're really good at it, but I've lost count of the number of times I've been embarrassed by your incessant, calculating efforts to move us up a rung or two."

"Embarrassed?" she spat out. "That's only your lack of imagination at work, Magnus. Most men would take pride in having such an enterprising wife. Most men would value my skill. Don't you know I was positioning you for the presidency of Cornell or Dartmouth? You can kiss those plums goodbye, Magnus, you stupid, stupid man!"

"I don't give a damn about prestige!" he yelled. "Can't you see that? It's not the preeminence of a position that appeals to me but the nobility of the work."

"I give up. I can't get you out of this one. You've probably screwed yourself with the Regents, but I don't care, and apparently you don't either. I'm leaving you, Magnus. I'm going back to North Dakota where the people are more…ambitious."

Chaucer was outraged by the crusade against the NCC. She had never attended worship there but knew that Magnus went to the congregation's textile service. Her anger came from viewing the NCC as a progressive institution and the protesters as right-wing reactionaries. As a consistent champion of liberal causes, Chaucer felt compelled to defend the church, which was after all, led by her friends Cloud and Terp Morgan, whom she had known since her undergraduate days at ASU.

Apart from the Christian humanist congregation she attended while in graduate school in Pittsburgh, Chaucer's experience with church had been problematic. She now thought of herself as an aesthetic Christian, appreciating ritual and symbolism of the Christian tradition and the great classical music of the Church. Certain historic doctrinal themes seemed elegant to her, and her biblical literacy was deep. But when it came to accepting doctrines as factual and the Bible as authoritative, she could not assent. This caused her momentary concern, but then she realized that the NCC was not a dogma-driven institution. In fact, Chaucer had considered visiting the naturist congregation for years. Now was the time. This was a *kairos* moment she was called to seize.

She stood before her bedroom mirror, assessing her nude body and finding innumerable minor faults. My muscle tone is loosening, she thought. Time to start exercising again. Peering closely at her upper thighs, she spotted faint stretch marks from her episodes of weight gain and dieting. Though no one else would notice them unless looking for them specifically, the existence of the tiny lines felt like her body's rebuke to her for not taking better care of it. Her mind jumped to women who had borne children. They've earned their stretch marks, she decided. For mothers those scars are badges of honor, but I don't have any excuse.

Chaucer had never felt shy about being naked in front of a lover and had experienced communal nudity in college and graduate school, but that had been more than a decade earlier, and her body had been younger and firmer in those days. Somehow the prospect of baring all in a public setting where hundreds of people gathered now seemed a bit daunting. "Courage, Chaucer!" she said out loud to the image of herself. "This is a justice issue, and you have to go through with it!"

The next Sunday she acted in solidarity with Cloud and other faculty colleagues by attending, without her clothing, the traditional service at the Sedona Natural Christian Church. She sat with Emily and Bookman, who were pleased at her participation but restrained their zeal to evangelize her.

During the fellowship time after church, Chaucer chatted with Cloud and Terp. "I found the experience spiritually refreshing," she said. "And intellectually stimulating as well. I could see myself coming back in different circumstances."

"Well, I like to think we are just as refreshing and stimulating when there are no protesters around the place," said Terp.

"And more peaceful too," said Cloud. "There's a bit of tension in the air right now, but usually an aura of calm pervades."

"Calm would be good," Chaucer said as a far-off melancholy look fell across her face.

Responding intuitively, but knowing nothing of Chaucer's extramarital involvement, Terp said, "We have lots of pathways on the property for strolling and contemplation. People often use them to work out their preoccupations. You're welcome to take a walk if you like."

Chaucer replied, "A contemplative stroll has a lot of appeal, but I'm not much of an outdoors person. If I have to be outside for more than a few minutes, I always wear a broad-brimmed hat and slather sunscreen on any exposed body parts." She chuckled. "I'm afraid if I became a naturist, I would quickly go bankrupt from the expense of all the bottles of sun lotion I would empty every day."

"We buy it in bulk at home," said Terp. "I know where you can get SPF 60 for a very low price. But contrary to common wisdom, most naturists spend more time indoors than out. You could become very active here and never see the sun, although that would be a shame. A little sun on the skin is quite healthful."

"Next time, I'll bring a hat and sun screen," said Chaucer.

Cloud laughed. "Next time has such an optimistic ring to it. I look forward to seeing more of you."

Now Chaucer laughed. "More? You can see *all* of me this very moment."

"I meant more *often*," Cloud responded.

"I know," said Chaucer. "I couldn't resist teasing."

"The truth is," said Terp, "It's very good to see more of *you*, and it will be a blessing to see you more often."

"Well, you've built yourselves a Shangri-La here among the red rocks that James Hilton would be proud of, and who can resist Shangri-La?" Chaucer said.

"Don't try," said Cloud. "I take it you've read *Lost Horizon* or at least seen the movie. No, as an English professor, you would have read the book."

"Both, actually," Chaucer replied. "I've read quite a bit of James Hilton, *Lost Horizon*, *Goodbye, Mr. Chips*, and so on. He created wonderful stories and called them novels. My main criticism of Hilton is his terseness."

"Yes," said Cloud. "His books seem more like treatments for screen plays than fully developed novels. Many writers go into tedious detail page after page. Hilton's failing was the opposite, leaving large gaps. I enjoy his books but come away wanting more."

"But they do make great movies, *Chips* and *Horizon* especially," Chaucer said.

"We could go on for hours talking books and films," said Terp, "but we need to circulate among the visitors. Excuse us, Chaucer."

"Go!" said Chaucer and shooed them away.

Across the fellowship hall, Chaucer thought she saw a familiar face but decided it couldn't be Helene Finn. She moved closer to investigate and discovered that it was indeed Helene, eating a piece of celery and chatting with a fellow parishioner. Chaucer called out her name and soon the two were locked in an embrace.

"Helene, you look stunningly beautiful," said Chaucer. "You have a golden tan and shiny long hair, but still with the glasses."

"Thanks, Chaucer," Helene replied. "Coming from someone with a long history of being gorgeous, that's quite a compliment."

"What are you doing now? Are you a doctor? Do you live in Sedona? How did you end up in *this* place?" Chaucer was full of questions.

"I am a pediatrician with a private practice in Sedona," Helene explained. "I opened the practice in June after leaving a large corporate practice in Los Angeles, and it is a growing but not yet a full-time endeavor. Many of my new patients have connections with the NCC, so I thought it a good idea to check it out. I love this church."

Chaucer wanted to ask about her friend's marital status but hesitated to find a tactful way to put the question. "Do you live alone?"

"I'm not married, if that's what you want to know," Helene said. "But I am in a semi-regular relationship with a neurologist in Phoenix. Neither of us has any current interest in matrimony."

Chaucer told Helene about being a professor at Anasazi and being divorced. No mention was made about falling in love with the college president, for Chaucer was beginning to think of that experience as history. An aura of star-crossed inevitable loss pervaded her psyche when she thought about Magnus.

At home that evening, Chaucer worked on notes for a lecture on her namesake Geoffrey Chaucer's *The Book of the Duchess*. As she did so, reflections on her own verse written in response to involvement with Magnus interrupted her concentration. The conclusion of Geoffrey's long poem struck her as an apt metaphor for the impetuous affair.

She made a Modern English translation of the last five lines of *Duchess:*

> *Thought I, this is so strange a dream*
> *That I desired in press of time*
> *To set this foolish dream in rhyme*
> *As best I could and quickly penned.*
> *This was my dream, now at its end.*

She considered sending it to Magnus without explanation and unsigned. There was no question in her mind that he would know who sent it and grasp the metaphor. But then she thought it would be a cruel thing to do. Though she felt vulnerable, ashamed, and abandoned by the emotional limbo he had created for her, she did not possess the needed vindictive streak. No, she thought, my words in response to his telephone call were painful enough.

Magnus, as usual, attended the contemporary service, and he especially needed the structure of prayer that day. Within an hour of the event, he had phoned Chaucer to tell her that Janett had left him. What remained unsaid was that he had dithered for months about his triangular predicament, unable to make any kind of decision until Janett had finally made it for him. He was too embarrassed to confess this failure of courage or decisiveness, about which he felt deeply ashamed. Rather, he naively hoped that a gracious and starry-eyed Chaucer would shout hooray and rush to his side.

Chaucer, however, was acutely aware of her lover's inability to choose and was deeply hurt by it. Something in her shadow wanted him to pay a price for dragging her through limbo. It would have been less painful, she thought, if he had simply and cleanly broken off their relationship and returned for good to Janett. Now that he was free, she was not sure she wanted to fall gratefully into his eager arms, and she told him so in blunt and resentful language. What she needed now was a time to be angry and resentful with no commitment to get over it. This was why Magnus needed prayer.

"Cloud told me to imagine life without either one," Magnus whispered to himself, as Jonathan Davidman skillfully produced Bach's meditative song "With You Beside Me" on an eerily resounding electronic organ. "Why didn't I see this coming?" He might have been tempted to fall into a depressed expression of abject misery had it not been for his guest seated at his right.

Pleased by his courageous defense of the church, Sigrid Yves, the attorney representing the congregation in its efforts to counteract the protesters, asked if she could accompany him to the service, and Magnus was grateful for her company. Sigrid was a fine conversationalist, and he fell into an easy exchange of words with her, but he was too wrapped up in recriminations about failing to be decisive on Chaucer's behalf that he was unable to detect anything more than friendly support in Sigrid's request to sit with him.

Chaucer Dickinson had been conducting an independent study of *Adventures of Huckleberry Finn*, and as a matter of pleasant coincidence, the discussion that week dealt with the idyllic motif of Huck and Jim rafting down the Mississippi River in the nude. Her two female students, Vera Toll and Terra Birtles, were inspired by the student counter-demonstrations against the puritanical crusaders and thus motivated, invited Chaucer to lead this particular conversation with them while all three relaxed without clothing in a dormitory lounge. She did so with glee.

A short time later, after the crusade against the naturist congregation had collapsed, Chaucer was leading another independent study with Vera and Terra, probing attitudes toward sexuality in the works of Geoffrey Chaucer. Taking a break from the academic analysis, Vera asked Chaucer what she thought of the anti-nudity protest.

"The attempted assassination of Cloud's father proved that the whole episode was morally and ethically ungrounded and the picket leaders were despicable," Chaucer said.

"Would you ever go to services at the church?" Vera pressed.

"Actually I have attended services there in solidarity with the NCC but I'm not a member," Chaucer said. "And to clarify my characterization of the crusade leaders, I do not think their followers are evil but simply sorrowful people who are misguided and ignorant."

"Vera and I carried anti-crusade picket signs," Terra said, "but we hesitated to attend the church. Not because of the nudity. That was the appealing part. But we thought we might embarrass ourselves trying to follow their rituals and wondered if they might come off all pious and holy to compensate for their lack of clothes."

"You needn't worry on either of those counts," said Chaucer. "The worship is elegant in its simplicity. You won't have any trouble following the order of service. And they are very much down-to-earth and not holier-than-thou."

"If you go again sometime, could we go with you?"

"I don't see why not," the professor said.

The following Sunday, Chaucer accompanied Vera and Terra to the NCC service, sitting with Helene.

"When Chaucer and I were in grade school," Helene told the coeds, "we lounged around naked in the attic of a house under construction."

"Ooh, so the teacher has a secret," Vera responded with a chuckle.

"It's hardly a secret if it's part of casual conversation," said Chaucer. "And you might be interested in knowing that Dr. Finn here..."

"Call me Helene," the physician interrupted.

"Helene then," Chaucer continued, "only became a pediatrician so she could see boys' weenies."

Helene guffawed. "Yes, well when I was fourteen, that was indeed part of my motivation for planning to go into medicine. But that mission was accomplished long before I ever got to med school."

"That's OK," said Terra. "Vera and I are roommates in a coed dorm, and we lounge around naked in our room all the time."

"And sometimes we see boys running down the hall to the showers with their weenies hanging out," said Vera.

"Give me an informal estimate," said Helene. "Do you see more circumcised or intact penises in your dorm?"

"Definitely more circumcised," said Terra. "Does that make a difference?"

"Indeed it does," said Helene. "I won't allow circumcisions in my practice. It's a barbaric ritual that should have been abandoned centuries ago. If parents want their newborn boys sliced up, I won't accept them as patients."

"I thought it was done for hygienic reasons," said Vera.

"Cutting off foreskin does not improve a boy's hygiene. That's a myth," the physician said. "The foreskin is full of blood vessels, sensitive nerve endings that enhance sexual pleasure, and important mucous membranes. Circumcision eliminates all that and exposes the glans to abrasions."

"What a bummer," said Terra. "I didn't know that."

Vera and Terra represented only two of an influx of Anasazi students who became new members of the Sedona NCC. They along with a few other students got to know the pediatrician well enough to become her groupies. Several of these students asked Helene if she would lead them in independent studies in various aspects of anatomy and disease. Thus agreement was quickly gained from the life sciences department, and Helene became an Anasazi adjunct professor. Her first independent study examined genital mutilation practices around the world, including male circumcision.

To rebuild her childhood friendship with Helene, Chaucer also began to attend church regularly. Within a few weeks she had become friends with the church organist, Jonathan Davidman, whose playing she considered artistically brilliant and whose wit she thought mordantly sharp. She liked the sibling feel to her growing relationship with the gay musician.

Since neither had a partner, they often went out together for dinner and films, as well as musical concerts at the college. Jonathan reminded her wistfully of her father's musical talent but Jonathan was more affectionate to her than her dad had ever been. The relationship also reminded Chaucer of the good parts of living with Ving but without the dishonesty.

Over lunch at a Mexican restaurant in town one day, Chaucer teased Jonathan about his stylish dressing habits.

"Are you stereotyping me?" Jonathan said.

"Maybe," she said. "If the shoe fits…"

"No, if the shoes are stylish," Jonathan said. "The most important thing is that they *look* good."

"I'm really grateful for your listening ear," she said, now serious. "You're such a good listener and comforter. You should be a pastor."

"What makes you think a church musician is not a pastor?" Jonathan replied.

"After all I've confided in you about my affair with Magnus, I believe you are a pastor regardless of your position description," she said.

"Thank you," he said.

"The thing is," she continued, "I will probably never get Magnus out of my system, but I'm really angry that he was such a wimp about his wife. Once Janett found out, how much courage would it have taken to say it was over?"

"Not everyone has the gift for breaking up," Jonathan said. "There is an art to it, and though Magnus is brilliant, he is no artist, and he is far too kind a soul to do it cleanly. I suspect his hesitation had more to do with essential niceness than lack of courage. He does project that Midwestern politeness thing. I think it's authentic."

"Oh Jonathan, that helps a lot. You have such a talent for parsing messy love affairs," she said and kissed his hand.

CHAPTER 27:
RED AND WHITE ROSES

Within that little Hive
Such Hints of Honey lay
As made Reality a Dream
And Dreams, Reality –

Emily Dickinson

Chaucer tried to fill her non-working time with writing more of her *Timberscape* fairy tale. As with her fiction writing endeavors in Vermont, she wrote and promptly ripped up every new page she produced. She was unable to get the chapter to go anywhere she judged worthwhile. The quartet simply do not like what I'm writing about them, she thought. This was to be the final chapter, and she wanted to wrap everything up elegantly, but although early on she had developed a structure for the book around the main characters sojourning in the four realms, she was not satisfied with any of the conclusions she conjured.

On one point, however, she was completely clear. She would not have any of the characters waking up from a dream. She toyed with the idea of having them drink spring water or eating berry bread as a way of bringing the twins back to Arizona, but could not figure out what to do with Hansel and Gretel. No matter how hard she tried, nothing she wrote seemed any good to her. And clearly, the four were not satisfied either.

The characters in her novel were trapped inside her brain in literary limbo, paralleling her own life in which she felt stuck in an unresolved relationship. Nevertheless, and despite the welcome insights of her friend Jonathan, she retained her anger at Magnus.

Some relief came from her attendance at the naturist church. Inevitably she felt better after each service. She paired up with Terp for a foot washing and reflexology session one Sunday afternoon, and the two reminisced about high school. Their experiences had been very different, because Terp did not date during those years. But they both had intellectual achievement on their teenage resumes.

"I was such a nerd," Terp said. "I read the New York Times and obsessively watched the evening news on television."

"Actually, so did I," said Chaucer. "I read the Phoenix Gazette, which was no match for the Times but informative nonetheless. And I tuned in to the CBS Evening News, even when my parents weren't watching it. There's at least one thing we had in common. I was nearly reverential about the news broadcast. For a long time I had a crush on Walter Cronkite."

Now Terp produced a full-throated laugh. "No way! So did I. I thought Uncle Walter was the sexiest man in America."

Chaucer snorted a series of giggles. "Well, he was sort of sexy in those days."

The combination of foot massage and laughter with a good friend prolonged Chaucer's sense of well being for the rest of that day. She went to bed in a mellow mood. The following morning, however, she was back in her limbo of funk.

After two months of living without Janett and Chaucer, Magnus was beginning to feel better about being alone. In the first weeks after both women had (in his mind) forsaken him, he had simply plodded through each day, doing what he needed to do without attention to detail or care about success.

Gradually, however, the veil of depression lifted, and he was able to imagine a satisfying life ahead. It would no doubt be solitary for the foreseeable future, but that had its compensations. He did not have to negotiate the use of his free time. There was no one he needed to coordinate with about errands or what to do with an evening. He did allow himself to dream about meeting someone someday, but for the time being, no one he could imagine approached the glorious reality of Chaucer. He assured himself that her aura would fade in time, and so he chose to be patient and let it pass of its own energy.

He had learned soon after Sigrid had joined him at church that she did indeed have an agenda, but it was not hidden. She sought him out as a friend and hoped that as a friend he would recognize her intellectual talent. What she wanted was the chance to teach occasional independent studies at Anasazi. When she told Magnus what she had in mind, he signed her up as an adjunct faculty member.

After separating from Magnus, Janett told a female friend on the Anasazi faculty about her husband's infidelity and with whom. From a distance in North Dakota, she relied on this friend for intelligence about the affair, and the friend made it her business to keep watchful eyes on Magnus and Chaucer. When her spying friend called to report that Chaucer had apparently dumped Magnus and he seemed to be moping around most of the time, Janett felt victorious. She did not want him back, but from her seat of triumph, she felt a tinge of pity for her foolish husband who now had no one and whose career was clearly stalled if not dead. To make things fast and simple, Janett filed for a no-fault divorce. All they needed to do was wait for the process to move through its stages.

Janett was also certain that she would find another talented man to mold into a successful executive much sooner than Magnus would expend the initiative to meet a suitable woman. Indeed, she already had her eyes on a high school classmate who was teaching at the University of North Dakota. The poor soul's wife died of cancer, and he needed encouragement and direction. She knew he would one day make a fine university president.

Chaucer stubbornly insisted that Magnus not try to communicate with her, because she needed time to assess her own life on her own terms. In fact, this assessment dealt with Magnus as much as it did Chaucer, but she did not reveal this to him.

Weeks of brooding produced this result in her mind. Magnus was a brilliant, careful, and diplomatic man who successfully balanced the odd mixture of faculty egos, student rebelliousness, and parents' anxieties, while maintaining a financially sound institution. He was a skilled college president, and therefore *should* be able to think clearly about personal relationships and make insightful decisions about them. But he was a flawed man. He suffered from a maddening inability to end a dysfunctional and unsatisfying marriage, presumably out of a medieval sense of loyalty and duty baked into him by his Scandinavian mother. Instead, he had passively allowed his manipulating wife to make the decision for him, which made Chaucer feel humiliated.

Magnus was not a perfect catch. And his inability to act when she needed him to be decisive thoroughly frustrated her. But there were two other factors to consider. First, she too was flawed, and no doubt had plenty of idiosyncrasies that would provide adequate counter-frustration for Magnus. Second, despite, or more likely because of his peculiar imperfections, she was madly in love with him.

Late Saturday afternoon, while he was fully occupied with his project to redecorate and refurnish the president's house to make it reflect more masculine tastes, Magnus experienced a sense of pleasure at his solitary endeavor. "All shall be well," he recited to himself. Peace descended upon his mind, and he sighed.

At that moment, the doorbell rang. As he had positioned himself between several large bookcases he was in the midst of rearranging, some maneuvering was necessary before he could make his way to the foyer. On the porch stood a young woman in a delivery service uniform, and when he opened the door, she handed him a long cardboard carton.

Inside the box were twenty-four roses, half red and half white. Tucked into the side was a card.

Dear Magnus,

I have tried very hard to maintain my anger at you. However, I am an abject failure in this effort. And the failure seems to stem from the very basic underlying fact that I long to hear your voice, and I ache for your touch, and I am foolishly and recklessly in love with you. I would be most grateful if you could forgive my inability to stay mad at you and instead graciously satisfy my need to be mad *about* you.

The card was not signed.

As he searched the kitchen for an adequate vessel for the flowers, the doorbell rang again. This time, Chaucer stood on the porch.

"I was in such a rush at the florist shop I forgot to sign the card. May I do that now?" she said.

He reached for her hand and pulled her into the house. "You can do that later; I recognized the handwriting," he replied and enfolded her in his arms.

A little past two in the morning, a thought jolted Magnus out of a deep sleep, and he sat straight up. "Oh my God!" he said.

This wakened Chaucer, and she pulled herself up beside him. "What's wrong?" she asked.

"I left the roses on the kitchen counter -without water," he confessed.

"They'll keep," she said. "And if they don't, they've served their purpose. Go back to sleep, my love."

Obediently, Magnus settled back down and quickly fell into peaceful slumber. For a while, Chaucer remained up, watching him sleep, overcome with gratitude not only that she loved him more than she had ever loved anyone else, but that now she would be able to sleep beside him all the time. She felt no sense of having won out over Janett but rather that she had now landed where she needed to be, and Janett was now free to pursue her own authentic destiny.

Over breakfast the next morning, Chaucer said, "The time away from you helped me clarify some very important things. You know how dysfunctional my family of origin is. It has certainly molded me into someone less than ideal. And I ran away from it, ran away from home to recover from it right into another dysfunctional marriage. So when I see signs of dysfunction, I get fearful. I've been yearning for a new home, but I don't want to be drawn into another abyss."

"And, I gather, the emotional bonds that tied me to Janett represented that fearful possibility to you," Magnus said.

"Yes," she replied. "But then I came to recognize that we're all messed up one way or another. But we can change. In judging my parents, I failed to take into account that some people do transcend their early experiences. Some people recover if they do the hard work necessary."

"I think you will find that I am a very hard worker," said Magnus. "For a time it was sheer terror for me believing I had lost you without the lifebuoy of Janett to keep me from drowning, but I learned to stay afloat. You were far wiser than I to insist on a season of solitude."

"We both have interior work to do, and exterior work, as well, on how to function in healthy ways even if those around us try to make us crazy," she said. Reaching across the table, she took his hand. "But after all the years of searching, I think I've finally come home."

Chaucer was so energized by settling in with Magnus, that she worked diligently and enthusiastically on completing *The Timberscape of Memory*. Now the words flowed, the way ahead for her characters became clear, and she brought the tale to what she believed was a satisfying conclusion.

CHAPTER 28:
DECISION IN TIMBERSCAPE

*"Well, now that we have seen each other," said
the unicorn, "if you'll believe in me, I'll believe
in you."*

Lewis Carroll

Wisdom gleaned from their experiences in the realms gave the quartet confidence that this time they would be able to find the spring source of the river. Bathing in it, they had come to believe, would unseal the door to the cave. They suspected also that the Golden Mind, the Spring of Memory, and the spring source all referred to the same place. Thus Kyp needed to stay with them as they searched.

As soon as they crossed into the Timberscape, the four decided it would be prudent to change back to their own original clothes, which they carried with them while wearing their self-selected Hearts uniforms of khaki slacks and blue polo shirts. If the opportunity to return home suddenly presented itself, they wanted to be prepared to do so in the garb they had been wearing when they arrived. The four disrobed to don their old clothes and immediately a strong gust of wind blew in from the north and carried all the garments off beyond sight.

"Oh my!" said Allys. "There go our old clothes and our Hearts attire too."

"Better your Hearts attire than your heart's desire,"

Aylwyn noted dryly and then added, "This hasn't happened since our first day here."

"This is a sign," said Gretel. "Perhaps it means that we should not return to Hearts."

"But what does it portend about returning to our birth lands?" Hansel asked. "Perhaps we may not be able to return but will be kept here forever."

"I don't think it means anything," said Allys. "We've lost our clothes before and always gotten them back. The winds in the Scape seem to have a mind of their own for blowing garments around."

Kyp was still wrapped in her sarong, which she offered to anyone who felt the need for covering. All four declined the offer.

Once again, they hiked naked through the forest and meadows, stopping to make crowns of vine as exercises in nostalgia evoking their first day in Timberscape four years earlier. Kyp wove a loose necklace of flowers, and as she had become warm from the hike, removed and folded the sarong and carried it like a purse.

The quintet moved southward toward the area where Pieter and Wendlich lived. Once there, they found the tree house but no one was home.

"Let's leave a note saying we are heading toward the spring at the source of the Gymnarykum," said Aylwyn.

"And also that we have learned magic and may be able to reverse their spells, so please try to meet us there," Gretel added.

This they did.

On the continuing journey, they again met Foxford and Ollam, now jointly tending a different ferry station.

"Oho, the foursome has become a fivesome," Ollam shouted merrily as the young ones approached. "Would you like to cross the river?"

"Yes please," said Allys. "And we have plenty of stories to pay the toll with."

"Then let's hear them," said Foxford.

As the raft moved slowly across the water, each of the five told a story about life in Hearts. Then they made their way to visit Cranna and Tovah, who were so delighted to see them that they prepared a great feast of thanksgiving, with berry bread and sweet gourds filled with seven grains all downed with tankards of honeyade.

Stuffed with food and contentedly setting out in search of the cave and spring, they soon discovered that all the trails had disappeared with no trace. All their contentment disappeared, too, as they circled for hours. Recognizing nothing of the landscape, they sat under a fig tree to consider their situation.

"One must laugh at the irony," said Gretel, "that we worried so much about going in circles while escaping from Spades, though there we made a straight path. Now in the friendly safety of the Scape, we are indeed going round and round."

"As frustrating as this is," Hansel offered in response, "at least our lives are not at stake here. No one is trying to imprison us."

"Don't be so sure," said Allys. "Maybe the disappearing trail is Timberscape's way of keeping us in captivity."

"This is no prison," said Kyp. "It is an enchanting residence. Have patience."

"Allys, you speak as if the Scape were a living thing," said Hansel.

"Maybe it is," Allys responded. "A living entity of some kind, anyway. I think it has a brain apart from the human and other beings here. I don't mean the Golden Mind. The whole place -trees, mountains, streams, and all- feels...conscious. It's like the land has an agenda."

"If so, there must be a reason for keeping us here," said Aylwyn.

"I think you are correct, Aylwyn," said Gretel. "But the reason remains a mystery. I have been inwardly speculating about our homes. Perhaps they have been destroyed. Perhaps we do not have homes or parents to return to. That could be why we are kept here and cannot leave."

"Yeah, I've been thinking along that same line," said Aylwyn. "But I didn't want to say anything to discourage anyone else. I have a dread feeling that we have been saved from some great disaster in our home world –or worlds as the case may be. The good news is that we are alive, but the bad news is we can never see home again, because home no longer exists."

"That is a thoroughly depressing thought," said Allys.

"Do you have a better explanation?" Aylwyn shot back.

"I certainly have a more optimistic attitude," Allys said forcefully. "I don't believe our homes have been destroyed. I can't abide the thought of Mom and Dad being gone. Whatever is keeping us from leaving, it doesn't have anything to do with disasters at home."

"I am inclined to endorse the more cheerful view of Allys," said Hansel. "And I sense she is right about the Scape having its own brain. All we can do is continue to search and not be discouraged by the difficulties of the journey."

"Point well made," said Aylwyn. "We've escaped from far worse in the last few years."

"Yes, I would rather act with hope than allow my own inner fears to dominate our efforts," said Gretel.

"Well then, let's get going," said Allys.

Eventually they spotted a chuckwalla sunbathing on a rock.

"You look lost," the chuckwalla said.

Hansel replied, "Yes, we are quite lost and do not know where we are."

"That's easily fixed," said the large lizard. "I can give you a map."

"Oh great! We are saved, after all," said Allys with a relieved sigh. "Let's see your map."

The chuckwalla ran into a crack between boulders and returned with a foot square parchment bearing an image of the place where they were standing. "Here you go. This shows your exact location. See, right there on the map are these very rocks."

Gretel said, "This will not help in the least. It only shows where we are but not where we want to go."

"It will show you everywhere you go," said Chuckwalla with a huff. "Look, step over here away from these rocks." They did so. "Now look again. See, the map still shows where you are, even though you have moved. It will show you exactly where you are, wherever that may be, so you will never be lost."

"Alas, that will not help us in the way we need to be helped," said Hansel.

"And precisely why not?" said Chuckwalla in frustration.

"Because," said Gretel with similar frustration, "we need to see where our destination is so we can tell that we are going in the right direction."

"Well, why didn't you say so," said Chuckwalla. "Where is it you want to go?"

"To the Spring of Memory," said Aylwyn.

"It just so happens I also have a map of the spring." Chuckwalla went back down into the crevice and returned with another map that showed the spring but only the spring and not the whole of the Timberscape or even the environs of the spring.

"I'm afraid this won't do either," said Allys. "We need a larger map so we can see where we are now and where we're going at the same time."

"At the same time? Why that is preposterous!" said Chuckwalla. "Who ever heard of such a thing? All that **really** matters is to know **who** you are each moment **wherever** you may be."

They continued tramping about all day, still quite lost. As dusk approached, they stumbled upon a gazebo with five mats and blankets, so they settled in for the night.

"This is a hopeful sign," said Gretel.

"It will be more so if an outhouse should be found nearby," said Hansel.

Upon rising in the morning, they found a small spring behind the gazebo and a five-seat outhouse a short way into a clearing to the west. After their communal ablutions and emergence from the outhouse, they were unsurprised that the gazebo had disappeared. Beyond where it had stood was a clover field bounded by a white granite cliff with a large cave in its face. The rock surrounding the entrance to the cave was painted in bright psychedelic colors forming an arc a yard wide.

"Whoa!" said Aylwyn. "It certainly doesn't look like the one we came out of when we first arrived here. But looks in this place can be deceiving."

"Let's see," said Allys. "This may be our ticket home."

As they approached the cave, the sound of laughter preceded a dozen longhaired and chubby young men and women emerging from it. Joining hands, they began exuberantly dancing in a circle across a patch of clover. They wore nothing but the flowers braided into their manes.

One of the dancers, a woman in dreadlocks, spotted the five and shouted to the group, "Hey, we have visitors. Make room in the circle."

Another with straight jet-black hair said, "Groovy! Join us, friends."

Various dancers dropped their hands to make separate spaces for each of them to enter, although the movement never stopped. All five jumped in to the dancing circle and took the extended hands of those on either side.

Gretel managed to speak, "Excuse us for crashing your dance party, but we are searching for the Spring of Memory. Could you help us with directions?"

At once the movement stopped, catching each of the five off guard, causing them to bump into the people to their left.

"Bummer, man," said a blond man. "Who needs memories? Just live in the present moment. That place does strange things to your mind."

"But it is really important for us to find the spring so that we can go home," said Hansel.

"This is home, man, right here. You can stay in our pad," said a woman with black hair streaked with silver. "The more the hippier. Stay away from that spring."

"Where exactly are we at the moment?" Aylwyn asked.

"Why the Cave of the Hippies," replied a female with red hair. "This is a sanctuary pad. Hey, we're just about to go inside and have some tea. Care to join us? It's really good stuff."

"Thank you," said Allys, feeling both pleased and leery of the easy hospitality. "But we would be really grateful if you could give us directions **before** we took tea."

"Truth is," said a man with curly brown hair, "we really don't know where it's at. That's not our bag. Of course, we don't **need** to know, because we're already home."

"Unfortunately, we are not. Do you have any neighbors who might be able to help us?" Gretel asked.

"There's Old Z," said a brunette with bangs. "Just follow the cliff-side trail for a couple of hours, or maybe a couple of days, I don't remember which. Eventually you'll find Old Z's cave."

"Tea time," said a woman with an afro. "Please come in."

"Thank you all the same," said Kyp. "But I'm in somewhat of a hurry and need to be on my way. I'm not speaking for my companions, though."

"Yes, thanks. It's kind of you to invite us," said Allys, "but we all have miles to go before we sleep."

"Well frost my butt," a platinum blonde said. "You bunch need to mellow out. It's your loss. But if that's the way you like it, all I can say is later dudes and dudettes."

"And if you get lost," said the ginger woman, "just come on back to the Cave of the Hippies and we'll help you forget about it with some really good tea and brownies."

"Yeah, later," said Aylwyn. "And thanks for the directions and hospitality."

"Here's the trail," Kyp announced and began hiking it. The other four waved cheerfully to the hippies as they followed Kyp.

A few minutes later, Gretel said, "Do you think we should have stayed with them for a time? Maybe they had something we needed to learn."

"Maybe," said Allys. "But my intuition says we got what we needed from them -directions to the cave of this mysterious Old Z."

At noon, Hansel spotted a dark patch in the white granite cliff about a hundred yards ahead. "Maybe that's the cave of Old Z," he said.

It was indeed the entrance to a cave, which they approached cautiously and peered into. All five of them jumped back in startled embarrassment when they saw a strange person sitting in the lotus posture meditating just inside the mouth of the cave. The lone creature was both male and female.

The person calmly looked up at the searchers and said, "Hello. I have been expecting you. My name is Zeitreise. I trust you enjoyed a pleasant night in the gazebo."

"Yes, and a curious morning at the Cave of the Hippies," Gretel said.

"A charming, good-hearted bunch," Zeitreise said. "And now you are here. Welcome to my home."

"Do any others live here with you?" Hansel asked.

"No, I am quite alone in my cave," Zeitreise said. "I am an eremite, one who prefers solitude. The land of my birth is the Realm of Hearts, but this is now my home forever."

"We apologize for intruding on your solitude," Allys said.

"Oh, no bother," said Zeitreise. "I enjoy company every now and again."

"Why were you expecting us?" Aylwyn asked.

"Every pilgrim, seeker, and lost soul in the Timberscape eventually passes by this spot," Zeitreise explained. "Besides that, the birds tell me everything, all the gossip about strangers from alternative realities. But come now, you must be hungry. Please step inside. I'll serve you a delicious lunch and my most refreshing tea."

Zeitreise ushered them into a pleasant living room with thick woven rugs for reclining on. "Make yourselves at home, while I rustle around the kitchen. I'll only be a minute."

Zeitreise, who appeared old but not ancient, soon returned with a platter of cups of hot tea, cucumber sandwiches, oranges, and chocolate chip cookies.

"The hippies offered us tea, but we were in a hurry, so we didn't accept their hospitality," said Aylwyn.

Zeitreise laughed. "Their tea is more...fragrant than mine. You might have done better to sojourn with them. And their brownies are out of this world! I am quite fond of the hippies down the trail. Of course, their boisterous, extroverted household is quite the opposite of my simple and ascetic homestead. But they are good neighbors and rarely intrude on my solitude."

"Out of curiosity, why did you leave Hearts to come here?" Hansel asked.

"Because I did not want to become a martyr," Zeitreise answered. "I was well on that path when I realized that martyrdom was not my calling. It would significantly disrupt my practice of meditation. Besides, I could not help people like you if I were dead."

"Pardon my words if they give offense," said Gretel, "but you look like an old woman who lives down the street in our village."

"No offense taken," said Zeitreise genially.

"In that case," said Aylwyn, "I'll add that you remind me of an old man on our street in Tempe."

"Well," said Kyp, "you do not remind me of anyone I have ever met. I think you must look like yourself."

"All of your impressions are accurate," Zeitreise said.

Hansel said, "The old woman in our village is widely believed to be a witch."

Allys said, "People think the old man on our street is an eccentric scientist, working on weird experiments like time travel."

"Are you afraid of your village witch and mad scientist?" asked Zeitreise.

In unison the four said, "No!"

"Then neither shall you fear me," Zeitreise said.

The meal was quickly consumed, after which the visitors told Zeitreise what they were looking for and asked if the old one had a map.

"A map will not do you much good, anyway." Zeitreise said. "Maps in the Timberscape only show you where you are and not where you are going."

"So we found out yesterday," said Aylwyn.

"But do not despair. I will personally guide you to the spring at the source of the Gymnarykum River so that four of you may bathe in it. Kyp, you do not need to find the source. You can bathe anywhere in the river to recover memory of a previous life. But you must have solitude when you do it, so you must now bid farewell to your friends and set out alone to the river."

Kyp cried amid the time of goodbyes because she did not want the four to leave the Timberscape and the Realm of Hearts forever. But mindful of her goal, she went off to complete her task.

As Zeitreise led the four through the forest, a short path appeared before them, revealing only the next few yards ahead. As soon as they had stepped onto it, the section behind them vanished into the underbrush.

"This path opening and disappearing looks to me like a sign that Timberscape has its own brain," said Allys. "Am I right?"

"In a sense, yes and in another sense, no," Zeitreise replied. "There is a collective consciousness here. Many interconnected brains, if you will. But that is not unique to this world. It is true for the place you four have come from. The various conscious entities respond to mental signals from those who know how to tap into the whole."

"And you know how," said Aylwyn.

"Oh, most certainly," said Zeitreise. "I would be a poor excuse for an eremite if I could not communicate with the universe and do wonderful things with my mind."

Before long, they came upon the cave entrance that Allys, Aylwyn, Hansel, and Gretel had come out of in the beginning.

"That's our cave!" Aylwyn shouted.

"And it's open!" Allys said. "Let's check it out."

Without further discussion, the four rushed toward the cave, but as soon as they came within three yards of the entrance, it sealed itself.

Zeitreise said, "That particular cave has a long history of passive aggression. It is overly sensitive and closes and opens again based on its mercurial emotions. It pays no attention to my desires. In that regard, it is very different from my serene cave. On the other hand, my cave does not lead anywhere outside. It only curves around inside the Timberscape of Memory."

"Could it be that this cave closed because we don't have the clothes we wore when we arrived here?" Allys wondered. "If we went back home naked, it would cause quite a sensation, and we would have a difficult time explaining how we happened to be that way. I can see the headline in the newspaper now: 'Teens found safe but naked.'"

"That is as good an explanation as any," Zeitreise said. "It is a suitable model that will suffice for the moment. Yet though the subject is an interesting one, let us not tarry in speculations over the motives of granite girded tunnels. Your goal is near."

Zeitreise led them around the base of the hill, and on the other side they saw a small stream of white water pouring forth from a bubbling spring, widening as it flowed in a coiled pattern.

"This is the source," Zeitreise announced with a note of pride in his voice.

As happy as they had been to find their cave, and as instinctively quick as they had been to approach it, now all four hesitated to enter the water.

"I detect reluctance," said Zeitreise. "I thought you were anxious to return home."

"Well," said Allys, "we do want to depart, but we are also hoping that Pieter and Wendlich will show up here so we can undo their enchantments."

"Right," said Aylwyn. "We've waited four years, so a few more hours shouldn't matter much."

Zeitreise replied, "The perpetual pre-pubescents will not come today. They are at the Diamonds border engaged in lobbing mud balls at fashion police from the protected cover of the Timberscape."

"That makes me sad," said Gretel. "But under the circumstances, we may as well enter the water."

"It has the opposite effect on me," Zeitreise said. "The image of fashion fascists spattered with slime seems an inherently humorous one."

"I don't mean the mud balls," explained Gretel. "That is indeed funny to imagine. Not being able to try our magic on Pieter and Wendlich is what disappoints me."

"Yes, yes, I know," said Zeitreise. "Rest assured that they will find what they need at the appropriate time. For the four of you, it is safe to proceed."

"I presume, then, that the absence of our clothing will have no effect on our return," said Hansel.

"You shall be suitably attired when you return to the lands of your birth," said Zeitreise.

"Do you mean by that that we'll be in our birthday suits?" asked Allys.

"Oh, why not leave a little something to be surprised about," said Zeitreise. "Where is your spirit of adventure?"

Aylwyn let out a great sigh. "Oh what the deuce. Let's be surprised then."

"Before we do this, I have a question," said Allys.

"Only one?" Zeitreise replied.

"A series of interconnected questions then," she clarified. "Carlos, our driver in Hearts, came here through a cave but was encouraged right away to go to Hearts. Wendlich and Pieter appeared here because of a spell and have remained in the Scape. Do all who come to this island enter through the Timberscape or do some pop up in various realms?"

"Only through the Timberscape" said Zeitreise. "As you have recognized, not all enter through the cave, but according to the laws of physical enchantment, entrance to Gymnarykum can only be gained through Old Mem, for it is the locus of rebirth."

"Well then," Allys continued, "We were rotated through all four realms, and I'll get to my question about that in a moment. But why do some stay in the Scape and others migrate to Hearts and presumably other realms?"

"There is a process of discernment with respect to new arrivals," Zeitreise explained. "Generally jackrabbits and mockingbirds handle this but bobcats and flickers participate on occasion. After sensing which realm the newcomers are best suited for, various residents encourage and assist the new ones to get there. In a number of cases the best place is the Timberscape itself."

"Where do most of them go?" Aylwyn asked.

"Apart from the special ones who stay here in Old Mem, the majority of arrivals seem best suited to Hearts," Zeitreise said. "A smaller number go to Diamonds and Clubs. Only the rare misanthrope is sent to Spades."

"OK then, now the big question: Why were **we** sent to **all four** realms?" Allys asked. "Are we so non-discernable that no one could figure out where we belong?"

"At the moment, I am afraid I cannot answer your big question," Zeitreise said with a deep sigh.

The four had been in Gymnarykum long enough to know nothing would be gained by pressing for more on this matter, so they ceased questioning.

An interval of silence prevailed, which was broken when Zeitreise softly said, "Shall we proceed?"

The four held hands as they processed slowly toward the spring. When they reached the water's edge, they closed their eyes for a moment of meditation. Just as they opened their eyes and simultaneously lifted their left feet to step into the water, a mockingbird swooped down before them and flapped its wings in their faces to get their attention.

The bird then announced, "In the interest of fair disclosure, I am required by ancient custom to inform you that should you depart under these circumstances, you will not be able to return to the Timberscape of Memory."

This news caused the return of their previous hesitation and they replaced their feet on the ground. As one, they turned to look at Zeitreise for confirmation. Zeitreise nodded enigmatically.

"Never?" Hansel said. "I had hoped to visit in the future, especially if I found conditions in our village too difficult. This place feels like home to me."

"After we tend to our parents," Gretel said, "we definitely want to return here again and hope that Allys and Aylwyn would do the same."

"I have informed you of the consequences in a timely manner," the bird said, "and thus I have fulfilled my ethical and moral obligation."

"Since you brought up the way things work, Mockingbird, I was wondering if it would be possible for all four of us to go home to the same place," Allys said. "We've grown very fond of one another, you see, and..."

"Yes, would that be possible?" Hansel enthused. "What are the rules for accomplishing that?"

"I spoke of ancient custom and consequences, not rules," said Mockingbird. "They are not synonymous. However, in answer to the question you have posed, there are ways to accomplish what you desire. However, this is not my question to answer."

Gretel addressed Zeitreise. "Is it your question?"

Zeitreise said, "No."

"But it's a really cool idea," said Aylwyn. "Still, if we all went home together, whose home would it be? Arizona or the forest south of the Elbe?"

Gretel said, "You have told us of the abundance you enjoy in your land, Aylwyn, so I would as soon go there...with you."

"But **whose** question is it to answer?" Allys demanded. "**How** can we cause that to happen?"

Mockingbird answered, "Any jackrabbit can easily handle that particular inquiry, although they are very hard to stop and interrogate."

"That we know quite well," said Hansel.

Then Zeitreise spoke, offering an alternative proposal. "Now that Mockingbird has given you the traditional fair warning, I am free to address the substance of your big question. On behalf of the other residents, I have been authorized to invite the four of you to remain with us and become joint rulers of the Timberscape of Memory. You have learned much in four years of sojourning in all parts of the enchanted island of Gymnarykum, and you have been agents of significant changes in Old Mem. It is now a less fearful place, and so the inhabitants desire you to live among us and encourage further evolution. The Timberscape would no longer be a neglected wilderness but a realm in its own right. If you agree to this, you will be able to travel home to the places of your birth when you are old and your children are ready to rule in your steads."

Gretel blushed and said, "We will have children if we stay?"

Zeitreise nodded. "Very likely."

"But animals don't need a government, and there are too few humans here to need ruling," Aylwyn said.

Zeitreise explained, "We have the usual complement of native born witches, wizards, and Tarot folk. Also, many disaffected people abide here, those who have run away from the four realms and are hiding in the forest. The great majority entered from Clubs, Diamonds, and Spades, although some from Hearts made pilgrimages and stayed, as well as a few more, like me, who abandoned Hearts to avoid martyrdom. There are also a good number from fabled lands who by magic spells were exiled here against their wills. And of course, we have among us those blessed ones who entered through the Transcendental Cave, such as yourselves."

"Is that the name of the cave we came through?" Allys asked.

"Yes," Zeitreise continued. "But returning to the subject of the many who reside in the Timberscape, we know what you did for Cranna, Tovah, Foxford, Ollam, Morey, Dis, and Ria. Those now in hiding would come out and join with the open ones if the birds announced the crowning of brave, kind, and wise tetrarchs. The Timberscape of Memory could become a place gently governed, not to destroy its wild beauty but to make it a place where people don't have to hide in shadows but can live as their authentic selves in the sunlight."

"But surely you, Zeitreise, should be the ruler of the Scape," Allys said.

Zeitreise bowed in acknowledgement of her words and said, "I am focused on inward things and have other concerns. Thank you for the vote of confidence, but I am an eremite, not a monarch. Simply being here with you four is trying my capacity for social interaction. It is very wearying. I will need to be alone for a long time to recover my energy once your fates have been decided."

"That sounds ominous," said Aylwyn.

"Not at all," said Zeitreise. "It is not a matter of doom but of opportunity. Nothing is predestined but much is possible."

"Surely the Timberscape would be less beautiful if it were tamed by rulers with regulations and laws," Gretel said.

"The goal is not to tame the place but to be less secretive and more openly aware of its reality," Zeitreise said. "Things have already improved around here with your brief sojourns. If you were here all the time, communications would be immeasurably better."

"People in Clubs, Diamonds, and Spades fear the Scape," said Allys. "Would we be expected to deal with issues of inter-realm intrigue?"

"Very astute," said Zeitreise. "That is apt to be a more difficult problem than governing denizens of the Scape."

"Fear is a basic motivation for war," said Aylwyn. "Are you hinting that one or more of the outer realms might invade the Timberscape? Are you looking for warriors to defend the place? Is that why we've come here?"

"We're not looking for a fight," said Allys.

"If this turns out to be about slaying some frightful beast," said Gretel, "I shall be greatly disappointed."

"Meddling in another country's war is foolish," said Hansel.

"I see that your wisdom is already on display. The probability of invasion is extremely remote," Zeitreise said. "It is not warriors we need but courageous healers. Your arrival here had nothing to do with preparing for battle and everything to do with living in peace."

Allys, Aylwyn, Hansel, and Gretel talked it over among themselves. They had been away from home four years, and their parents probably thought they were dead.

Hansel said, "I have been harboring the notion that my parents have likely perished in the famine. It is possible that Gretel and I would return to an abandoned village. This is why traveling with Allys and Aylwyn to the bountiful land of Arizona holds such appeal to me."

"That has been my thought also," said Gretel.

"Well reasoned," said Mockingbird. "Yet it represents only part of what you are thinking."

Hansel blushed and then straightened his posture and turned to face Allys. "Mockingbird is correct. The time has come for me to confess, dear Allys, that I am in love with you and would gladly accept Zeitreise's offer in order to stay here or anywhere on earth with you."

"I love you too, Hansel," Allys said. She fell into Hansel's outstretched arms and they heartily embraced and kissed.

"All four must agree unanimously," Zeitreise said.

Aylwyn said, "Gretel, I've been in love with you since I

first set eyes on your face and my heart was aching at the thought of never seeing you again."

"I am so delighted at your pronouncement," said Gretel. "The same is true for me."

Gretel and Aylwyn also embraced and kissed.

In unison the quartet said, "We will stay!"

Then Mockingbird explained the implications of this decision. "When you return to your birth homes in old age, if you choose to do so, you will appear there at the exact moment you first entered the cave, rather than many years into the future. I could not tell you this before you made your decisions to stay or go."

"But what about Hansel and Gretel?" Allys asked. "Will they even have a home to return to?"

Mockingbird said, "Their village was still in place at the time they became lost in the forest. Everything will be as it was."

"Why couldn't we all go to Arizona? What if we wanted to stay together, all four of us, and retire in the warm winters of Phoenix?" Aylwyn asked.

"As I explained before, you need to ask a jackrabbit how to do that," Mockingbird said.

"That implies that it **can** be done," said Hansel.

Mockingbird replied, "I did not say that, you only inferred it."

"But you didn't deny it either," said Aylwyn.

"Let's not worry about that right now," said Allys. "We may learn many things to help us with that issue in the years to come. Surely the jackrabbits will obey their monarchs to stop and answer a few questions."

Hansel thought he saw Mockingbird smile doubtfully at what Allys had said, but before he could decide whether it was physically possible for a bird to smile, Mockingbird began to sing a beguiling song and four more mockingbirds flew in, each with a golden crown dangling from its neck. They shrugged off the unembellished crowns into Zeitreise's raised hands.

The eremite then told the birds, "Fly throughout all Timberscape and announce the news that a coronation to initiate the tetrarchy will commence at dawn tomorrow!"

<><><>

At the coronation, the four processed to a ledge above the Spring of Memory wearing only their crowns of vine. Royal finery, robes, stoles, jewelry and such did not exist in the Scape, so they were otherwise quite naked. During the ceremony at which Zeitreise officiated, mockingbirds flew down and removed their botanic headpieces. Thereupon Allys, Gretel, Aylwyn, and Hansel knelt and bowed in a posture of prayer. Tovah, Cranna, Ollam, and Foxford then stepped forward to place the glistening but undecorated and gemless crowns upon the heads of the two sets of twins.

Cranna and Tovah approached Aylwyn and Hansel and chanted in unison, "We set these symbols of office upon the heads of those who appreciate, respect, and love the female body. Rule wisely."

Foxford and Ollam moved toward Allys and Gretel and similarly chanted, "We set these symbols of office upon the heads of those who appreciate, respect, and love the male body. Rule wisely."

Zeitreise then declared, "As four monarchs in one, you represent the equality of all sexes. Love, respect, and appreciate us all, bodies and minds, and lead us all with honesty and compassion." The eremite then presented each one with a willow basket filled with all of her or his original clothes, including undergarments, socks, and shoes. "When the time is full, you will need these to return to the places from which you have come."

Pieter and Wendlich attended the coronation. Afterward, they joined the four at the feast.

"I'd like to try out a reverse spell I learned in Hearts," said Allys. She touched their heads and pronounced, "Malediction reverso."

Immediately, Pieter and Wendlich transformed into eighteen year-old bodies with all the necessary secondary sex characteristics. They shouted in joy, bowed to Allys, and then rose and embraced each other. They asked the tetrarchs to marry them, and a ceremony was improvised on the spot. In the spirit of spontaneity, they also performed weddings for Cranna and Tovah and for Foxford and Ollam.

Morey also attended the ceremony with his lover, Stella, who had remained faithful during his captivity. So too did

Dis and Ria, who were now quite happy working with gilded flickers to deliver free flowers to random souls. Kyp came as well. She had learned in the river that in her previous existence she had been the first woman to live in the Timberscape of Memory.

"What was your name, Kyp, when you were the first woman?" Allys asked.

"Oh, I was called Lilith," Kyp said. "She was the first **human**, not just the first woman, to venture into the Timberscape and actually **explore** it."

"Who was the first man?" Aylwyn wanted to know.

"That's complicated," Kyp explained. "The second person to arrive here was like Zeitreise, having both male and female parts. That was Evadam. Lilith actually had a boy child by Evadam, who technically became the first man here. They named him Jubal."

"We learned about those mythical people at the University of Hearts," said Hansel.

"According to the voice of the Gymnarykum River, they are not myths but truly alive within my mind," said Kyp. "Especially Lilith."

"Without doubt, many wondrous things are truly alive in the human mind," said Gretel.

To this wisdom, all assembled creatures, human and otherwise, shouted amen.

Allys married Hansel, and Gretel married Aylwyn in a double ceremony officiated by Zeitreise, but wisely they honeymooned in separate locations along the Universal Sea in the Realm of Hearts.

Within a month, they were comfortable in their role as joint rulers, because no creature in the Timberscape of Memory treated them like royalty. They decreed there would be no bows and no reverent addresses. No one was allowed to call them "your majesties" but only their names. This, of course, well suited the egalitarian ethos of the Timberscape. It also served them well that their decisions as tetrarchs were not based on acquiring power but on maintaining hospitality.

And they all lived many years in peace and harmony, with just enough mystery to make each day an intriguing adventure.

CHAPTER 29:
FLOATING

Go, little book! Go, my small tragedy!
God grant thy author yet before he die
That he perchance produce a comedy!
Geoffrey Chaucer

On her thirty-seventh birthday in April 1987, Chaucer received a phone call from a man who said he was a former FBI agent, Milford Miller. He had investigated her in the 1960s and 1970s, and now he wanted to talk with her about what he had done. He had retired to Sedona, which was why he chose her to call among many people he needed to make amends with.

Chaucer invited him to meet her at her campus office. When he entered the room she said, "I recognize you. You're the agent who interviewed me about USARMI."

"Yes," he admitted. "And the reason I want to meet with you now is that I am a recovering alcoholic, currently working on step nine of the Twelve Step program. That means, wherever possible, making direct amends to people I've harmed."

She offered him tea, which he accepted. For a time they both sipped the warm beverages quietly. Then Chaucer said, "I'm not aware of being harmed by you."

Miller replied, "I pursued investigations on many private citizens who were simply exercising their rights of free speech and freedom

348

to criticize the government, and now I am ashamed of what I did. Since I can't locate and apologize to most of these people, in a sense you represent all of them. I am truly sorry. Will you forgive me?"

She found it surprisingly easy to say yes. "I forgive you, but ever since you called, I've been wondering about my FBI file. Is there any way I can read what's in it?"

"Under the Freedom of Information Act, you can request a copy," he replied. "A copy will be sent to you -eventually- but don't hold your breath. Also, it will likely be heavily redacted to cover the identities of agents and other items embarrassing to the Bureau."

"So I would not be able to determine which entries you were responsible for and which were written by others," she said.

"You could figure out what I wrote about my interview of you," he said. "If you're good at linguistic, syntactical, and rhetorical analysis, you might be able to identify other items that I wrote. Let me confess that I am not proud of what I reported and how I misconstrued your statements."

"I see," she said. "And actually, I am good at that kind of analysis."

"I should also add that the Bureau's interest in you has long since been abandoned. Yours is an old file, interesting only as history," he said.

"Thank you for coming to see me," she said. "If I should get my file, may I call you to discuss it?"

"I would only answer questions about my own work, and then only in ways that do not violate confidentiality rules," he replied. He handed her his card. "But feel free to contact me."

Reflecting on the matter later, she decided it was not worth the aggravation to request her FBI file. "If I did," she told Magnus, "reading it would probably raise my blood pressure, so why do something that will only make me angry."

Magnus Bergen's divorce had become final in March. At a small naturist ceremony in June, Cloud pronounced Magnus and Chaucer husband and wife. Helene Finn and Terp served as witnesses. As she had done when married to Ving, Chaucer kept her own name. There had been no Chaucer Valborg and now no Chaucer Bergen.

Together, Chaucer and Magnus formally joined the Sedona NCC congregation, the first time that Chaucer had been an actual member of any social organization, church or otherwise. Chaucer joined by total immersion baptism, while Magnus opted for the renewal of baptism ritual.

For their honeymoon, they traveled to Australia, visiting Sydney and per the recommendation of Cloud and Terp, spent a week at the Queen's Paradise resort at Cairns.

In August, Chaucer discovered that she was pregnant.

When the condition was medically confirmed she told Magnus, "I've been so happy with my life that I let down my guard on birth control. I've never been pregnant before and was not expecting it, so I overlooked the initial signs. I assumed my late period was simply a late period, since they have been erratic lately anyway."

"How far along are you?" Magnus asked gravely.

"Six weeks," she said.

The idea of producing a child with the man she loved was romantically exciting to Chaucer, but the thought of a bearing a child with Cystic Fibrosis who would die young terrified her.

"As painful as the subject is," said Magnus, "we need to talk about abortion. I am inclined to argue for it."

Chaucer responded, "It is unlikely that I am a CF carrier. The odds are greatly against me being one."

"The odds for Janett were also slim, but she was," he said.

"I could get carrier-testing to confirm one way or the other," she offered. "Then, assuming good news, we wouldn't have to worry."

"However, a first pregnancy at thirty-seven is riskier than at a younger age," he said. "The chances of *something* going wrong are greater, even if it's not CF."

Chaucer was surprised at herself for wanting this child even though she had previously been quite certain that she had no desire to be a mother. She informed Magnus that she needed time to think and pray about ending the pregnancy.

Two weeks later the decision was taken from her, when a spontaneous abortion occurred. She was deeply saddened but also relieved. Magnus reflected the same feelings, and on the spur of the moment, he made an appointment with his urologist for a vasectomy. Chaucer went with him to provide emotional support for his decision.

"Why didn't you get a vasectomy after Kit was born?" Chaucer asked him on the way to the doctor's office.

"Janett opted for a tubal ligation," Magnus said. "I offered to get fixed, but she insisted that she be the one to get her tubes tied. I think it was a way for her to have more control over her own destiny."

"And now it's your turn," said Chaucer.

Enfolded in her husband's arms in their bed later that night, Chaucer speculated about God's will regarding the miscarriage. "Was this some kind of punishment?" she asked. "Was it my karma?"

"It would be my karma too," Magnus said, "except that I don't believe in karma."

"Neither do I, really, nor do I believe that God wills this kind of event," she said. "More likely, I think a miscarriage demonstrates the wisdom of the body knowing that something is wrong with the fetus. I read somewhere that as many as half of all miscarriages are caused by chromosomal abnormalities, and twenty to thirty percent of all pregnancies end in miscarriage, in many cases without the women even knowing they were pregnant."

"You know that I love you deeply and want you to be happy," Magnus said. "If you want a child, we can adopt."

"As a teacher, I have hundreds of children, although not of an age to cuddle and change diapers and watch them learn to walk," she said. "Thank you, but the truth is that except for one brief moment, I have never wanted an infant.

"But I do want to talk about what this means in a religious sense. Spontaneous abortion due to abnormal chromosomes kicks holes in the theology of those who claim every conception is God's intention. If that's so, then God must be responsible for all the abortions as well."

"Hmmm," said Magnus. "In the aftermath of Kit's death, I gave up on the idea of God's presence at conception. If God is involved in conceiving every child, then God must be a messy, mistake-prone deity who prodigally creates abnormalities and encourages unsuitable people to produce offspring. I can't believe in a God like that."

"No, neither can I," Chaucer agreed.

<><><>

A week after the miscarriage, Chaucer received word from an editor at the Strange Angel Press that ***The Timberscape of Memory*** would be published in a lavishly illustrated format. She had lost one child but was about to give birth to another literary one, twins actually. However, the editor wanted Chaucer to write an epilog describing what happened when and if the two sets of twins returned to their real homes. Chaucer thought the suggestion was great and agreed to write the additional material.

The publisher also arranged with nationally known fantasy and science fiction artist Encantadora Santa Alma Askeladd to make the illustrations for the book. Chaucer and Encantadora found it easy to confer closely, because Encantadora lived in Sedona at Angel Nest, the home of Cloud and Terp Morgan.

Chaucer thoroughly enjoyed posing for Dora's work on her fantasy novella. Clothed, she became the model for Kensinga, the Queen of Hearts, and in the nude she became Stella Tarot, Star of the Major Arcana. Magnus agreed to sit for Encantadora as Kenilworth, King of Hearts. Chaucer also prevailed on her friend Kelly Fife to pose for the intersex character Zeitreise.

Cloud and Terp planned a surprise for Chaucer and Magnus. At a luncheon arranged for them at Angel Nest, a tall, intersex guest appeared. Cloud quickly described the attributes of the Merven species.

"Hello, Chaucer and Magnus," the visitor said. "My name is Sojourner, and I have met both of you in your minds but never before in the flesh."

"I don't recall ever encountering you, even mentally," said Magnus.

"No, my interaction with you has been sympathetic monitoring more than anything else," Sojourner said. "I spent a lot of time consoling you when Kit died."

"Now that you say that," Magnus said, "I do remember a sense of compassionate presence during that time."

"Yes, well that is an important part of my calling," said Sojourner. "But you and I, Chaucer, have carried on great conversations over the years."

Chaucer swooned in her chair and then sat up straight. "My God, are you Riff?"

"Indeed, and I must confess that I rather like the name Riff," Sojourner said. "Cloud used to call me the Old One, and Terp, in her youth, called me Big Head. Riff is much more imaginative, don't you think?"

"I thought you approved of Big Head and the Old One," Terp said.

"Oh, I did indeed," Sojourner said. "But Chaucer needs to tell you what Riff stands for."

"Real imaginary friend forever," Chaucer rattled off.

"So you can see how I would appreciate that appellation," said Sojourner.

"Right as usual," allowed Terp.

"Let me offer sympathy, Chaucer, on the unexpected termination of your pregnancy and congratulations on the publication of your book," Sojourner continued. "And also compliments to you and now Magnus as well on your mostly vegetarian diets."

"Are Merven vegetarian?" Chaucer asked.

"Yes, although we include dairy milk, yogurt, and cheese, but not eggs," Sojourner explained.

"Why?" Magnus asked.

Sojourner replied, "Many children like to play with their food before eating it, and this is harmless fun. Unfortunately, the people who raise animals for food today like to torture their food before killing it. They would claim efficiency to justify what they do, but it is torture nonetheless. This is not harmless fun but reflects a pernicious evolutionary trend among humans. Neither humans nor Merven have the teeth of carnivores, but humans have chosen to become omnivores as an expedient method of obtaining protein."

"You make me feel guilty," Chaucer said.

"Not intentionally," Sojourner said. "I don't condemn humans who eat meat, but would be thrilled to see a trend away from it."

<><><>

When Cloud and Terp told Magnus and Chaucer about their out-of-body experiences that they called floating, Chaucer said, "I've been doing that for years, but I discounted it as an actual phenomenon. I assumed it was some kind of mental projection."

"Then our intuition was right about introducing you to the practice," said Terp.

"Well, I'm astounded," Magnus said. "I had no idea my wife and my pastors engaged in such paranormal activities."

"Would *you* like to learn how?" Cloud said to him.

"Whoa! Let me think about that for a moment," Magnus replied. He bowed his head to reflect on the matter and quickly raised it again. "I'd better learn how if I am ever to have a prayer of keeping up with you three."

"Well, I don't know how to induce it," Chaucer said. "It's always happened without my trying."

Terp and Cloud began their tutorial on out-of-body travel by having Magnus and Chaucer lie supine on yoga mats and practice meditative breathing. From there they proceeded to mental techniques.

Chaucer quickly learned how to induce floating at will and happily embraced the experience as more than simply dreaming she was free of her body. After a few failed attempts, Magnus caught on and also became adept at the art of leaving his body. As weeks passed, Chaucer and Magnus joined Cloud, Terp, and other Angel Nest residents on floating expeditions throughout the region.

The new year, 1988, was punctuated by triumph and tragedy.

The Timberscape of Memory was released and sold far better than the publisher had expected. The illustrations by Encantadora Askeladd were a major reason for the book's success, Chaucer told people, but the work of her imagination took hold in the literary ether, and the book's popularity grew by word of mouth recommendations.

During another luncheon at Angel Nest, Sojourner conversed with Chaucer about her writing. "I very much enjoyed your fantasy novella and found Zeitreise a compelling character," Sojourner noted. "However, I could not help wishing that Zeitreise had been introduced at an earlier point in the narrative and given a fuller and more activist role."

"If I had met you in the flesh before publishing it," Chaucer replied, "I very well might have expanded Zeitreise's presence. However, it would be necessary to contort the plot quite a bit to introduce the intersexual eremite earlier in the story. But on second thought, I think Zeitreise is much like you, mostly hovering in the shadows. That's where your activism occurs. So I don't think I would change Zeitreise's story after all."

Sojourner laughed heartily. "Indeed! And I humbly confess that your author's reasoning is superior to my desire to promote the character I most closely identify with."

One of Chaucer's English students, Pier Bendary, proposed an independent study of the process of writing *Timberscape*, and Chaucer agreed to be interviewed by the students who signed up for the course. They delved not only into her writing methods but also her research methods and the effects of the extended time intervals between chapters on the finished product. Then they asked her about the real subjects and objects of the political and social satire in her narrative. She challenged the students to do their own historical research and to write papers speculating about possible precipitating events and public figures the author may have had in mind as she produced her satire. The resultant papers made Chaucer laugh out loud, especially the ones in which the speculations were accurate.

Chaucer decided to end the term by staging a dramatic reading of *Timberscape*. A student commented that given the centrality of nudity in the narrative, it would be appropriate for everyone to be naked during Chaucer's recitation. Pier suggested a refinement on this that they should wear clothes when the quartet wore clothes and strip when the quartet stripped. The professor thought that continually dressing and undressing during her reading would be aggravating, so she agreed to do her part nude while the students put off and put on garments according to the flow of the story.

This independent study developed into a regular course offering each spring, and her oral presentation of *The Timberscape of Memory* on the last day of class attracted a cult following, as a nude Chaucer read her book, while students and many guests stripped and dressed according to a cheerful choreography. Some went so far as to don attire worn by the quartet in the realms. They brought livery, French and English maid outfits, lacy pink panties with peignoirs, olive drab boxers and camouflage hunting vests, as well as khaki slacks with sky blue polo shirts. In unison with Chaucer, fans recited from memory their favorite passages.

Ving called Chaucer one day to say how much he and Crandall had enjoyed **Timberscape**, which led to her inviting them to dinner for more literary conversation. From then on, Ving and Crandall became regulars in the Chaucer and Magnus social circle. This included their church activities, so the gay couple soon joined them for services at the naturist church. Ultimately, Ving and Crandall became members of the Sedona NCC.

Norah telephoned her daughter and wondered if she had any free author's copies that she might autograph for Banky and herself.

"I'm afraid I don't, Mom," Chaucer replied. "All I have is my own personal copy. But if you buy the book, I'll gladly sign it for you."

"I'll do that," Norah said. "Getting a freebie was a long shot, but I needed to ask. But while we're on the subject, since you have an in with a publisher, could you put in a good word for me? I've arranged my poems into an anthology, and I'd like to get it in print. The manuscript is just shy of 700 pages."

Knowing that collections of poetry were nearly impossible to publish, especially lengthy ones, Chaucer replied in a kindly voice, "Good for you, Mom, keeping up with your writing. I can't promise anything, but I'll mention it to my editor."

"Thank you, Chaucer," Norah said.

Then a few weeks later came tragedy. Chaucer received word from her father that Spenser had been killed in a motorcycle accident. He had not been wearing a helmet in the one-vehicle crash.

"The evidence is not conclusive," Banky said, "but it could have been suicide. He had been going through another one of his spells of depression over being unemployed. But it could've just as easily been carelessness. He had done a few gigs playing sax in a retro rock band, which he enjoyed. So he wasn't totally down."

"Since you're uncertain," Chaucer said, "I assume he left no note."

"Spenser was not much for writing down anything," Banky said, "even phone messages."

"Let me know when the funeral service will be," she said. "I want to be there."

"There won't be one," Banky said, his voice now suppressing rage. "After all the time and effort his mother and I spent supporting him, and he never lived up to his potential. He doesn't deserve a funeral."

"What are you going to do then?" Chaucer asked.

"He's being cremated this afternoon," Banky explained. "We'll scatter his ashes someplace appropriate."

"And where might that be?" Chaucer asked. "I'd like to be present for the scattering."

"I'll get back to you on that," he said. "Your mother is so angry about our fair-haired boy's callous stupidity that she's inclined to dump his ashes in the garbage disposal."

"Oh no, you wouldn't do that," Chaucer gasped.

"We just might," he said.

Chaucer told Cloud about her desire for a memorial service for her brother and her parents clear opposition to the idea. When she heard nothing from them about strewing the ashes, she called again and Norah told her she had indeed emptied Spenser's ashes into the garbage disposal.

Cloud offered to conduct a memorial service in Sedona in the NCC chapel on a Saturday afternoon. Chaucer called her sister and learned that Marlowe was also appalled at their parents' behavior. Marlowe, Grant, Harrow, and Millay flew in for the memorial, arriving Friday night and staying until Monday morning. Since Spenser had spent time with the Archers in Vermont on several occasions when he was attempting to get his life back together, Marlowe wanted to offer remembrances of him.

At the service, after Cloud's opening prayer and scripture reading, Marlowe walked to the lectern and said, "It is fitting to honor the memory of Spenser Dickinson with words from his namesake, Edmund Spenser. The poet began one of his sonnets with these lines that remind me keenly of our troubled brother:

> *Oft when my spirit doth spread her bolder wings,*
> *In mind to mount up to the purest sky,*
> *It down is weighed with thought of earthly things,*
> *And clogged with burden of mortality."*

Chaucer then read lines from Christopher Marlowe:

> *"Cut is the branch that might have grown full straight,*
> *And burned is Apollo's laurel bough."*

After a meditative pause, she continued, "Now we will never know what might have been. Spenser had so much talent and showed off a bit of it with his music, but he was never able to handle parental adulation. We who knew him shall not now have the opportunity to rejoice with him at eventually finding redemption in this life. Our only consolation is that he is no longer tormented by personal demons."

Grant Archer then stepped forward with his guitar as Harrow trailed carrying a high stool, which he set behind his father and returned to his pew. Grant leaned back on the stool and briefly tuned his guitar. Without saying a word, he strummed and began to sing Leonard Cohen's "Hallelujah." As his voice steadily rose in intensity through the plaintive and powerful chorus, Marlowe and Chaucer wept. Following the final, throbbing hallelujah, Cloud pronounced a simple benediction.

The few attending the memorial had worn clothing for the event, as it was not a naturist service. Later in the day, still dressed in mourning attire, they ate picnic food at the campus residence of Magnus and Chaucer, and the subject of the NCC came up. Marlowe expressed fascination with the naturist congregation that her sister had joined.

"Tell me about this nudist church," Marlowe said. "I want details."

"If you really want to know what it's all about, the best way is for the whole Archer family to come to Sunday morning worship and experience it firsthand," Chaucer replied.

Now fondly remembering the carefree nudity of her hippie commune days, Marlowe in turn looked at Grant, Harrow, and Millay with an unspoken question in her eyes.

They unanimously agreed, and the next day, Magnus and Chaucer escorted the Archers to the NCC service.

"Wow!" said Marlowe to Terp during fellowship time conversation following worship. "What a transcendent experience!"

Grant, Harrow, and Millay expressed similar sentiments.

"Does the NCC have any congregations in Vermont?" Marlowe asked.

Terp said, "Our denomination has no congregations anywhere in the Northeast, but we've been talking about expanding there. Our denominational ethos is Western and Pacific, but growth is always on the agenda. For year-round outside activities, the New England climate is a concern, but our congregations usually meet indoors, so there is no inherent reason not to do a new church development in Vermont."

"We would be willing to serve as the core of a new congregation," Grant said.

"And as for the geographical ethos, we do live in *southwestern* Vermont," Marlowe quipped.

"We have dear friends who spend their summers in a cabin in Vermont," Terp continued. "They might be willing to help you get a congregation growing." Terp gave them contact information for Argyle and Ruth Watts.

"I've heard there is a coed Quaker summer camp -a farm and wilderness camp- somewhere in Vermont where children and teenaged youth are allowed to swim, use the sauna, and other appropriate activities, such as sunbathing, in the nude," the pastor added. "They've been practicing a limited form of naturism since the 1950s. You might check into that also."

In March 1990, Jonathan Davidman died following a long struggle with AIDS, and thus Chaucer and Magnus attended yet another memorial service for someone who had passed away prematurely. Chaucer was so grieved by the loss of Jonathan that she decided she would not like his successor.

"He was a such great soul, such a good-hearted person. And no one could ever match Jonathan's skill with the organ," she told Magnus. "He was simply superb with a keyboard. They will never find anyone to play as well."

But in this pronouncement, she was mistaken. Jonathan's successor, Rowan Gordon, had been one of Jonathan's organ students, and Chaucer was blown away by his playing, particularly Handel's "Halleluiah Chorus" from "Messiah," "The Holy City" by Michael Maybrick, and "Jerusalem" with music by Sir Hubert Parry set to William Blake's text. In church on Sunday, people stayed in their seats after worship to listen to Rowan's postludes and then stood and applauded. Chaucer was among the first to rise for the approbation.

Predictably, Chaucer befriended Rowan and learned his story.

"I dropped out of San Francisco Conservatory of Music," he told her, "and toured as keyboardist for a rock band, got strung out on drugs and riotous living. I was in rehab three times before it took. When it did, I dropped out of the band and moved to Sedona to recover health and live simply. I've joined the New Age Personship, where Coventry Ford is Convener. It's a place where I can be in touch with my higher power and stay sober."

Years passed by in contented living for Chaucer. Her work at Anasazi was fulfilling. For the spring semester in 1996, she facilitated an independent study with Cloud and Terp's daughter Zara. Zara wanted to examine the sexual euphemisms and double entendres in the work of Geoffrey Chaucer, Shakespeare, and the King James Bible. The professor-student discussions on that subject brought great laughter to both women.

One day, Zara said to Chaucer, "***Timberscape*** is so successful, you should write another book. Have you thought about it?

"I've played with some ideas," Chaucer said. "At one point I considered writing a modern, female version of ***Robinson Crusoe***."

"Great idea! That would be in keeping with your island motif,"

Zara said. "Defoe's novel is a classic but his thick prose gets in the way and could use some updating. And a female protagonist is exactly what's needed. You should do that."

"Yes, but I have a problem with it. Every time I've tried to outline the story, it turns into a depressing tale of descent into madness. The effects of years of isolation would not be pleasant to describe."

"That's your extroversion asserting itself," Zara noted. "My first thought when you mentioned the subject was a sojourn in paradise. Such wonderful solitude."

"The idea makes me shudder," Chaucer said.

"Then that's why you need to write it, to face your fears," said Zara.

"I'll give it some more thought," Chaucer replied with a dismissive tone.

She did think about it but never wrote the book.

In the winter of 1997, Ving's father died of a stroke. His mother inherited the business and wasted no time merging it with Ving's to form a super travel agency. Ving kept the name Exotic Journeys for the Sedona location, however.

That spring, Zara did another independent study with Chaucer, exploring the premise that the English language existed prior to the Anglo-Saxon invasion and that therefore Anglo-Saxon is not the source of Middle English but simply an external influence on it arising from the circumstances of Angles and Saxons ruling much of the country. Zara made a strong case for her idea.

In the fall, Zara approached Chaucer and her colleague Bookman Donne about doing a joint independent study with them. "I'd like input and guidance from both male and female perspectives," Zara explained. "You see, I had a particularly vivid dream about the myth of creation in the Bible. Actually, there are two myths woven together, one in the first chapter of Genesis and the other in the second chapter."

"I am very familiar with those competing passages," Bookman responded.

"So am I," said Chaucer.

"Excellent," said Zara. "The vision that came to me in a dream was a third creation myth. What I propose to do is write a mythic

poem of a thousand lines, with guidance from the two of you as I
work on each section. It will extend from the creation of humans to
the end of the age. I have an outline that I'll include in the written
proposal for the IS."

After studying Zara's outline, Chaucer and Bookman agreed to
the independent study to review and critique her work as she
produced *The Third Song of Creation, a Myth in Five Seasons*.
The professors spent more time affirming Zara's work than offering
editorial advice.

Magnus retired from the presidency of Anasazi College in June 2001,
and he and Chaucer vacated the president's residence. They bought a
home in Sedona, a rambling ranch style house made of stone that
was once the home of an artist married to a poet. The walls of nearly
every room had built-in bookshelves, which suited the new owners
very well. Chaucer named their new home the Bookery.

Prasada Pratyaksha was named interim president while a search
committee looked for a successor. Magnus was pleased by the
interim appointment, although he worried that it meant Prasada
would seek a position elsewhere when the interim ended, which
would be a huge loss to Anasazi. Applying his usual optimism to the
matter, he thought that she could easily get a position at NAU or
Prescott College and still live in Sedona.

Cloud chaired the search committee for the successor to Magnus.
After a year and a half of diligent effort, the committee was unable
to find anyone who excited them or was as effective as Prasada. Then
news came to them that Prasada was being recruited by Northern
Arizona University to be dean of the Liberal Arts College and this
pressed them to action. In a unanimous decision, they turned to her,
though she had not applied for the position, and asked her to accept
the presidency permanently. She accepted.

Magnus was very pleased when she was named his installed
successor and was further delighted when Prasada asked him to lead
independent studies in library science. It felt very good to be
teaching again. The biggest surprise about being back in the
classroom came when a course he taught on the craft of handmade
bookbinding proved to be very popular, and he was asked to repeat

it in subsequent semesters.

Prasada also named Chaucer chair of the English department.

CHAPTER 30:

FIFTY-NINE YEARS LATER

Halfway up the cliff is a mist covered cave.
Homer

The golden children rejoiced when they saw each other again, kissing and caressing each other.

Jacob and Wilhelm Grimm

Wearing the now tattered and moth-eaten clothes they had on when they first arrived in the Timberscape, the gray-haired quartet stepped into the Transcendental Cave and quickly found the chamber with stone benches where both pairs had spent the night so many years past. The cave had long since worked through the issues that had led it down the path of passive-aggression, and its entrance remained invitingly open. From the central chamber, the couples made their way down a passage toward the exit they had been told would lead them home.

For a time on that fateful day long ago, all four had been in the stone room together, although they did not know it, because they had been occupying different dimensions of the space-time continuum.

Earlier on the day of their departure from Timberscape, they had made tearful good-byes to their children and grandchildren. Their sons and daughters had long since found mates and taken over the tasks of governing. Each couple, Aylwyn and Gretel and Hansel and Allys, had produced boy and girl twins, and the four twins now ruled as a tetrad with their spouses as consorts.

Over the years, the quartet had carried on earnest conversations with various jackrabbits about the laws of fantasy world physics and metaphysics. One specific subject of inquiry had to do with whether they could or should return to their places of origin or whether it was possible to go as a foursome to the Arizona cave entrance. None would answer the question directly. On this subject, all jackrabbit answers were consistently equivocal, as were those from Zeitreise.

Now, on the verge of returning to the lands of their birth, they realized that they could not bear to be parted in old age. Thus they would risk going as a foursome, not knowing what would happen. Would Hansel and Gretel turn into five hundred year-old bodies and crumble? How would Allys and Aylwyn be able to explain the presence of Hansel and Gretel to their parents? Saying they found these refugees in a cave would sound extremely lame. And how would they explain that their clothes were practically in shreds? But in the face of deep love none of that mattered. They had to stay together, and they would deal with whatever consequences developed.

When Allys, Aylwyn, Hansel, and Gretel reached the mouth of the cave, it was obscured in a thick mist, but when they poked their heads through the obscuring cloud, all four saw the column of rock that had allowed Allys and Aylwyn to reach the cave the first time.

"That's an excellent sign," said Aylwyn. "If we can all see it, it means we're all in the same universe."

As if waiting for their appearance, the needle bent forward and allowed them to step onto it, providing a means for climbing down to the base of the cliff.

Holding hands, Allys and Hansel went first and then turned to reach out to Aylwyn and Gretel. Together Aylwyn and Gretel stepped onto the rock column, and as soon as their feet were securely in place, both couples embraced with great joy.

Noticing a change in her hair, Aylwyn stepped back and cried out, "Look at you, Gretel! You're fourteen again."

"And so are you," Gretel answered.

The same was true for Allys and Hansel.

A second later, something popped in the atmosphere and Hansel and Gretel disappeared.

The hearts of the Arizona twins cried out in pain.

"Well, there's part of an answer," said Aylwyn with deep anguish in his voice.

"Look at your clothes," said Allys through tears. "There's another answer."

Their clothing had been restored to its original condition.

So shaken were they by the loss of Hansel and Gretel that their muscles trembled as they descended the stone needle, and they had difficulty finding the trail they had left nearly three score years before to pursue a jackrabbit. When at last they did locate the path, they wiped the tears from their faces and hiked back to the camp.

Upon reaching it, the fourteen year-old twins found their parents still napping. Soon, their parents awoke.

Dad said, "What have you two been up to while we dozed off?"

"Just exploring the area," said Allys.

"There's a rock needle and a high cave up the side of a cliff over that way," Aylwyn said as he pointed in the appropriate direction.

"You look upset," Mom said. "Is something wrong?"

In this case, the literal truth simply would not suffice, thought Allys, but the spirit of the truth would. "Oh, we've been talking about what it must feel like to be old and lose someone you love."

"That's an odd subject for young people to discuss," said Dad. "But show us this needle and cave you found."

The twins retraced their steps with their parents in tow and found the rock needle without difficulty. But no cave could be seen in the cliff face.

"It was way up there," Aylwyn said, pointing to the spot but not completely surprised that the entrance was no longer visible. "I guess it must have been a mirage."

"Sometimes the sun can play tricks on your eyes," Dad explained.

Safely back at home, Allys and Aylwyn realized that though they had lost Hansel and Gretel, they had retained the memories of a lifetime in Timberscape. If this were some kind of hallucination, both had seen exactly the same one. Ditto for a dream. They believed it was neither and were grateful for the remembrances.

Though back in their adolescent bodies, they had accumulated in their minds the experiences and learning of geriatric adults. Thus, their years in high school proved easy, without any of the teenage angst or feelings of inferiority or lack of self-confidence normally associated with those years, which their friends found exasperating and smug and their parents found odd. Still, they painfully missed Hansel and Gretel.

After graduating from high school, Allys and Aylwyn enrolled at Vortex College in Camp Verde, Arizona. The first day on campus they met another set of twins who had come from Germany to study American culture at the experimental college. Except for contemporary hairstyles, they were nearly perfect images of Hansel and Gretel at age eighteen. Their life experiences were different, though, because they had been born in the second half of the twentieth century and had never known famine.

The German students even exhibited the fairytale twins' mannerisms, as well as notions of having lived long ago in a mysterious place called the Timberscape of Memory, as if in a previous life. Hans and Greta had undergone psychotherapy for the rare condition of experiencing identical hallucinatory fantasies about a past life in a fairy tale world. However, despite extensive examinations, the psychiatrist could never explain the phenomenon. What most perplexed those close to them, however, was their tendency to behave like impatient parents with their age peers, while doting like grandparents with younger children.

As if they had known this would happen, the quartet laughed and embraced.

It goes without saying but will be said anyway: They lived happily ever after. Fifty-nine years later, the two married couples went hiking in the Superstition Mountains and found a cave in the face of a cliff.

CHAPTER 31:
OLD PHOTOS

I would not paint – a picture –
I'd rather be the One
Its bright impossibility
To dwell – delicious – on –
Emily Dickinson

Nude photos of Chaucer taken when she was sixteen were published on the Internet in 2005. Her high school boyfriend, Chuck Wallace, had read ***The Timberscape of Memory*** and was so taken with the imagery of the characters' nakedness that he posted the pictures on his website as a true portrait of the artist consistent with the text of the author's book.

Chuck did not think he was doing anything to discredit or embarrass Chaucer. He included a narrative describing the photos as pictures of the beautiful woman who had written a wonderful novel about clothes-free fairytale characters. He noted what he perceived were similarities between the photos of Chaucer and Encantadora Askeladd's illustrations of Allys, pointing out the shape of their faces, body contours, and posture. Chuck also saw similarities between Chaucer and Gretel, for example the eyes, nose, and mouth. Oddly, Chaucer had not posed for the illustrations of either of these characters.

In one of the shots, Chuck had superimposed a photo of a jackrabbit beside Chaucer's feet looking up at her with a quizzical expression on its face. It was done so well that a casual viewer would consider it an actual photo of Chaucer and a jackrabbit.

An avid fan of *The Timberscape of Memory* who was a former Anasazi student emailed Chaucer with a link to Chuck Wallace's web site and advised her about the shots. "PS," he added, "if you google the title of your book, one of the hits that comes up is Chuck's. He is now an accomplished documentary cinematographer in Los Angeles."

Chaucer and her husband held differing views on what to do about the photos. Being somewhat old-fashioned as well as somewhat feminist, Magnus wanted to press charges against the former boyfriend, not because of the nudity but because Chaucer had been underage at the time the shots were taken. "This is classic child exploitation," he said. "And by the way, did you sign a release for publication?"

"No release," she said. "I didn't know there was such a thing way back then."

"Aha!" he crowed. "We have him nailed."

Laughingly, Chaucer said, "Chuck was underage then too. Instead of contacting the police, I think we should add the photos to the Anasazi catalog as a recruiting tool for the English department."

Magnus said, "Do you have any idea how many boys fantasize about seeing their favorite teacher naked?"

"I'll take that as a rhetorical question," she replied. "However, the universal practice of apodyopsis is not exclusive to males."

"I'm not familiar with the term," he said.

"It means mentally undressing people or imagining what they look like naked," she explained. "The phenomenon is extremely common among the textile population."

Magnus said, "But imagine all the young men in your classes grinning because they don't need to imagine it, because they've already *seen* the professor naked. And some young women as well, I suppose."

"They can see me naked any Sunday at the NCC," she said. "If any of them get cheeky, I'll invite them to church, and then maybe they'll grow up a bit about naturally bare bodies. Or they could come to my annual reading of *Timberscape*. Many have, and I've seen them naked too in that context."

"As I well know," confessed Magnus with a sigh.

The negatives and an original set of the prints were still in her possession. Chaucer got out the photographs and selected one for matting and framing to hang in their bedroom. She was unfazed that nude images of her were available on the Internet. Indeed, she was pleased to see visual evidence of how beautiful her body was back then, because at the time she had thought of it as flawed. She chided Magnus for being, oxymoronically, a prudish naturist. This made him laugh and agree that she was handling the situation in a more mature manner than he.

Chaucer sent a thank you email to her ex-boyfriend's web site, including the comment, "It is simply amazing what photographers can do these day, even without the negatives."

Chuck replied with an offer to set up a scholarship at Anasazi College for students to take courses in photography and cinematography. Chaucer passed this on to Prasada, along with his request to explore the feasibility of making a film documentary about Chaucer as well as other faculty members at Anasazi who participated in the Sedona Natural Christian Church. His final comment was:

I would love for **The Timberscape of Memory** to be made into a film. Of course, I am the perfect cinematographer for such a project. I'm itching to do a fantasy film to match my vision against luminaries like Andrew Lesnie who directed filming for **The Lord of the Rings** trilogy as well as John Seale, Roger Pratt, and Michael Seresin, respectively cinematographers for the first three **Harry Potter** films. I plan to send copies of your book to every Hollywood producer I know. I've got a documentary on naturism under my belt, filmed at Mira Vista Resort in the northwest of Tucson near Marana. The only snag I foresee is not the nudity per se but the ages of the main characters. The casting department would have to find baby-faced eighteen year-olds to look fourteen, because too many District Attorneys are incapable of distinguishing between art and child abuse.

<><><>

An unexpected package was delivered to the Bookery two weeks later. As Chaucer supervised, Magnus (who claimed expertise in the art of opening cartons) carefully slit the tape on top, raised the cardboard flaps, and reached in to lift out something in white wrapping tissue, whereupon a spray of compressed packing peanuts attacked and clung to his hand. "Damn! I hate those things," he swore, trying to shake them off. Chaucer laughed.

Once the paper was pulled away, they saw a framed eighteen by twenty-four inch enlargement of naked Chaucer and the jackrabbit. She was so pleased with this gift from Chuck that she took it to her campus office and hung it on the wall above her desk.

Terp and Cloud stopped by to visit her one afternoon soon thereafter, and when they walked in and saw the photograph, Cloud exclaimed, "Wow! Nice jackrabbit!"

About the Author

Kenneth Alan Moe was born in Phoenix, where from an early age he experienced mystical events. At age ten he began writing poetry. His working life has included service in the U. S. Army as a prisoner of war interrogator, in the corporate world as an insurance investigator, and as a mainline Protestant minister.

Consistently underscoring it all, for more than half a century he has practiced the vocation of writer, evolving through pencil, pen, manual and electric typewriter, and computer to produce reams of fiction, non-fiction, and poetry. Moe's novels reflect his staunch advocacy for feminist and gay rights issues.

About Strange Angel Press

Strange Angel Press is a consortium of writers who act as editors, advisors, and cheerleaders for one another. We pool our collective experiences and talents to help participating writers with the art, craft, and discipline of fully telling the stories that have inspired us to put words to paper.

Visit our websites:
strangeangelpress.com
facebook.com/StrangeAngelPress
facebook.com/HereticsInOccupiedEden

NO SUCH THING AS COINCIDENCE...

The Rider had chosen him. The knot of darkness would billow out of his chest like a mist of writhing tentacles, to feed, flay and kill. Its goal, its need... its passion bled through his dreams as he slept. Salvation would only come once he brought the Rider to its desire.

Now bound to the deadly spirit, Evan Michael's only chance for survival lay with two witches from the Order of Magdalene: women who could bind the Rider to prevent it from feeding and help him avoid the authorities.

If they failed, he would be executed in front of a live television audience.

But, the Rider's passion was to kill the Abbess, the leader of the Order of Magdalene.

If they succeeded...

Available in Paper and Kindle editions on Amazon.com

STRANGE ANGEL PRESS

www.ingramcontent.com/pod-product-compliance
Lightning Source LLC
Chambersburg PA
CBHW050906250626
47155CB00001B/120